A WEEK WITH THE BEST MAN

ALLY BLAKE

THE FAMILY HE DIDN'T EXPECT

SHIRLEY JUMP

MILLS & BOON

First Published in Great Britain 2019
by Mills & Boon, an imprint of HarperCollinsPublishers,
1 London Bridge Street, London, SE1 9GF

A Week with the Best Man © 2019 Ally Blake
The Family He Didn't Expect © 2019 Shirley Kawa-Jump, LLC

ISBN: 978-0-263-27253-6

0719

MIX
Paper from
responsible sources

FSC
www.fsc.org
FSC™ C007454

This book is produced from independently certified FSC™
paper to ensure responsible forest management.

For more information visit: www.harpercollins.co.uk/green

Printed and bound in Spain
by CPI, Barcelona

A WEEK
WITH THE
BEST MAN

ALLY BLAKE

To the people and places that
make me feel like I'm home.

CHAPTER ONE

CORMAC WHARTON SAT on the curved boot of his classic car, shoes hooked a half-metre apart on the gleaming bumper, elbows resting on knees, as he watched his dog, Novak, sprint off into the small forest to his right; a streak of sleek caramel fur in search of the stick Cormac had thrown. And had been throwing for the past forty-odd minutes while he waited for the visitor to arrive.

The sound of a car belting along Beach Road beyond the high bougainvillea-drenched walls of the Chadwick estate had him sitting up, listening for a slowing engine.

Alas, it was not to be.

So, Cormac waited. And would continue to wait. For he was best man to his best mate, Grayson Chadwick, and this was wedding-related-waiting, so it was his job to help out on such occasions. Not that he wouldn't have done so under normal circumstances. It came down to friendship. Loyalty. Respect. Balance. Duty. The pillars upon which Cormac believed a person could build a good and honest life.

Harper Addison—Maid of Honour and The Person Cormac Had Been Waiting Forty Long Minutes For—appeared to have other ideas.

With only days to spare until her sister Lola's big day, Harper had *finally* deigned to drag herself onto a plane to join them. She hadn't condescended to actually let anyone know she was even on her way until she'd landed. Then, refusing to wait for someone to pick her up in Melbourne, she'd hired a car instead to meander down the Great Ocean Road to Blue Moon Bay at her leisure.

Lola claimed she didn't mind not knowing exactly when

her sister would arrive. That she understood how busy her sister was. Cormac knew better. He knew all about keeping the family peace.

A crunch of claws heralded Novak's return as the dog bolted across the bright white gravel driveway, ears flapping, fur gleaming in the summer sun, before coming to a panting halt. Her tongue lolled around the mangled stick as she looked up at him, all liquid eyes filled with adoration and trust. It was a hell of a thing, even from a dog.

"Good girl," Cormac said, and Novak carefully placed the damp stick into his upturned palm. He gave her silky ear a rub. "Ready?"

Novak's nose quivered.

"Fetch!" he called as with a flick of the wrist he launched the stick. It whistled winningly as it soared through the air and into the bush beyond. And then Novak was gone, a rocket of joy bounding off into the shrubs.

When Cormac looked back to the driveway it was to see an unfamiliar car pulling through the gates.

"Here we go," he murmured as with hands flat to the warmed metal he launched himself to the ground. There he twisted at the waist and stretched his arms over his head, before running his slobber-covered hands down the sides of his jeans.

Not a hire car, he saw as it rounded past him. A long black Town Car, the kind that came with a driver and windows so dark he could not see inside. For the hour-and-a-half drive from Melbourne it was a little too much. Even for Blue Moon Bay, which was not short on folk with more money than sense.

So, what did that make Harper Addison?

Cormac tried to call up a mental image of what she'd looked like in high school.

A year or two below him, wasn't she the one who had hung around the bottom of the D-Block staircase, tin in hand, collecting coins for whatever down-on-their-luck soul had appeared in the news that week? He saw unruly brunette curls, ripped jeans, smart mouth and a frown.

Lola Addison, on the other hand, was a sweetheart; bright, happy-go-lucky, with an easy irreverence. His hazy recollection of Harper felt about as far from Lola as one could get.

The Town Car pulled to a halt at the bottom of the wide stone stairs leading up to the house. A moment later a silver-haired driver in a peaked hat and black suit alighted from the car and shuffled to the back door before opening it with a flourish.

Then, like something out of a classic Hollywood flick, a woman's shoe—the colour of champagne with a heel like an ice pick—uncurled from inside the car to stab the graveled ground.

The second shoe dropped, followed by a pair of long legs.

The woman attached to the legs came last, a hand tipped with shiny black fingernails curving over the top of the door as she disregarded the outstretched hand of the driver and pulled herself to standing, slammed the door shut and stared up at the Chadwicks' house.

Not an unruly brunette, Cormac noted as sunlight flowed over sleek, caramel-blonde waves, kicking out sparks of bronze, of gold. And no ripped jeans either, but a long, fitted, expensive-looking coat—far too much for a southern summer's day—embroidered with the same champagne colour as those killer heels.

Clearly not the bolshie rebel he thought he'd remembered. Unsurprising. For him, those later high-school years were pretty much a blur.

The driver moved in to ask her a question right as a mobile-phone tone sounded loudly in the restive silence. She stayed the driver with a hand as she answered the call with a clear, "Yes?"

Was she for real? Cormac coughed out a laugh. Then

ran a hand up the back of his head as he counted down the hours until the wedding. The hours he'd have to make nice with his counterpart in the lead-up. When he could have been working. Surfing. Staring into space. Any of which would be a better use of his time.

Friendship, he reminded himself. *Loyalty. Respect. Balance. Duty.*

The driver glanced Cormac's way, his face working as if unsure what his next move ought to be. Cormac lifted his hand in a wave and half jogged towards the car to take the passenger off the poor guy's hands.

As if she'd heard his footsteps encroaching, the woman turned.

Cormac's pace slowed as if his batteries had drained, till he came to a complete stop.

For the woman was a fifties femme fatale brought to life. A swathe of shining hair curled over her right eye. Shadows slashed under high cheekbones. Full nude lips sat slightly apart, as if preparing to blow a kiss.

Cormac found himself engulfed in an instant thwack of heat. Like a donkey kick to the gut, it literally knocked the breath right out of him.

Then she flicked her hair from her face with a single, sultry shake of her head, said something into her phone before dropping it into a structured bag hooked over one elbow, and then both of her eyes met his.

A flash of memory hit like a rogue wave, and he knew he'd remembered her right.

He saw himself bounding down the D-Block staircase with Gray, Adele, Tara and the rest of the school gang at his heels. There she was, the unruly brunette, homemade posters covered in pictures of flood or famine tacked to the post behind her, collection tin in hand, eyes locked on his with that same unrelenting intensity.

A wet snout pressed into Cormac's hand and he flinched.

Eye contact broken, he glanced down. Novak leaned against his shin, his knee, his thigh, looking at him as if he was the greatest thing on earth.

"That's my girl," he murmured, giving Novak a scratch under the chin, before pulling himself the hell together and striding over to meet the woman he'd been waiting for.

Cormac Wharton.

Of course, *his* had to be the first familiar face Harper saw upon arriving back on home soil for the first time in a decade.

Her breath had literally stuttered at the sight of him ambling towards her. It had taken every ounce of cool she had not to choke on it.

Harper glanced back towards the Chadwicks' gargantuan house, hoping Lola might still come bounding towards her, arms out, hair flying, exuberantly happy to see her. Alas, she understood what Cormac's presence meant: the Chadwicks had enlisted him to babysit. And nobody in this part of the world said no to the Chadwicks, least of all Cormac Wharton.

Her fault, she supposed, for making her arrival a surprise. But the moment she'd fulfilled her rocky last contract, she'd wanted to get on the plane and fly away as fast as she could.

Pulling herself together, Harper turned her attention back to the man in question. Dark sunglasses covered half his face. A bottle-green Henley T clung to the broadest shoulders she'd ever seen, and his jeans fit in all the right places. His haircut hadn't changed—all preppy, chestnut spikes. The sleek toffee-coloured dog trotting at his side was new.

He looked good. Then again, Cormac Wharton had always looked good. Dark-eyed, with charm to spare and a smile that lit up a room, he'd claimed the attention of every girl in school. Including, she deeply regretted, her.

"Ma'am?"

Harper turned to find her driver still standing beside the car, awaiting instructions.

"Sorry," she said, shaking her head and offering a quick smile. "Sam, wasn't it?"

"Yes, Sam's the name. And no apologies necessary. I'm used to passengers coming off long flights. May I help take your luggage inside?"

"No. Thank you. I'm not staying. Not here. This was a quick stop in case my sister was here. Seems she's not. You were kind to drive me this far, so I'll point the way to the hotel and then you can head home."

"Not at all, ma'am. It's always lovely to find myself in here. Dare say it's one of the prettiest places on earth."

The driver's smile dropped a smidge when a shadow fell over the car. A shadow in the shape of Cormac Wharton.

The back of Harper's neck prickled as it always had when he'd walked by. She shut down the sense memory, quick smart. Enough water under that bridge to require an ark.

Seeing no use in putting off the inevitable, Harper turned, bracing herself against the impact of the man, up close and personal. He'd taken off his sunglasses, hooking them over the top button on his shirt revealing an array of frightfully appealing smile lines fanning from the edges of his deep brown eyes. Then there was the sun-drenched warmth of his skin. Sooty stubble shading his jaw. And the fact that, at five-foot-nine—plus an extra four inches in heels—she had to look up.

No longer a cute jock with a knee-melting smile, Cormac Wharton was all man. Just like that a warm flutter of attraction puffed at the dust shrouding her ancient crush.

"Cormac Wharton," she said, "as I live and breathe," her neutral tone owing to years spent working as a professional negotiator.

"Harper Addison. Good to see you." His voice was the same, if not a little deeper. Smooth with just a hint of rough that had always brushed against her impressionable teenaged insides like the tickle of a feather.

For a second, she feared he might lean in to kiss her cheek. The thought of him entering her personal space, stubble scuffing her cheek, warm skin whispering against hers, was enough for her to clench all over.

Thankfully he pulled to a stop, rocking forward on his toes before settling a good metre away. His dog stopped, sat, leaned against him. A female, for sure.

"I'd hoped Lola would be here," Harper said.

Cormac shook his head, his dark gaze not leaving hers.

She waited for an explanation. An excuse. It seemed he was content to let her wait.

"Right, then I'll head to the hotel." She turned to Sam, the driver, who moved like lightning, hand reaching out for the handle of the car door before Cormac's voice said "Stop."

Sam stopped, eyes darting between them.

Harper's gaze cut to Cormac.

He said, "Dee-Dee and Weston are expecting you to stay here."

She shot a glance at the Georgian monstrosity that was the jewel in the immoderate Chadwick Estate. It looked back at her. Or, more specifically, down on her. Dee-Dee and Weston Chadwick might be richer than Croesus, but they couldn't pay her enough to stay under their roof. Water under the bridge didn't come close.

"I've booked a suite at the Moonlight Inn for the duration," she said, softening the refusal with a smile. "I'll be perfectly comfortable there."

"Your comfort isn't my concern."

Harper's smile slipped. "Then what, exactly, is your concern?"

"Gray's comfort. Dee-Dee's and Weston's. And your

sister's. Lola's had a room ready for you here for some time now, on the assumption you'd arrive sooner. Not with only days to spare."

Harper had been in transit for over twenty-four hours. And was still a mite tender after the rare, personal unpleasantness that had tinged the last negotiation job she'd completed in London.

All she wanted was to see her sister. To hug her sister. To see for herself that Lola was as deliriously happy as she said she was. And to do so beyond the long reach of the Chadwicks and their associates.

Tangling with a passive-aggressive Cormac Wharton hadn't been on her radar. Yet he'd just up and slapped her with the trump card; the *only* thing that would make her change her mind: sisterly guilt.

Jaw aching with the effort to hold back all the retorts she'd like to fling Cormac's way, Harper turned to her driver, her voice sweet as pie as she said, "Change of plan, Sam."

Sam squared his shoulders before flicking Cormac a dark glance. "Are you certain, ma'am? If it's still your intention to leave, all you have to do is ask."

She glanced at Cormac right as his mouth twitched. Nothing more than a flicker, really. Yet it did things to his face that no other smile in the history of smiles had the power to do; pulling, like an insistent tug, right behind her belly button.

"Thank you, Sam," she said, deliberately turning her back on the younger man. "You're a true gentleman. But if my little sister wants me to stay, then that's what I'll do."

Sam clicked his heels together before heaving her suitcase and accompanying bags to the ground. She feared hauling them up the stairs to the Chadwicks' front door might do Sam in, so before he could offer she pressed a large tip into his hand and sent him on his way, hoping she'd made the right choice as she watched the car meander slowly up the long gravel drive.

"I think you have a fan there," said Cormac, his voice having dropped a notch.

Harper tuned to Cormac and held his gaze, despite the butterflies fluttering away inside her belly. "Where *is* my sister?"

"Catering check. Wedding-dress fitting. Final song choices. None of which could be moved despite how excited she was that you were finally coming home."

Harper bristled, but managed to hold her tongue.

She was well aware of how many appointments she'd missed. That video-chatting during wedding-dress-hunts wasn't the same as her being in the room, sipping champagne, while Lola stood in front of a wall of mirrors and twirled. That with their parents long gone from their lives she was all Lola had.

Lola had assured her it was *fine*. That Gray was *such* a help. That the Chadwicks were a *total* dream. That she understood Harper's calendar was too congested for her to have committed to arriving any earlier.

After all, it was the money Harper made from her meteoric rise in the field of corporate mediation that had allowed Lola to stay on in the wealthy coastal playground of Blue Moon Bay, to finish high school with her friends, to be in a position to meet someone like Grayson Chadwick in the first place.

And yet as Cormac watched her, those deep brown eyes of his unexpectedly direct, the tiny fissure he'd opened in Harper's defences cracked wider.

If she was to get through the next five minutes, much less the next week, Cormac Wharton needed to know she wasn't the same bleeding heart she'd been at school.

She could do this. For Harper played chicken for a living. And never flinched.

"You sure know a lot about planning a wedding, Cormac," she crooned, watching for his reaction.

There! The tic of a muscle in his jaw. Though it was

fast swallowed by a deep groove as he offered up a close-mouthed smile. "They don't call me the best man around here for nothing. And since the maid of honour has been AWOL it's been my honour to make sure Lola is looked after too."

Oh, he was *good.*

But she was better.

She extended a smile of her own and placed a hand on her heart as she said, "Then please accept my thanks for playing cheerleader, leaning post, party planner and girl-friend until I was able to take up the mantle in person."

Cormac's mouth kicked into a deeper smile, the kind that came with eye crinkles.

That pesky little flutter flared in her belly. She clutched every muscle she could to suffocate it before it even had a chance to take a breath.

Then something wet and cold snuffled under Harper's coat and pressed against the back of her knee. With a squeak, she spun on her heel to find Cormac's beautiful dog standing behind her. Panting softly, tail wagging slowly, it looked at her with liquid brown eyes that reminded her very much of its owner.

She was surprised to find a soft, "Oh," escape her mouth.

"Harper," Cormac's voice rumbled from far too close behind her, "meet Novak. Novak, this is Harper."

"Novak?"

"After the great and glorious Kim."

"The actress? From *Vertigo*?"

A beat, then, "One and the same."

Spending more of her life in planes and hotels than her high-rise apartment, Harper didn't see a lot of dogs these days, so wasn't sure of the protocol. What could she do but wave? "Hello, Novak. Have we been ignoring you?"

Novak's tail gave a quick wag before she sat on her haunches and— *No. Surely not.*

"Is she…smiling?" Harper asked. "It looks like she's smiling. Can dogs even smile?"

She looked over her shoulder to find herself close enough to Cormac to count his lashes. There were millions of the things…long, plentiful as they framed those deep, molten-chocolate eyes.

When she didn't look away, his eyes shifted slowly between hers, lingering a beat before shifting back. Then he smiled. Turning her thoughts to dandelion fluff.

Then suddenly he was leaning towards her, a waft of sea salt, of summer, tickling her nose. Then he leant down to grab a couple of her bags, hefting the long handles over his shoulders as if they weighed nothing, and the moment passed.

She reminded herself—stridently—that he might look like the boy she'd thought worthy of secret teenaged affections, but those affections had gone up in smoke when she'd discovered he had it in him to stick in the knife. And twist.

Harper grabbed the handles of her last couple of bags and took a discreet step away.

Not discreet enough, apparently, as Cormac's cheek kicked into a knowing smile before he said, "Could you have brought any more baggage?"

Honey, you have no idea.

"Come on, then," he said, and with that he crunched over the white gravel and up the huge front steps of the big house.

The impressive Georgian-look manor was the first house built on the bluff over Blue Moon Bay by Weston Chadwick's father. When the next generation relocated the head office of their world-famous surf brand to the area, making the holiday estate their permanent home, the sleepy town had fast grown into a haven for wealthy families looking for a sea change.

Those who could keep up with the Chadwicks thrived. Those who couldn't…

"Come!" Cormac called.

Harper's eyebrows rose sharply, until Cormac's dog trotted up the stairs and she realised the command had not been for her.

Cormac and dog disappeared inside the double front doors as if they'd done so a thousand times before. Which they likely had.

Rumour had it that Cormac had moved into the Chadwicks' pool house right after high school. Then he and Grayson had gone on to take law together at Melbourne University before Grayson had taken his place on the board of his family's behemoth company, while Cormac opened up his own firm, servicing one client: the Chadwick family.

By the look of things, insinuating himself had been a smart move. As Harper made her way up the front steps, she wondered how much of his soul he'd had to give up to do it.

None of which made Harper feel any better about the fact that her little sister was about to marry into that world, that family, for good.

Well, she'd see about that.

Through the impressive two-storey foyer, walls unexpectedly lined with some pretty fabulous modern art, Harper kept eyes front as she followed Cormac up one side of a curling double staircase.

She found him in a large bedroom suite, leaning against a chest of drawers as he played with his dog's ear.

Her bags had been placed by a padded bench at the end of a plush king-sized bed. Sunshine poured through large windows draped with fine muslin, picking out shabby-chic furnishings and duck-egg-blue trim. A vase of fresh gardenias sent out the most glorious scent.

The room was elegant and cool. It suited her to a T.

Lola, she thought, her chest tightening, knowing Cormac hadn't been kidding. Her little sister had decorated the room with her in mind.

Harper slowly unwrapped the tie around her waist and hung her coat over the back of a padded chair, leaving her in a neat cream shift with a kick at the hem and her ubiquitous heels.

Cormac cleared his throat. She looked his way to find him watching her, his deep, rich brown eyes still holding the glint of affection he held for his hound.

"So," she managed, "am I meant to stay in here until Lola arrives, or have you been given further instruction as to what to do with me?"

Something flickered across his eyes, but was gone before she could take its measure. His hands slid into the front pockets of his jeans, framing all he had going on down there. Not that she looked. Then he pointed a thumb over his shoulder towards the door. "You hungry?"

"I'm fine," Harper lied, for she was starved. Sharing a meal was a tactic she often used mid-negotiation to soften up the combatants. And she would not be softened. Not by him.

"Then I guess we could stand here making awkward conversation till someone gets home."

Harper glanced deliberately at her watch. It was two in the afternoon. On a Monday. "I vote no."

"Hmm. Big shock." He took a step towards the door. "If we're up to our throats in my famous ham and mustard sandwiches there'll be no need to make small talk. Let me make you something. Let me feed you."

She wondered how often that line worked. By the gleam in his eye, probably every time. She actually found herself wavering towards his suggestion when a bang, a crash, a flurry of voices preceded the thunder of feet taking the stairs two at a time.

Then a whirlwind of blonde hair, yoga gear and running shoes rushed through the door and launched itself at her.

Harper's knees hit the back of her bed as she fell, laughing despite herself.

While Lola hung on tight and cried, "You're here! You're really here!"

After a quick mental scan to make sure nothing was broken, Harper hugged Lola back. Hard. Drinking in the feel of her little sister, the hitch of her voice, the scent of her skin.

She squeezed her eyes shut tight when she felt the sting of tears. Not now. Not here. Not with an audience. Their story had always been a personal one. The two of them against the world.

"Of course I'm here," Harper said through the tight clutch at her throat. "Now get off me before I crumple. Or before you bruise yourself. You are getting married this weekend, you know."

Lola rolled away, landing on her back. "I'm getting married this weekend."

Harper hauled herself to sitting, fixed her dress and swiped both hands over her hair. "So the rumour goes."

A noise, movement, something had her looking back towards the door to find Cormac leaning in the doorway. Watching her.

When their eyes met he smiled. Just the slightest tilt of his mouth, but it filled her with butterflies the same.

She felt her forehead tighten into a scowl.

For she'd been hanging out for this moment, this re-union with her flesh and blood, her heart and soul, her Lola, for so long.

And he—with his history, his link to the Chadwicks and his knowing eyes—was ruining everything.

"Oh, hi, Cormac!" said Lola as she crawled to sit beside Harper on the bed, before leaning on her like a puppy. "I didn't see you there."

He tilted his chin and gave her a wink, his stance easing, his eyes softening, his entire countenance lightening.

"Have you two been getting reacquainted, then? Chatting about the good old days?"

"Not sure we had much in the way of 'old days', did we, Harper? You were—what, a year or two below me at school?"

"A year below," she said, her voice admirably even. Then, with a deliberate blink and a turn of her shoulders, she cut him out of the circle.

She took one of Lola's hands in hers and pulled it to her heart, then pressed her other hand against her little sister's face. And she drank her in like a woman starved.

The last time she'd flown Lola to holiday with her in Paris, she'd still had apple cheeks. Now they were gone. New smile lines creased the edges of her mouth. Her hair was longer too, more structured, blonder.

And shadows smudged the skin beneath her bright blue eyes.

Late nights? Not enough water? Or some deeper concern?

When their family had fallen apart all those years ago, Harper had done everything in her power to shield Lola from the worst of it. Taking every hit, fixing every problem, hiding every secret, so that Lola might simply go on, having the blessed life she'd have enjoyed otherwise.

Meaning Lola knew nothing about the part the Chadwicks had played in it all.

Here, now, seeing her sister in the flesh, Harper knew—it was time. It was time for Lola to know the truth.

"How you doing, Lolly?" Harper asked, her voice soft, her expression beseeching. "Truly."

At which point Lola's bottom lip began to quake and she burst into tears.

CHAPTER TWO

HARPER PACED UP and down the long wall of the Chadwicks' library. A clock somewhere struck seven, and her eyes flickered to the open doorway as she waited impatiently for her sister to appear.

It had been hours since Lola had burst into tears.

In the several beats it had taken Harper to come to terms with the fact her sister was sobbing in her arms, Grayson Chadwick had filled the doorway of Harper's room.

With a grunt he'd lumbered inside, climbed up onto her bed and wrapped them both in a bear hug.

At which point Lola had come up laughing, wiping her tears, looking from fiancé to sister with shining blue eyes, claiming she had no idea why she'd broken down. Likely nervous excitement, over-stimulation, and pure joy that Harper was finally here.

Harper hadn't pushed it. Not then. Not there. It had been clear Lola had not wanted to appear upset in front of Gray, which rang all kinds of fresh alarm bells.

Lola had pushed away from the bed. "You must be exhausted. If you look in the bedside drawer you'll find I've left you a little relaxer."

"Wow, you guys are close," Gray had murmured.

Lola had smacked her fiancé, her hand bouncing off his pec. "Not that kind of relaxer, you degenerate. A *yoga nidra*. I bookmarked links to some awesome guided meditations in my favourite yoga book so she can centre herself before heading down for dinner. If I know my sister, and I do know my sister, she'll need it to handle your parents.

I'll come find you in the library," she'd said, pointing a finger at Harper. "Seven p.m. sharp."

Then they'd piled out of her room, Cormac the last to go.

"A little prolonged relaxation should never be underestimated," he'd said with a nod towards her bedside drawer, before he'd caught her gaze, delivered a knockout smile, rapped a knuckled fist against the doorway and was gone.

Harper swallowed. And rolled her shoulders.

The moment she had her little sister alone Harper would get to the bottom of Lola's tears. Would see how much Lola really knew about her future in-laws. And then she would fix everything.

A scrape of shoe against floor had Harper turning to the library door and once again staring down Cormac Wharton.

He'd changed into a charcoal suit, sharp white shirt open at the neck, no tie. He looked slick and relaxed. Debonair and yet with the unshaved scruff on his jaw a little rough around the edges. Forcing her to admit—if only to herself—that, while the boy had been swoon-worthy, the man was a far more dangerous beast.

She said nothing as she waited for his gaze to finish its travels over her.

She'd chosen a fortifying dress in which to meet the Chadwicks; midnight-blue and dramatically detailed, with a full skirt and fitted bodice, the sharp horizontal neckline and long sleeves leaving neck and shoulders bare.

Cormac's eyes paused at her ankles, her waist, her décolletage, before they swept swiftly back to hers. Her breath snagged in her throat as their gazes clashed.

"Evening, Harper," he said as he prowled into the room.

She nodded, not yet trusting her voice. And began to pace as well. "No sign of Lola on your way down?"

"I wasn't upstairs. I only just arrived back."

She shot him a look. "Quick commute from the pool house?"

"The pool house? I haven't stayed there in years. How did you even know about the pool house?"

Dammit. Harper feigned interest in the wall of books when her attention was wholly on where he was in the room relative to her. "Lola talks. She keeps me up-to-date with the goings on in Blue Moon Bay."

"But that was before Lola's time. You been keeping tabs on me, Harper?"

Double dammit.

"Hardly."

Cormac stopped prowling to flick a speck of lint off the back of a chair and she came to a halt. When he began pacing once more, so did she. The smile tugging at the corners of his eyes grew into a grin as it became all too obvious they were chasing one another around the couch.

Harper sat on the soft leather lounge and reached down to pick up a book from the coffee table, as if she'd been planning to do so the entire time.

Cormac moved to take the other end of the same chair, lifting an ankle to rest it on a knee, stretching a lazy arm across the back of the seat, his fingers curled mere inches from her bare shoulder. "I wouldn't have picked you as a fan of bird-watching."

"Hmm?"

Cormac motioned to the book she was pretending to admire.

She placed it back on the table and gritted her teeth.

"You're right about Lola," Cormac said.

Harper couldn't help herself; she glanced his way, cocking a solitary eyebrow to show her care in anything he had to say was limited.

"She talks," he said. "She talks a lot about you."

"And I talk a lot about her." Or she used to. Harper struggled to remember the last time she'd met someone new, someone she felt comfortable enough to talk about her sister with. "She's my everything. And has been for a very long time. The fact that we live on opposite sides of the world hasn't changed that."

"I'm going to tell you what she says about you too," said Cormac, "because you looked a little delicate when we left you in your room earlier. Like you could do with a boost."

Harper opened her mouth to tell him where he could put his boost, but Cormac got there first.

He leaned forward, resting his elbows on his knees, and looked back at her as he said, "I've never met anyone as proud of another person as Lola is of you."

Harper's mouth slowly closed.

"She talks so highly of your work, your ambition, how much you've sacrificed for her, we'd be forgiven for believing the sun shone out of your very eyes."

Harper shifted on the seat. Blamed the softness of the cushions.

"She loves telling the story of how you didn't freak out when she ditched her physio degree with a semester to go, even though you'd paid her way through uni. Goes on and on about how amazing you are. How happy she is that you're her sister."

He stopped there, as if waiting to see her reaction. As if he knew exactly how much she'd "freaked out" behind closed doors. And she had—calculating the costs, the overtime she'd put in to pay for it all, worrying how Lola might create a future for herself instead.

Only the relief in Lola's voice, the joy, as she'd spoken about her decision had brought Harper's outrage level down from eleven to a solid seven, which was pretty much her baseline.

Cormac's gaze remained direct and unrelenting.

If she'd managed to keep her frustration and disappointment from Lola, then she'd damn well keep it from him. Her smile was worthy of the Mona Lisa as she said, "It's true. I am amazing."

A muscle flickered in Cormac's cheek. "So it would seem."

"Yet after what happened upstairs earlier, would you say that my little sister is truly happy?"

His eyes narrowed, and slowly, slowly he leant back in the chair. Then he waved a hand in the air and asked, "What is happiness?"

When Harper realised she didn't have a ready answer, she said, "I imagine it's different things to different people."

"Then for me it's a hot morning, an empty beach and a long wave."

Harper cocked an eyebrow.

"There's a *chance*," said Cormac, "it could be the exact same ingredients for Lola, but you'd have to ask her yourself."

And she would. When she could get her sister all to herself for any length of time. Till then…

"Look, I know you're in deep with the Chadwick family, so I'm talking to the wrong person about this, but right now you're all I've got. I need to know that Lola's okay. I need to know that she's making the right decision."

Cormac breathed out long and slow. She could all but see him picking her words apart and putting them back together in his mind. Then he said, "And if I said I couldn't make any promises, what exactly would you do about it?"

Harper opened her mouth to tell Cormac exactly what she would do, when Cormac looked at something over Harper's shoulder. His face creased into a smile. With teeth. And eye crinkles. And pleasure. Before he pulled himself to standing.

"Well, if it isn't the folks of the groom!" Cormac said, holding his arms wide.

Every question fled from Harper's head as she spun

so fast her neck cracked, giving her no time at all to pull herself together before Weston and Dee-Dee Chadwick glided into the room, leaving her unprepared for how over-whelming it was to see them again.

They looked much as she remembered them. More grey in the hair, of course. More weather around the eyes. But still dripping money and success and ease. As if they had not a care in the world.

Harper was too busy noting the deep smile creases branching out from the edges of Weston Chadwick's bright blue eyes as he took Cormac in a long hug, a hug fit for a son, to see Dee-Dee coming for her.

Cool, ring-clad fingers gripped Harper's upper arms, pulling Harper to Dee-Dee's cheek. "Darling Harper. We are all so glad that you're finally here."

There was that *finally* word again. Had they made a pact to use it any chance they had?

Dee-Dee turned Harper this way and that. "Aren't you an absolute treat? Not much of Lola in you, but enough. In the eyes, perhaps. And, no doubt, the heart."

Floaty, blonde and elegant, Dee-Dee Chadwick had an unexpectedly kind touch. Warm. Enveloping. Motherly. Not that Harper would know. She hadn't seen her own mother since she was five.

The urge overcame her to twist away. To gain distance. Only her years spent as a star player in the field of corpo-rate manoeuvring had taught Harper the value in smiling politely. While plotting quietly.

"Thank you for putting me up, Mrs Chadwick. Though I'd have been fine staying in a hotel—"

"Nonsense. We are to be family after all. And no call-ing me Mrs Chadwick. It's Dee-Dee."

"Then thank you, Dee-Dee," Harper managed, right as Lola traipsed through the wide doorway, mouthing *Sorry!* as she dragged Gray into the room.

Harper shook her head and mouthed *It's okay.*

"Weston, darling," said Dee-Dee. "Stop talking business, this is a family gathering. Come meet Lola's sister,
Harper. Fresh in from her high-powered job in Dubai."

"High-powered, you say," said Weston as he ambled to
Dee-Dee's side, placing a hand in the small of his wife's
back as he looked into Harper's eyes.

Harper's breath burned in her lungs. Her back teeth
ground together. Every inch of her skin felt as if it were
crawling in microscopic bugs. For this man had been the
cause of so much pain in her family. Did he remember?
Did he care?

"She's a corporate negotiator," said Lola, sidling up
beside them, her hand still locked tight in the crook of
Gray's elbow.

"For?" Weston asked, attention already beginning to
slide away.

Harper knew just how to get it back. "The highest bid-
der."

Weston blinked and seemed to see her for the first time.
"That so?"

Harper wondered if Weston Chadwick recognised her
father in her eyes. In her heart.

"And isn't she luminous?" Dee-Dee gushed. "Look at
her skin."

"A benefit of not living under the Australian sun all
your life," said Weston, his deeply tanned skin creasing
as he smiled.

All Harper could think was that the only reason
she'd had to leave this place was in order to chase the
highest bidders, was so that she'd make enough money
to provide Lola with every opportunity the Chadwicks
had been able to gift their son. And the only reason that
had become her responsibility was because of him. Her
sister's future father-in-law.

"And that dress," said Dee-Dee, cheerfully. "So strik-
ing. Not that Harper wouldn't look just as beautiful in a

hessian sack." Dee-Dee looked around for agreement just as Cormac moved into her line of sight. "Cormac, wouldn't Harper look lovely even in a hessian sack?"

Cormac glanced around the group before his gaze landed on Harper. She still couldn't get used to it; those familiar deep brown eyes looking right at her.

It was a relief when he broke eye contact to do as Dee-Dee requested and determine whether she would look good in a hessian sack. His eyes dancing over her with speed and ease. Nothing at all untoward to an untrained eye.

Only Harper read body language for a living, noting the rise and fall of his chest, the flaring of his nostrils, the way his throat worked.

Cormac liked what he saw.

Seeing that flare of attraction in the eyes of any other man, she'd have been flattered and moved on. In the eyes of Cormac Wharton it was a threat to life as she knew it.

Harper shook her head just a fraction. Please, no. Don't go there. Don't answer. Don't make this week more complicated than it already is.

Cormac smiled, his voice a rough rumble that skittered down Harper's arms as he said, "I for one would love to see Harper in a hessian sack."

Gray's laughter was like a sonic boom. Though he quickly sank into his gargantuan shoulders when his mother slanted him a Look.

"I am truly disappointed in all of you. Harper is going to think we are a bunch of yokels," said Dee-Dee, pointing a finger at each man in her midst.

"Not at all," Harper said, hoping they'd all now move on.

She had no problem being centre of attention, but only when she was prepared, armed with not a single question she did not already know the answer to. And Cormac's *"And if I said I couldn't make any promises, what exactly would you do about it?"* rang in her head like a promise. Or a portent.

Lola cleared her throat. "Sorry to break up the fun, but after all the wedding stuff I did today I'm famished." She winked at Harper, who could not have loved her sister more.

"Of course," said Dee-Dee. "Let's head into dinner." She took her husband's arm as he escorted her from the room.

Then Lola put her hand through Gray's elbow and allowed herself to be swept out the door as well, like something out of a royal procession.

"Miss Addison?"

Harper turned to find Cormac beside her—eyes front, one arm behind his back, the other crooked her way. As if he'd read her mind.

She laughed before she even felt it coming. Then, with a long outrush of breath, she placed her hand in the proffered elbow.

Though she took the first step, leading him out of the room.

But his legs were longer, and he wasn't wearing heels, meaning soon he was a smidge in front. So she picked up the pace. He lengthened his strides to match. And soon they found themselves all but jogging.

When Harper's high heel caught on a knot in a rug and she had to grip on to Cormac's arm to steady herself, Cormac shot her a look.

Giving in?

Never.

Yet they called a silent truce. For now. Walking at a sensible pace.

And in the silence Harper felt the warmth of him beneath her hand, even through the layers of clothing. Felt his leg as it brushed against her skirt. Felt her pulse quicken

when he let go a quick hard breath, as if he too was un-
duly affected by their proximity.

Not that it mattered. All that mattered was Lola. Making sure she was happy. And that she would continue to
be so once Harper left. Meaning she had to get to the bottom of Cormac's cryptic quip while she had the chance.

She licked her lips. Swallowed. And said, "Cormac?"

He glanced down at her, catching her up in his deep,
warm brown eyes. And for the life of her she couldn't remember what she'd been about to say.

When an eyebrow cocked and a smile started tugging
at his mouth, she had to say something. She went with,
"How far away is the dining room?"

"It's a big house." Cormac's cheek twitched, bringing
his dimple out to play. *Have mercy.*

Whatever he saw in her eyes made him breathe deep.
Then his gaze travelled down her cheek, her neck, paus-
ing on her dress. His voice dropped a fraction as he said,
"You didn't actually pack a hessian sack, did you?"

Harper shot him a look that would flay the top layer
of skin off a less self-assured man. While Cormac only
grinned. A quick flash of teeth that had her heart slamming against her ribs, hard enough to make her wince.

"Good," he said. "For a second there I thought I'd have
to track one down too in an effort at maid-of-honour-best-
man solidarity."

"No need," she said. "For the sack or the solidarity."

"Is that so?"

"You stand for Gray. I stand for Lola."

"There was I, thinking that's the same thing. Why do
I get the feeling you don't?"

Right. *That* was what she wanted to talk to him about.
"Earlier, before the Chadwicks arrived, when I asked if
you thought Lola was happy, that she would be okay, what
did you mean when you said you couldn't make any promises?"

Cormac lifted his spare hand to run it up the back of his neck. A sign of frustration, no doubt. With her. But it wasn't her job to make his life easier. It was her job to protect her sister.

"You're not going to cause trouble this week." It was a statement, not a question.

"I'm not a troublemaker, Cormac. I'm a fixer."

Cormac's gaze was unreadable.

Voices murmured ahead as they neared the dining room; a long table covered in elegant settings of fine china and huge floral centrepieces was visible through a pair of double doors.

"Who else is coming?"

"Just us."

"All that view is missing is a pair of armoured servants holding swords," Harper muttered.

"Night off."

"Ah."

Harper's pace slowed, the thought of having to play nice with the Chadwicks turning her legs to jelly. She may even have tightened her grip on Cormac's arm.

She felt Cormac's gaze slide to hers before his voice came to her, low and slow. "Harper."

"Mmm?"

"Dee-Dee was right. Even without the hessian sack, you look immoderately beautiful tonight."

Harper's gaze skittered to his. She hadn't needed to hear it to know Cormac was thinking it, for so far he'd not felt a need to hide behind propriety. Yet hearing those words from that mouth were the worst kind of bittersweet.

She'd have melted if he'd as much as gifted her a smile when she was sixteen. Now a distraction of this kind was the very last thing she needed.

When she said nothing, he went on. "And by immoderately, I mean unfairly. With relish. As if to dazzle. To create shock and awe. Why do I get the feeling this is your version of playing dirty?"

Because you're too smart for your own good.

Harper thought she might have found an ally, but she'd thought wrong. Cormac Wharton would have to be watched, and handled, very carefully indeed.

She lifted a hand to fuss with the perfectly straight lapel of Cormac's jacket. "For a small-town boy, you clean up okay yourself."

After the briefest of beats, Cormac murmured, "Look at that. We can play nice."

And he leaned in to her, just a fraction. Enough that she was forced to flatten her hand against his chest. Felt the steady thump of a strong heart through her fingers as they stood, toe to toe. Who would flinch first? Not Harper. Never Harper.

"Hurry up, you two!" Lola called from inside the dining room.

Harper pulled her hand away right as Cormac leant back. The game a draw. Though the skin of her palm tingled as if she'd held it too close to an open fire.

Something flashed across Cormac's face before he hid it behind a smile. Then, sweeping an arm ahead of him, he said, "After you, my lady."

Harper couldn't help herself; she curtsied, earning an ear-to-ear grin that had her blinking to clear her eyes, before they joined the others.

CHAPTER THREE

HARPER DID NOT sleep well.

The bed was wonderful, the sheets soft and heavy, the mattress the perfect level of firmness.

And yet her dreams sent her tossing and turning.

Dreams of Lola chained to the floor à la Princess Leia in Jabba's palace, while the Chadwicks laughed and shovelled mounds of exotic food into their gobs.

Dreams of waking and not knowing which time zone she was in. Or which city. Whose bed.

Dreams of deep, dark eyes, a smile that made her knees turn to water and a mouth carved by the gods.

She'd woken with a start, sheets tangled around her limbs, sweat sheening her skin.

After a quick shower, liberal use of her serious wasabi eye drops and a strong black coffee by way of the Chadwicks' day chef—yes, *day chef*—she put on her face, skinny grey jeans, delicate cream heels and a frilled white top. With a yawn, she tossed the necessities into her buttery leather tote and made her way downstairs to find Lola bouncing around the foyer a mite before half past eight.

Lola barrelled into Harper's arms, wrapping her in such a hug she nearly tipped them both over backwards. Harper soon realised how long it had been since she'd experienced prolonged human contact, shaking hands with a room full of suits before dismantling them across a boardroom table notwithstanding.

When Harper peeled herself away the return of lung function brought forth another yawn.

"It's the sea air," Lola said with a grin. "It's therapeutic. Calming enough, even you might relax."

Harper poked out her tongue. "I grew up here, remember."

"Oh, right. I'd forgotten you were ever a child." Lola nudged Harper with a shoulder. "Now, I get you don't feel the same way about Blue Moon Bay as I do. Fair enough, too. I was too young to remember Mum leaving, or to fully understand the repercussions when Dad made such a hash of things."

At Lola's casual mention of the defining moments of Harper's young life she took the hits. As she always had. Keeping Lola protected from the worst of it. Only now she hoped she hadn't been too thorough at keeping her in the dark.

Lola went on, oblivious, "Today is my chance to rectify that. To help you see the place through fresh eyes. To undertand how deeply I appreciate everything you've done for me in helping me follow my bliss. Why being here, being a part of this community, being a yoga teacher, being Gray's wife, beats making big bucks working nine-to-five somewhere."

Lola's eyes widened as she realised her faux pas. "Not that there's anything wrong with nine-to-five! It's just not *my* thing."

Harper laughed. She hadn't worked less than an eighty-hour week in as long as she could remember.

Which was okay, because the career Harper had forged out of necessity was her bliss.

She loved the satisfaction that came with taking what seemed like an untenable situation and finding a way to make all parties happy. Or at the very least come to an agreement. No ambiguity. Complete transparency. A deal signed. She also loved that it paid more than enough for her to give her little sister whatever life she wanted, no matter how different it was from her own.

"So fresh eyes, hey?"

Lola clapped her hands together and bounded on the

balls of her feet. "Yes! It's going to be great. We'll do some wedding stuff along the way—to the tailor to check out our dresses, and a bar to check out the band who'll be rocking the wedding. But I also have a few secret plans to make you fall in love with Blue Moon Bay."

"Did you say *band*?"

"Only the best band in the bay."

"And the Chadwicks are okay with that?"

"Of course they are." There was no glancing away. No fussing with her thumbnails. No signs that she was lying and the Chadwicks were actually horror in-laws.

Yet the back of Harper's neck tingled.

The Chadwicks were as good as royalty in this community. And they had one child. One *son*. There was no dimension she could imagine in which they would not impose their influence over his wedding.

Then there was the fact they had refused to let Harper pay a cent towards the big day, asking for her blessing to allow them to pay for it all.

But what if it went deeper than that? What if they were doing so out of guilt? Was this their way of trying to rectify their part in the mess of years before? If so it wasn't nearly enough.

It took Harper's elite-level self-control to say, "I imagine a string quartet to be more to their taste. Or the Melbourne Symphony Orchestra."

Lola blinked. "Possibly. But it's my wedding."

"Yours and Gray's."

"He did his part with the proposing and being so gorgeous I had to marry him." Lola took Harper by both hands. "Harps, everything is fine. Everything is fabulous! You're so used to fighting for me you're looking for bad guys to smite. But I'm happy. This will be the wedding of my dreams."

The thing was, apart from the waterworks the day before, Lola did seem happy. And so very young.

It was early days. Better to eke out the truth rather than smack Lola over the head with it. Harper hooked her arm through Lola's elbow and said, "So let's do this."

Lola dragged her through the double-storey foyer, and out the front door. At which point Harper took a literal step back.

The same sky-blue, open-topped sports car Cormac had been sitting on the day before was now perched on the gravel outside the front door, its engine producing a throaty purr.

The man himself lounged in the driver's seat. No sitting, or slouching, for Cormac Wharton. For the gods had gifted him an overabundance of ease which only turned Harper's tension up a gear.

Cormac shifted, looked over his shoulder.

Dark sunglasses covered his eyes, bringing his jawline into relief. And his mouth. That same gorgeous mouth that had been doing things to her in her dreams that made her blush, even now.

"Our chariot awaits!" Lola proclaimed, her good cheer carrying on the wind as she dragged Harper down the stairs. Then she leapt over the car door to sit in the back seat alongside Novak, the dog, leaving the front passenger spot for Harper.

"Morning, ladies," Cormac rumbled.

"Hey, Mac," Lola sing-songed. "Thanks for the lift."

"You bet. Harper?"

Harper was busy trying to figure out how to get in the damn car as it seemed to have no door handles. Cormac opened the door from the inside, the muscles in his tanned forearm bunching winningly.

With a smile that felt like more of a wince, Harper slid onto the soft cream seat to find the leather already warmed by the biting southern sun. A subtle breeze kicked at her hair until it stuck to her lipstick. And she could feel Cormac's gaze burning a mark into her cheek.

"You all right over there?" Cormac asked, laughter lighting his deep voice.

Harper glanced sideways to find him watching her from behind his dark shades. He tilted his chin, motioning to where she held her bag like a shield. She slid it into the footwell.

With a grin, Cormac gunned the engine and took off down the drive.

"Nice car," Harper allowed.

"Nice?" he said, his face pained, before running a hand over the leather dash. "This is an original, metallic blue, 1953 Sunbeam Alpine Mark I. You can do better than *nice*."

She could. She just didn't want to. The best she would offer was, "Reminds me of the one in that movie. With Grace Kelly and Cary Grant."

"Oh, my life!" Lola said from the back seat. "Harper you have no idea what you've just done."

Harper glanced at her sister. Then at Cormac, who had dropped his sunglasses to the end of his nose to look at her as if he'd never seen her before.

"What? What did I say?"

"He's obsessed with Hitchcock movies," said Lola. *"Obsessed."*

"Right. Novak," Harper said, pointing a thumb at the dog, who wagged her thin tail.

Lola groaned. "Poor guy actually believes this is the car used in the filming of *To Catch a Thief*."

"Really?" Harper asked, unable to withhold her interest. Had Grace Kelly actually sat in this same seat? No, from memory, she had been the one driving.

"The provenance is unprovable," said Cormac, gazing dreamily over the inside of the car. "But the research I've done leads me to believe it really could be the one."

When his eyes once more found hers, they narrowed. "Don't tell me you're a sceptic."

"I'm not much of a believer in fairy-tale endings."

Cormac lifted a hand to his heart, as if he'd been shot. "I ache for you. I truly do." At which point he pushed his sunglasses back into place and slowed at the Chadwicks' front gates.

Giving Harper the chance to deal with the fact that Cormac Wharton had just told her he *ached* for her. She had to move past this erstwhile crush of hers, and fast. The man was far too astute, and if she wasn't careful he'd soon figure it out.

"Buckle up, kids," Cormac said. "The sun is out, life beckons and the waves wait for no man!"

Waves? What waves? Harper didn't have the chance to ask, as Cormac zoomed out onto Beach Road, pressing them back into their seats.

As they curved around the mouth of the bay, heading back towards town, the car rumbled smoothly beneath them, the sun filtered through the thin trees dappling the bonnet.

The air rolling in hot waves over the windscreen and whipping past Harper's face smelled of sea salt and scorched sand. Of sunscreen and coconut oil. Of bonfires and summers that lasted for ever.

"Everything okay?" came Cormac's voice.

Harper didn't realise her eyes were closed until she snapped them open.

"You sighed," he said, his voice low. "Dreamily."

Had she? "I was…lost in memory."

"That's what today's all about," said Lola, leaning forward to poke her head between them. "Harper's been away too long to remember how amazing it is here. Today's mission is to make her fall in love with Blue Moon Bay all over again."

All over again.

If she was honest her childhood had been mostly wonderful: a kaleidoscope of lazy summers and snug winters, lit with the smiles of a permanently joyful little sister and their wildly charismatic father, who'd told her daily that he loved her more than the moon and stars.

Before he'd lost everything and bolted, making it clear that love wasn't enough to tether him. She wasn't enough.

"Shouldn't be too hard," Cormac said, his warm voice sweeping away the discomfiture of those memories. "This is the best place on earth."

Harper laughed. Sure, Blue Moon Bay was ostensibly appealing with its craggy cliffs and blustery bluffs, world-famous surf beaches, stunning homes and quaint village shops, but come on.

"You disagree."

"Oh, you weren't kidding."

Cormac shot her a glance, the edge of his mouth lifting. Even a hint of that knee-melting smile made her pulse jump.

"I prefer somewhere nearer an international airport for a start. With consistent Wi-Fi coverage. A greater variety of cuisine. Style. Culture. Need I go on?"

Cormac whistled long and low. "I do believe we've been dissed."

Lola's laughter was short and sharp. "You think?"

"So, where are these havens of style of which you speak," Cormac asked. "Give us names. Paris? Verona? Madrid?"

"For a start."

Lola perked up. "What do you reckon, Mac? Is she right? Mac's been to more countries than I even knew existed. Yet he chose to come home."

What was that, now? So far as Harper knew, Cormac had left high school, moved into the Chadwicks' pool house, skated through university and found himself in a cushy position too good to give up. It seemed she'd missed some steps.

Then again, at one time he'd given her good reason to believe the worst of him.

"Is this true, Cormac?" Harper pressed. "In between

the gnarly waves, throwing a stick for your dog and baby-sitting for the Chadwicks, did you truly find the time to see the world?"

A muscle ticked in Cormac's jaw—a classic sign of discomfort—before he shot her a dark look. Enjoying having him on the back foot for once, Harper wriggled down into her seat and waited.

"Yeah," he said. "I truly did."

He deftly changed down through the gears as they hit the edge of the cliffs overlooking Blue Moon Bay's rugged coastline, one side of the road dropping away to a giant curving hole that seemed torn from the edge of the continent.

Harper thought he was done, until he said, "After uni I studied in England for a bit. Worked in bars, restaurants, sold balloons in Hyde Park to earn cash to backpack every chance I could."

Lola tsk-tsked. "Seriously, Mac? Way to downplay. By 'study in England' he means he went to Oxford on a Rhodes Scholarship."

Harper's gaze whipped so fast to Cormac she nearly pulled a muscle.

"It was around the time Gray and I got together," Lola added when it became clear Cormac wouldn't. "Poor Gray, pining for his friend, started coming to the gym where I worked. One day he took my yoga class and that was that. Then Cormac broke Gray's heart by not coming straight home after Oxford. Harps, remember that Christmas I couldn't come to you in Dubai?"

Harper remembered.

"Gray and I had gone to Boston to surprise Mac. Why were you there, again?"

Cormac gripped the wheel a little tighter. "My MBA."

Harper blinked. And blinked some more. And it had nothing to do with the wind.

None of this was sitting well. Like a piece from the

wrong puzzle, it didn't fit into the picture she'd built up—
or down—of him in her head.

And the worst of it? With the advantages he'd had, he
was wasting it all. The top-class education, the compre-
hensive world view; he should have been living the kind
of life she'd scraped and fought and bled to achieve.

So what on earth *was* he doing in Blue Moon Bay?

Looking for answers, her gaze tripped over the dry
brush covering the cliff-face, the sandy dirt spilling onto
the edges of the pockmarked road as they reached the end
of the bite and slowed to a stop at an intersection.

"Well," she said, motioning to a big, battered sign pointing the way to The Oldest Working Lighthouse in South-
Eastern Australia. "That's gotta add bonus points."

Cormac turned to face her, his eyes hidden behind his
sunglasses. But she felt his look all the same. Flat, assessing, and not altogether cool.

"Are you sassing us, Harper?"

"I'm just saying it all comes down to taste."

"Which is your way of saying we have none."

"Pretty much."

With that Cormac laughed, the sound deep and throaty
and sexy as hell. Then he lifted his sunglasses onto his head,
sending his hair into a mass of shaggy chestnut spikes.

"Lola," Cormac said, eyes never leaving Harper, "your
sister is most definitely sassing us."

Lola said, "And yet I am not deterred."

"Mmm…" Cormac murmured, those warm, dark eyes
of his holding her in their thrall. "Neither, it seems, am I."

He took off, curling around the bend and onto the long,
winding stretch of road heading into town.

His expression had been light but something in the
tone had Harper's heart ricocheting off her ribcage as if
she was back in the grip of teenage crushdom. And, by
the smile still creasing his cheek, she had the awful feeling he sensed something of it too.

Mad at herself, and him, and life in general, Harper turned bodily towards the window.

She should be better at this. She spent every working day facing down boardrooms full of powerful people with axes to grind and fear for their futures. She stood tall against their antipathy, not a single barb or sharp glance piercing her armour, she was that sure of her position.

Facing Cormac Wharton should be no different. For she was on the side of right and he was on the side of wrong and that was that.

A small voice of dissent chirped up. And for the first time that day she remembered the contract dispute she'd most recently left behind.

She'd purposely taken on a much smaller job than normal; representing a group of investors looking to buy out a small string of Italian restaurants in London that were in financial trouble with the plan to manage them more efficiently and take them international.

The original owner, the man who had started the brand from scratch, had been amenable to negotiation. His son, not so much. Especially once Harper been brought on board to end the talks quickly.

The son of the owner had somehow tracked down her private mobile number, leaving a string of awful messages accusing her of being soulless. A robot. Closed off to any real human emotion.

Yes, she saw things in black and white, separate from any emotional attachment, but that was her forte. Her research into both businesses had been thorough and flawless. Her recommendations equitable.

And yet those accusations had shaken her. As if the man tapped into some deep vein of unhappy truth she'd hidden from herself.

Once the deal was sealed she'd left without sticking around for the after-party. Back in Dubai, she'd packed fast and taken a car to the airport; the bad taste in her mouth a result the negotiation and not the fact she was heading back to Blue Moon Bay.

And if it wasn't for Lola, her gorgeous, smushy, beloved little Lolly-Pop, she'd never have stepped foot in the place again.

As wounds—both fresh and ancient—throbbed inside her, Harper closed her eyes to the sunshine and breathed, knowing she'd need to conserve her energy for whatever else this place threw at her today.

Harper knew herself to be organised. She had to be, what with international travel, shifting time zones, having to research every client to the nth degree, but Lola was a revelation.

The morning passed by in a blur of visits to the florist, the baker, the candlestick maker. Seriously. A local artisan had produced custom-made candlesticks wrought into the shape of driftwood for the reception table centrepieces.

While Lola chatted to the woman who was hand-printing the seating chart, encouraging her to come to a yoga class, Harper watched Cormac through the window. He stood outside the surfboard shop across the road talking to a guy with blond dreadlocks and skinny brown limbs. Novak sat on his foot, looking adoringly at her lord and master.

"The blonde or the brunette?"

Harper jumped out of her skin when Lola suddenly popped up beside her.

"Which one were you checking out?"

Harper scoffed. "Please."

Cormac made a rolling motion with his hand and the surfer dude laughed so hard he had to bend over to catch his breath.

Harper asked, "What do you think those two could possibly have to talk about?"

"Those long boards by the front door are made by one of the Chadwicks' subsidiary companies. Knowing Cor-

mac, he's most likely checking how Dozer—the blonde—
is doing. If they're selling. If he can do anything to help."

"Why would their lawyer need to do that?" Unless
something untoward was going on.

"He doesn't *need* to, he just does. Cormac knows every
employee by name. Every supplier too. Makes everyone
in the Chadwick family of businesses feel like more than
a cog in the wheel. That they are all important."

Harper narrowed her eyes. "But what's in it for him?"

Lola laughed and gave Harper a hug. "Oh, Harps, my
favourite cynic. I do love you so."

A cynic? She wasn't a cynic. She was a realist. In reality people usually did things to serve their own ends. She
classed herself in that group as well. Her motivations were
black and white- she did what she did for Lola. Dammit,
she was fine with that.

When Cormac turned to jog across the road, slowing to
wave a Kombi van through in front of him, Harper quickly
turned away from the window. But not before catching a
knowing glint in her sister's eye.

"Ready?" Cormac asked as he strode in the door, dark
eyes taking in Lola, who was trying to hide a grin, and
Harper, who was trying to hide the heat that had risen in
her cheeks.

"Ready as she'll ever be," said Lola, moving to hook a
hand into the crook of Harper's elbow and drag her from
the shop.

CHAPTER FOUR

CORMAC STOOD BY Gray's Jeep, wetsuit unzipped and hanging low from his hips as he waxed down his surfboard, not watching Harper and Lola doing yoga on the beach.

Or, to be more exact, Lola did yoga while Harper tried not to fall over. Or bend too far. Or snap in two.

"So what do you think of the elder Miss Addison?" asked Gray as he ambled around the car, wetsuit zipped up, board under one arm, half-eaten apple in the other hand.

"She's all right, I guess."

The moment the words left his mouth Cormac knew he'd played it too cool. Gray might not be as over-educated as Cormac, but he was no dummy.

Gray leaned against the car. "*All right*, you say? Sure, if a face that would once have been carved into the bow of a ship could be considered '*all right*'."

Cormac continued rubbing wax over the plane of his board.

Gray grinned. "Seems really smart too, don't you reckon? Scary smart. Quick tempered, though. A little sharp on the palate but elegant with it. Graceful but tough. Killer combination."

"Maybe you're marrying the wrong sister."

Gray laughed, delighted to have finally nudged out a response. "Nah. I'm good. I love my little bundle of sweetness and light. Harper is far too cool for the likes of me. By that I don't mean *cool*. I mean hot fury banked behind an icy mask. That one's pure kryptonite for poor saps who seek out a challenge."

Gray shivered dramatically, like a St Bernard shaking water from his coat.

While Cormac felt his gaze drag back to the women on the beach in time to see Lola performing a headstand, feet wriggling gleefully.

Harper, on the other hand, stood with her arms crossed, shaking her head, her entire body a study in tightly coiled suspicion. It ought to have been enough for him to dismiss her out of hand.

For he was easy going. Look at him, waxing a surf-board on a week day. Sure he'd done three hours of work before the rest of the gang were even awake, and he'd do more tonight once his babysitting duties were done. But he was extremely content with the balance he'd achieved in his life.

In fact, he'd have gone so far as to say he had life pretty much figured out.

Relax. Look up. Breathe. Be kind. Do good. Figure out what you love to do and do it more.

So why did seeing Harper walk out of the Chadwicks' house that morning make him feel like a racehorse locked in a stall?

Why, every time she came near, did he feel a need to brace himself, as if readying for a jolt of static shock?

Why did watching her now feel as if he was staring at sunlight glinting off the bonnet of his car, forcing him to blink against the intense bursts of light? Yet he couldn't look away.

In the distance, she squared her shoulders and lifted her chin to stare out at the horizon.

And it hit him.

The first time he'd seen *Rear Window*, he'd been four-teen years old. He still remembered the moment Grace Kelly first appeared on screen, her shadow falling omi-nously over Jimmy Stewart as he slept on, unsuspecting.

He'd found himself stunned by those sultry eyes, the mouth slightly open, décolletage bare as she leant in for a kiss.

But it was her cool detachment as poor Jimmy tried to lift himself out of his wheelchair to follow her kiss when she pulled away that had made him feel as though some switch had been flipped inside of him. As if he'd been given a glimpse into the mysterious, dangerous, world of Woman.

That was Harper Addison.

She was nothing so simple as a challenge. She was a tectonic shift.

"Earth to Mac," Gray said, his laughing voice now sounding as if it was coming from a mile away.

Cormac blinked and sniffed in a breath. Then he held up a hand to his face as if he'd been looking beyond the sand to the waves. "Better get cracking if we hope to find a decent curl."

"Funny, I've never seen you so intensely interested in a curl before." Then he reached out and slapped Cormac on the arm. "Relax. I get it. And I'm okay with it."

Cormac rubbed the board so hard the wax went flying out of his hand and rolled down the scrubby bank, collecting sand and dirt as it went. "Mate, I'm not hot for your fiancée's sister. Nothing is going to happen there. So get over it."

Curled darkly beneath the sudden sharp twang to his voice, Cormac heard his father. It took the edge off his aggravation as thoroughly as a bucket of iced water.

Plucking his board from the sand and hefting it under an arm gave Cormac an extra few seconds to summon up a smile. "You're projecting."

"You think?"

"Tell me you're not imagining us buying houses in the same street. Having Sunday barbeques. Our kids growing up as cousins."

Gray's eyes widened. "Whoa. I hadn't even thought that far. But how amazing would that be? You should totally marry her."

Cormac brought a hand to his chin and pretended to consider it. "Nah. I'll pass."

"Whatever you say." Gray tossed his apple core into the bush beside the car, then turned and jogged down the rickety stairs criss-crossing the dunes leading down to the beach.

Cormac breathed out hard. Closed his eyes against the sunlight a moment while he pulled himself together. Then whistled for Novak to stop investigating the scrub and follow him down the steps.

And not for the first time he thought, *Thank goodness for Gray.* A guy who'd never raised a fist to Cormac. Or even his voice. A guy whose family had been nothing but open, and warm, and welcoming, even when Cormac had been angry, confused and scared. Without them, who knew what path he'd be on now?

Which was why coming back to Blue Moon Bay had never been in question. Not really. The moment they'd offered him the job, he'd accepted. For he owed the Chadwicks more than loyalty. He owed them his life.

When Gray reached the girls he shoved his board into the sand before creeping up behind Lola and lifting her bodily, swinging her in the air.

Novak danced around them as Lola's squeal was caught on the wind.

Harper stopped mid-lunge, her hands coming up onto her hips before she shuffled her bare feet together. Her pale jeans had been rolled up to her knees. Her fussy top was now tied around her waist, leaving her in a lacy tank-top. As she heaved in a breath Cormac was gifted with a peekaboo sliver of skin and a flash of belly button.

Who knew an outie could be enough to make a man have to breathe deep in order not to embarrass himself?

Harper turned right as Cormac shifted his surfboard in front of him all the same, her long ponytail whipping around her face. Small curls had sprung up around her hairline. Her cheeks were stained with colour, her hazel eyes bright.

One of the thin straps of her top slipped down her shoulder, revealing just a hint of a curve of a strapless bra. Half-cup. Heaven help him.

"Your thing," he grunted, glancing determinedly at her shoulder.

"My what?" she asked, brow furrowing.

"Your—thing."

Words having deserted him, Cormac moved in, lifted a hand to slide her strap back into place, his knuckles grazing hot, sweat-dampened skin, before he drew his hand away.

Keeping his gaze up wasn't enough to stop his heart from pounding. To ease the blood rush behind his ears. To dampen the urge to slide the strap back off her shoulder, to run his palm over that soft, sun-kissed skin.

Harper's chest rose and fell in short sharp breaths. Heat shimmered in her bright eyes. Mutual attraction spread like a fog, curling around them till they were both enveloped.

Then she cleared her throat, readjusted her top and shook her hair out of her eyes before going back to glaring at him for all she was worth.

What had he promised Gray? *Nothing was going to happen there.* He'd actually believed it as he'd said it. As if saying it would make it so. But, up close and personal, he knew it wouldn't be a given. It would have to be a choice.

Somehow Cormac found a last remaining scrap of cool, enough for him to dredge up a smile as he asked, "Having fun?"

Lines dug deep into the skin above her nose. "What do you reckon?"

"You know, that's the first time that you sounded like a real Aussie."

She narrowed her eyes like a cartoon villain. "What's that supposed to mean?"

Figuring baiting her had to be safer than touching her, he said, "You're all uppity-woo now. Posh-tosh with that non-accent of yours. Almost as if you've purposely scrubbed away any evidence of where you came from."

Harper's eyes went from comically narrow to wide with shock. "I'd never have imagined the day I heard Cormac Wharton say 'posh-tosh' or 'uppity-woo'. It was worth coming back just for that."

And then she laughed. The sound unexpectedly raw, husky and brash. It shot heat straight from his ears to his groin. When her laughter subsided, it left a smile behind. The kind that kicked at just one corner of her mouth. A mouth that was pink, soft and far too kissable.

Cormac took a subtle step back, turned his surfboard horizontal, used it as a shield. "Going to have a dip?"

She glanced out at the churning waves, the wind having picked up over the past couple of hours. "You're actually going out there. Looks...dangerous."

"It is. And yet I go anyway."

She rolled her eyes. "So brave."

"Nah. Just hooked. I head out every day if I can. Ups the dopamine. Great workout. Great excuse for a big breakfast after." He patted his flat belly. Watched as her gaze went there. And stayed.

Her eyes darkened. Her jaw twitched. Her chest rose and fell again. This staying-away-from-her thing was not going to be easy. But whoever said self-sacrifice ought to be?

"This'll be my second time today, in fact. Gray slept in. So here we are."

"Gray does love his sleep," said Lola, appearing with Gray's hand in hers, before tipping up onto her toes to give her fiancé a kiss.

Cormac saw all this out of the corner of his eye, unable

to keep his gaze off Harper. Meaning he didn't miss the contempt that tugged at the corner of her mouth.

It wasn't for Lola. It was clear she adored her little sister as much as Lola adored her. Meaning the disdain was all for Gray.

Cormac's sense memory snapped into gear, his muscles tightening with the readiness to step physically between a loved one and a threat. A theory he'd been skirting around until that moment shifted into sharp focus, and the final reason Harper had him feeling on edge fell into place.

Her questions about Lola the night before, asking how happy she was, had not been casual. Harper was not on board with Lola marrying Gray, and he had no doubt that over the next few days she'd do something about it.

For he'd known people of her ilk before, prepared to voice their opinion even if it made them unpopular, because being right was more important to them than being judicious.

Harper had it in her power to unhinge everything. To make Lola doubt. To cause trouble for the Chadwicks. To hurt Gray. Add enough pressure and any family could be made to tear apart.

He stepped in, ready to take action, when Lola perked up and said, "Come on, Harps, let's go for a walk. Go surf, boys. The day is still young and there is much left to do."

Harper's wince was infinitesimal. Though when her face cleared there was none of the animosity he'd seen towards his friend. Just her usual heady mix of fire and ice.

"Can we take Novak?" Lola asked.

Cormac tipped his chin up the beach and Novak took off, bolting along the sand before turning back with a "hurry up" bark. And the women followed, Harper's hips swaying hypnotically as she navigated the soft sand, caramel ponytail swinging beguilingly behind her.

"Kryptonite," Gray said, his fist exploding while he

made the accompanying sound of a bomb, before running down into the water and out into the waves.

Realising he wasn't fooling anyone, Cormac watched the women work their way up the beach for a few more moments before he tore his gaze away and made his way to the water's edge.

Once knee deep he threw his board down and his body after it. It might not be the cold shower he needed, but it would have to do.

The car was relatively quiet as they rounded Beach Road on the way back to the Chadwick estate. Lola had gone in Gray's Jeep, leaving Harper and Cormac alone.

Unfortunately, it only made her more aware of Cormac in the seat beside her. The warmth of his thigh near hers. The nearness of his hand as he changed gears. The fact that she *knew* he was feeling it too.

Never in her life had she met a more confounding man.

First there was his geography. Well-travelled, and internationally educated, he chose to live in the back end of the most remote habitable continent on earth.

And she was extremely wary of how close he was to the Chadwicks.

Then there was the hurtful memory of the last thing he'd said to her all those years ago.

For some reason she got the feeling he didn't seem to like *her* very much either, yet she'd found him devouring her with a glance more than once.

Not that she'd acted any better. Watching Cormac come out of the surf, water droplets raining over him like diamonds, his chest bare, board shorts clinging to strong brown legs, she had felt as if she'd swallowed sand.

No matter the unexpected spark between them, there was nothing to be gained by revisiting her old crush. She had to be vigilant. Keep her focus tight. On Lola and the family her sister was hoping to marry into.

They hit the coastline, land dropping away to the squalling Southern Ocean on their right and rambling up into the sky to Harper's left. Shadow and light flickered over her face, forcing her to shut her eyes. And jet lag mixed with the emotional see-saw of the past couple of days finally took over.

In a sleepy half-awake state, Harper found herself once more swimming in memories. Like Polaroid pictures, the images were a little fuzzy and out of focus. But the location was clear: high school, tenth grade.

Part of the school extension programme, Harper had been able to join the year above for one class per term. Once it had been biology with Cormac.

Harper, thankfully, had been partnered with the top student in the class, an industrious girl from Torquay who bussed in every day.

Thankfully, because without her steering Harper might well have spent every lesson staring at the back of Cormac's gorgeous head.

He'd been partnered with Terence "The Bug" McIntosh. Named for the thickness of his oversized glasses.

Harper—who knew Terence a little from when she was collecting money to save the bees—knew that Terence liked the nickname. Bugs were his favourite people. But that didn't make him less ripe for the attentions of those with an eye for bullying.

While Cormac's friends made it clear they thought it hilarious he had to sit with The Bug, Cormac had ignored them all.

In fact, he'd taken the time to make friends with his lab partner—this kid half his size, with a face full of spots and interests a million miles from Cormac's own. Laughing during class, stopping to chat to him in the halls, throwing his arm around the kid's shoulders, marking him as a protected species. Together they'd delivered a hilarious and well-researched final presentation that Harper had watched with both hands over her cheeks lest the whole class see her adoration for Cormac written all over her face.

Harper came to with a start. It took a moment to remember she was in Blue Moon Bay, Cormac's car rocking beneath her as he drove her back to the Chadwick estate.

"It's the sea air," Cormac murmured.

She turned her head to find him watching the road. One arm resting on the open window, the other hand a light touch on the steering wheel.

He shot her a quick smile, and she had one last flashback to high school; a time of constant study, keeping down a weekend job, volunteering, navigating her dad's mercurial moods. Even on her most challenging days, that smile had never failed to chase her blues away.

"The sea," he repeated. "The sunshine. The fresh air. It does something to a person. On a cellular level."

She waited for a punchline. But he was serious. He wanted her to know this place was important to him.

Before she could ascertain why it mattered that she understood, they slowed, pulling around the white brick walls leading to the gravel drive of the Chadwick estate.

The Jeep had beaten them there. Lola and Gray watched Cormac and Harper pull up, all bright, guileless gazes and big, toothy smiles. The monstrous house loomed behind them.

"The two of you look like an ad for healthy, wealthy living," Harper muttered while she unclipped her old seatbelt and fiddled unsuccessfully with the door handle.

"Thanks," said Lola.

Gray burst out laughing. "Honey, I'm not entirely sure she meant that as a compliment."

Harper stopped wrestling with the handle as she caught Gray's eye. Well, well, well. Not as simple as he seems.

As if he knew exactly what she was thinking, Gray tipped his head in acknowledgement.

Before she could react, Cormac reached across her lap, grabbed the inner door handle and clicked it open.

At the wash of warmth from his nearness, his drinkable scent catching her out, Harper stilled right as he drew his hand back. The backs of his knuckles caught on the frills of her shirt before brushing lightly, softly, achingly over her breasts.

The whole thing happened in less than a second, yet Harper remained frozen. Her breath stuck in her lungs, the frills of her shirt swaying under her nose like some teasing reminder.

Then her eyes went to his.

He gave her an easy smile, no teeth, as if simply waiting for her to hop out of the car. Only the flare of awareness burning in the depths of his eyes, and the way his hand gripped and ungripped the steering wheel, indicated he'd felt the touch too.

"Thanks?" she said.

"You're welcome?" he said, copying her faulty inflection. Despite the attempt at humour, his voice was deep and throaty and coarse. The voice of a man barely holding himself together.

"Come on, Harps," Lola said, her sing-song voice coming from a million miles away.

Spell broken, Harper swallowed and hopped out of the car on shaky legs.

"We need to get changed, put on some lippy and get ready to lose several decibels of hearing."

"We're going out *again*?"

"We're going to hear the wedding band play!" Lola threw her hands in the air. Behind her Gray copied the move.

Harper heard Cormac's door shut but deliberately did not look back. Maybe that was the key. Not looking at him at all. No getting lost in those deep brown eyes. No imagining how his springy hair would feel between her fingers. No holding out for even a glimpse of that smile.

Out of sight, out of mind had worked for the past decade; it'd have to work now.

"Go make yourselves pretty, boys," Lola said. "Give us half an hour and we're all yours." Lola turned to Harper with a grin. "It'll be a double date!"

"Yay!" Harper said, throwing her hands in the air in imitation of the lovebirds, before following Lola into enemy territory to prepare for the next level of hell.

CHAPTER FIVE

HARPER SHOWERED, CHANGED into a cream bustier, black pencil skirt and pearlescent stiletto sandals, taking time to turn the beachy frizz into smooth, Veronica Lake waves. Cormac had been right in suggesting she dressed to dazzle. But she it wasn't her version of playing dirty. It was her version of armour-plating.

Gray drove this time, escorting them in his old Jeep, to the next town over—bigger, more touristy, full of bars.

Their bar—The Tide—boasted dive-bar chic, all crumbling brick and flaking black paint on the window frames. The deep base sound of rock music thumped through the walls.

Lola took Gray by the hand and dragged him past a long line of people to the front door, where a bouncer the size of a yeti stood holding a folder.

"Seth!" said Lola. "I haven't seen you in class for too long."

The bouncer took one look at her and melted. "I know, Miss Lola. I've been busy."

"How's your neck?"

"Not good."

"Come. Next week. Promise me."

He blushed. "Promise."

"Excellent. I have these three cutie-pies with me. All right?"

The bouncer's lovey-dovey smile hardened as he ran beady eyes over Gray, then Cormac. He seemed to save his longest glare for Harper.

"That's my big sister, Harper," Lola said. "She's here

for my wedding this weekend. Hey, Seth, you should totally come!"

Harper opened her mouth to reprimand Lola for making such an unconsidered request. There were seating plans to consider. And catering. Fire hazards. Lola had been that way her whole childhood—saw a tree, had to climb the tree, saw a dog, wanted the dog, even if it was at the end of someone else's lead. Their father's light ran through her blood, but thankfully none of the dark.

But then she looked to Gray. Let him be the bad guy here. For Lola was his responsibility now, or she would be come Saturday afternoon.

Gray shrugged. "Sure. The more the merrier. We'd love to have you there."

Harper gawped. Then saw the delight in Lola's eyes. Not a new kind of delight, but a warm and familiar glance. As if she knew exactly the kind of man she had and was grateful for it.

Harper felt herself soften towards the big guy. If he knew Lola that well, enough to realise how happy a yes at such a ridiculous request would make her, then maybe...

Then Harper remembered Grayson was a Chadwick. Which made him the wrong man for Lola, no matter what.

The face of the man who'd sent her the awful phone messages slid unbidden into her head, his voice cracking as he accused her of seeing in black and white. She shook him off. She did believe in absolutes. In right and wrong. In the fact that it was easy for a man to say yes when they owned the whole damn town.

"Ease down, soldier," Cormac murmured, his deep voice rolling over her, his hand clamping gently over her wrist.

She pulled her hand away, the skin burning from his touch. Shocked that her intentions had been so clear.

"Bite me," she shot back.

"Any time, anywhere."

Her gaze clashed with his. She could all but see the sparks that now seemed to be multiplying between them. She definitely felt them.

Cormac's smile was slow and smouldering. Knowing. Before he casually motioned to Seth the bouncer, who had lifted the velvet rope to let them through.

Once inside, Lola grabbed Gray by the hand again as they made their way down a long, dark hall, leaving Harper and Cormac to bring up the rear. Harper kept her distance, not wanting to make accidental physical contact again. Especially not in the dark with his *Any time, anywhere* rolling through her mind on a loop.

Until they spilled out into the bar proper. Despite its less than enticing exterior, the inside was beautifully kitted out. A large room with wood columns throughout, an empty stage at one end, a long, clean-looking bar with mirrors behind and elegant drop lighting all round.

The bouncer wasn't for naught, as the place was packed. On a Tuesday night too. That was beach living for you.

"This cosmopolitan enough for you?" Cormac asked, leaning close so he could be heard over the music.

Harper caught his scent—freshly cleaned male skin, with a tang of sea air still clinging to his hair—before she leaned determinedly away.

"It's no Cavalli Club," she said, referring to her favourite place to grab a cocktail to celebrate a contract fulfilled.

"I'd suspect nothing ever is." His smile was quick. A flash of white teeth in the darkness before he turned away, looking for Lola and Gray through the crowd. Spotting them, he reached back with a hand.

Harper stared at it.

"I won't bite," he said, not needing to lean in for Harper to understand. "Not right now anyway."

His hand closed around hers—warm and a little rough. As if perhaps he didn't spend his days merely chauffeuring bridal parties around town. And every time his skin shifted against hers she felt it. All over. As little triggers all over her skin. And waves of warmth beneath.

Chatting and charming as he went, Cormac forged a path through the crowd till he found Lola and Gray at a small reserved cocktail table near the stage.

Lola had already scored a bottle of bubbly; Gray was pouring out the glasses. When he lifted his glass and drank deeply, he caught Harper's eyes. Said, "Soda water."

Once again Harper felt the world shift a little off its axis as Gray surprised her. Had it been that obvious she'd been ready to add another sin to the list? First a Chadwick and now a drunk driver?

Harper lifted her glass to Gray's and said, "Chin-chin."

Gray grinned, lifted his glass, tapped it heartily to hers, and drank.

After one glass of the very good bubbles, Harper agreed to another. She must have been thirsty after the heat of the day, as it was gone before she remembered drinking it.

Then a tray of milky-green shots appeared from no-where. Amarula and some peppermint liqueur; she didn't catch the name. She tried one—it was good. It would be rude not to have another.

"Isn't this fun?" Lola asked.

Harper nodded. Being out with her sister as adults wasn't something they'd managed before Harper had moved overseas. She'd been too busy studying, working to save for Lola's university, for rent, food, Lola's ski trips, surfboards, fun money and all the extras it took to fit in in Blue Moon Bay.

"What's your favourite cocktail?" Lola asked. Then, before Harper could answer, she shouted, "Pina coladas all round!" The tables near by shouted happily along with her, so Gray—with his deep pockets—ended up buying pina coladas for the entire bar.

By the time the band started up, Harper was well and

truly sozzled. Her vision was hazy, her insides buzzed; she couldn't seem to stop smiling.

So glad was she to be with her sister in the flesh. So glad the bar wasn't a dive. So glad she'd picked the shoes that as comfortable as they were dazzling.

She actually felt...*happy*.

Why had she been in such a grump? Blue Moon Bay really was pretty. She'd had a lovely day rediscovering the place. Gray seemed nice, if not a little dull for her tastes. And it was becoming clear that he knew, and adored, her sister. The Chadwicks—despite their past misdemeanours—were excellent hosts. There was nothing wrong with having your own chef! And, disruptive dreams aside, the bed was like a cloud to sleep on.

As for Cormac Wharton? Harper blinked and across the table he came into focus.

He looked *good*. More than good. Slick grey jacket over white T-shirt. Jeans that fitted just right. Thick chestnut hair in those adorable spikes. Low light creating sexy shadows under his puppy-dog brown eyes. He looked all broody and delicious, like a modern-day James Dean.

What kind of name was Cormac, though? Although she could talk...

Most of the boys at Blue Moon High had names like that. Blane. Preston. Braxton. Like the bad guys in a John Hughes movie.

Corm. Mac.

He looked up, questioning. Had she said that out loud? She sucked on her straw and squinted a smile his way.

He blinked, the broody furrows in his brows clearing as his face split into a smile. And not just any smile. *The* smile. Like sunshine on a rainy day. The moon coming out from behind a cloud. A unicorn appearing in a dell.

The one that made her heart feel as if it was locked in a fist.

Whoa. So there was happy and then there was precarious. Harper let her drink drop and breathed out long and slow.

Cormac's furrow slowly returned. He cocked his head, questioning. But what could she say? That she'd happily look at him all night long? That she'd once thought him the most beautiful boy in the whole world? That she wondered what a girl had to do to make that *any time, anywhere* promise come true?

"Let's dance!" Lola cried, then grabbed Harper by the hand.

Needing a little cooling off, Harper took one last sip of her cocktail before reaching back with her drink. Cormac reached back and grabbed it. She gave him a grin of thanks. When he smiled back, her stomach flipped a full three-sixty degrees.

She lifted her hand to her mouth and blew him a kiss.

He blinked, reached out and caught it, and pulled it to his heart.

It was all so ridiculous Harper laughed, feeling it from her belly button to the outer reaches of her skin. Inside that happy little bliss bubble, she let Lola drag her wherever she pleased.

Which turned out to be the dance floor.

"There's a band!" Harper said, only just noticing the stage was now full.

"My wedding band!" Lola shouted, giving them a big wave.

The lead singer waved back, and the band played… something. A few somethings. All of them fabulous.

It had been so long since Harper had danced. Or listened to music on purpose. Or carved out time to just let go.

With the disco lights dancing over her eyes, the thump of the bass resounding through her bones, her sister at her side, she danced till her top stuck to her back, till the balls of her feet ached, till her body no longer felt less like a tightly wound rubber band and more like a warm, wet noodle.

What other sisterly experiences had they missed over the years? Birthdays. Work days. Drunk days. Sad days. So many hazy, lazy summers and winters so brisk it felt as if Antarctica was on your doorstep.

Harper caught Lola's eye. Then her hands. Then pulled her into a hug.

Lola stopped dancing and hugged her back.

"I love this song," Harper said.

"Love you too, Harps."

Before Harper could digest all the feelings she was feeling, Gray appeared, taking Lola's hand and sweeping her out of Harper's arms and into his own.

Watching them together Harper smiled when she felt as if she might burst into tears.

She shifted from foot to foot beside them until the buzz began to fade. Then she slunk through the crowd. Feeling squidgy. Off kilter. As if she'd left something behind.

She found Cormac at the bar, the pool of light from the pendant lamp above carving shadows onto the strong planes of his face. When she dragged herself up onto the bar stool next to him he didn't budge. Moreover, he didn't notice.

"Hey," she said, bumping him with a shoulder. Though her sense of balance was such she didn't so much bump as lean.

Meaning when he looked over at her, she was snuggled up against him. Close enough to see every tangled eyelash. The smudges beneath his beautiful eyes. The slight bump in the bridge of his nose. The stubble fighting its way to the surface despite the fact he'd shaved. The sensual seam between his lips.

When she felt drool pooling beneath her tongue she used the bar for leverage, pushing herself away.

"Well, that was fun," she shouted. Then realised she no

longer needed to as the acoustics at the bar were awesome. "The dancing. Fun. The band's really good."

"So why aren't you still out there?"

"Gray and Lola…" Harper waved a hand towards the dance floor. And felt that same sad feeling break over her again. But she didn't want to feel sad, not when she'd been feeling so good.

So she pressed her shoulders back, lifted her chin and said, "Don't you love this song?"

Cormac coughed out a laugh. For once there was no humour in it.

"Not a favourite?" Harper asked.

"Not." He took a mighty swig from his designer beer, before staring across the bar into nothing.

Harper looked around. Where was charming Cormac Wharton and what had this curmudgeonly stranger done with him?

Funnily enough, while his vibes were very much "stay away from the bear", Harper found it a relief. With no need to brace herself against the constant charm offensive, she could finally relax.

She settled more comfortably on the bar stool, caught the bartender's eye and asked for a big glass of iced water.

"Sure about that?" the bartender asked, leaning a forearm on the bar and giving her the twinkle eye. "Can't tempt you with something a little more exciting?"

He was handsome, and she was well-pickled, so she gave him the twinkle eye back. "Get me that glass of water and you'll see how excited I can be."

As the bartender poured her drink, Harper could have sworn his pecs danced, one after the other, behind his tight black T-shirt.

Then again, she couldn't exactly trust her eyesight. She felt squiffy. And hot. Her hair stuck to the back of her neck. She pulled the top of her bustier away from her chest and blew a stream of air into the gap.

When she looked back to the bartender his eyes had dropped to her chest. Oops.

Gently tugging the top of her bustier back into place, she spared a quick glance at Cormac. And got nothing. No gulp. No gawp. He was too busy staring moodily into the middle distance to score a flash.

When the glass of iced water appeared in front of her she crooked a finger at the bartender. "My friend here doesn't like this song, but I do. You can be the tiebreaker. So what's the verdict? Good song, or the worst?"

"Good song," the bartender agreed, twinkling with all he had.

"See?" Harper said, slapping Cormac on the arm.

Cormac refused to respond.

So Harper poked him in the arm. Then the shoulder.

When she went for his cheek he caught her finger in a closed fist and slowly brought it back down onto the bar.

Their eyes caught. When Harper found herself drowning in pools of melted dark chocolate she breathed in so fast, so deep, the wires inside her bustier strained against her ribs.

Out of the corner of her eye Harper noted the bartender moving away to flirt with someone else.

"You have good reflexes," she said, her voice sounding a little more awed than she'd meant.

"You're drunk," he said, one eyebrow raised, a half-smile on his face.

With her mental barrier no longer in place, Harper felt the power of it like a sucker punch, sapping the air right from her lungs.

"Pfft," she said though her lips were a little numb, so it sounded more like a raspberry. "I'm a grown woman who has had a couple of—" *several* "—legal alcoholic beverages. For which I will not apologise."

She lifted her spare hand to brush away a lock of hair that had fallen into her eyes. When it fell back into place she shook her head. When her brain jiggled like jelly she stopped.

Cormac let go of her finger and held up his hand in surrender, before lowering it to wrap around his drink.

Harper sat on her hand in an attempt to suffocate the fizzing feeling left over from his touch. "So… Cormac."

"Yes, Harper."

"Hmm? No, I mean, *Cormac*—is it a family name?"

He swallowed a sip of beer and shook his head. "My mother chose it. After Cormac McCarthy. The author."

"Me too! I mean, I wasn't named after Cormac McCarthy. Obviously. But people often believe I must have been named after Harper Lee. Though I wasn't. Which isn't the same thing at all, is it? Quite the opposite."

Harper knew she was rambling. But, now that she'd let down her guard, she was struggling to remember where she'd put it.

"My sister got the short end of the stick there," she managed. "Being named after someone famous."

"The Kinks song?"

"Bugs Bunny's girlfriend."

Cormac shot her a look that put the bartender's twinkle eye to shame. The life force behind those deep brown eyes of his so strong, so vibrant, so rich, Harper curled her toes into her shoes to distract herself from the heat washing though her.

"So, McCarthy," she managed through a tight throat. "He wrote *The Road*, right?"

"That he did. But my mother was obsessed with one of his earlier books—*Blood Meridian*."

"Ah."

"You've read it?"

Harper read company accounts, stockholder documents, investigative reports. If she had a spare half-hour on a plane she answered correspondence, checked in with erstwhile clients. She hadn't read for pleasure in years.

Which, in that moment, felt kind of sad. And again she felt a wave of a kind of lost feeling come over her—as if she was missing out.

"Have not," she admitted.

"It's a brilliant book. A modern classic. But it's not pretty. About a kid with a ken for violence, whose mother dies during childbirth."

"Jeez," Harper said on a long, loud breath before she could hold it back. "Sorry. That's…"

"Dark?"

"I was going to say intense." And unexpected.

Seeing him in high school, anyone would be forgiven for imagining his was a life full of ease, and comfort and love. After the…incident, it had made it easy to despise him, believe he had no clue what it meant to struggle.

Now she felt as if she'd peeked through a crack in his front door. That she'd seen things he hadn't wanted her— or anyone—to see. And the edges of the neat and tidy box she'd put him in began to fray.

At the *thunk* of glass on wood Harper jumped.

Cormac had let his drink drop to the bar. Under his breath he said, "My mother is not a dark person. Circumstance played a part. Environment. Ill-fated choices."

Silence settled over them, as it was her turn to fill it. But there wasn't enough alcohol in the world to override her deeply ingrained aversion to getting personal. Harper's knee jiggled and she glanced back to the dance floor, figuring it the lesser of two evils.

Then Cormac sighed, used both hands to rub his face, before tugging them through his hair, leaving spikes in their wake. After pressing his fingers into his eye sockets, he once more looked out into nothing.

It had been a long time since a man had turned to her for solace. Either because she wasn't the kind of woman who attracted men who wore their hearts on their sleeve. Or because she'd avoided them at all costs.

Harper swallowed as a wave of regret broke over her. What if the son of the London restaurateur was right? Was she an empty, soulless, robot? Ice cool. Untouchable. Closed off to human emotion. Didn't the fact she kept half a world between herself and the person she loved most say it all?

Whether it was the rum—and bubbles and green stuff—speaking or if she'd truly had some sort of epiphany, Harper finished her iced water in one go, turned to Cormac, leaned her chin on her palm and said, "Tell me about it."

Cormac blinked several times then looked her way.

"Your mother," Harper said, forcing the words through numb lips. "Darkness. Ill-fated choices." She leaned in and gave Cormac a nudge with her shoulder. She'd sobered up enough to bounce back. "Think of me not as Harper Addison, Lola's dazzling big sister, but as a ghostly apparition, a stranger, a ship passing in the night. I'll be long gone by this time next week, so anything you say goes with me."

Cormac's gaze remained snagged on hers, thoughts too deep to catch slipping and shifting behind his corrupting eyes.

Then, with obvious effort, he dragged his gaze away, lifting his hand to call for another beer. Only when it was in front of him did he say, "That song."

"Which song?"

He tilted a chin towards the band. "The one you like so much. My father would play it *ad nauseam* the nights he was holed up in his study. I should like that song, as at least it meant there was a wall between him and my mother. And yet the warm, fuzzy feelings remain at bay." He lifted his drink to the heavens, as if offering a toast, then downed three large swallows.

"I'm taking it your dad was no peach."

Cormac coughed out a laugh, though he didn't look her way. As if imagining her a stranger was the only way he could get the words out at all. "Not so much. He was more of a mean bastard, actually."

Harepr breathed, and forged on. "Did this have something to do with your mother's time in the dark?" A nod, then, "He blamed me for drawing her attentions away from him. He blamed her for my existence. He blamed us every chance he got."

He lifted his drink to his lips, then stopped. Put it slowly on the bar before pushing it away.

While Harper's throat tightened. Her insides twisting and squeezing. And it had nothing to do with the number of drinks she'd had.

She ached for all the things he hadn't said. The confessions between the words. The grey area she usually had no time for. It was shaky ground for her. Terrifying, actually. But in her experience the only way out of the bad stuff was through.

"We, Lola and I, were brought up by our dad."

Cormac glanced her way, his eyes still warm, despite the subject matter. How did he do that? How did he keep his compassion when she had so little?

"Where was your mum?"

"She left. I was too young to really remember." Saying the words out loud, she felt like an overblown balloon. One slip and she'd burst. "But our dad, he was formidable."

Images of her father chased one another like drops of liquid mercury. "He'd take us out of school to spend entire days at the beach. He'd happily learn the dances we choreographed for him. Or wake us at midnight for chocolate feasts."

"Sounds like a hell of a guy."

"He was. Most of the time," Harper amended. "When he was on top. When things were bright and shiny. But when things got shaky, when things didn't go his way…"

The memories flipped over on themselves. "Like the time he came home with a litter of kittens, forgetting Lola was allergic. Or the times he forgot to pick us up from school at all."

"Was he violent?" Cormac asked, his voice rough.

Harper glanced over to find his attention completely hers, the man's charisma like a heat lamp, making her burn.

"Never that," she said. *Not, I imagine, like yours.* "He was…unreliable. Disorienting. Even during the good times, I felt as if I was walking on eggshells, always waiting for the ground beneath us to suddenly drop away."

Harper leant her elbows on the bar, and dropped her chin into her hands, her head suddenly too heavy for her neck to support.

Had she *really* felt that way? Even as a little kid? She must have. She'd simply never voiced it, as it would have made it real. It would have messed with the good memories of her dad she'd secretly let herself keep.

"I wonder now if there was something else there. Some undiagnosed condition. Bipolar perhaps? Something…"

She turned her head slowly, her brain following at a lapse. Saw Cormac watching her.

"I'm so sorry. We were talking about you, about *your* dad, and I totally hijacked things."

Cormac smiled, as if he too felt lighter than he had ten minutes earlier. As if talking to her had actually helped. "It's called a conversation, Harper. It's what grown-up people do whilst getting to know one another better."

"Is that what we're doing?"

"So it would seem."

Harper swallowed, trying to press down the uncomfortable feelings swelling inside her. And said, "Your dad—he was violent, wasn't he?"

Cormac picked up his beer, the bottle dangling between his fingers, the amber liquid swaying and sloshing against the glass. And after a beat he said, "He was an angry man."

"Why was he angry?"

"That I don't know. All I know is that he got off on making others feel insignificant. As if the only way he felt important was to make sure everyone else did not."

Harper remembered the conversation she'd had with Lola in the shop that morning. About how Cormac went out of his way to make sure everyone who worked for the Chadwicks feel as though they mattered. She'd seen herself that he'd done the same at school. And now she understood why.

He knew what it felt like to be marginalised. And, rather than give in, rather than believe it, he redressed the cosmic imbalance by making sure everyone else he ever met felt seen. Heard. Felt the glow of his attention.

She'd known he was special when she was a teenager. Now, having lived in the world, she knew how truly rare that quality was.

"I'm so sorry," she said. For his childhood. For thinking his motives were purely selfish. His closeness with the Chadwicks could not be put aside, but it was a strange kind of relief to know that he wasn't all bad.

"He died," Cormac said, without inflection. "Heart attack a number of years ago."

Harper nodded. "And your mum?"

"Has moved on admirably. She remarried a perfectly nice man with a bald patch and a caravan."

He pulled his phone out of his back pocket and slid it along the counter. Under a contact labelled "Mum", complete with a picture of an attractive woman with a short grey pixie haircut, was a message that had come through only a few minutes before.

Sorry, buddy, won't make it to Gray's wedding. Loving the reef so going to stay a while longer. Love, Mum. XXX

She glanced at Cormac to find him staring through the phone. "You were really hoping she'd come."

Cormac breathed out long and slow. "I was really hoping she'd come."

"How long has she been away?"

"A year. And a bit."

"She sounds like she's having a great time. Which is nice for her."

Cormac looked into the mouth of his near-full bottle, as though searching for an answer. He let out a sharp breath, as if he was letting something go. "I'm not sure why I even told you all that."

"Because I asked?"

He sniffed out a laugh. "Maybe."

In the onset of quiet, Harper heard the music had gentled. She glanced out towards the dance floor to see Lola and Gray slow dancing.

Wasn't that all anyone wanted in life? Someone who listened. Someone who stuck around.

Since the moment she'd looked into Cormac's eyes by the car outside the Chadwicks' house, there had been something there between them. She'd thought it the zing of latent attraction. Now she wondered if it went deeper. What if they'd recognised in one another the look of someone who had it all together, while inside they were both secretly hanging on by their fingernails?

Harper swallowed against the rising tide of something that felt a hell of a lot like tenderness and reached for her water.

"Way to bring the mood down, Wharton," she said, before having a gulp. "Just saying."

Cormac burst into laughter.

She caught his eye; saw light, brightness, oodles of charm. And her epiphany faded like mist on a morning lake. Either he actually *did* have it together, and tonight was a rare anomaly, or he was the best at hiding it she'd ever seen.

Either way the spell was broken. She couldn't help but grin. Then soon joined in the laughing herself.

When they both settled down, Cormac asked the bartender to take away his untouched beer and ordered two more iced waters. Then they sank into an easy kind of quiet.

Until Cormac said, "You, Harper Addison, are an unexpected wonder and delight. When you're not all sniping and stubborn, that is."

His words whistled lightly through the air before lodging in her chest. "Well, you, Cormac Wharton, are far deeper than you at first appear."

Cormac coughed out one more laugh, taking the insult hidden inside the compliment for the mood-lightener that it was.

He held out his glass. She clinked hers against it.

And they drank.

Harper's heart felt strangely light. Lighter than she remembered it feeling in a very long time. Even as they sat close enough now that every time one of them breathed in, their arms brushed.

Yet neither made a move to pull away.

And, blinded by the light, she found herself saying, "So what do you really think of the happy couple? And this time I want the truth."

CHAPTER SIX

CORMAC GLANCED AT HER, then past her towards the dance floor. Something flashed over his eyes. A different kind of pain from the one he'd dealt with earlier. For a second it felt like a mirror of her own; that sense of missing something.

"Come on, Cormac," Harper pressed. Go hard or go home. "Tell me what you really think about Lola and Gray as a couple."

"I think they are madly in love."

"Do you?"

His eyes narrowed. "What's going on behind those gorgeous yet devious eyes of yours now?"

Ignoring the "gorgeous" comment, or at least tucking it away for later, Harper said, "Come on, Cormac, you're a smart guy."

"Why, thank you."

She shot him a look. "You know Gray far better than I do, so tell me if I'm wrong in thinking his only ambition is finding the next wave."

Cormac did not tell her she was wrong.

"A man like that is not ready for marriage. For forging a future. And what about fatherhood? You can't seriously tell me you think this wedding ought to go ahead."

"I can," he said, lifting his water in salute. "And I will."

Then he let his glass drop as he looked deeper into her eyes. So deep she wondered if he might fall in.

Then he sat back far enough he had to grip the bar to keep his seat. He ran a hand through his hair, and Harper tried not to stare as it flopped back down into an adorable spiky mess. "You're serious."

"Of course I'm serious! This is my little sister. My flesh and blood. The only family I have left."

"What could you possibly have against Gray?"

"I don't have anything against him, *per se.*" *His parents, on the other hand...* "Though for one thing, he's not the sharpest tool in the shed."

Cormac physically recoiled. Then looked off into the middle distance, muttering, "You're unbelievable."

"Lola is pure potential. She is far brighter than what she is currently doing. Which is my fault. I see that now. I gave her too much leeway. When she finally figures that out she'll regret this. She'll regret him."

Cormac shook his head.

"Then tell me what I'm missing. Convince me. Why should I think Gray is good enough for my sister?"

"Because he's Gray! Sure, he might appear a little laid-back. But so are half the guys who live around here. He might not be the most driven of all men, but he is all heart. Harper, he's a good man who adores your sister. What more could you possibly wish for?"

Harper breathed out hard. In a negotiation, when tempers were high, this would be the moment she tore the opposition's argument to pieces. But "good man" who "adored" her sister? The guy had just swept her legs out from under her.

Till Cormac added, "And Lola could not ask for better in-laws than Dee-Dee and Weston."

At that Harper snorted.

Dee-Dee seemed lovely. But Harper knew, she *knew*, what kind of man Weston Chadwick was. The depths he'd sink to in order to keep himself top dog.

Cormac did not appreciate her snort. She saw it in the cut of his shoulders. The sharpness of his gaze.

She wouldn't get any more insight out of him now. She'd drawn the lines and they stood firmly on either side.

She pushed her stool back.

Cormac twisted on his stool, blocking her. "Where are you going?"

"To the ladies' room. The dance floor. The other end of the bar. What does it matter?"

"Don't do anything stupid, Harper. Don't do anything you'll regret."

Harper's hackles rose into needle-sharp points. When he breathed she felt it brush over her cheek and the rest of her woke as if dragged from a deep sleep.

His gaze shifted from one eye to the other. "What on earth could you possibly have against the *Chadwicks*?"

No. Not now. She had to talk to Lola about this first.

Cormac turned to look around the bar as if searching for reinforcements, and his knee knocked into hers before sliding past her thigh. Not that he seemed to notice.

Harper, on the other hand, noticed. Every inch of her that hadn't been touched felt cheated.

When his gaze once more found hers, he was close enough that she could feel his frustration. Like a heat wave washing over him, washing over her.

His voice was low, ruinous, as he said, "Tell me this: what does Lola have to offer the best friend I've ever had? The sweetest guy I've ever known? Apart from a bitter and confused sister she never sees and two MIA parents with murky pasts?"

He'd gone so deep, so fast, Harper blanched. For she felt herself flung back into the awful past couple of months at work, then right back to high school as if she'd been dragged there by icy claws.

"Wow," she managed, frantically trying to haul every self-protection measure she had back into place. "You really went there? Talk about going dark."

A muscle beneath Cormac's eye flickered, but she took little pleasure in the hit.

"Look, I have nothing to prove to you, Cormac. We don't need to be friends. The only thing I care about, the only thing in the entire world, is making sure my sister is happy."

Cormac lifted a hand to rub it over his face before glancing off to the side. "The worst part is, I think you actually believe it."

Harper reared back. "Excuse me?"

"If that's all you cared about, why have you been gone so long? If that's all you care about, why can't you simply be happy for her? Hell, if that's all you care about, why aren't you out there dancing with her while you have the chance? Why are you sitting here, jousting with me?"

While Harper mentally batted at his every accusation, Cormac laughed, the sound throaty and rich, but completely lacking in humour. Then he tipped forward, elbows on the bar, face landing in his palms. After a moment he gave his face a good rub before swinging his dark gaze back her way.

His hair was mussed, his eyes wild, and heaven help her she found herself so caught up in the heat of the man, she forgot for a second why he was looking at her that way.

Then he pushed to his feet and held out a staying hand. "Hang on a second. Could it be… Are you *jealous?*"

"What? No!" Harper took a deep breath. How had this turned so quickly? Persuading people to her way of thinking was her bread and butter. Why did Cormac Wharton have to be the one man who refused to drink the Kool Aid? "I'm not jealous. Not of them."

"Then what's the problem? Because I'm struggling to understand you, Harper. Try as I might. But every time I think I see a glimmer of humanity lurking beneath this slick, cool, ice-princess exterior you use as some kind of weapon and shield all wrapped up in one, the next second I wonder if I'm looking for something that just isn't there."

For all that his tone was even, his voice calm, his words hit Harper right at the heart of her.

Heartless. A robot. Out of touch with human emotion. Empty. Devoid. Not enough. Nothing at all.

Every bad thing she'd ever been called, every bad thing she'd ever feared about herself, every piece of her heart she'd closed in, tied off, cut away in order to protect herself, swam to the surface. And it was suddenly too much.

"Screw you," she said, pressing him back so she could get the hell out of there.

He opened his mouth to respond, but Harper leaned in, pointing a finger in his face. "If you dare say *any time, anywhere*, I will hurt you."

Harper was too fired up to catalogue his tells, to decide if his slow breathing was a sign of him being in control, or fighting as hard as she was to find it.

Either way, she turned, shot a rather unladylike symbol over her shoulder and made to walk away.

But Cormac grabbed her by the arm. "Wait."

When she turned, glaring at where he held her, he eased off, but did not let go.

He swore beneath his breath. "You... I don't know why, but you drive me places I never go. Places no one else has come close..."

He took a deep breath and looked deeper into her eyes. "I'm sorry."

Harper braced herself as the backs of her eyes began to burn. "I don't care."

"You clearly do. Which proves my last statement wrong right there. Should never have said such a thing either way. Blame it on the beer, or the heat, or my mother's message, or that damn song. Or simply blame me."

Harper's lungs grew tight at the emotion in his words. At the wildness in his eyes. At the clutch in his voice as he said, "You do something to me, Harper."

Harper's knees gave way as if the ground beneath her feet had cracked.

Then he said, "You push my buttons in a way I can't explain."

When he saw he still had hold of her he let go as if burned, running his hand through his hair again.

You do something to me. How was she supposed to respond to that?

Her chest rose and fell. She could feel her blood racing beneath her skin. Hot and maddened.

"It's fine," she gritted out. "I mean, it's not fine. But whatever."

When he continued looking like a kicked puppy she slowly deflated, her anger leaving her in a trickle. It wasn't as if she'd been sweetness and light, after all.

She waved a hand his way, in a kind of blessing. "You're forgiven."

With a twitch at the corner of his mouth, Cormac bowed ever so slightly. But his voice was still raw as he said, "Why, thank you, milady."

When he straightened up she could have sworn he'd moved closer, for suddenly they were toe to toe. It would take nothing to lift a hand to his chest—that well-sculpted chest, with all that warm brown skin and its smattering of sun-kissed hair—to feel if his heart beat at anything like the pace hers did in that moment.

She watched, as if from a distance, as she did just that, her hand falling over his heart. She felt the throb, like a distant thud against her palm. Then she felt it quicken. Beat harder. Reverberating through her palm until it might as well have been her pulse. Her heart.

"Harper," he said, his voice rough.

"Do I really do something to you?" She lifted her eyes to his.

Eyes that had gone so dark she couldn't tell the chocolate from the black.

"You really do."

From one heartbeat to the next, the hastily built wall she'd tried to construct between them fell away.

"Well, that's...nice."

He laughed, the sound rumbling from his chest to hers by some kind of sexual osmosis. "Harper, I can assure you, the last thing you make me feel is nice."

Right back at ya, she thought, paying hard attention to the conflict in his eyes. The same conflict she felt riding roughshod through her entire body.

She'd wanted to touch him so badly. Wanted him to touch her too.

She wanted to keep scrapping with him. And boy, did she want to run.

His hand lifted to brush the hunk of hair that had been bothering her behind her ear, and there it stayed. Big and warm and secure.

His thumb traced the edge of her face, his eyes following the move. His chest rising and falling as he breathed deep.

She leant into his touch, just a little. Feeding on the unexpected tenderness like a woman starved.

When his eyes found hers, the blatant emotion therein made her ache all over.

But this was Cormac Wharton. He'd never looked at her, much less this way.

What if it was the beer? And the heat? And his mother's message? And the song? She began to wonder if she'd simply wandered into a perfect storm.

Until his gaze landed on her mouth.

The hunger in his eyes was unmistakable. Specific. Real.

She was in grave danger of sighing. In grave danger of crying.

"I'm going to kiss you now, Harper," he said, his voice ragged. "Just so you know."

There was time to pull a Harper and make light. It would allow her to save face. To keep her distance. To have the chance of getting through the rest of this week in one piece.

But this was Cormac Wharton. The boy who'd once held her heart.

The boy who'd broken it too.

No, she remembered as he shifted closer, as his spare hand stole around her back, as his hand delved deeper into her hair. As his body pressed up against her own, all muscle and heat.

This was no boy.

Cormac Wharton was all man.

Thank goodness, she thought as his lips closed over hers.

She'd imagined this moment more times than she could count. Imagined how he would taste, how he would feel. How she would feel.

As Cormac sipped on her mouth as if it was the sweetest thing he'd ever tasted she felt struck. Every cell jolting as one. Like lightning unable to find earth.

Cormac soon turned her to nothing but sensation. Heat. Pleasure. Somehow she found the wherewithal to slide a hand around his neck and another into his hair.

It was thick and soft and perfect.

Her lips opened on a groan. And Cormac took complete advantage, sliding his tongue over the seam of her lips, seducing them open. Not that he had to try too hard. She was all in.

Feeling it, Cormac hauled her closer, wrapping her up so tight she felt the evidence of exactly what she did to him.

Swamped by need and heat and desire so rich and warm, she felt it take her under, every thought dissolved into mist.

Until her leg wrapped around his, and her skirt pulled too tight against her thigh. While in a bar. In Blue Moon Bay.

Harper came back to reality with a thud.

Her eyes snapped open. She squinted against the brightness of the dome of light above the bar.

Cormac must have felt her freeze, as with one last kiss that made her insides go into free fall he pulled back. Looked into her eyes. And her heart squeezed so hard it hurt.

"Ow," she bit out.

And Cormac quickly stepped back, holding her lightly as if knowing exactly how boneless he'd left her.

"You okay?"

The only bit of her that hurt was the big, throbbing muscle behind her ribs, so she said nothing as she carefully extricated herself from his hands.

"Are you okay?" he asked again, and she shot him a look.

"Of course I'm okay."

Something acute flashed behind his eyes. "Okay."

"Just…" What? What could she possibly say? That she was shaken by how easily he'd taken her apart? That her whole body now ached for the lack of him? "Just, don't do that again."

A beat slunk by. His voice went deep as he said, "Which part exactly?"

"All of it."

"All of it? Right. Okay. You bet," he said, stepping away. Giving her space. Putting his hands in his pockets and leaning against the bar as if he hadn't a care in the world.

You bet? Really? As if it was nothing? As if he'd felt nothing? As if it meant nothing?

It had been as if he'd known her. Kissing not only with his mouth, but also with his touch, with his mind. She felt rearranged. As if her atoms were no longer where they had been before.

She wished she could simply turn and walk away, only

her knees were no longer in optimal working order, so she had to regroup.

Harper stood tall, as tall as she could with the backs of her knees tingling like crazy and her heart threatening to beat right through her ribs. And she pointed a damning finger Cormac's way.

"You might be Gray's best man, and I might be Lola's maid of honour, but that does not mean we have to fall into some cliché by getting it on this week."

"Getting what on?"

"You know what I mean."

"I know that you kissed me."

"You kissed me!"

Cormac's smile said, *You know it. But you kissed me right on back, sweet cheeks.* He pressed away from the bar and took a step her way.

Harper's first instinct was to take a step back, knowing deep in her heart that, despite her demand not to kiss her again, if he came close enough for her to get even a whiff of his scent she'd be back to climbing him like a tree.

But her next instinct—her stronger instinct—forged from necessity and experience, was to be strong.

For Harper never flinched. Even if it killed her.

So she stood her ground as Cormac crooned, "I've never been a best man before, so I'm not sure of the rules."

"There are no rules."

"Glad to hear it. Because that kiss has been coming for days."

Years, Harper thought, then bit her lip to stop that gem from spilling free.

"How about this, then: now that's out of our systems, let's agree to play nice for the rest of the week? I'll endeavour not to bite back if you push my buttons, while you can…"

Cormac waved a hand in front of her, as if incorporating every part of her in whatever it was she was doing wrong.

"So you'll try not to bite. While I'll try not to be quite so me."

He leant back and smiled, as if she had it in one. "Truce?"

Truce? *Truce?* The damnable man held out a hand. As if expecting her to shake it!

If it meant she could finally extricate herself from the hash she'd made of the evening, what the hell else could she do?

Harper grabbed his hand, shook it twice and blurted, "Now I'm going to dance. Out there."

"Go get 'em, tiger."

"I shall," Harper said, before turning on her heel and blindly disappearing into the crowd.

On the dance floor she found a spot on her own, closed her eyes and danced. Numb with the fact that fighting with Cormac was better than making love with any other man.

And if that wasn't the most messed-up thing she'd ever admitted to herself, she didn't know what was.

In the wee hours of the next morning, after the girls had wobbled into the Chadwicks' house together, Cormac whistled for Novak, who came bolting through the front doors of the manor before sticking to him like Velcro.

Only to find Gray leaning against the hood of the car.

His friend didn't waste any time getting to the point. "So you kissed her."

Dammit. "You saw that, huh?"

"You guys sucked up so much energy the lights flickered in the bar."

He'd have believed it too. For that kiss... Hell. He'd not meant to, even if he'd wanted to. He'd fought it, even as every word out of her mouth roused him. But the fever in her eyes, the way her breath caught whenever she found him watching her, the way she lifted her face to his, like a sunflower to the sun…

Cormac scratched the back of his neck. "Did Lola—?"

"Nah. I had her well distracted."

"Good." He opened up the car and Novak leapt in, taking up her usual spot on the back seat.

"Not so fast," said Gray, holding the door before Cormac could close it. "Wasn't it only a few hours ago you told me nothing was going to happen there?"

"Yeah."

"So, what happened?"

Cormac closed the door and leant against the car beside his oldest friend. "You want details? Need some pointers for your wedding night?"

Gray coughed out a laugh, before shooting Cormac a single hooked-eyebrow glare.

Cormac looked towards the house. Lights on in several rooms. Not Harper's; hers was around back. The fact he knew that spoke volumes as to the trouble he was in.

"She said stuff. Asked questions. Brought things to the surface. She talks. A lot. Only way I could think to shut her up."

"Fair enough," Gray shot back. "And if she says stuff again, talks too much again, what's the plan?"

"I think it's pretty clear there has not been a clear plan for me where Harper is concerned."

"You think? Look, you tell me it's just a best-man-maid-of-honour thing and I'll leave it well alone. More power to you both. We can look back on this in years to come and laugh and laugh. But if it's something that I need to worry about, something that might rebound onto my darling soon-to-be bride in *any* way, then I might have an opinion on the matter. Fair?"

Cormac hadn't been kidding when he'd said Gray was all heart. The guy rarely had strong opinions bar when to eat and who his people were. But when he did, he meant it.

Cormac nodded. "Fair."

Gray nodded back. Slapped his friend, hard, on the back and pressed away from the car. "All righty, then. See you at the lunch tomorrow?"

"Yeah, about that. I was hoping to beg off." A break from the partying, and from Harper, time to shake off the effect of her, would do him good. "I know your folks forbade me from going into the office this week, but they have an international business that needs running..."

Gray held up a hand as he backed away towards the house. "You are not sending me in there on my own, buddy boy. I will see you tomorrow at twelve. Don't be late."

"Aye-aye, Captain."

CHAPTER SEVEN

FORGOING A TRADITIONAL rehearsal dinner, the bride and groom had booked the entire *See Sure* restaurant for a family and friends lunch.

It had taken a shovel-load of concealer and mighty amounts of water to make Harper look and feel human after the night they'd had.

That, a killer navy halter dress held up behind the neck with a big satin bow, and her favourite fringed ankle-boot heels had her poised to meet Gray's mighty collection of guests, as well as Lola's far more meagre set, for a sea-food buffet.

Harper had to admit a more stunning locale could not have been procured if she had been around to find one herself.

Abundant swathes of sheer white chiffon and tiny fairy lights were draped from the moulded ceiling, leaving glimpses of whitewashed walls. Small bowls of lush succulents had been scattered down the long table, while white and gold place settings glinted and sparkled in front of the fifty-odd rustic wooden chairs.

It was fresh and casual, with glints of sophistication. It was Lola. Not Lola of the yoga pants and baseball caps, but exactly as Harper saw her.

Someone else had done this for her. Someone else who knew Lola that well.

Harper had been struggling since she'd arrived, owing to a sense of inevitability as the days rolled forward until Lola would no longer belong only to her.

Only, looking around at the smiling faces of those Lola

deemed close, Harper realised that moment had long since passed.

Harper could live with that, so long as she knew for sure that this was the best possible path for Lola's future.

Today, her focus would remain sharp. If Lola showed even the slightest tell that she was anxious—twitchy gaze, tight voice, fingers tripping over one another as a way to disperse excess nervous energy—she'd instantly find a way to tell her the truth about the Chadwicks. And about their father's last days at home.

Harper kept her radar on as she met Lola's yoga friends—high on holistic health and Insta-fit likes—as well a couple of Lola's mates from her incomplete university degree.

The rest of the women at the table were already familiar to her. There was maudlin Marcy, ditsy Dana and sly Serena—the *über*-rich girls of Blue Moon Bay High and members of Gray and Cormac's high-school clique.

No tenacious Tara, though, Harper noted. Interesting. Except, *not*. What did it matter to Harper if Cormac and his high-school girlfriend were still tight or not? Not a jot!

As for Cormac, he sat sideways on his chair at the other end of the table, cradling a coffee rather than a beer, as if he too was doing what had to be done to recover from the night before. He listened intently as the guy beside him told a story, suit jacket over a dark T doing him all sorts of favours.

Not that she was watching him. Or constantly reliving that kiss. Or wondering if he was too.

Harper turned in her seat as a woman plonked herself into the chair beside her. *Adele*, Harper thought, quickly glancing across the table at Lola. Was this the sign she'd been looking for that things weren't as they appeared?

For Adele had been Queen Bee of Blue Moon Bay High. And Gray's high-school girlfriend. Now she was leaning over the table to touch hands with Gray's mother, blowing air kisses to Gray's father.

"Harper," said Lola. "You remember Adele."

Adele stopped shuffling in the seat and gave Harper a quick once-over.

Adele held out a hand, which Harper shook. "The pleasure is all mine."

"Adele's family owns this joint," Lola said. "When she offered it up for the day we couldn't have been happier. Right, honey?"

Gray looked up at Lola's voice and smiled.

"Wedding gift sorted," said Adele with a wave of her hand. Then she turned on her chair, her knee bumping Harper's. "Harper Addison. What's your story? Where did you disappear to after the hell that was high school?"

Harper looked at Adele again, to find no irony on her face. Just open interest.

"I'm a freelance corporate negotiator," she said, "based out of Dubai."

Adele nodded. "Dubai, I know. The rest went right over my head."

"She flies all over the world," said Lola, her voice carrying so that others listened in, pride tinging every word, "to sort out corporate squabbles, messy mergers and contract negotiations. Think Fortune 500 companies, even governments. They bring in my big sister when things go really sour. She's the last word."

"So, you're a total badass. In heels."

For all that Harper tried to dislike Adele, she failed. "Damn straight. Though most of the time it's less Wild West and more like being a stern kindergarten teacher, only the students are stubborn fifty-year-old millionaires."

"Huh," Adele said. "And did you look like this in high school?"

"Same bones. Less gloss."

"I hear that. Were you one of Gray's swooning aco-lytes, by any chance?"

Harper looked to Lola and said, "No. Never."

Lola shrugged. "I wouldn't blame you if you were. He was hot stuff in high school. So many of my friends had crushes on Gray."

"And yet I was not one of them," Harper insisted, re-alising how much of the table was now looking their way.

Even Gray, who gave her a wink. A wave of his hand. *All good.*

While Adele was not to be deterred. "If not Gray, who was your high-school crush?"

Harper should have seen it coming. But after the hot days and long, restless nights she was off her game. She didn't even feel herself turn towards Cormac until it was too late.

Her eyes brushed over him for a heartbeat. Maybe less. But it was enough, and in case anyone at the table missed it Adele lifted a hand and pointed a finger Cormac's way.

Harper's gaze flicked back to Lola in time to see her eyes widen. As if all her Christmases had come at once.

Then Harper caught Adele's eye and shook her head. Just once.

A flicker of understanding warmed Adele's eyes, before she clapped her hands and shouted, "Okay, kids, enough of the polite wine. Shots all round!"

A bevy of nattily dressed waiters brought trays covered in an array of fierce-looking shots and conversation once more filled the room with its warm buzz as Harper's mo-ment in the spotlight was fast forgotten.

Lola grabbed a shot, downed it fast, then stood and said, "Wee time," to no one in particular.

Harper was on her feet in an instant, the loud scrape of her chair sending curious gazes her way. She offered a tight smile to the table at large, her own gaze snagging on Cormac, who now watched her in that warm, intense way of his.

Had he seen? Had he heard?

She shook her head, shook him off and followed her sister to the bathroom.

"Lolly?"

"Harps!" Lola said on a sigh. "Isn't this the best day ever? I'm so happy you're here. So happy everyone is here."

"Everyone?"

The toilet flushed and Lola stumbled out. "Of course!"

When Lola waved her hands under the tap and nothing happened, Harper turned it on for her. And asked, "Even Adele?"

"Especially Adele. She's the best. She knows everybody. She put me on to the cake lady. Told me the name of this amazing guy who custom-makes wedding rings. She even manages the band who are playing at the reception. Such a cool chick, don't you think?"

"That she is." How to put this? "It doesn't bother you that she and Gray used to…"

Lola blinked. Then burst out laughing. "That was ages ago. Besides, Adele is gay! Or bi, I guess, if you take the Gray anomaly into account."

"Right." She had wondered, what with Adele looking at her as if she was lunch.

"Adele got Gray through Chemistry and he got her through teenagerhood with uptight, unforgiving parents. From the look of things, she's quite taken with you. If you're keen." Lola waggled her eyebrows.

Harper levelled her with a look.

"Well, how am I supposed to know? I haven't seen you in years. And you never talk about the men in your life. You could be gay, or married with seven kids, for all I know."

Harper didn't realise she was holding her breath until her throat felt uncomfortably tight.

She moved to take Lola by both hands. "I'm not gay, honey. Or married with seven kids. Or seeing anyone right now. But when I do see people they are men. And if you have any other questions about me, about my life, ask away."

A smile tugged at the corners of Lola's mouth. "Did you seriously have a crush on *Cormac* in high school?"

Harper's instinct was to deny, deny, deny. But this was Lola. She'd made the decision to be honest with her little sister about their past, meaning she had nowhere to hide.

Quickly checking to make sure the other stalls were empty, Harper said, "Yes."

"That's awesome! Did you write his name all over your school books?"

Harper's eyes closed in mortification. "Yes. I imagined what our kids would look like. The whole gamut."

Lola shot her a sly look. "So what about now? Crush still alive and kicking?"

Harper shook her head, no. For what she felt for Cormac was nothing so plain and simple as a crush. It was far more complicated in the way adult things tended to be.

"But he's so hot," Lola encouraged.

"Lola, come on."

"Watching him surf is one of life's great pleasures, don't you agree? And he's funny too. Dry. And seriously smart. Loyal. Sweet as pie. According to the Chadwicks, he's a lifesaver. I've heard them say more than once that they owe their current success to him and only him."

Harper channelled Teflon, allowing Lola's words to roll off her back.

"If you need for me to put in a good word, let Cormac know you're available, I will."

"Please don't."

"Are you sure? Because I really wish I could see you as happy as I am."

Lola's words, and the truth of them in her eyes, hit Harper like a harpoon, right through the belly.

Was Lola happy? How could she really know for sure? Her world was so limited. Harper should have encouraged her to travel more, before she met Gray. She should have taken Lola with her...

This time Lola took Harper by the hands. "Are you happy, Harps?"

"If you're happy, then I'm happy," said Harper, using the same mantra she'd used on Lola for the past decade. "It's that simple."

And it had been that simple. It really had. It had kept Harper going when it had all seemed too hard. When she'd doubted. When she'd failed.

Only now she was here, back in this place, seeing Lola not as the needy teenager, but as a woman who had moved on, made decisions, made friends, made plans, put down roots, fallen in love—she should have felt triumphant.

And yet Harper felt...lost.

For what had Harper done in the same time?

Worked. Worked. And worked some more.

She had money, she had respect, she had a closet full of fabulous clothes.

But she had no people in her life. No roots. She had no plans bar the next couple of contracts. She'd spent more time in the past two years to London and back than she did in her own apartment which was really nothing more than a place to keep her dry cleaning.

"Okay, then," Lola said as she fixed her ponytail in the mirror. "Ready?"

For what? Harper nearly asked. Going back out there with those girls who'd never looked twice at her in high school? With the man who'd ruined her father's life? With the boy who'd twisted her heart in his fist, who had become the man who was fast making inroads in that same direction yet again?

Not even close.

But Harper was good at putting on a brave face. Always had been. Always would be. "Let's do this!" she said.

Then Lola took her by the hand and led her back out into the big, bad world.

The hens' night and bucks' party turned out to be a joint affair.

With the older generation saying their goodbyes around five, the lights in the See Sure faded, a disco ball dropped from the ceiling, the wait staff cleared away the tables and a dance floor and DJ appeared as if from nowhere.

Trays of jelly shots did the rounds. Someone handed out wigs, novelty headbands. A face-paint artist painted tattoos onto arms, butterflies onto faces, even six-packs onto less-than-toned bellies.

Harper danced just enough to keep Lola off her case, but drank nothing but water. She made sure to eat whenever a tray of nibbles came around. And she kept herself alert. Frosty. All the better to avoid any more accidental revelations of any kind.

And somehow, she managed to avoid Cormac all night long.

Until Lola bundled her up to an old-fashioned photo booth, right as Gray made his way out.

"Your turn!" Lola said, forcing Harper inside.

Harper flapped the dusty red curtains away from her face as she stumbled inside. Only to find Cormac already there, making to stand. When he looked up and spotted her, he stopped; knees bent, hands glued to his thighs, too tall to fit in the booth upright.

"Hi," he said.

Panicked, she tried to back out, but someone's hands—

Lola's, no doubt—grabbed her backside and gave her a shove.

Meaning it was either stumble onto the small bench seat beside Cormac or end up splayed against him like a starfish. She chose the seat.

After a mortifyingly long wait, Cormac did the same. She shuffled over. Made room.

Not enough though. With nowhere to put his long legs, he settled his thigh against hers, sending little shock waves up and down her side.

"So now what?" she muttered.

"It takes a few minutes to warm up. A red light comes on. And then we smile. Easy."

Harper looked around the room, feigning interest in the dark glass behind which the camera no doubt resided. In the seventies wood panelling on the walls. In the strips of photos, showcasing all the different kinds of faces one might care to pull.

"Having a good time?" Cormac asked.

"Hmm?" said Harper, turning to Cormac as if she only just remembered he was there.

His eyes smiled a half-second before his lips did the same. "Are you having a good time?"

"Sure. You?"

His pause was telling. As was the deep breath in, and heavy breath out. When, rather than answer, his gaze travelled away from her eyes, tracing her face, he might as well have said out loud that none of it mattered to him. Until now.

You do something to me, Harper.

Everything had shifted off its axis when he'd said those words to her the night before. Sitting there next to him in the quiet of the booth, the sounds of the party roaring like a storm outside, there was no denying he'd done something to her too.

Not only on that fateful day in high school, when his

words had forged the backbone that had put her in good
stead through her twenties. But this week. He was doing
something to her right now, just by sitting there.

When her eyes meandered back to his it was to find
him watching her, smiling as if he'd been watching her
watch him for some time.

She swallowed. "How many minutes does it take to
warm up?"

"Some," he said, his throaty voice filling the booth.

Harper wriggled on the seat, though it only served to
rub her up against him all the more.

"Am I the only one who feels like I'm back in high
school? Forced into a closet for a game of five minutes
in heaven?"

He said nothing to that, merely stared at her as shadows
of smoke swirled into his eyes. "I never played. Did you?"

"Once. Tenth grade. Samuel Clifford's party."

"Who did you end up in the closet with?"

"Samuel. Everyone ended up in the closet with Samuel."

Cormac threw back his head and laughed, the deep
sound reverberating in the small space before bouncing
about behind her ribs.

"And this feels like *that*?"

"It feels like something," she murmured. She leant forward, squinted at the tiny array of instructions. "Nothing
will happen unless we press that button."

"You don't say."

"Hang on, you knew that because you've done this already."

"While you've been flitting around like a humming-
bird all night, doing everything in your power to avoid
me." Frown lines creasing above his nose, he turned his
big body towards her, his leg brushing slowly against hers.
"If you don't want to be here, Harper, all you have to do
is open up the curtain and go."

She looked towards the curtain—red velvet, pocked

with moth bites—heard the murmur of voices, music, laughter outside.

For all her bravado, and talk of preferring big cities with plenty on offer, she was an introvert at heart. Far happier to sit up in bed on a Saturday night with a juicy corporate report than partake in the nightlife of whichever city she was in. No chance of making friends that way. No chance of losing them either.

Then there was the fact that Cormac was beside her. All warm, and big, and combative.

Her toes curled in her shoes. And she stayed.

"Mmm…" Cormac rumbled. "That's what I thought."

She shot him a glance out of the corner of her eye. "I'm just taking a moment. It has nothing to do with you."

"Of course. I'd never have dared suggest you prefer my company above all others'. Consider me put in my place."

Harper opened her mouth to soften her statement, before figuring she'd only dig herself a bigger hole.

After a couple of long, interminable beats of silence, Cormac said, "Nothing wrong with taking a moment."

"I know."

"Nothing wrong with showing concern for your sister."

She shot him a look, saw it filled with understanding and insight into how things had unfolded between them the night before.

"Nothing wrong with feeling vulnerable either. Or tired. Or fed up. Or nervous. Or out of place. Or scared."

"I know that too," she lied. How could she convince others she was bulletproof if she couldn't convince herself?

"Then, why pretend?"

"Pretend what exactly?"

"To have it all so under control."

"Who says I don't?"

He shot her a look. As if he knew her. Understood her. As if he cared.

"I'm talking about the heels, the hair, the matching bling." He reached up as if about to run a curl through his fingers before letting his hand drop. "Being so together at work is one thing. It no doubt requires for you to appear in command. But nobody can be expected to be this perfect all the time."

Harper blinked. Her gaze catching on his as he finished a slow, meandering mapping of her face. How did he do that? Was she really that transparent? Or only to him? And had Cormac Wharton just called her perfect?

She *knew* better than anyone she wasn't that. Though for her entire childhood she'd tried to be the "perfect" daughter. Her grades had been impeccable, the house always pristine. She'd won awards for math, debating, her charity fundraising. Even her lemon yoghurt cake at the town fair. Because she'd known, deep in her heart, that her father was hanging on by his fingernails too.

Clearly it hadn't been enough.

She glanced down at her hand to find she'd been picking at the edge of a fingernail, chipping the glossy black polish away, something she hadn't done since she was a kid. And said, "I'm far from perfect, Cormac."

"I'm well aware."

"Wow. You didn't even have to think about it."

His grin was fast, a flash of humour and heat. And in the small, enclosed space Harper felt as if her heart had grown a size too large.

"Nobody is," Cormac said. "We are all slovenly, frustrated, confused animals, trying to be civilised. And that's okay. It's the fact that we try to be better, that we learn from our mistakes, that moves us up the evolutionary scale. We are a lot—the people in this place. So if you're tired, if you've had enough of us, tell us so. Or go grab a patch of quiet. The Chadwick grounds are vast. Plenty of places to get lost."

Harper's instinct was to sit tall, to deny that she had a

clue as to what he was talking about. But in the protection of their little booth she let out a large, exhausted sigh. "Thanks. I'll do that."

His next smile was smaller, less flash, and yet it hit deeper. Warming her from the inside out.

"So, I have news," he said.

"Such as?"

"You had a crush on me in high school."

Harper froze.

"When Amy heard Adele she told Tad, who told Weston, who told me. I figured it was nothing more than Chinese whispers but by the look on your face... Wow. It's true."

Realising she'd just given herself away, Harper only groaned louder.

The entire booth shook as Cormac sat back in the seat. Harper's gaze crept sideways to find him sitting with his head against the wall, looking at the ceiling.

"How did I not know this?" he asked.

"Nobody knew! Okay, so people probably knew. But everyone was too scared to call me on it. You probably don't remember, because it's now clear you had no idea who I was, but I was a bit scary in high school."

His head tipped sideways, until Harper found herself tangled in those intense dark eyes. Then his gaze narrowed as it moved to her hair, her cheeks, her mouth.

"I remember darker hair, wild curls. Doc Marten boots. Flyers and demands for action. And you were one of those really smart kids, the extension kids, right? Were you even in my biology class once?"

Harper scrunched up her face. "Yeah, that pretty much covers it. While you…"

She couldn't help herself—her gaze travelled over his face, cataloguing the changes in him: the firm jaw, the lines at the corners of his eyes, the scar cutting through his right eyebrow. Before also finding all the things that had drawn her to him in the first place—the smiling mouth, the size of him, as if he could protect the world, and those warm, magnetic eyes.

"You were like this handsome prince. Your whole gang always laughing and leaning all over one another, ruling the school. It was pretty seductive for a serious loner like me."

Cormac's gaze hardened for a fraction of a second. "I was lucky to have them. But you know we weren't all that we seemed."

She did. Now. But those memories were hard to budge.

"Anyway, back to that crush of yours—"

"No. Uh-uh. That subject is closed. It was many years ago when I was young and stupid."

"I can't imagine you were ever all that young. Or stupid for that matter. Hang on, I remember a speech. Wasn't that you who accused the school board of fascism because of the sexist uniform policy?"

"Yep. That was me. I was quite the little radical." Her dad had loved it. Loved her sticking it to the man.

Ironic that after he'd left it had been those radical instincts that had saved her; in scrapping, in fighting, in keeping a low profile so that Lola wasn't taken away from her.

Harper wondered what else he might soon remember. Such as the last thing he'd ever said to her before leaving school. When he'd dismissed her so wholly, as if she was no more than a fly buzzing by his ear.

She dared not ask. Not when his eyes dropped to her mouth and made her feel anything but irrelevant.

"So, are we going to do this?" he asked, his deep voice curling beneath her defences.

Harper's gaze dropped to his mouth too and she remembered how it had felt on hers. She wanted to. God how she wanted to. But if there was ever a time when she needed to see the world in black and white, this was it.

"I'm not sure that I can."

"We are making up our own rules, remember?"

"Then my number one rule is to not do anything I'll soon regret."

"What's to regret? You have a thing against devastatingly handsome lawyers?"

"I have a thing against devastatingly handsome lawyers with dibs on themselves."

"So, you do think I'm handsome. Knew it!"

He punched the air like a jock after a touchdown and Harper couldn't help but laugh. Then she said, "Let me put it this way: Lola. Gray. Enough said."

His voice dropped as he said, "Did it not occur to you that Lola and Gray conspired to get us in here together?"

Harper opened her mouth to deny him then thought about how Gray had come out of the booth right as Lola had shoved her in. "It's more complicated than that."

"How?"

"I...can't."

"You...won't. It's not the same thing. Huh."

"What?"

"I never would have thought of you as a coward, but here we are."

Harper knew he was goading her. Calling her chicken in order for her to bite back and give him what he wanted. But this wasn't school. Thank goodness.

She was a grown woman.

And he was all man. God, the scent of him filling the cramped cubicle was like fresh laundry and sunshine, with an undercurrent of male desire.

She didn't realise she'd been staring at him, while nibbling at the inside of her bottom lip, until Cormac's gaze darkened, nostrils flaring, throat working.

Then he said, "Just so we're clear, when I said, 'Are we going to do this?' I meant, 'Are we going to take the photos?'"

"You did not."

A smile spread slowly over Cormac's mouth. Then he leant over to touch the magic button. On the machine. Not her magic button. That would have been—

Harper shook her head as a wave of sensation rushed over her, threatening to make her swoon.

The machine began to whir as it warmed up, loaded the film, or whatever it did to ready itself.

"I never knew you enough to give you a lock of hair, so we'll get you your keepsake today," Cormac said. "Every girl with a crush deserves one—it's the least I can do."

"Seriously—"

A flash went off, filling the small box with light and—
Click.

"What? Was that a photo?" Of her gawping at Cormac while he smiled gorgeously towards the lens?

"Next one's only a few seconds away," he warned, shuffling to put his arm around her.

"I can't believe I'm doing this," she muttered as she tucked herself into his side. The heat of him washed over her, his scent filling her lungs. She puffed out a breath between pursed lips and—
Click.

"I wasn't ready!" she cried.

"Just sit still and smile."

"Okay."

At the last second, he turned and kissed her on the cheek.
Click.

"Cormac!"

She turned to chastise him, only to find him so close they bumped noses. She froze. He nudged her nose once more, this time with purpose.

Then he leaned in and kissed her, this time pressing his lips gently, so gently, against her lips.

And whatever she'd been about to say slipped right

out of her head as sweet, painful longing overtook every other feeling.

Click.

Harper's eyes flickered open, slowly, unsurely. To find Cormac on his feet and sweeping the velvet curtain aside.

While Harper couldn't move. The sounds of the party slowly came back to her—laughter, music, chatter. The ground beneath her feet felt unstable, as if it was tipping and swaying. As if she didn't know which way was left any more. Which way right.

Things didn't just happen to Harper, not any more. She'd made sure of it. She was her own boss. She took on the jobs she wanted to take on. She had no problem with saying no. She was in charge of her destiny.

But this place was undoing her. This man… He worried she wouldn't let herself feel vulnerable. Nervous. Scared. With him that was *all* she felt.

If she didn't get a handle on things and soon, she feared she might never quite get a hold of the strong, grounded, serious parts of herself again.

It was time to take back control.

She reached up and grabbed Cormac's hand. He stopped, looked back at her, eyes questioning.

"You want to get out of here?"

He didn't even hesitate, didn't draw breath as he said, "Hell, yeah."

CHAPTER EIGHT

DESPITE THE WARM summer weather, they were about as close as one could get to Antarctica while still remaining on mainland Australia, meaning a crisp chill had well and truly fallen over Blue Moon Bay.

Cormac changed down a gear as they neared the coastal road gouged into the cliff-side.

Beside him Harper pulled up the collar of the jacket he'd insisted she borrow, and leant back against the head-rest, watching the sky. He snuck a glance before the road became too precarious. Drank in her hooded eyes, long, tip-tilted nose and those tempting full lips.

He knew how soft those lips were. He knew the taste of them, the heat. He knew the sounds that came from them as she melted in his arms.

She folded her arms over her chest and sighed.

"Don't get stars like this where you live," Cormac said.

"We get great stars. Have you been to Dubai?"

"Stopover only." He couldn't remember on the way to where. Once he'd left home at eighteen, with only days to go before he finished high school, he hadn't stopped there. Studying abroad, and working all hours so he could see the world.

So he could keep moving. So he didn't have to look back.

"Did you never think about staying in the States?" she asked. "Or England? London could well be my favourite city."

Cormac swallowed. It had been his too. "I'm pretty sure we've covered this ground already."

She waved a hand his way. "That was before."

Before what exactly? Before they'd taken off in his car after disappearing from a party they should not have disappeared from. Before they'd kissed. Before they'd begun to find ways to be together as much as humanly possible.

"What is the answer you're looking for, Harper?"

She breathed out, long and loud, and said, "I don't know."

Excellent. Then they were both on the same page. Because he had no clue what he was doing here either.

Leaving Gray's bucks' night without saying a word was not like him at all. He'd spent his adult life taking pains never to put his own needs over the needs of others in an effort to make sure he never even came close to becoming his father.

Now he was in the car with no idea as to where they might end up.

Then, like a little gift, he saw a familiar turn in the road.

He slowed, shifted down a gear. The low-slung chassis juddered as they edged onto the dirt road and curled their way up the hill. Peering through the darkness, he found the two painted posts that pointed the way to the spot he was looking for.

The shale crackled under his tyres as he slowed to a halt just before the land dropped away once more, and the lights of the town shimmered down below.

"Where are we?' Harper asked. Then she sat bolt upright, his jacket falling a little off one creamy shoulder before she hooked it back into place. "You're kidding me, right?"

"What?"

"This place. This is…" Her voice lowered as she said, "Kissing Point."

He leaned a mite towards her, his voice dropping to match. "And we're the only ones here. So why are we whispering?"

She looked around, and sat back in her seat. "How many girls you must have brought up here."

"Just one, mainly."

"Right. Tara Parker."

Cormac's mouth twitched. He'd taken the "high-school crush" thing with a grain of salt. But all these years later she remembered the name of his senior girlfriend? Well, what do you know?

Deciding to see how deep it went, he lay back against the headrest and said, "Ah, Tara. Oh, how you brought happiness and light to a young man's life."

Harper's look was blistering. "Wow. Heartfelt. Are you still in touch?"

Cormac turned a little to face her, his knee bumping hers. She noticed. Eyes widening. Breath hitching. But she didn't shift away.

"We are," he said. "Social media. We occasionally bump into one another at the supermarket, or a party every now and then. She married Josh Cantrell."

Harper's nose twitched. Not a Josh fan, then. Cormac didn't blame her. The guy was a douche.

"They have four sons under the age of five."

"Four? Good lord."

"Amen." Then, "You really want to know why I came home?"

"Yeah," she said, "I really do."

He considered his words. Considered making a joke, which was often his way when things edged towards tension.

In the end he went with the truth. "I had an epiphany."

"Did you just?"

"Oh, yeah. A big one. The kind that smacks you across the back of your head so hard you see stars. I figured out the meaning of life."

"Wow. So it was a *big* epiphany."

"The biggest."

"Care to share?"

"The meaning of life? Sure. It's about figuring out what makes you happy and doing more of that."

He waited for Harper's zinger, for offering such an idealistic notion was sure to invite derision. But it never came. Instead she watched him with those quixotic hazel eyes of hers.

Then she lifted a hand to swipe a lock of hair from her cheek. A shaking hand. And he wished he knew what the hell he'd said. Something that had made it past that big, thick wall of self-protection she wore like a walking safe room.

Yet he was well aware of how she reacted when pushed, so he let it be, looking out across the lights of Blue Moon Bay instead.

Keeping his voice light, he said, "For me that means surfing. This glorious old car. Old movies. True friends." He paused, holding the last on the list on the back of his tongue, as it had always felt like a private need, a secret too close to home, before he felt as if she needed to know it, more than he needed to hold it in. "It also means doing good work, for good people, that makes me feel of use."

He spared a glance for Harper, to find her looking out across the town. "What makes you happy, Harper?"

She breathed in deep, breathed out hard. For a moment he thought she was too caught up in her thoughts to have heard him, before her brow furrowed and she said, "Money in the bank. Mostly for the freedom it brings with it, but also the ability to buy shoes without checking the price."

"I hear that."

She lowered her eyes as a smile flashed across her face. Then added, "I love crisp, clean sheets. Room service. A long, hot shower under a showerhead with oomph." Cormac turned to face her a little more. Watching her eyes as she spoke; her cheekbones—the kind Hitchcock would have killed to light; the curve of a mouth built to drive a man out of his mind.

She turned to face him too, her eyes lit with an inner fire as she said, "I love standing in front of a boardroom filled with suits and knowing that I'm in control. That I am there because those smart, powerful, lauded people caused a right mess, and I'm the only one who can fix it. And when all's said and done they legally agree to follow my recommendations and do as I say."

That he did not doubt for a second.

"But it's not about the power trip. It's about making things right. About turning what has become an explosive situation that could break people into a fair, thoughtful compromise in which nobody loses their house."

Cormac's next breath out was tough.

She presented to the world like a professional ball breaker, but he'd known she was more. He wouldn't have been so drawn to her if beneath the implacable exterior he hadn't been able to sense her big heart.

But, he wanted to know, did any of those things make her *happy*?

Her voice seemed far away as she said, "But you know what?"

"What?"

"I would gladly give all of that away if that's what it took to make sure Lola was happy."

"She is."

She swallowed, her throat working as she said, "So it would seem."

"So what will you do now? Where does all that fierce focus of yours go?"

She opened her mouth and shut it again, doing a fine impression of a fish out of water.

"More long, hot showers, perhaps? More time to squish suits under the heels of your expensive shoes?"

Her mouth tightened, her focus coming back on line. "Like you can talk."

"What does that mean?"

Her chin rose, heat swirling behind her sultry hazel eyes, as she said, "What is it you do exactly? I mean, from what I've seen you surf, you chat up the customers and you drive people around. But there has to be more."

Cormac laughed, the sound coiling deep inside of him and holding on tight. He was a smart man. He knew how she reacted any time they came anywhere close to intimacy. She was baiting him to keep him at arm's length.

Hell, he'd just admitted to himself that he did the same thing, only he used humour to keep anything too close to real conversation at bay.

This push-pull dynamic was completely new to him. She was abrasive, stubborn, and she made him itch, but the attraction was undeniable. Damn scary, in fact, how fast it had come on. How deep it already went. Especially when he still wasn't all that sure he trusted her.

By this point he was acting on gut instinct alone.

The same instinct that had him saying, "The Chadwick companies are more than just a clothing brand. We are sports equipment designers. We own manufacturing plants, real estate, restaurants, shipping and logistics businesses as well as many other concerns. We work hard to put as much business back into the region as we can, in order to keep the local economy booming, but we also build and serve every community in which we run. We employ thousands of workers across the globe. All our products are made using adult labour with fair pay. We run more than one charity under the Chadwick umbrella—medical research, domestic violence shelters, educational scholarships—with ninety per cent of all monies raised going direct to the beneficiaries. And of all that I am lead counsel."

He turned to Harper to find her watching him, eyes wide and gleaming in the moonlight. No wonder. His words had scattered like artillery fire, ready to take out anyone who dared deny the veracity of his speech.

"You want to know what I do, Harper? While—after years spent keeping this entire town afloat—the Chadwicks finally get to enjoy their well-earned retirement, and Gray—my big, kind, sweet, loving best mate—enjoys the hell out of his blessed life like the trust-fund kid that he is, I run the damn lot."

"Cormac, I didn't mean—"

"Yes, you did."

Cormac ran a rough hand through his hair.

What the hell was it about her that made him feel the need to prove himself? To make her believe that he was content, settled and damn well happy? When deep down she made him feel it was time to shed his skin.

If only he could get her out of his head. If only he could keep his eyes off her. Stop touching her whenever the chance arose, as if making sure she was still there. If only he could pinpoint what it was about her that had swept him up so fast, so hard.

Then maybe he could figure out which parts of him she'd left untouched, untattered, unchanged, and he could rebuild from there. He'd done it before when he'd been nothing but a shell of a boy. He could do it again.

"Look," he said, doing his all to gentle his voice, "I've tried to be pleasant. Tried to be welcoming. Tried to be accommodating for your sister's sake, for the sake of the Chadwicks. But enough is enough, Harper. You've had it in for me from the moment you arrived. What I want to know is why."

He could all but see the invisible quills popping up all over her skin. Protective measures locking into place. Then, before he even felt her move, she was outside, the car rocking as she slammed the door behind her.

She turned only to toss his jacket into the back seat,

as if shedding him as well, before she paced to the front of the car.

Her silhouette cut into his view. Moonlight poured over her bare shoulders, glinting off the silken sheen of a dress that hugged her curves like a second skin, turned her movie-siren hair to silver.

The air around her shimmered with her intense energy. He'd never met anyone who held on as tight. Who was as impossible to crack. So why the hell did he keep trying?

He gripped the steering wheel as too many emotions to count slammed over him like a series of rogue waves. Went to slam his wrists against it, before stopping himself at the last. Breathing. Temper gentling.

He kept trying because, while he might not yet trust her, he trusted himself. His instincts were decent. His motives genuine. He would not have been so drawn to her without good reason.

Cormac alighted from the car, shut the door carefully, walked to her, before hitching himself up onto the tough old bonnet.

When she finally turned, levelling him with a look, he patted the spot next to him.

As he'd known she would she held out a beat, before leaning back against the bonnet next to him. Because, strange as it was for such a short acquaintance, he felt as though he *knew* her. And, knowing her, he only wanted to know more.

The breeze rustled her hair, sending a waft of her heady scent his way.

"Harper, I need you to talk to me. Did Lola tell you something about me that doesn't sit right? Is it something to do with my father? Did you know him back then?" Not that, please let it not be that. "Or was it something at school? Did I not take your causes seriously? Did I hurt your feelings in some way?"

There. The brisk lift of her shoulders. Harper said nothing, her face a case study in elusive shadows, but with a sinking feeling in his chest Cormac realised that while trying to make light he'd somehow hit the mark.

What the hell had he done? His last couple of years of school were a blur in his memory. A haze. While things had spiraled out of control at home, he'd become cocooned in his group of friends.

Never before had he wished he could remember it all. He'd blocked it out deliberately; the shouting, the fights, the bruises, the terror that this time might be the last. The feeling that his soul was trying to burst out of his skin. He knew he'd growled at poor kids who got in his way. Stopped listening when a friend was telling a story. He'd skipped school. Stolen beer. Drunk it while skipping school.

Somehow, he'd managed to keep it together, enough to look after his mum. Enough to finish with grades and friendships intact. Enough to finally put an end to it.

But if going back helped him figure out why Harper sometimes looked at him like he had horns, he'd do it.

"Tell me."

"Why? So you can throw it in my face? Been there. Never want to go there again."

Battling a chaotic mix of concern and frustration, Cormac crossed his arms, the cotton stretching tight over muscle and bone. His voice was quiet but the intent clear as he said, "Are you just going to leave that there like a little time bomb? Or do you plan to tell me what that's supposed to mean?"

She lifted her chin. "It's nothing."

"It sounded pretty specific. Did I cut in front of you in the lunch line? Did you ask me to a school dance and I was already taken?"

She'd have been such a spitfire back then. Full of hope and promise and snark. Why hadn't he seen her? Noticed her? Especially if she'd had a crush on him. The very thought of which was messing with his head, big time.

He'd been a swimming star, part of the "in" group, and he'd had all his features in the right place. He'd seen enough John Hughes movies to understand those ingredients all but ensured that girls would giggle behind their hands as he and his mates walked past.

And yet knowing that one girl in particular had harboured feelings for him made him feel as if the fabric of his life was being stretched out of shape.

"Harper, sweetheart. Just tell me."

For a moment he thought she hadn't heard, or was going to refuse him again, but then her voice came to him, soft but clear.

"It was late in your last year of high school, right before graduation. You must remember the scandal. My family's scandal."

"I promise you I'm not making light, but I remember very little of that time." He swallowed, knowing there was only one way she'd believe him. "My father… That year was his worst."

She glanced his way, her eyes impossible to read in the semi-darkness. And she said, "Mine too. My dad lost everything—every cent we had and then some—in a shady real-estate deal."

Harper's father—*Lola's father*—had gone *broke*? No. Surely he'd have remembered that. Or at least learnt about it since. If the Chadwicks knew they'd have said something, for they'd never held back business talk in front of him. They'd always treated him as if his opinion mattered. Taught him that, armed with knowledge, he could make a difference.

"It was all over the news," Harper said. "All over the school. My father lost millions, not only his own money but also that of a number of local mum and dad investors, too."

When her gaze swept to his, moonlight glowing at the edges of the dark depths, he found himself holding his breath.

"It was awful," she said. "Everyone knew. It was too much for Dad to bear, and he left."

"Left."

She nodded.

"I don't understand. You were what, sixteen? Lola younger again. Your mother wasn't around and he *walked out*."

"And never came back."

Her eyes remained focussed on his. Watchful. As if trying to decipher how much he was hiding from her about not remembering. As if he wasn't the only one who struggled with trust.

"Wow, you *really* don't remember, do you?"

He shook his head. And once again said, "Tell me."

"News spread fast, as it does in this place, and the scavengers arrived the next day to clear us out. I don't even know who they were. I thought it was the bank, but looking back it couldn't have been. Loan sharks, perhaps. Worse. We were probably lucky we weren't cleared out with the stuff.

"I only managed to fill a couple of backpacks as they took everything. Our furniture. My stereo. Lola's soft toys. Even the family photographs. I'm sure they had lost money in Dad's deal, as it was personal.

"Anyway, I had to find Lola and myself somewhere to sleep. I negotiated with the market on Haynes Street. I already worked there after school and weekends only from that time on I'd do so for use of the vacant space above the store and a grocery allowance.

"I didn't realise till we were getting ready for school on the Monday that I'd only packed clothes for Lola. The only clothes were the ones on my back- old jeans and an ancient Bowie T-shirt of my mum's. I washed them every night. Wore them to school still damp if necessary. One day I was sent home—half-day suspension, no less—because my shirt was too short. Only because it had shrunk from so many washes."

"The speech," he said, under his breath. "The one about sexist uniform policies."

She blinked at him, a ghost of a smile flickering across her lush mouth.

"The shop owner downstairs heard and gave me a bag of hand-me-downs. And they started paying me my wage again as well. Thank goodness, because it meant Lola had money for excursions and birthday parties and dental check-ups. All the while I had to avoid any questions about guardianship."

Cormac ran a hand through his mussed-up hair. He'd thought he'd kept his family turmoil under wraps, but where he'd had his friends to protect him, she'd gone through it on her own.

No wonder she was still so overly concerned about Lola's welfare—she'd been raising her since she was a kid herself.

He had questions. But he kept them to himself. She needed to get this out. He waited, and he listened, all the while his gut roiling with anger at her father, and at his town that had made a sixteen-year-old girl negotiate to put a roof over her head.

All the while dreading the part he'd played in the story she told.

She held her arms around herself, shaking so hard her teeth rattled.

"You're trembling," he said, sliding off the car to be next to her.

"I'm fine."

"Let me get the jacket." He made to move and Harper's hand reached out and grabbed his wrist.

"Stay."

He stayed. He also took her hand in his and held it between his own, rubbing it and blowing hot air over her chilled skin.

She watched him as she said, "It was a few weeks after. I saw you at that table under the oak tree—"

"Behind the science block."

"Right. You were sitting on the table, feet on the bench, legs jiggling with pent-up energy. You were wearing your Jurassic Fart T-shirt."

Cormac grimaced. He didn't remember much from that year, but he remembered that shirt. *If she remembers that much detail, this is going to be bad.*

"You were wild-eyed. Unfocussed. You looked like you wanted to climb out of your skin. I'd never seen you like that before. You looked… You looked how I felt. Your friends, on the other hand, all sat on the grass nearby, joking, lying all over one another, not a care in the world. The fact that none of them saw you, saw how tragic you looked, well, it made me angry. So…"

She glanced at him then, chin ducked, eyes blinking. First time he'd ever seen her look shy. He moved in a little closer, ran his hand down her forearm and back up again, thawing her out an inch at a time.

"So I went up to you. And I asked if you were okay. You looked through me like I was some kind of apparition. Then one of the others, a boy—not Gray, Josh—jumped up and loped over. Said something like, *'What's up, Addison? Begging for the whales? The spotted owl? Or lunch money?'*"

"What the—?"

Harper waved it off. As if in the grand scheme of things Josh the douche had barely left a mark. "A place like Blue Moon Bay High you can't get away with wearing the same clothes every day before it becomes a point of conversation. Then he turned to you and said, *'What do you reckon, Wharton? Should we give her what she wants?'*"

Cormac's jaw hardened. "Please tell me I told him where to go."

"Not exactly." Harper's next breath in was short, sharp; as if the sensation burned. "You looked me dead in the eye and said, *'She's nobody. She's not getting anything from me.'*"

Cormac stilled; his entire body felt like ice, only now it was her warm hand in his keeping him tethered.

He slid his hand up her arm, and gently tugged her closer. Right into the curve of his body. He waited for her to twist away. Would let her go in an instant if she did. But after a moment she gave in, settling into his side, her head tucked under his chin.

"I said that?" he asked, his words muffled by her hair.

She nodded against his shoulder. "Word for word."

Cormac closed his eyes and tried to picture the time, the day, the way it might have unfolded. It wasn't hard. She had recounted it in excruciating detail.

"Josh wasn't exactly a friend of mine," he said, his voice rough. "He was a drifter in the group. He could be a git even at the best of times. And for some reason he always treated me more like competition than a friend."

"Tara," Harper said, her voice a husky whisper.

Of course.

Cormac breathed in the scent of her hair, letting his mouth rest against her crown a moment before he said, "If Josh thought you meant something to me, he'd have made your life hell."

Harper's face tilted to his, and she stared hard into his eyes. He wondered what she saw. What she made of him. Then and now. It floored him how much it mattered.

"But I *didn't* mean anything to you," she said. "And yet… Are you telling me you were trying to *protect* me? Even so?"

"If Josh was about to cause trouble, with anyone, taking the fun out of it was always a good way to deflate it."

Harper's deep eyes gleamed in the low light. Her arm rubbed against his chest as she breathed in and out. Her skin, no longer ice-cold, burned him everywhere they touched.

And then she laughed, the sound closer to a sob. Laughed and laughed and laughed. Before, with a groan, she leant forward, her face falling into her hands.

Cormac's hand slid to her back. To the satiny touch of her dress. Beneath the thin fabric he felt the delicate curve of her spine. Felt her every breath.

He opened his mouth to ask if she was okay, then closed it. She wasn't okay. It had been clear from the moment she arrived. Only now he knew why.

She pulled herself upright. Cormac's hand slid to her hip. He took the chance to pull her closer. She let him. Melting against him as if she no longer had the strength to hold herself up.

Eventually she said, "My life took a turn that day. I hardened up, my focus becoming a pinpoint of determination. I'd show my mum, I'd show my dad, I'd show you that I wasn't someone to walk away from, to dismiss. I wasn't nobody."

Cormac had been made to feel worthless in his life. Told by his father on a near daily basis in the end, how disappointing he was, how insignificant, he'd come all too close to letting himself give in and believe it.

The good people in his life—the Grays, the Adeles, the core gang—had been the reason he'd been able to break free.

From what he'd gathered she'd not had that. She'd been too busy trying to hold her family together to make friends like his. To think he'd been the one who made her feel small when she'd had no people, no support—he felt as if claws were tearing at his insides.

"Harper."

"What?"

"Look at me."

She heaved in a deep breath and looked up into his eyes, fierce and utterly wondrous. And something ferocious and unstoppable stampeded through his chest.

Gray thought her a Hitchcockian ice queen, but Cormac knew better. Harper Addison was pure fire. And that fire of hers had lit something within him, stoking the embers of the slow burn of a life he'd thought was enough. The life he'd thought was exactly as he wanted it to be.

She'd wrapped an invisible fist around something deep and primal inside of him and yanked him out of complacency without even trying.

Cormac's hand travelled slowly up her back, catching on the ribbon at her neck before sliding back down. He saw smoke drift into her eyes—eyes that were wide open, exposed—and felt change in the very vibrations in the air.

Her crush was not merely a thing of the past.

His crush, on the other hand, was brand new. And all the more mercurial, unwieldy and unsettling for it.

He wanted to kiss her, more than he remembered wanting anything in his entire life. It took every gentlemanly bone in his body not to take advantage.

For there were more things to say.

"While it doesn't excuse the way I made you feel that day, will you allow me to give you some context?"

She nodded. "Okay."

"It was right around the time you described that I finally convinced Mum to leave my father. I'd spent a rough few months working her up to it, securing a room in a domestic-violence shelter. I took the day off school to drive her there—three hours away to a place he'd never find her. At eighteen, six-feet-two and male, I wasn't allowed to stay with her which was hard. But she convinced me I had to go home, to graduate with my friends. And I wanted to see the look in his eyes when he realised she was gone."

Harper asked, "What happened?"

"It went as was to be expected." He lifted a hand to his forehead.

Her fingers followed, tracing the pale line that slashed through his eyebrow. "Your *father* did that?"

And more. Before then, before he'd come home to find his wife gone he'd been lucid enough to make sure the scars would be well hidden. "Broken bottle. He was aiming for my throat. Swing and a near miss."

"Except for the black eye."

"Hmm?"

"I remember now. You had a black eye. That day. It was so unlike you it was why I'd found the courage to go up to you in the first place. I was a sucker for a lost cause."

He tried again to imagine her. A girl with a heart big enough to put aside the horrors she was dealing with to check on him. While his friends—too distracted by all the end-of-high-school excitement—hadn't noticed a thing.

"I slept in the local park after the bottle incident," he said, his voice sounding far away to his own ears. "The noises you hear outside your window as a kid are nothing compared to being up close and personal."

Harper said nothing. She simply turned in his arms until she leaned flush against him. One hand sliding over his shoulder, the other gathering his hand and holding it to her chest.

"The next day Gray took one look at me and dragged me back to his folks' place. They offered me a room in the house, but I couldn't take it. I'd been trapped for so long, I feared I'd wake in the middle of the night and smash a window to get out. So they gave me the pool house—a room of windows and light—for as long as I wanted it."

"The pool house," she murmured. "It always sounded so decadent."

Her voice reverberated through his chest.

"It was the Chadwicks' pool house. Of course it was decadent."

Her eyes lifted to his. Maybe it was the moonlight play-ing tricks, but there was no wall up now. Only so much tenderness his breath stuck in his throat.

Her voice was husky as she said, "No wonder you're so enamoured of them."

"The Chadwicks are the reason I'm here today. All three of them. They are the reason I came back here, to the edge of the world. Without them...who knows what might have become of me?"

Harper's dark eyes flickered between his. "For so long I've dreamed of telling you off for how you treated me. Mostly because you left before I had the chance."

Her voice cracked on the words "you left". And no won-der. Her mother had left. Her father had left. How many times could that happen to a person and they still forged on? Only she'd more than forged on, she'd flourished. She'd shown them all.

"And now?" he asked.

"I've always believed my life took a turn that day. A turn on a misunderstanding, as it turns out. Does that make my entire life a sham?"

He reached up and unhooked a strand of golden hair from her eyelashes. "It makes you human."

"Who knew?" Harper said, her voice husky, her eyes darkening. There was a softness about her he'd not seen before. A yielding.

And Cormac knew in that moment that he was in deep, deep trouble.

He'd told Gray nothing would happen between him and Harper because he'd believed it wasn't worth the trouble.

Now he knew nothing could happen between them be-cause he might never get over it.

For Cormac was a man who held on to those who'd marked him in some way, taking on the cuts and bruises along with the laughter and light. For they had all helped forge the man he'd become.

He knew if he let Harper in, she'd carve him to pieces. And when she left she'd take whatever pieces of him she wanted.

"Thank-you for telling me," he said, his voice rough.

She nodded.

"It's late. We should get word to Lola and Gray, let them know we're okay. Then I should get you home."

At mention of Lola, he felt the shift. All but saw the wall slide back down between them.

"Right," she said, gently pressing away. "Let's do that."

Once completely free of him, she ran a hand over her dress, fixed her hair, until everything was perfectly in place once more. Then strode around the car and hopped inside.

His phone buzzed. A quick check of the message had him frowning. "Dammit."

"What's wrong?"

He leapt into the driver's seat without opening the door, and had the engine ticking over in a second. He looked over his shoulder as he made a quick turn and took off back down the dirt path.

"Mind if we make a quick stop? The alarm has gone off at my place."

"Your place?"

"My house. My home."

"So you really did move out of the pool house, then? I thought you were kidding."

The snark was back. Though it was half-hearted. As if she couldn't quite tap into it any more. As if things had shifted too far towards something intimate. Something real.

Cormac carefully navigated the rutted path as they made their way back towards the coastal road. And felt a sense of inevitability fall over him at the thought of taking her home.

CHAPTER NINE

HARPER FELT AS if her life had been shaken like a snow globe. As the flakes settled, everything looked different.

Her father had always been fickle. When he fell short it was a disappointment, but not a shock.

Cormac had been her constant. A shining light in her topsy-turvy world. So much so she'd built him into something unrealistic. A person without fault. Without pain. Without troubles of his own.

And the first time he'd faltered she'd cracked.

Only Cormac *hadn't* faltered; he'd been trying to protect her even as he'd lived inside his own pain.

What if she'd known? What if she'd taken another step towards him, rather than walking away? Might something have been forged from that moment, rather than being broken?

So deep inside her own head was she, Harper paid no attention to where Cormac was taking her until the car rumbled to a stop.

"Back in a sec," he said as he hopped out of the car to meet a security guard before the men headed inside.

Harper slid numbly out of the car, gaze dancing over a gorgeous big liquid amber tree—tyre swing and all—in the pristine front yard. Front porch. Gabled roof. Big, neat suburban home.

Harper was halfway up the path when the security guy came back out. He smiled, tipped his hat and jogged back to his little white hatchback, but not before slowing to have a quick look over Cormac's far cooler wheels.

"Hello?" Harper called as she stepped through the open front door.

"Back here."

Harper followed Cormac's disembodied voice up a wide hall boasting pale wood floors, and warm, creamy walls. She spied couches and rugs in living spaces, a tidy open-plan office. Fireplaces everywhere. And in a media room a wall of movie posters—art deco takes on *Vertigo*, *Rear Window*, *Dial M for Murder*.

The house was both elegant and comfortable. But what stood out most of all was the sheer scope for just one man.

It was not a house for a bachelor. It was a house for a family.

Still unbalanced from earlier, and now even more so at having to place this piece into the Cormac puzzle, Harper found the man in question turning lights on in a large chef's kitchen.

"No burglar?" she asked.

He glanced up, his expression unreadable as he watched her walk towards him. "Just a dog who can open fridge doors." Then he held up a carton of orange juice, the drink dripping from a hole in the corner.

Harper saw movement out of the corner of her eye and turned to find Novak lying on a big, soft doggy bed, looking guilty.

"Who's a clever girl?" Harper said on a laugh.

Taking it as an invitation, Novak slunk up to her, leaned gently against her leg and looked up at her for a pat. As Harper looked down into the dog's liquid eyes, she felt herself fall in love, just a little bit.

When she looked up to find Cormac standing still as a statue, watching her, brow furrowed, eyes dark and consuming, she didn't steel her heart against the sight of him nearly quickly enough.

"So this little piece of suburbia is really yours?" she asked.

"I bought it for my mum, actually."

"She lives here with you?"

"No," he said with a wry smile. "She's only been here once. The day I planned to surprise her with the place.

Before I had the chance, she told me she was getting re-married. To a guy I'd never even met. She was standing about where you are, right now."

Harper took a step sideways. "Yet you kept it."

"I'd bought it for her." The words were simple, the sentiment anything but.

Cormac Wharton was no cardboard cut-out to drool over. He was far deeper than she'd given him credit for. He was a man who put great stead in his place in the world. His purpose. His tribe.

His family.

No wonder he'd found the Chadwicks so compelling—with their big smiles and warm hugs.

After the craziness of their childhood, no wonder Lola had too.

"Did you tell her?" Harper asked, very much needing a distraction. "Did you end up telling your mum what you'd done?"

Cormac shook his head. "Didn't seem right to burden her. Not when the point had been to gift her her freedom. I wonder though if she'd have taken it anyway. If one of the reasons she's been away so long is that she looks at me and sees him."

Him. His father.

Harper's father had been imperfect. But he'd tried to make their lives fun and bright and joyful. Tried to love them enough that the rest didn't matter.

While, from what Harper could glean, Cormac's father had hit his mother until Cormac was big enough to take the brunt. And he'd taken it, refusing to leave until he could convince his mother to do the same.

Yet under the kitchen down lights Cormac couldn't hide the shadows in his eyes. The regret, the hurt, the sliver of uncertainty that maybe his mother was right.

"You want to know why I had such a crush on you in high school?" The words spilled out of her before she even felt them forming. "It wasn't because you were cute, though you were that. It wasn't because you were popular, though I never heard anyone say a bad word about you. It was because you were kind. To everyone from the grounds-keeper to the principal."

Always quick with a joke, with a smile and a way to lighten the mood, Cormac didn't budge. So Harper did, taking a step his way.

"At my house we'd have chocolate cake for dinner one night, nothing at all the next. The place could have been filled with balloons and streamers and glitter all over the floor when Dad was in a good mood, or deathly quiet if he was having one of his 'dark days'. Never knowing what I'd come home to, high school for me was a torrent of quiet tension. Except when I saw you."

A muscle ticked at the edge of his jaw. And Harper kept walking towards the kitchen.

"You have a way of making people feel calm, Cormac. Feel safe. Feel as if it's all going to be okay. There is no possible way your mother looks at you and sees anyone but you."

She turned the corner of the bench on her last word, only to stop at the sight of the devastation on the kitchen floor. "Wow, that dog of yours doesn't do things by halves."

Cormac blinked at her. Then laughed. Then ran a hand over his face. Then let out a little growl. Sexiest five seconds of Harper's entire life.

He watched her then, across the kitchen, for a heartbeat. And another. Before he breathed out hard. And asked, "Are you thirsty? Hungry?"

Harper was both. At least, she told herself that was the gnawing feeling in her belly. That big, empty hole that hadn't been there a week ago.

"I could eat."

"Then go," he said, angling his chin towards the front room. "Sit. Put on a movie. I'll finish cleaning then I'll whip something up." He didn't reiterate his plans to drop her home after.

Then again, neither did she.

"You cook? More than your famous ham sandwiches you once tried to tempt me with?"

"I reheat," he said, poking a thumb at his freezer. "I'm pretty damn good at it too."

With a smile and a nod she turned on her heel and moseyed back to the front room, where she turned on the TV and scrolled through his movie library till she found the one she was looking for.

She kicked off her shoes and tucked herself up on the couch, smiling as Cary Grant and Grace Kelly's names appeared on the screen.

Cormac picked up the opening strains of *To Catch a Thief* within the first couple of bars. He smiled. The woman had taste.

His subconscious spoke up. *Clearly. She had a crush on you, after all.*

His foot moved and slipped slightly in a blob of cream. Crush magnet or not, he still had to clean his own damn kitchen.

His kitchen; not his mother's. It was time he got used to that fact.

To the fact his mother had done exactly what he'd always hoped she could. To stand up for what she wanted. To turn her back on the past. To find a way to be happy.

He'd just never imagined it would mean turning her back on him.

A woman screamed in the front room—a woman in the movie, not Harper.

Harper. She'd been left by her mother, *and* her father. Both before she was even an adult herself. And, rather than giving in, she had chosen to fight for the right to forge a life for herself. A highly successful life, by the sound of it. All the while making sure Lola had the chance to do the same.

When had Cormac last fought for anything? Fair pay, yes. Workers' rights, sure. But something real to him? Something personal?

He'd spent years priding himself on his contentment. But contentment was easy. It didn't ask too much of a person. While Harper... Harper expected more.

Harper was real. As real a person as he'd ever known. And once upon a time she'd thought the same about him.

How does she see you now? How does she feel about you now? What does it matter? She'll be gone in a few days, and you'll be here. Always here...

His subconscious sure was chatty tonight.

Cormac motioned to Novak, who hustled over, panting happily, ears flicking up and down, between guilty and delighted. He reached out and gave her ear a quick rub. She blinked, one eye at a time.

"Have at it," Cormac said.

Novak did as instructed, delicately lapping up the edible bits while Cormac cleaned up the rest. Then he let her out into the big back yard to do her nightly security check.

The soundtrack of the movie grew louder as he neared the front room. And there he found Harper, curled up on his couch, fast asleep.

Her cheek rested against the back of the couch, her hair tumbled over one cheek, her bare feet curled around one another.

He laughed under his breath at the way she white-knuckled the cushion cuddled to her chest. Tightly wound, even in sleep. As if the world might scatter into a zillion tiny little particles if she wasn't there to hold it all together.

He found the remote and tuned the sound to low, then he slowly sat on the empty end of the couch nearest her head, draping his arm along the back of the couch.

The movement unsettling her, she woke. Eyes flickering open. Whole body stretching. Elegant, graceful, and beguiling.

When her eyes snagged on his they stuck. For a second or two, she was completely open, her eyes drinking him in, her face softening into a smile so true it made his heart twist.

"Hi," she said, her voice husky and light.

"Hi."

"What happened?"

"You fell asleep."

"I did?"

"Mmm-hmm. I'd chastise you for daring to do so during one of the best movies ever made but I have the feeling you needed the rest."

She shifted, pulling herself upright until her face was level with his. "How long was I out?"

"Not long."

"I was dreaming."

"About?"

Her gaze roved over his face before landing back on his eyes. "I'd rather not say."

She didn't have to. It was written all over her face.

"Can I ask you something?" she said, looking around the room. "I know why you stayed, but what brought you back in the first place? Was it a girl?"

"No, Harper. I didn't come back for a girl."

"So, you're not living here, alone in this big family house, because you're pining for the one that got away?"

"And who do you imagine that might be?" he asked, voice soft, low.

Her lips snapped together, as if only just realising how much she was revealing. "I'm just trying to build a profile here."

"A profile?"

"I meant picture."

"No, you didn't."

"Fine. It's what I do. I research everyone in the room so I know what I'm up against."

"And you're planning to go up against me?"

The double entendre was not subtle. The waggling eyebrows made it even less so.

Harper managed a deadpan stare. "Do you wish things had worked out differently with Tara?"

"Did I not mention the four sons under five?"

He saw the smile hit her eyes first before it tugged at one corner of her lush mouth. Cormac's gaze dropped to the tug. Stayed as Harper said, "Even so."

He tugged on a curl, as if using it to lever himself forward. Her nostrils flared, but she didn't back away.

"Harper, are you asking if I still have feelings for my high-school girlfriend?"

"I'm merely making conversation."

"I'd not have pegged you for a fan of small talk."

"Needs must."

A slow smile spread across his face. "Interesting saying, that one. *Needs must.* Why is that that you *need* to know if I'm seeing anyone? Why *must* you know if there's anyone I'm longing for? Only one reason I can think of."

She licked her lips before asking, "And what's that?"

"Because that crush of yours is still well and truly alive."

She breathed out hard, her molten gaze dropping to his mouth.

He waited for her to fight him, for she was nothing if not a fighter. He waited for her to deny every word, for denial was a fair part of her repertoire. But she didn't. She sat there on his couch, hugging his cushion. And for the life of him he couldn't remember his own name, much less the name of any other girl he'd ever met.

"Here's something for you to mull over," he said, sliding his hand deeper into her satiny hair. "I have a crush on you, too."

Her lips opened on a sigh.

"And if you don't want me to kiss you till neither one of us remembers how we got here, now's the time to tell me."

Out of the corner of his eye he saw her grip soften on the cushion, before she flung it across the room.

Then she reached up, slid a hand around the back of his neck, and she kissed him. Open-mouthed. Soft, sensual, hot as Hades.

With a growl he took her in his arms, shifting until she lay beneath him on the couch. His thigh between hers. Her leg wrapping around his, trapping him. Claiming him.

Then, like teenagers, they couldn't get enough of one another. All harsh breath and clashing tongues. Roving hands and raging lust.

Needing to calm things, to centre himself, before he lost himself entirely, Cormac ran a settling hand over her shoulder, down her bare arm, till his hand reached her thigh, her bare thigh. Her satinydress had ridden up until his thumb brushed the slightest, most delicate hint of lace before it gave way to the curve of backside.

Afraid it might end him, then and there, he kept his hand moving until he found her hand, took it, lifting it to his lips. Placing a kiss on the tip of each finger, before resting his lips on her palm.

She watched him, chest rising and falling, eyes bright. Overly bright, as if she might be about to…

With a shake of her head she broke eye contact, then pushed him to sitting. There she wasted no time before undoing the buttons on his shirt.

"Harper," he said, lifting a hand to cup her cheek.

"Shut up, Cormac," she said, shaking his hand away. "Anyone ever told you you talk too much?"

Cormac coughed out a laugh, the sound barely making it past the tightness in his chest. "Not a single living soul."

When her eyes found his they were full of fire. Desire. And something else. Something deep and raw and old as the cliffs keeping Blue Moon Bay from tumbling into the raging ocean below.

This woman, he thought as he somehow managed to stop himself from tearing the shirt from his back. To let her do the work. Understanding on a cellular level that a semblance of control was necessary to her. Even while handing it over was unnerving to him.

She slid his shirt down his arms, her thumbs scraping against bare skin as she took her time. Eyes roving hungrily over his chest. His bare stomach. The aching bulge in his jeans. Her hands stopping when they reached his wrists. Trapping him with his shirt so that he couldn't touch her. Like Jimmy Stewart, stuck in his wheelchair, while the most beautiful woman in the world shadowed over him.

"Harper," he murmured. "You are every fantasy I ever had, all rolled into one."

Only this was real life. The woman before him all too real. No ice in her eyes, no wall between them, only heat, and desire, for him.

He leaned in, holding her eyes with his, before he kissed her softly. Gently. Tenderly. Meaningfully.

Waiting until she began to sigh, and moan, and melt, before carefully pulling a hand free so that he could touch her, run his fingers down her neck, undoing the ribbon at the back of her dress, until the silken slip of nothing pooled at her waist.

Their eyes caught. Neither of them breathed. As if hovering on the brink of something. This their final chance to pull back. To slink back to the safety of their respective corners.

Then Harper lifted her hand to Cormac's cheek, her thumb brushing over his bottom lip before she followed up with a kiss. A caress. An admission.

Then she lay back. A vision of loveliness. Of surrender. To this. To them.

* * *

When Cormac woke it was to a quiet house. The TV was turned off. Novak snored softly on the rug. He didn't need to call out, to search the house, to know that Harper was long gone.

With a groan he unpeeled his long body from the couch, replacing the cushions that had fallen to the floor, before sitting and resting his face in his hands.

How had she managed that? Uber? The town-car guy from Melbourne who'd been so clearly smitten with her? She might well have walked, for all he knew. If she'd wanted to get out that bad, she'd have found a way.

A thought came to him and he was on his feet, padding barefoot to the garage, only breathing out upon finding his beautiful blue Sunbeam slumbering safely there still.

Closing the door, he looked about his big house. He only lived in three or four of the rooms; the rest had never been touched except by a cleaner once every couple of weeks.

But now it seemed cavernous. Empty. A clock ticking somewhere upstairs marking the long seconds as he tried to measure how he felt.

All too quickly landing on restless. Off kilter. Discontent.

Cormac swore beneath his breath as he picked up the clothes strewn about the lounge before jogging up the stairs to his bedroom. Heading straight into the *en suite,* he dumped his clothes in the hamper, before turning the spray to full hot.

She needn't have stayed over if that had been her concern. Hell, he'd have been happy to take her wherever she wanted to go. Well, not happy, but resigned.

At the very least she could have woken him. Said goodbye.

But even as he thought it he knew it wasn't her way.

She might have been a revelation in the quiet dark of night, offering him a rare glimpse at the tender heart of her.

But in the bright light of day she was a runner. It was in her blood, after all.

CHAPTER TEN

LOLA TURNED HER face to the sharp summer sunshine. "Can you believe this weather? I mean, tell me, have you seen skies like this anywhere else in the world?"

Harper grimaced as she tugged the spike of her left heel out of the lush lawn leading out to the Chadwicks' extensive rear gardens. "Hmm?"

Lola dropped her hands to her yoga-pants-clad hips. "You're the one who said you wanted to get some fresh air—now you're acting like you're allergic."

"I know. And I do." She did want fresh air. Or at least some space to talk to Lola without wondering if someone was about to walk in the room. The nature she could take or leave.

Harper winced as something landed on her shoulder.

Lola leaned forward to flick away the small leaf, then tucked a hand in the crook of her arm. "Come on, Harps, let's just walk and you can tell me why we're out here when you're ready."

Lola yabbered away about the lemon icing she'd chosen for the wedding cake, and the gorgeous local bubbly they'd chosen over imported champagne.

Harper tried to concentrate, but she couldn't stop her mind from wandering to Cormac. His couch. To making love to Cormac on his couch.

For that was what it had felt like. Not sex. Not a one-night stand or an itch that had needed scratching. But sweet and gentle. Tender and thorough. It had also been seductive, and hot, and gravely intimate. Consuming. Till every cell in her body, every ounce of her soul had come together to ride the wave of heat and feeling and emotion.

When she'd woken to find herself curled up in Cormac's arms, she'd felt as if she'd been jolted with an open electrical wire and when she'd come back to earth all of her cells had settled in the wrong place. A place that craved his protection, his warmth, his intimacy.

"Harper, what's got into you?" Lola asked. "First you disappear on me last night without a word. Then you don't come home. I knew you were with Cormac and he's the last person in the world who'd let anything bad happen to you, but what the heck is going on?"

"Nothing. I'm fine. Just worried about you."

Way to deflect.

Though somehow it worked. "Harps, I'm on the countdown to marrying the man of my dreams. What could I possibly have to worry about?"

As openings went, it was too good to pass up.

Harper looked back at the house, looming ominous and regal on its agrestic bluff, and she felt a flicker of guilt. Her mind went to Cormac and his stories of how the Chadwicks had saved his life. To Gray, and the way he looked at Lola, with such tenderness and indulgence.

But then she saw herself as a sixteen-year-old girl, sitting on the floor of the downstairs bathroom, trying to stop her father crying, while he shouted the name Weston Chadwick, crying into his hands as he blamed the man for ruining his life.

She would never forgive herself if she had brought Lola this far only to let her down at such a critical moment.

"Lola, honey, can we talk seriously for a moment?"

Lola's eyes flickered before she said, "I know what this is about."

"You do?"

"It's Cormac. It's not just a crush for you. You're smitten with the guy."

"That's not it at all—"

"But it's true."

"Fine. Yes. I guess. But—"

"You guys totally got it on last night, didn't you?"

Harper gawped, no longer in control of her faculties.

"Ha! I knew it!" Lola snapped her fingers. "I was totally sure you'd deny it. When I told Gray I reckoned the two of you had left the party to find somewhere a little more private he was all, *'Nah, they can barely look at one another without biting each other's heads off.'* While I said, *'He looks at her like a lion looks at a baby gazelle—like he wants to swallow her whole.'* And I was right!"

Which was when Harper knew her innate ability to hold her emotions in check had been stuttering for some time. Badly.

Lola grabbed her by both hands, forcing Harper to look her in the eye. "Don't look so stricken! This is the kind of thing we should be able to talk about. Not only your work, and my work, and if I have enough money, and if I'm eating my vegetables. Sisters should dance together, and cry together, and talk about boys. And you need to let me support you as much as you've supported me."

Harper sniffed, gaze flickering between her little sister's eyes. "When did you suddenly become a grown-up?"

Lola shrugged. "Oh, a little while back now."

She didn't say it happened while Harper was on the other side of the world, but the truth of it hovered between them all the same.

Till Lola said, "Enough garden, don't you think? Shall we head back?"

Harper nodded. And on the amble back to the house they talked about work, and they talked about Gray. But they also talked about some of the fun times they'd had as kids, and some of the hard times too, the subjects shifting and changing with the dappled sunshine lighting the path ahead.

Harper realised she hadn't managed to tell Lola the

truth about the Chadwicks. About their part in her dad's downfall.

She'd find another moment. Soon.

Right now she just wanted to relish the newness of this feeling. Of this different version of sisterhood. For the relationship she'd been so fearful of losing might not be lost. It would simply change. For the better.

"So how was he?" Lola asked as they neared the back steps leading up into the house.

Harper didn't need to ask who. A beat went by before she said, "Transcendental."

"Lucky girl."

"Tell me about it."

"Now go rest. We have the pool party this afternoon. And a fun kids-only evening planned for tonight."

"Will do." A morning off from the wedding fun, from Cormac, was a huge relief. For Harper needed some time. Space. To sort out her head without him there, messing with her algorithms. "Now, how tight is your wedding dress?"

"Tight enough."

"Pity. I ordered a pair of punnets of macadamia ice cream to be delivered here from Ice-Ice Baby for just a moment such as this. I guess I can eat yours too. Take one for the team."

"Harps, there is no dress in the world tight enough to stop me eating Ice-Ice Baby's macadamia ice cream."

Arm in arm, they jogged up the back stairs of the palatial home and made a left towards the kitchens.

By that afternoon the Chadwicks' back yard had been turned out in a French Riviera meets Beach Blanket Bingo theme for Lola and Gray's pre-wedding pool party.

Rows of jauntily angled striped umbrellas threw patches of shade over the bright green grass. While waiters all in white delivered trays of cocktails and nibbles to the guests clad in everything from Alain Delon open-necked shirts to Sandra Dee pedal-pushers.

"Just a few hundred of your closest friends?" Harper asked.

"Business associates, mostly," said Lola, waving madly as she spotted Gray weaving his way through the crowd, looking dapper in tight board shorts and yellow shirt to match Lola's yellow mini-dress, passing out cigars to anyone who'd take one. "Local community members. The Chadwicks' reach is vast. We wanted the wedding to be intimate. So, this is the compromise."

"Does it worry you that the wedding can't possibly compare to all the pre-wedding parties?"

Lola laughed as she jogged down the stairs, turning to say, "Not a single bit. Now, come on! Let's party!" before she leapt into Gray's arms.

He caught her, twirling her around. Those nearby clapped and laughed. While Lola smiled up at her man as if she was the happiest person on earth.

Seeing Lola happy had been her life's mission for as long as she could remember, and yet Harper found herself having to look away as a strange pain bit behind her ribs. Harper smoothed her hands over her floaty, one-shouldered white dress, before taking the plunge and joining the party.

Dee-Dee Chadwick caught her eye, giving her a big smile and a wave. Weston Chadwick was surrounded with men in linen suits, all laughing at some joke he'd made. When her stomach clenched at the sight of him, Harper looked away.

Gaze dancing over the crowd, Harper searched for a familiar head of preppy chestnut hair. It had been several hours since she'd last seen Cormac. He hadn't called. Then again, neither had she.

Then, weaving her way around the deckchairs by the pool, she found him standing over a BBQ, flipping steaks.

It was so distinctly Australian, so familiar and reassuring, it snagged on something primal inside of her. Then he lifted a beer to his mouth and drank, his lashes batting his cheeks and his throat working against the bubbles. And she had to swallow lest the saliva pooling under her tongue ooze out the corner of her mouth.

As if he'd felt her staring, Cormac turned his head and looked straight at her. And she felt stripped bare. Then steam sizzled between them, obscuring her view of him as if he were a mirage.

With a quick word to one of the others, Cormac handed over the tongs, put down his beer and came to her, every step matching the beat of her heart.

"Harper, you look…stunning."

"Thanks. You too."

And he did. She couldn't have told a soul what he'd been wearing that day but the warmth in his eyes, the intimacy in his smile, made her heart go *kersplat*.

What had she been thinking, sleeping with this man?

Adoring him from afar was one thing. It was safe, harmless. A little heartbreak the worst thing that could come of it.

But, having been with him, having felt his heart beat beneath her hand, having seen the heat in his eyes as he was inside her—she feared for how it would feel to see this end.

With a hand at her elbow he moved her a little further from the barbecue and prying ears. "I wish you'd woken me before you left last night."

"You were out for the count. I thought it best to let you sleep."

"No, you didn't," he murmured, stepping a little closer. Close enough she could see the shadows in his eyes. The sexy stubble shading his jaw. "You turned tail and ran. And there I'd been thinking we'd both had a good time."

"We did. *I* did. I just…" Her words petered out, as she

had no excuse apart from pure and unadulterated panic about feeling too much.

"It's okay." He lifted a hand, brushed his knuckles over her cheek.

It sent a sharp tingle sweeping through her body, wild and wanton and needy. She took a step back. Only she'd misjudged, her foot reaching out and finding...nothing.

Her heart leapt into her throat. Her hips shot back, her hands scrambling for something, anything to grab onto. Finding Cormac's shirt.

Instinct had her gripping on tight. His eyes widened. He stepped into her. Her balance gave way and together they tumbled into the pool.

Cool water rushed into her nostrils, into her mouth. Until a pair of strong hands gripped her under the arms and dragged her to the surface.

Harper came up spluttering, her hair all over her face, her hands busy keeping her dress from floating up to her neck. Especially now the entire party had moved to the edge of the pool. Some faces wide with surprise. With embarrassment. Others laughing.

And there, front and centre, Weston Chadwick.

His voice—big and booming—carried across the yard as he said, "In case you haven't met them yet, I give you Harper and Cormac—our maid of honour and best man. And apparently contenders for the family synchronised swimming team. Anyone else want a dip, feel free."

Barely a beat went by before a few men took off shirts, and women slipped dresses over their heads—thankfully revealing swimwear beneath.

Smart move, Harper thought, knowing her bikini was still inside.

Then hands were pressing the swathes of lank wet hair from her face. Cormac's hands. His touch gentle but sure. The pads of his palms deliciously rough. The goosebumps trailing in their wake making her shiver.

Then his hands lingered, smoothing over her skull as if looking for bumps.

When they trailed down the sides of her face, his thumbs smoothing over her temples, his little fingers resting along the edges of her jaw, there was no pretence of examination in the touch. He touched her because he wanted to. He touched her because he could.

She held her breath. Wondered if she might hold it for ever.

"If you ask me if I'm okay," Harper gritted out, "I will scream."

His gaze dropped to her mouth, his nostrils flaring, and she knew he was remembering another way he'd proven himself able to make her scream. Then a smile crinkled the corners of his eyes and he said, "I know you're okay. You'll always be okay. No matter what. It's one of the reasons I can't get enough of you."

With a firm hand, Cormac herded her towards the far edge of the pool, away from the crowd. While Harper was so busy trying to digest his last words, she let him.

He heaved himself out of the pool first. Muscles in his arms bunching, clothes sucked tight to strong legs and a grade-A backside. To think she'd run her hands over all that, again and again, as if committing his shape to memory.

Then he ran a hand over his hair, droplets flying into the sunshine. When he looked back at her, her brain refused to believe he was real.

He pulled his shirt over his head the way men did—two hands behind his neck and tugging forward—before rolling it into a ball and tossing it onto a spare deckchair.

She couldn't *not* stare at his chest, with its spray of dark hair, his washboard stomach, the happy trail that arrowed into his tight shorts. It was right there after all. While every other part of her was soaked through, her mouth went dry.

Then he leaned down and held out a hand.

Harper bit her lip before saying, "I'm not sure I can."

A flicker of humour lit the depths of his eyes. "And why is that?"

"I'm wet."

"So I see."

"This dress is rather…thin. And I'm not wearing any togs." Or a bra, for that matter.

His gaze lowered, that muscle in his cheek clenching as he realised it too.

"Would you prefer I closed my eyes?" Before waiting for an answer he did just that, waggling his hand her way, before squinting one eye open, just a tad.

"It's not you I'm worried about. You've seen it all already."

His eyes popped open. Dark, warm, and full of the knowledge of her.

Knowing it was several hours before sunset, a time when she might exit the pool in semi-darkness, Harper figured her only choice was to suck it up and get the hell out.

No way was she going to let him heave her out of the pool like a seal. She hiked her dress up into a knot at her thigh and waded to the shallows. Water dragging at her, she stepped out as gracefully as possible—meaning not in the least. Tugging her dress down as best she could, she made a beeline for the house.

She felt Cormac fall into line beside her.

"I'm fine," she said; "I don't need an escort."

"Super. Neither do I."

She tried to ignore the titters as they walked through the crowd. But she didn't have enough hands to cover the bits of her the wet white dress revealed.

Out of the corner of her eye she saw Dee-Dee Chadwick rushing over, and Cormac holding out a hand, his head shaking just a little. And just like that, Dee-Dee stopped.

"Can you hold up?" he said.

"I'd really rather not."

"Harper, wait for one second," Cormac said, his frustration with her coming through loud and clear.

She stopped so fast he had to back up.

"What?"

Shaking his head at her, he looked at her as if she was nuts. As if she was stunning, and funny, confounding and nuts.

Then he held out a towel he must have gathered along the way, flicked it out flat and wrapped it around her shoulders. It was soft and warm from the sun.

Holding her by the upper arms, his face mere inches from hers, Cormac said, "I'm going inside with you. We are both getting out of these wet clothes. And then we are going to have a discussion, you and I."

We'll see, she thought. Without a word they made their way up the stairs, turning as one towards her bedroom.

He slowed as Harper headed into the bathroom on her own. When she caught sight of herself in the mirror she let out a squeal.

"What?" he called, rushing to the door.

"I look like a nightmare."

Cormac leant in the doorway. "You look like a water nymph."

She looked at him in the mirror.

"A mess of a nymph, sure. A little insecure. A little out of control. Beautifully fragile."

Cormac couldn't have used a more terrifying word to describe her if he tried.

"Don't you mean brittle?" She'd had that one hurled at her more than once. Enough times she'd wondered if they might be right.

"No, Harper. I don't."

She caught his gaze in the mirror. Raw, honest and scorching hot.

"Don't look at me like that."

"Like what?"

"Like you're waiting for me to take off my wet dress."

"But I am waiting for you to take off your wet dress."

She laughed. Then hiccupped. As if the gods wanted her to know things could still get worse.

Cormac took a step inside the bathroom. Walked up to her, gently placed his hands on her upper arms as he caught her eye in the mirror. Goosebumps shot up all over her skin and it had nothing to do with the water still dripping down her limbs.

"I thought I made it clear the other day, Harper, that you don't need to pretend to be so perfect. Not with me."

The urge to ask why, why not with him, was so strong it filled her throat so that nothing came out.

He lifted a hand to sweep a wet hank of hair off her neck, his hand resting in the dip at her shoulder as his eyes rose to hers.

She hiccupped again.

Cormac smiled.

And the words spilled free. "I am a mess."

"That you are."

"I don't mean the hair. Or the dress. Or the make-up running down my face."

"I know."

"You do?"

He nodded.

"I came here on a mission," she said, lifting a hand to her heart. Not that she'd tell him what it was. For she'd still not completed it. "But from the moment I stepped out of the car I've felt...disorientated."

Cormac breathed, his hand lifting to tuck around hers, the backs of his knuckles pressed over her heart. He waited, as if weighing up whether or not she could handle what he was about to say.

"Is it wrong for me to say that I'm glad to hear that?"

"Yes, that's wrong!"

Harper hiccupped again and Cormac grinned. A flash

of white teeth. Of crinkling eyes. Good lord, the man was hot.

"Why, thank you," he said, surprise lighting his voice. And Harper realised she'd said the last bit out loud.

With a groan she tried to sink her head to her chest, but Cormac caught her chin with a finger and lifted it so she had no choice but to look into his eyes. Then he turned her in his arms so there was no mirror getting in the way.

For a few moments they simply drank one another in. Then Cormac said, "While I never saw you coming."

Harper swallowed. "What does that mean?"

"It feels like a million years ago that I was sitting on my car, muttering under my breath as I waited and waited and waited for Harper Addison, the bolshie, curly-haired do-gooder in the ripped jeans. I had no idea I was really waiting for you."

She wanted to look away, she needed to look away. For, locked in Cormac's gaze, she had nowhere to hide.

Then Cormac said, "I can't rightly say what is happening here, with us, because I've never been here before. But I feel as if I see you in a way I've never seen anyone before. That you see me in a way no one has seen me before. From the moment you stepped out of that car, and levelled that blistering hazel gaze my way, I have been under your spell. I can't decide if that's wondrous or disastrous."

"Disastrous," she said on a sigh. "Definitely disastrous."

"Okay, then. Glad we got that sorted."

A single note flickered in the back of her brain—a reason she should push him away. Like flotsam in a post-storm sea, it bobbed on the surface a moment before it sank beneath the calming waves and was gone.

Harper felt the tears fill her eyes a mere moment before they spilled warm and wobbly over her cold cheeks. Who was she? She didn't recognise this emotional being in Cormac's arms. Would she ever know herself again?

"Cormac, I—"

"Harper!" Lola called from just outside the room.

"In here," Cormac said, holding her as if he realised she'd collapse without him.

Lola burst in, her eyes full of concern. "What happened? The girls told me Cormac pushed you into the pool." She glared at Cormac, eyes dark and ferocious. Lola as protector; that was new.

Harper quickly swept fingers under her eyes, as if trying to clean up her mascara. "Not exactly how it went down. Though I'm okay if you don't wish to disillusion them."

In the mirror she saw Cormac slip from the room. Felt the loss of him like a phantom limb.

"So you both fell in the pool."

"Mmm- hmm."

"Who took who with them?"

"I took him."

Lola nodded. "Nice."

"She's wet, remember," Cormac's voice called from the bedroom. "And shivering. If you don't get her out of those wet clothes, I—"

"Hey," Gray's deep voice joined the chorus of rescuers. "Lola has this, right, honey?"

"You bet I do, sweetie! You look after Cormac."

"I'm fine," Cormac called back, laughter tinging his deep voice. "I'll be fine."

Lola shut the door with a decisive click before turning on the bath taps.

For someone who was very much used to taking care of herself it was discombobulating. But nice, she realised, no longer having the wherewithal to fight. Really nice. She ran her thumbs beneath her eyes again before letting Lola look after her for once.

CHAPTER ELEVEN

"OH-OH!" LOLA SING-SONGED. "Watch out for a temper tantrum! My sister is *not* a good loser."

"Not a good poker player, you mean," Cormac murmured as he dealt out the cards to the remaining players.

While Harper, who was an extremely adept poker player—her years of learning to read facial tics and tells standing her in good stead—watched as her chips were swept into a pile by Gray. So open-faced a novice could read him, he'd landed a full house and she'd missed it completely.

Harper barely managed to keep it together as he glared Cormac down. "Seriously?"

"What? Are you insinuating it's my fault?" Cormac asked, hand to heart, glint in his eye.

As if she was about to tell the whole table that she'd been distracted by the man playing footsie under the table. How he'd brushed the edge of his hand against her thigh more than once. That every time she'd caught his gaze it had been hot enough to make her blood sizzle.

"Not at all," she said, her voice cool. "You are a paragon of fair play, Mr Wharton."

The corner of his mouth twitched. "A paragon? You do flatter me so."

She quickly pushed away from the table as her cheeks heated condemningly. "Drink, anyone?"

The others—Lola, Gray, Adele and a few others from the old gang—who'd been too busy focussing on their cards to even notice her byplay with Cormac, muttered a range of orders.

Harper headed past the pool table in the huge upstairs

games room to the bar, where the barman—yep, they'd kept on an actual bartender after the pool party—poured out the range of cocktails and spirits and Harper's sparkling water.

She glanced over her shoulder to find Cormac watching her, his gaze on her backside. She slunk a hand to her hip. His gaze shot to hers. After which he shook his head, slowly, tellingly, everything he had done to her, everything he still wanted to do, written all over his face.

She spun back to the bar, struggled to catch her breath. To still the thunderous beating of her heart. Which was near impossible when every time she even glanced at the man her very atoms danced and twirled and near spun off into the ether.

Never track down a teenage crush, she thought; a life lesson that ought to be gifted to every woman upon entering adulthood. Along with other absolutes such as the need for financial independence, a quality skin-care regime and shoes that stunned but also fit like a glove.

Speaking of which, Harper nudged off a high heel, curling her toes against the back of her calf. Then asked for a Manhattan. She needed something strong to get her through the rest of this night. For the happy couple didn't seem in any hurry to get to bed, even though the next day they were supposed to be getting married.

Drink in hand, she turned on one foot as she lifted out the stick, and caught the maraschino cherry between her teeth.

Cormac—who was now sitting back in his chair—watched her openly. Eyes dark, breaths long and slow.

Harper bit down on the cherry, her tongue darting out to catch a stray drip as it burst in her mouth.

"Fold," Cormac said, his voice subterranean. Then he threw down his cards, pushed back his chair and strode over to the bar to join her.

Harper quickly tried to find her other high heel with

her bare foot but it was nowhere to be found. Meaning she had to balance on one heel, or crane her neck to look into Cormac's face.

So precarious was her self-control when it came to the man, she reached out to grip the bar, choosing precarious balance over giving up high ground.

"Need a hand?" he asked, motioning to the tray of drinks.

"Sure."

He nodded. But didn't make a move bar grabbing his lemon, lime and bitters and taking a sip, turning to lean a hip against the bar himself, so that his body curved towards hers.

She felt his warmth ease over her, around her, into her. It was like nothing she'd ever felt. As if her skin was too tight to hold in all he made her feel.

The fact that she had no control whatsoever over any of it, that another person was able to make her feel so much without her explicit permission, was unsettling. And—she would only ever admit this to herself—rather wondrous.

"Harper?" He nudged her with a knee, then left it there. Touching her. Connecting them. She could feel his energy racing over her skin.

"Hmm?"

"You ready and raring for tomorrow?"

His words were innocuous enough, but Harper knew what he meant. Was she ready to let her little sister go?

"Raring might be pushing it."

"Come on," he said. "Who doesn't love a wedding?"

Having given up on finding her shoe, she'd plopped her bare foot onto the floor. "You mean that, don't you? You are actually looking forward to it."

"Of course I am. The chance to watch two people declare in front of everyone they know—and a few people they don't—that despite the impediments, despite the over-whelming evidence that it is near impossible to sustain, they choose happiness. They choose eternal love."

Harper searched his face for laughter, and found none. "You, Cormac Wharton, are a romantic."

"Unashamedly."

Harper coughed out a laugh. She swallowed the sound, while inside her head it turned into a sob.

She—a realist, a doubter, and fine, a cynic of the highest order—had fallen under the spell of a *romantic*. An honest one. Who said what he felt and meant what he said.

What must that feel like? To have that kind of freedom? To feel that safe in your place in the world?

Harper's entire life had felt like a game of chicken and refusing to flinch first.

Only with Cormac, she'd flinched. She'd flinched bigtime. She'd flinched so hard it had knocked her off her axis. Made her forget who she was, what she stood for. He dragged her focus. Made her stumble. Her heart tumble. Until she found herself falling—

Wait, no, she thought, shaking her head. Not *falling*. She wasn't *falling* for him. She was attracted to the man. Who wouldn't be? She even liked him. A great deal.

But falling for the guy would be nothing short of selfdestructive, a streak she did not inherit from either parent, thank you very much.

Across the room Lola slammed her cards on the table and growled. While Adele threw her winning hand onto the table and leapt out of the chair and did a fine impression of an NFL player, post-touchdown.

"I hate this game!" Lola cried, and it could have been Harper sitting there.

Because they were sisters. Family. The only real family either of them had. The only ones who'd never turned their backs on each other. Who'd loved one another no matter what.

Harper didn't want freedom. Not from her. And yet it was coming at her anyway.

Tomorrow Lola would be married. The cord would be cut. And Harper would be truly adrift.

If Lola was grown-up enough to marry, she was grown-up enough to know the truth.

"Whatever it is you are plotting," Cormac said, "stop."

Harper pretended to ignore him as she took a step forward and motioned to Lola.

"You have that manic look in your eye, the kind that makes you look like you're planning world domination." Cormac wrapped a gentle hand around her arm. "What are you up to, Harper?"

"Nothing that concerns you."

"I doubt that very much." His words came with a growl. A growl that tapped into her very marrow.

"Lola!" Harper called.

"Yeah?"

"Need some air?"

Lola ran her hands over her face and pushed her chair back. "Sure."

Harper led her little sister out the door onto the balcony. They were high enough to see over the gardens to the ocean beyond, but the moon was hidden behind a bank of cloud, meaning they could only hear the crashing of the waves against the cliff below.

Lola lifted her face to the sky and took a deep breath. "Can you believe that tomorrow I will be Mrs Grayson Chadwick?"

"Or he could be Mr Lola Addison?"

Lola shot her a look.

"It's been done."

"I'm sure. But not this time. Not by me. I'm happy to take his name. To fold myself into his family."

Harper sucked in a breath through her teeth.

It must have been loud enough for Lola to hear, as she

spun and took Harper by the hand and said, "That came out so wrong. I only meant that they've been like family for so long already. Not taking over from you, but as well as you. It's helped, having them, what with you being so far away. I need to belong. To some place. To someone. I'm not like you."

Holding on for all she was worth, Harper managed to say, "There's something I've been meaning to talk to you about. About Gray."

"Gray?"

"His parents actually. And Dad."

"What do Gray's parents have to do with Dad?"

Here goes, Harper thought, nearly one hundred per cent sure this was the right thing to do. "The deal. Dad's deal. It was their fault."

"What are you talking about? Dad lost money, not them. It was awful, but it was unforeseen."

Harper bit her lip, the words clogging her throat. She'd kept Lola in the dark, keeping the family secrets for so long. To protect her. Meaning it was her fault they'd ended up here. Now she had to do her job and fix it.

"I'm certain Dad made that deal on the advice of Weston Chadwick. And when it all went bust he took no responsibility, leaving Dad out to dry."

Lola reared back as if slapped. "That's so not true."

"Not according to Dad."

"You've…?" Lola swallowed. "You've spoken to him?"

"Not since he left, no."

When Lola had rung to say she was getting married, the first thing Harper did was hire an investigator, on the quiet, to track their dad down. To tell him? To invite him? To show him they were both okay despite him? They'd had no luck. She could only hope he was living off the grid somewhere. She could only hope he was happy too.

"Oh."

"But back then—the day he came home broken, torn

apart—he said so. Over and over again. That it was the Chadwicks' fault. That Weston Chadwick was to blame."

"I remember," Lola said, her voice barely a whisper.

"You do?"

"I thought it was a dream, or a made-up vision of some sort. Most of my memories of Dad feel like that. Blurs of memory, or fantasy. I have no clue how much is real. But I remember him crying in the bathroom, you kneeling at his feet, gripping his hands, begging him to tell you everything so you could fix it. And him…" Lola swallowed. "Dad saying that he wished he'd never met Weston Chadwick."

"But you were so young."

"Not that young. I'm only three years younger than you."

"You were always such a happy kid, Lolly. Even during that whole mess. I hoped it all went over your head."

Lola shrugged.

"You see, then, why you can't marry Gray."

"What the hell?" Gray's voice cut across the open space as Adele, Gray and Cormac spilled out onto the balcony, drinks in hand.

Harper's gaze snagged on Cormac's as he slowly shook his head.

"Lola," Harper said.

But Lola gave her a pained look before going to Gray. Harper reached out to grab her hand, to bring her back, to finish the conversation, but her sister slipped through her fingers.

"It's okay," Lola consoled her fiancé. "You just walked in at the wrong moment."

"When would the right moment have been?"

Lola glanced back at Harper, who said, "Tell him. Tell him what I told you. See if he denies it."

"Denies what?" Gray asked, moving to stand in front of Lola. As if needing to protect her—from Harper!

But Lola held up a hand, staying him. "Don't worry about it. She's so used to having control over my life, it's hard for her to stop."

Was she serious?

"For what it's worth, I never wanted to 'control' your life, Lola. It wasn't my childhood dream to work three jobs to pay for rent, food, clothes. Or to hide from Social Services, who'd never have let me look after a thirteen-year-old when I was still underage myself. I wasn't given a choice. Did I say a word when you dropped out of university, a course that I'd paid for, to become a yoga instructor? When you shaved your head? When you came this close to legally changing your name to Bowie?"

Lola's eyes flashed, as if she had more to say but didn't know where to start.

"No," said Harper. "I didn't. But I can't keep quiet about this. I can't stand by and watch as you marry a Chadwick."

"Hey," Gray growled.

Harper hadn't noticed Cormac edging her way until he took a step in front of her. Protecting her. Gray noticed, eyes narrowing at his friend, who had clearly just taken sides.

It was Harper's turn to hold out a hand, to stay him. These men! Had they no clue at all? This wasn't about them.

"Lola," Harper said, "I will stand by you no matter what choices you make for your life. I just want you to have all the facts. I want you to be sure."

"Listen to yourself, Harps. I can't believe you're playing negotiator with me."

"I'm not *playing* at anything."

"Tell me you're not trying to talk me down from the ledge. Grayson is not my version of leaping off a tall building. He's the man I love. Come on, Gray, it's nearly midnight anyway and if you see me a minute after I'll turn into a pumpkin."

Gray gathered Lola into his arms and they left. Adele and the others who'd been watching on from the sidelines seemed to have melted away.

Leaving Harper. And Cormac. And the cool of the night closing in.

"Harper," he said, his voice deep. And disappointed. That cut like nothing else. "What the hell did you just do?"

"I had to tell her the truth."

"What truth?"

"That your precious Chadwicks are the reason my father lost everything."

Cormac ran a hand through his hair, the spikes popping up in its wake. "Says who?"

"Said my father."

"With what evidence?"

Harper looked down at her feet. Her *foot*. She was still wearing only one shoe. She kicked the other one off and watched it bounce pathetically off the balustrade. "He told me so. The night I found him sitting on his bedroom floor in tears. The night before he disappeared for ever. I'd never seen anyone cry like that. Like every tear was a piece of his soul. He looked terrified. Said he'd screwed up and this time there was no way out. And that everything was Weston's fault."

Cormac moved to stand by her, not close enough to touch, but close enough for her to feel him all the same. He leant his arms over the balustrade, looking out into the dark, moonlit grounds. And he said, "From that you took him to mean that it was on Weston's explicit advice that your father made that investment. And after it went bust Weston took no responsibility for his part."

Harper thought back, tried to squeeze more details out of the memory, but she could only come up with the low points. "I did. I do."

"Harper, please tell me you have some kind of physical

evidence. Phone records. Recordings. A note in Weston's handwriting admitting culpability. Because if you don't…"

"He *told* me. His sixteen-year-old daughter. While he wept on my shoulder." Harper breathed in deep. "He tried so hard… To be a good dad. To be a success. But that investment… It broke him. When he told me, I went to hold his hand… He had a razor blade clutched in his palm. I had to pry it away from him. Don't tell Lola that part. She can't know. Ever."

She quickly glanced at Cormac to find his dark eyes on her.

Then with a growl he reached out and dragged her into his arms.

She sank into his hard embrace, the simple act of his arms around her taking the edge off the chill she didn't realise had its grip on her. He rubbed a hand up and down her back until the shakes came under control.

"He was such a sweetheart of a man, Cormac. He tried so hard… I tried so hard to make it easy for him to love us, to love me, but it wasn't enough. I wasn't enough."

Cormac shushed her softly, his breath wafting past her ear, creating new goosebumps all over her body. She turned her head till she leant against his heart.

When the silence became too much, she asked, "Do you believe me?"

He held her tighter. "I believe that you believe it. But Harper, you're making big assumptions. Distorted through the lens of a devastated teenager looking for someone to blame other than the father she adored. You have to find a way to undo this."

"Undo what?"

He breathed out hard before pulling away and looking deep into her eyes. "The grenade you just threw at Lola and Gray. The night before their wedding. You have to fix it now."

She blinked. "That's up to Lola."

"To do what?"

"To decide where her loyalties lie."

Cormac let her go so fast she stumbled, before catching herself on the back of a wrought-iron chair, the metal freezing against her hot palms.

"Weston Chadwick is a good man. A great man. The best man I've ever known. And a better father than yours and mine put together. Your accusation was serious. And Lola, Gray and I weren't the only ones to hear it. Our friends were inside. And some random bartender. Did you forget that? We can only hope the others decide to let it go. If not…"

"What? Are you going to sue me for defamation?"

His eyes flickered between hers, the muscles in his jaw working. "I am his lawyer."

"Wow. So it's come to that now." Harper began to pace, pressing a hand to her temple, which had begun to pound. "You're unbelievable."

"While you're so caught up in your own way of seeing the world you don't think. You just act. Without thought for how it affects those around you. Do you have any idea the kind of permanent damage that can cause?"

When she said nothing, Cormac shook his head. "You truly don't get it, do you? And I thought my father was self-absorbed. But you, honey, you take the cake."

"Whoa. Did you just compare me to your *father*?"

Cormac's expression was dark and sharp. Not a scrap of his usual charm. "I found your bravado enchanting. The way you see the world as something to conquer, in a way I wished I could. But you've gone over the edge here, you've gone too far. I don't know what the hell I was thinking, getting mixed up in all this."

Feeling utterly trapped, by her own words, by her feelings for Cormac, Harper lashed out. "In what, exactly?"

"This," he said, taking a step forward.

Harper gasped in a breath, her entire body bracing for his touch. Craving it.

But it never came. His mouth twitched as he held his ground.

While the empty places inside Harper filled with a rage she couldn't contain. "We aren't *doing* anything, Cormac. We made out a couple of times and rolled around on your couch. That's it."

"You're kidding me," he said, his face blank, shadowed in the semi-darkness. "That's how you see our past few days together?"

"Of course. What did you imagine would happen after tomorrow? In the time it takes for you to wax your surfboard I build and destroy companies. My life is structured. Settled. Take that house of yours. Do you not understand the pressure you put on any woman who walks through that door? It's like vodka for the ovaries. But I'm not the kind of woman who'd be content to settle down and play house. To pop out a couple of perfect, polite, high-achieving kids and imagine that will make me happy. While you…"

She took a breath.

"You might have everyone else fooled, but I saw right through the Mr Laid Back Happy Easy Charm act you have going on. You are so restless here it's a miracle you can stand still. I can feel it every time you look at me. You *yearn*, Cormac. For more, for different, for something. Only you don't know what. I know how that ends. I could never fall for a man like that."

Cormac stood so still after her tirade, she wondered if he'd heard her at all. Then his voice came to her ragged and worn as he said, "You done?"

Harper nodded.

"Then I'm glad I realised that's how you felt. Before…" He brought a hand to his mouth and turned away.

Harper swallowed, but couldn't stop herself from asking, "Before what?"

"No. You're not getting that from me too." Cormac's head dropped, his body a study in disillusionment. "I hope I'll see you tomorrow at the wedding, and only because I hope there'll be a wedding at all."

He walked towards the open doorway leading back through the games room.

What had just happened? How had that fight even begun? How had it spiraled out of control so fast? That was really it?

"Cormac," Harper called. "Cormac, come on."

But he disappeared without looking back.

"I did what I thought was best," she called, clueless as to whether anyone heard her. "I did the best I could!"

Her words wafted away on the night breeze. The taste left in her mouth bitter and acrid, leaving her feeling sick to the stomach.

The options as she'd seen them had been black and white—not tell Lola and fear for her for the rest of time, or tell her and hope she'd raised her to make smart choices.

She'd done what she thought was right.

And once again it wasn't enough.

CHAPTER TWELVE

It was right on midnight by the time Cormac threw his keys onto the hall table, the clattering sound echoing in the lofty space.

He deliberately did not look into the media room, or at the cushion he'd found Harper clutching only the night before, as he marched down the hall. He didn't even bother turning on the kitchen light before he went to the fridge for a beer.

The snap of the bottle top echoed in the emptiness of the big house. "Vodka for ovaries", as Harper had called it. Cormac slowly put the drink on the bench, untouched, and gripped the cool countertop.

How the hell did she do it? Cutting straight to the heart of him. And why Harper? Why not some sweet, lovely, modest girl who kept all the contradictions she saw within him to herself?

Why? Because what would have been the point?

She was right. Cormac hadn't kept the house hoping one day his mother might come home. He'd kept it for himself.

If you build it she will come.

"She" being some imaginary woman content to settle down and play house. To pop out a couple of perfect, polite, high-achieving kids who would fit in nicely in the fantasy future he'd imagined might negate his own rotten childhood.

A fantasy was all it had been, for such a life would bore him to tears.

No wonder he'd been treading water. He'd been waiting for more. For different. For a tectonic shift. For someone

who would see through him—to the good and the bad—
and want him anyway.

And, like all men who ought to have been more careful in what they wished for, he'd found her.

Only he hadn't realised it until he'd seen Harper lash-
ing out at his oldest friend, at the family who'd taken him
in, and he'd chosen her side. Without thought. Without a
pause. He'd stepped into her corner.

Protecting Harper had been a case of pure instinct. Protecting her from Gray and Lola. And from herself.

For she'd made a great hash of things.

He'd seen no choice but to impugn her ridiculous asser-
tions. Even if it had meant her pushing him away. For she
was too stubborn for her own good. Stubborn and fierce
and so very fragile.

It had seemed better to make himself the target—for
her anger, for Gray's, and for Lola's—or she'd never forgive herself.

Only now he hoped he hadn't gone too far.

Cormac picked up the beer and drank. Grimacing as
the bubbles burned his throat.

He'd gone for the jugular in accusing her of acting before thinking. Of strong-arming, like his father.

When the truth was, seeing her cornered he'd been
the one struggling against a ferocious rise of emotions he
couldn't control.

Anger, frustration, fear; feelings he'd spent his life
striving to avoid. By living simply. Wanting little. To the
extreme of living in a sleepy town at the bottom of the
world surrounded by people who only saw the good in
him.

For in the back of his mind he'd always wondered,
and worried, at what point his father had turned from a
functioning man and into a monster. Was it genetic? Pre-
determined? Or a slow and steady series of choices?

Despite the fact he felt as if he'd been flattened by

a steamroller, the silver lining to tonight's fracas wasn't negligible. With emotions high, loyalties stretched, things could have spun so far out of control. Yet he'd kept his head. As he always did. As he always would. For those were *normal* emotions. *Human* emotions. It was the way you dealt with them that made you the man you were.

The abundant love Harper felt for her sister made her the woman she was. But tonight it had threatened to swamp her. To pull her under.

She needed to shake off her past as much as he needed to rid himself of his.

It was the only way they could move forward. Whatever that meant.

Somewhere in the house a wall creaked. A gecko made a clicking sound. His fridge began to whir. A soundtrack to loneliness.

First thing Monday he was putting the house on the market.

But what about now? Now what the hell was he supposed to do?

Go to bed and sleep it off? Not going to happen.

Not while Harper still filled his head. That burr in her voice when she'd asked if he believed her. Her body sinking into his. Her cheek against his heart.

He wondered if Harper had ever asked such a question before. Of anyone else. If she'd ever been that vulnerable with another person. He would have bet everything he had that he was the first.

Because he was more to her than a roll on the couch. And she meant more to him than anything.

Anything.

As wrong as Harper had been, everything she'd done she'd done out of love. Knowing it could backfire. Knowing she'd be the bad guy. Knowing Lola might choose Gray, and never talk to her again. She'd been willing to sacrifice the most important thing in her life, because she believed it gave Lola a better chance at a happy future.

Which said it all really.

He ran a hand through his hair and paced down the hall. Stopping when he had no clue where he was going. Only knowing that he had to do something.

What if there was a kernel of truth to her assumptions? What if Weston *had* been somehow involved in her father's bad deal?

If being a good person was about making hard choices then that was what Cormac would have to do.

He checked the time. A little after midnight. Too late by any stretch of the imagination, especially considering the man's only son was getting married the next day.

Yet he picked up the phone and made a call, knowing that it would change everything, no matter which way the chips fell.

Harper lay on her bed, a pillow over her head, her thumbs pressing gently into her temples.

Like gravel shifting through wet cement, she had to keep the gritty flashes of memory rolling about inside her head lest they solidify into a sharp, chunky, heavy mass she'd never be able to shift.

What had she been thinking, having that conversation the night before Lola's wedding? How could she have imagined it would go anything but badly?

Why? Because she was so used to having to make hard decisions on her own. That life had been forced upon her, when the father she'd loved had let her down.

He hadn't hit her, as Cormac's father had hit him. But he'd damaged her all the same.

A gentle knock sounded on Harper's door.

She peeked out from under the pillow to check the time on her phone and saw it was a few minutes after one in the morning. And that Lola had sent her a text a few minutes before, asking if she was awake.

She pulled herself to sitting and said, "Come in."

Her door opened slowly and Lola's face poked through the door.

"You should be asleep," Harper said, moving over to make room.

Lola crawled up Harper's bed to sit cross-legged beside her. "Like you can talk."

True. For Harper was fully dressed. Her bed still made.

"What's up?" Harper asked, finding herself unable to ask if Lola had heard her. If she'd decided to call the whole thing off. If so she'd be the bad guy and stand up in front of the crowd and tell everyone so that Lola didn't have to.

Only after the way Lola had clung to Gray, who had protected her as if she was the most precious thing in the world, the thought of the wedding not going ahead felt hollow.

"Stuff," Lola said after a while. "Thoughts. Imaginings. Memories. Mostly of Dad. Even while I want to smack him right now for all he put us through, I still kind of wish he could be here tomorrow. Mum, too."

Harper breathed out slowly. It was the best she could do considering the lump of lead that had suddenly pressed down on her chest. She patted the pillow beside her and they lay down side by side, curled in towards one another.

"Do you remember how we used to sleep this way?" Harper asked.

"On that God-awful mattress on the floor in the rooms above the convenience store."

"The mattress was perfectly serviceable."

Lola rolled her eyes. "Always so sensitive. It was a terrible mattress. The springs dug into your back if you slept near the edge. And the apartment—do you remember the smell?"

"Mothballs."

"That's right! But it did the job of keeping us together. And I never truly thanked you for making it happen. So, thank you, Harper, for always looking out for me."

Harper felt something shift inside her at Lola's words. Shift and settle. "You're welcome."

"Now, can we agree that those days are long behind us, that you did an amazing job of raising me, even before Dad finally left, and that it's time for you to let me go?"

Harper laughed, even as a tear rolled down her cheek, wetting the pillow. "I think I can do that. If not, I'll do my best to pretend."

"Atta girl."

She had to ask. "You're still marrying Gray, then?"

The look Lola gave her was so grown-up. "Of course I am. Whatever his father did or did not do, it does not reflect on Gray. He's his own man. My man."

Harper's mind went straight to Cormac before she could stop it.

Never, not once, had she believed that Cormac's father's actions reflected on him. Or only so far as to show how extraordinary he was, having come out the other end of such a terrible formative experience so strong, resolved, balanced, kind and loving.

It was only fair that he gave Gray the same benefit of the doubt.

"I like Gray," Harper said, and meant it.

Lola's face lit up. "Me, too." Then she said, "May I say, I've noticed signs of you having become a proper grown-up now too."

"Have you, now?"

"Apart from tonight's massive spontaneous combustion, of course. I mean, you managed to stay out of the commotion downstairs without stepping in with your negotiator hat, which was huge for you—"

"Hang on," she said. "What commotion?"

"You really didn't hear it? Dee-Dee and Weston. And Cormac."

"Cormac's back?" She'd heard his car drive away over an hour ago, kicking out gravel he'd left so fast.

Lola shook her head, and Harper's disappointment was like a living thing.

"Cormac rang Weston about an hour ago. It got loud. Heated. His voice carried all the way from the library. Knowing Gray would have fallen asleep the moment his head his pillow, I went to check on Dee-Dee then scurried downstairs to make sure Weston was okay. Only to find him talking on the phone... about Dad."

"Our dad?"

Lola nodded. "From what Dee-Dee and I could gather, he was telling Cormac everything he remembered about Dad's bad deal. Then he'd pause to listen. Then Weston would rub his forehead and try to remember more. It got pretty intense."

Harper rolled to look at the ceiling, as her heart thumped so hard it felt as if it was trying to push out of her chest. "Did he admit to anything?"

"Only that he knew of it after the fact. That he'd called Dad in, offering to help bail him out, anonymously, at least with the smaller local investors. That Dad had accepted. And that was the last time he'd seen him."

Harper breathed out long and slow.

"Harper, I believe him."

"I think I believe him too."

Yet somehow, in the quiet of the night, it didn't even matter anymore.

What mattered was Cormac. She tried to imagine what had been going through his head when he'd made that phone call. With nothing to go on but her hunch.

She knew Cormac would stand up for anyone and everyone if he thought he could help. He was just that kind of man.

But this was bigger than that. He'd stood up to his hero tonight. A man he claimed saved his life. For her.

"I've been thinking about it and I reckon I know why Dad said all that stuff about Weston," Lola said. "Dad would have been happier with a simpler life. Life in a place where keeping up with the Chadwicks wasn't a consideration. I think he'd have liked living in that one room above the convenience store with us."

That thought settled over both of them like a blanket, gathering memories as if they were dust bunnies.

On a yawn Lola said, "Not a dull moment when you're around, Harps, I'll give you that. We're going to miss you when you go back to your fancy life."

"We?"

"Me, Gray. Cormac. I think he might have a little crush on you too."

"I'll miss you all too." The thought that Cormac had already said his goodbye squeezed like a fist around her heart. "More than words can say."

But Lola had already fallen asleep, her dark lashes soft against her cheeks, her breaths even. Her little sister was going to be just fine.

As for Harper? Living out of her big, empty apartment in Dubai and spending her days bending powerful business people to her will seemed like another life. A life she'd relished. But the real satisfaction had come from it giving her the ability to give Lola everything she'd ever wanted.

Only now she realised Lola would still be happy living in a tiny flat above a convenience store. So long as she had Gray there with her.

That was what Cormac had tried to tell her. The meaning of life he'd stumbled upon at a far younger age than she had.

Find what makes you happy and do more of that.

Maybe it was time she found out what really made *her* happy.

And, as though a veil had been lifted, Harper saw the grey between the black and white. And with it a million new colours too.

Cormac, she thought, his face swimming before her as her eyes slid closed and sleep began to take her under.

So smart, so kind, so hot she couldn't even think his name without coming over all woozy and feeling like the floor was tipping out from under her.

She had to tell Cormac…something. About being best man to her maid of honour. Best man she'd ever known.

CHAPTER THIRTEEN

By THREE THE next afternoon most of the guests were seated in gilded chairs on the Chadwicks' lawn overlooking the bluff. Others milled about, partaking in chilled flutes of local bubbly or prawn gyoza and salmon blinis.

The grass was green, the sky an uninterrupted cerulean-blue dome, the waves crashing dramatically against the jagged rocks below. Only the slightest breeze took the edge off the crisp warmth of the day.

"How you doing?" Gray asked.

Cormac came to from a million miles away, blinking against the glint of sunlight reflecting off the second-storey window at the rear of the Chadwick mansion. Harper's window.

"Me?" he said, clearing his throat of the gruff note. "Isn't that meant to be my question to you?"

Gray's smile spread slow and easy across his face. "I'm great. Looking forward to the next bit."

For Gray that might have meant seeing Lola, eating, or whisking his new bride off to Nepal—to check in with a few of the Chadwick factories and attend a surprise yoga retreat for their honeymoon. For the man was easily pleased. Cormac figured that came with being very wealthy and very loved.

Cormac had never felt that level of ease. It was why he'd had the same group of friends since high school. It took a lot for him to trust.

He looked out over the guests and caught Dee-Dee and Weston—standing shoulder to shoulder, as they always did, as if they couldn't bear to be outside of touching distance from one another—watching him.

He felt a sliver of remorse for the phone call made late the night before. Not for making the call itself—he stood by that decision. He wished he'd waited. Then maybe he'd not have come at the man with such heat, such feeling, such emotion.

Over Harper.

She provoked him like no one else. Finding soft spots, bruises he'd thought long since healed. Pressing till he was forced to say *enough*. Or to own up.

Harper.

Who'd seen that his ease, his contentment, was skin deep. When those who'd known him longest, those he'd thought had known him best, had taken his smiles at face value.

Harper.

Who had walked into his life and shaken it to pieces. Until he could no longer see it the same way he had a week before.

Dee-Dee lifted a hand, waving at him.

Cormac did the same. Then he dropped his hand over his heart, sending her his love. For she was family—if not of his blood, then in spirit.

Even from a distance he saw her smile, and her sniff, before she took a tissue from her purse and dabbed it over her eyes.

Cormac let go a long, slow breath. His life would never look the same from this day on because it wasn't.

The house he'd called a home now felt like nothing more than a roof over his head.

After the wedding the Chadwicks would announce their retirement. He'd been running their operations for years and knew they planned to make it official. He'd thought that was what he wanted. But now he wasn't so sure.

Gray and Lola would be married, meaning their lives would shoot off on a different trajectory. A life of couples' dinners and snuggling on the couch and pretty soon children. Nappies and sleepless nights. Birthday parties and scraped knees and new friends who inhabited that world.

And while a week ago such thoughts all strung together would have sent him hurtling into the surf in order to distract himself, standing beside Gray, the sun on his face, his future uncertain, Cormac felt loose. Relieved. Free.

Once more his eyes cut to the second-storey window. To Harper.

The harpist who'd been playing rock songs at the edge of the dais stopped mid-song before launching into the opening strains of Pachelbel's Canon.

Cormac dragged his eyes back to Gray, who was busy chatting with Adele—high-school girlfriend, and current wedding celebrant. "Gray, mate, you're on."

Gray looked to Cormac blankly a moment before his eyes filled with joy. "It's happening?" he asked.

"It's happening."

Gray grabbed Cormac and yanked him into a bear hug. Cormac gave as good as he got.

"Love you, brother," Cormac managed through the tightness in his throat.

"Right back at you, brother."

Pulling apart, they turned as one to face the aisle between the gleaming gilt chairs. A path of soft pink rose petals split the guests in their floral dresses and summer suits.

The view was so bright, so cheerful, it was as if the world had been washed clean. Or that was how it looked to Cormac: fresh, new, full of possibility.

Then the doors at the rear of the house swept open and Cormac's next breath in didn't make it far. His heart beat so fast he could hear it in his ears. And Harper stepped out onto the terrace.

While the guests wore a cacophony of colour, Harper had been poured into a subtly sexy, shimmering, pale grey number that clung to every part of her it could. Never thought he'd see the day he'd be jealous of a dress, but there it was.

Gray swore softly beside him. "If that isn't the most beautiful woman on the planet, I don't know who is."

"Hmm," Cormac murmured, in full agreement.

She looked like a dream. His dream. Dazzling on the outside, tough as nails, with a soft centre.

Then he blinked and saw the bride heading down the petal path a few steps behind her big sister.

Cormac huffed out a laugh. For Lola—a down-to-earth girl who swore, drank beer and lived in yoga pants and baseball caps—looked like a princess in the most wedding-dressy dress imaginable. And she grinned from ear to ear, showing more teeth than a person had the right to have.

As they neared the business end of the aisle, Harper slowed by Dee-Dee and Weston. She leaned over and said something, then held out her hand to Weston, who after the barest hesitation shook it heartily. While Dee-Dee leapt to her feet and hugged her for all she was worth.

If Cormac hadn't already been aware of how impressive the woman was, watching her swallow her pride and make peace with the Chadwicks pushed him right over the edge.

Gray, clueless as to the whys of the happenings, grumbled, "Can't they walk faster?"

Then, with a growl, Gray suddenly took off down the steps. Cormac reached out to grab him before deciding to let him go. The guests laughed as Gray grabbed a shocked Harper, placing a big kiss on her cheek, before running to Lola and lifting her into his arms, and rushing her back up the aisle and plonking her on the dais.

"There," he said. "Better. Let's get this thing done."

Adele's face twisted a moment before she said, "Ah, one thing's missing."

Harper had stopped in the middle of the aisle, catatonic gaze stuck on Lola, throat working, as if she didn't quite know what to do.

Cormac told Novak to stay—for the rings were hanging from a small box attached to the dog's collar—then jogged down the steps and went to Harper.

He'd planned to take her hand, and place it in the crook of his arm and lead her the rest of the way. To make it appear as if it was a part of the ceremony.

But when he caught sight of the smudge of a tear beneath her right eye, he was undone. All pretence went flying out the door.

He was done. Gone. Head over heels. He was hers—if she wanted him or not.

After the way they'd left things the night before he couldn't be sure of the reception he'd get, so he simply followed his gut. Slipping a hand around her waist. His hand jolting when it met skin.

"What the hell?" he murmured, twisting to look at her back, to find by some kind of miraculous design it was bare from a ribbon at her neck to her lower back.

Needing every ounce of social grace he could muster, he let his hand splay over her back as he pulled her gently, fully, against him.

When her deep hazel eyes focussed on him, and she let out a sigh, some final piece shifted into place inside the new landscape of his mind.

"You ready for this?" he asked.

She shook her head.

"Yeah," he murmured. "Until about five minutes back I realised I wasn't really ready for it either. Since we're making up the rules as we go along, let's decide to get through it together."

He slid his hand an inch further around her waist, gave her a tug towards the dais. One high heel shot forward, followed by the other, and together they walked up the aisle.

Forgoing tradition, Cormac walked Harper to Lola's side and stayed there, knowing Gray didn't need his support today. Gray wouldn't have cared if a spaceship took every last person there so long as he had his girl.

And in that moment Cormac felt the same.

Once the ceremony was over the party began.

A big white tent had been filled with long farmhouse tables draped in gauze and covered with every kind of food under the sun. While the band started up under an adjacent marquee.

Harper made to follow the happy couple, until Cormac took her by the elbow and dragged her off the back of the dais.

"What about the photos?"

"No set shots," Cormac said. "Photographers—plural— are moving through the crowd taking happy snaps all night long."

He really did know more about the wedding plans than she did.

"So where are we going?"

"Somewhere with less people," Cormac muttered, smiling at guest after guest who tried to flag him down.

"Can we slow down just a mite?"

He glanced back at her, his eyes hot. Dark. Too dark to read.

"This dress won't take another big step."

Cormac's gaze slid down her body, leaving spot fires in its wake. Then he slowed. "I do like that dress."

"I like your suit," she said. Though what she really meant was that she liked the man wearing it.

"Cormac—"

"Photo?"

A man with a big camera suddenly appeared in front of Harper. She squealed, and leapt into Cormac's arms.

A second later her pulled her closer and said, "No thanks." He patted his chest. "Already got one."

"One more can't hurt," said the photographer with a smile.

"Not now, mate," Cormac growled and the man slunk away. Leaving a clear run to a secluded spot beneath an oak tree at the edge of the lawn.

Once there he lined Harper up with the trunk, his hands searing through the slippery fabric of her dress before he stepped away, running his hands down the sides of his suit pants.

While she felt as if her belly was full of butterflies, her head with dust motes, Cormac looked even more discombobulated. She had to smile. "Thank you."

"Hmm?" he asked, his hand at his mouth, finger tapping manically against his bottom lip.

"For helping me through that. Seeing Lola up there, about to get married, I froze. But watching her grinning at Gray, hearing the vows they made..." Harper let out a great big sigh. "It was like watching the final piece of a puzzle fall into place."

"I know what you mean," Cormac said, focussed on her as if he couldn't bear to look away.

She remembered the revelation she'd had just before falling asleep in the early hours of that same morning. When deciding it was time to figure out what really made her happy.

Cormac's phone call to Weston had rushed through her like a waterfall of hope. The way he'd walked with her down the aisle, held her to him like something precious, looked at her as if she was the only person in the world, had given her hope wings.

Looking at Cormac looking at her now, she had no need to wonder any more.

Her voice was a little rough as she said, "Why did you pat your jacket when the photographer asked to take our picture?"

He looked at her then, face blank. Not a tell in sight. But she knew him too well. "Come on, Cormac, fess up."

His mouth curved at one corner, and her heart flipped over on itself. "You really can see right through me, can't you? I'm going to have to remember that in future."

In future. Meaning he saw a future between them.

She shook her head, even while every other part of her was saying yes, yes, yes! "Stop trying to distract me." She reached for his jacket, flapping open the lapel and patting the inner lining. "What are you hiding in here?"

Her fingers slipped into the pocket and came out with—

"Oh."

For inside Cormac's jacket was the thin strip of black and white pictures of the two of them together, taken by the photo booth at the bucks' and hens' night.

"Where did you get these?"

"I grabbed them the moment they were taken."

"And you kept them?"

His face softened, his expression indulgent. *Of course I kept them, Harper.*

"Why have you got them on you today?"

"I've had them on me ever since that night." He lifted his hand, placing it over the now empty pocket. Over his heart.

She looked down at the pictures. In the first image she looked so stressed. While he looked straight out gorgeous, with his knee-melting smile and warm eyes.

In the second she appeared exasperated. While he looked as if he was having too much fun.

In the third... That was right. He had kissed her on the cheek. Her mouth had sprung open, and her eyes were wide with surprise.

In the last picture she had turned to chastise him, only to give him prime opportunity to kiss her. Gently. Sweetly. Lips only just touching. Her eyes had fluttered closed, her whole body was leaning into his and her hand gripped his shirt. And even in the grainy black and white, and all the shades of grey in between, she could see his smile.

She ran a thumb over the image. To think that woman in the picture—the woman giving herself so freely, so completely, so honestly, so vulnerably—was really her.

"About last night," she said, taking a moment to choose her words carefully. For the consequences were great. "I said some things, a great many things, that weren't exactly true. Or, maybe to be more precise, do not rightly explain how I feel."

"About?"

She looked up to find him standing before her—one hand in his trouser pocket, the other resting by his side. So handsome her heart ached.

"About you."

He breathed in deep, and waited for her to go on.

"I fear I might have made you think that you meant nothing more to me than a couple of kisses."

"And a roll on the couch, don't forget," he said, ambling closer. Sunlight dappling his suit through the leaves above. Playing shadow and light across his face. "I believe those were your exact words."

"Mmm… So they were."

"Are you suggesting you may have misrepresented your feelings?"

The man was a master at word play, probably what made him such a great lawyer, but Harper was a go-getter at heart. And if she didn't get soon she might spontaneously combust.

"Big time," she said.

His eyes flared with heat. His gaze drifting over her face before settling on her mouth.

"I've been fighting it since the moment I saw you sitting on the hood of your ridiculously romantic car. Heck, I've been fighting it since you walked the halls of Blue Moon Bay High, a smile on your face, a whistle as you walked, giving yourself to anyone and everyone in your path. I can't fight it any more. And I won't. I'm in love with you, Cormac."

His gaze, which had been roving over her dress as if trying to figure out a way to get through it one stitch at a time, lifted to her eyes.

Then he came to her in three strides, his hand reaching behind her neck as he pulled her to him and kissed her like a man drowning, and she the last drink of water on earth. When she moaned, and pressed herself all up against him, he wrapped an arm around her back and hefted her into his arms.

Aeons later the kisses slowed, softened, until they clung to one another with the barest touch of their lips.

"You love me," he said, his voice rough.

"Like nothing else. I've never felt that way before. But I know it. I know it like I know my own name."

"I believe you."

"You do?"

He nodded, his forehead sliding over hers. Then he slowly lifted his face away, his gaze snagging on hers. He slid her hair from her face, then traced the edge of her jaw. All the while looking at her as if he couldn't believe she was real.

She said, "I don't expect you to—"

He leaned down and silenced her with one more kiss. The kind that made a girl's knees forget how to work.

Then, reaching for her, cupping her cheeks, he looked from one eye to the other and said, "Harper, you must know that I'm in love with you too."

Harper swallowed lest she let out the sob that threatened to undo her completely. Then she threw her arms around his neck and held on tight.

In the distance people chatted, music played, food was devoured, and Lola and Gray's wedding party went on as if the entire world had not shifted beneath their feet. As if the boy Harper had a crush on all those years ago, the one whose smile had given her respite from the craziness of home, hadn't just told her he loved her.

As she pressed her face to his shoulder, as he held her tight, she laughed out loud.

"What's so funny?"

"I'm leaving tomorrow, Cormac. I have a plane to catch and contracts to fulfil." It all felt so insignificant compared with this, but she'd made promises. She'd never been one to walk away from a commitment and wasn't about to start now.

"While the Chadwicks are retiring and plan to announce my taking over as CEO of Chadwick Corp."

Harper leant back the better to see his face. To check if he was as indifferent to the idea as he sounded. "Cormac, that's amazing!"

"I'm not taking it on."

"Why on earth not?"

He grinned. Shook his head. "Only you would show your regret at having to leave all this then berate me for feeling the same way."

"Why?" she asked, slapping him on the chest. "Talk to me."

"You know why."

Harper lifted a hand to her chest. "You're giving it up…for me? No. You will not sacrifice something you've worked your whole life for, for me."

"Why not?"

"I'm not…" She swallowed the words that had been about to leave her mouth. Words she'd spent her entire life telling herself she didn't believe.

"You are more than enough, Harper. You're everything. To me. I can see your brain whirling, and I need you to stop. To listen, to believe me when I say that this is what I want. I'm going out on my own. Going to use that mighty education of mine to do good. I can start with pro bono for some of the Chadwick charities. Then reinstate my licence to practise in the UK. Or the United Arab Emirates, perhaps. It's been a while since I've been to Dubai."

Harper swallowed, the world so bright and shiny and colourful she had to squint. "But you love your job."

"I love doing good work that satisfies me. The Chadwicks will be fine. I'll even help them scour the world for someone amazing to fill the position. Or who knows, it might even light a fire under Gray, give him the chance to take on his birth right."

"Or not," Harper said.

Cormac grinned, and ran a finger over her forehead, trying to smooth out the frown. "So what do you say?"

"I say... Okay!" she said, her voice light as air.

"Okay?"

"Yes. Okay. To everything. Anything. We've been making up the rules as we went along, so why stop now? I want you to come with me. As soon as you can. And I want to come back here, too. As often as possible. To see Lola more. To get to know Dee-Dee and Weston and Gray. For if they love Lola and they love you then they can't be all bad."

"Who loves me?" Cormac asked, feigning deafness in his right ear.

"I do."

"What was that? I missed it."

"I love you, Cormac Wharton," she said throwing her arms out and shouting for the whole world to hear. "Cutest boy in school. Hottest man in town. Did I mention how much I like you in that suit?"

He brushed a stray lock of hair behind her ear, his eyes following the move, his fingers delving into her hair, cupping the back of her head and staying there. Then his gaze swept back to hers. "I love you too, Harper Addison. You stubborn, fierce, mercurial, gorgeous creature. Did I mention stubborn?"

"Since we met again? Several times."

Cormac leaned down and kissed her right as she lifted onto her toes and kissed him, the photos that somehow magically tracked the course of their relationship in four frames clutched in her hand.

"Do you think it's time we headed back?" he asked, lips brushing against hers.

She shook her head, even as she said, "Yes. We'd better."

He slung an arm about her shoulders and pulled her close and together they made their way back to the wedding party. Slowly.

"So this crush of yours," he said.

"Mmm?"

"Do you think it might last this time?"

"I think it might."

"Hmm. That's what I was afraid of."

Harper tipped her head to his shoulder. "Any advice on what we can do about it?"

"I have a couple of ideas," he said, his voice muffled as he kissed the top of her head. "Actually, more than a couple. A veritable cornucopia. As far as I see it, we'll have to work our way through them until I've exhausted you. I mean, your crush."

Harper couldn't wait. "Confident, much?"

"Are you suggesting I have no reason to be?"

Harper spun out from under his arm, taking his hand in both of hers as she walked backwards near the edges of the party.

"Please," she said, pretending to chew gum as she affected her most 'high school' voice. "You're not all that, Cormac Wharton."

He lifted an eyebrow in patent disagreement.

Fine, she thought. He was all that and more.

How much more she could not wait to find out.

EPILOGUE

CORMAC TURNED OFF the upstairs shower, muscles eased from the hard, hot spray, feeling a little more alive despite the lack of sleep the night before.

He'd have to do something about that. About the fact he couldn't keep his hands off Harper. He was a fit guy, running now since surf wasn't as close to home anymore, but even he needed some sleep in order to be a functioning member of society.

At some point he'd do something about it. Not now. Now things were pretty much perfect. Not that he'd say that to his girl. She was so determined to believe perfection was an impossibility. It could be his secret to bear.

He grabbed his toothbrush and brushed, thinking about the text he'd send Harper when she got to the airport.

Though she was heading into the restaurant on the way. Her company's first ever investment—a small elegant Italian seafood joint down the road from their new Chelsea digs.

She was a silent partner with an ex-client and his son. Or had they been opponents in a contract dispute just before she'd come home to Blue Moon Bay? He'd never quite been able to get the gist. Apparently they'd sold up a string of restaurants but Harper had convinced them that with her help they could create something wonderful, something new.

Though he wasn't sure she'd grasped the *silent* part, as she visited every time she was in back in London, pored over the financials, the contracts with suppliers, making damn sure it remained efficient and in the black.

And the place was doing great. The father and son who ran it seemed really happy, so he let her be.

Especially since she seemed really happy too.

Grinning as he wiped condensation from the mirror, he stopped his hand mid-swipe when he heard Harper's voice. Raised, in frustration.

Cormac grabbed his towel, wrapped it quickly around his waist and took off out the bathroom door, down the stairs and out the front door.

It was a summer's day in London, which was nothing like a summer's day back home, and Cormac's toes curled at the chill that met his bare feet.

Cormac could hear Harper's voice, strident and sure, coming from the miniscule front garden but he couldn't see her at all.

It had only been a matter of time before some neighbour made the mistake of trying to tell her where to park the Sunbeam, or how high to let the roses grow, clueless as to the fact they'd be dealing with the Negotiator.

Thankfully he was known for his charm, and was ready to leap in and clean up the mess.

"Harper?"

After a beat, she said, "Down here."

He bent over the railing to find her on her hands and knees on the grass, one sexy high heel poking out from behind her skirt-clad backside. Cormac fixed his towel and leant on a newel, prepared to put up with the cold when it came with such a view.

"Come on, sweet puppy," Harper cajoled. "Give it to me."

Her Maltese terrier pup, Marnie, stood about a metre away, Harper's other shoe hanging from her mouth. They'd engaged in a battle of wills ever since Harper had brought her home. But they were besotted with one another at the same time.

Novak watched on from the sidelines, though after seeing Cormac she ambled up the stairs and leant against his leg.

Cormac made a kiss-kiss noise. Marnie's ears pricked before she came bolting up to him, dropped the shoe and jumped around on her back feet.

Cormac lifted her up, gave her a kiss, then plopped her back inside the house, shutting the door behind her.

Harper blew a stream of air from the side of her mouth then pulled herself to her feet. Or, more precisely, her foot. "Of course, the dog has a crush on you too."

Cormac grinned and held up a shoe with a heel that could take out a vampire. "Looking for this?"

Harper limped up the stairs, fixing her suit as she went. And, hell, if he didn't want to drag her inside and unfix it. But he knew she wouldn't want to miss visiting the restaurant on the way to the airport, so he leaned down to help her on with her shoe, before sliding a hand up her leg, up her hip, around her back and pulling her in for a kiss.

A car horn beeped as a black cab pulled up just beyond their gate.

Harper's gaze was gorgeously fuzzy as she pulled away slowly from his kiss. "Two more days in New York to get this contract to bed. Then I'll be home tomorrow night. I have nothing lined up after this so I'm all yours for as long as you want me."

"I'll be waiting with bated breath till you come home."

"Right here?" she asked, her hand going to his towel and giving it a quick tug.

"I won't move an inch."

She pressed up against him a little more, and he moved more than an inch.

Knowing she was close to fulfilling the contracts she'd had in place after Lola and Gray's wedding, he'd cleared his schedule as well. "Since we have a rare break in the calendar, how about we go home."

She blinked. "Home-home?"

They hadn't been back to Blue Moon Bay in six months, and he knew she was itching to see Lola even more than he was ready to see his friends and family.

Cormac nodded. "Winter will have hit Blue Moon Bay by now. The fires will be lit. We can rug up against the brisk wind coming in off the bay."

Harper breathed out hard. "Yes, please. But what about—?"

"Adele and Wilma will look after the dogs." Adele had hooked up with one of Lola's yoga-teacher friends at the wedding, an English girl, and had made the trek north not long after Harper and Cormac had done the same. "It'll be a Hampstead holiday for them too."

"Gotta love a man who thinks of everything."

"Love you too." And saying it to this woman never got old. "We'll head off at the end of the week, giving you just enough time to pack."

The cab driver beeped again. Harper turned and shot the driver a look. He lifted his hands in surrender, grabbed a magazine and hunkered down in his seat.

"Go," Cormac said, reaching down to hand her her small suitcase from the landing.

She gave him a quick kiss. Then reached around his neck to give him a kiss hotter than any summer's day he'd ever known.

While he fixed his towel, Harper jogged down the stairs in her killer heels, slid into the cab and was gone.

Cormac watched the car till it turned the corner. Breathed in a lungful of London air, before heading inside, Novak at his heels.

He didn't tell her the flights had been booked weeks before.

Or that he'd tracked down the photo booth from Lola and Gray's party, and paid an exorbitant amount of money to have it waiting for him in the Chadwicks' pool house.

That it was plugged in, stocked with film, ready and waiting for Cormac to lead Harper inside.

For there was where he planned to offer her the diamond ring he'd had sitting in his sock drawer for months. Where he would ask her to be his wife.

Grinning from the inside out, Cormac hit the kitchen to grab an apple. And glanced at the strip of black and white photo-booth photos stuck to their fridge. Photos of Harper looking stressed, then frustrated, surprised, then melting into his kiss, while in every picture he looked like a man who was happy to wait for his girl to catch up.

He moved them over a little to make room for the new strip he'd bring back once their trip home was done. Pictures he had no doubt would show two people crazy in love.

It's a big fridge, Cormac thought, and he couldn't wait to fill it with photos of his family. And friends.

And Harper. His woman. His love. His everything.

Upstairs Cormac went; a man with a plan, a smile on his face, and a whistle as he walked.

* * * * *

THE FAMILY
HE DIDN'T
EXPECT

SHIRLEY JUMP

To Barb and Donna,
two of the smartest and best friends I could
ever ask for. Here's to more laughs and
a lifetime of cocktail Fridays.

Chapter One

Dylan Millwright sat in his Jeep, parked on a slight hill. Stone Gap, North Carolina, lay before him, lazy, content and still in the late October sunshine. When he was eight, he'd climbed the side of this hill with his older brother and felt like he'd conquered Mt. Everest. When he was sixteen, he'd brought Mary Alice Hathaway to this very hill and mistaken lust for love. At seventeen, he'd quit high school and crested the hill once again, but this time vowing to leave the small town where he'd grown up in his rearview mirror forever.

Forever had lasted a little over ten years. Then Uncle Ty had called, said *I need you, kid*, and Dylan had dropped everything. There were very few people in the world that Dylan would do that for. Uncle Ty was at the top of the list. Dylan had no idea how long he was going to be here, or what Uncle Ty needed, but that was okay. Dylan was used to living by the seat of his pants, with no more formal commitment than a handshake.

He looked out over the town one last time, then drew in a deep breath. Then he climbed back into his Jeep and headed down the hill and into downtown Stone Gap. Not much had changed, as if the whole town was caught in a time warp. Sadie's Clip 'n' Curl still marked the beginning of Main Street, followed by the ice cream parlor, a couple diners, Gator's Garage, Betty's Bakery, Joe's Barbershop...

Small-town America, on a first-name basis with everyone.

Hopefully he wouldn't be caught in this Norman Rockwell painting for very long. Dylan paused at the intersection with Juniper Street, took a left, then pulled into the parking lot of a long, low-slung building. The white paint was fading, peeling, and the roof had a few broken shingles. The morning rain had left the grass richly green and knocked a few light branches to the ground. The sign out front looked brighter than Dylan remembered, but still said the same thing, like a promise he could depend upon:

Millwright Family Children's Community Center

Uncle Ty and Aunt Virginia, who'd never had children of their own, had opened the center two decades ago. Kids from all over came here, filling the game rooms and the basketball courts out back, mostly after school and always on Saturdays. Dylan himself had spent many an afternoon here, often after a fight with his parents or yet another grounding for breaking a rule (or ten). Uncle Ty and Aunt Virginia had always welcomed him with open arms, providing a refuge for kids who really needed one.

A month ago, Aunt Virginia had died. Dylan had been hiking in Colorado and didn't get the message until after the funeral. Then Uncle Ty had called, his voice breaking with grief, and asked Dylan to come help.

He headed inside, his eyes adjusting to the dim interior, and his ears to the din. A couple of teenage boys were playing ping-pong at the scarred table with the Swiss cheese net in the rec room. Two others were immersed in an older generation PlayStation or Xbox. Another few were sprawled across the battered leather sofas, watching a football game. The teenagers, a motley, kind of scruffy crew, barely noticed him enter. At a set of small chrome and laminate tables on the left, a quartet of little kids were making some kind of craft with Mavis Beacham that involved a whole lot of glue and a tub of colorful beads.

As soon as she saw Dylan, Mavis got to her feet and opened her arms. "Dylan Millwright, as I live and breathe! What are you doing here?"

Before he could answer, she was drawing him into a tight hug. Mavis was an ample woman, the kind that embodied welcome. She'd been his neighbor when he was growing up, and had always made time for both the Millwright boys, keeping a jar of their favorite peppermints by her door for whenever they passed by.

"Tell me you're staying at the inn while you're here,"

Mavis said. "Della Barlow and I turned Gareth Richardson's house into something amazing. You'll love it there."

Leave it to Mavis to not even ask Dylan about staying with his brother. She knew him well, and had seen the squabbles between the boys. He smiled at her. "I wouldn't dream of staying anywhere else, Mavis."

She cupped his face between both her palms. "I'm glad you're home, Dylan. Real glad. Your uncle needs you."

"I'm glad I'm here, too, Mavis," Dylan said. He didn't correct her on calling Stone Gap home. She loved this town far more than he ever had, so he let that go and instead gave her a quick kiss on the cheek.

Uncle Ty was sitting in his office, behind a wide plate-glass window. He looked up, saw Dylan and started waving as he got out of his seat and came around the door. "Dylan! You made it!"

Dylan crossed the room and gave Uncle Ty a big hug. His uncle was five foot nine, a few inches shorter than Dylan, and used to be nearly as wide as he was tall. But since the last time Dylan had seen him, his uncle had lost at least twenty pounds. He had a friendly, open face, and though his graying hair was thinning a little and receding a lot, he still looked younger than his sixty years. As long as Dylan had known him, Uncle Ty had been a kid at heart. "Good to see you, Uncle Ty."

"You too, son. You too." He patted Dylan's back. "I've missed you."

"I've missed you too." Dylan drew back. "I'm really sorry about Aunt Virginia."

Ty's eyes filled. "She was one of a kind. Lord, I loved that woman."

"Everyone who met her did, too," Dylan said. Aunt Virginia had had one of those larger-than-life person-alities. The kind of woman who welcomed perfect strangers into her home and fed them pork and beans on a Saturday night. The kind of woman who knit-ted blankets for the homeless and baked pies for the poor. She'd been the lifeblood of the community cen-ter. Even though the rooms were still teeming with ac-tivity, it felt as if some of the air had gone out of the space, but Dylan didn't want to say that. "Looks like the place is as busy as ever. And exactly the same as when I was here."

Uncle Ty chuckled. "You know me. Change is a four-letter word. I don't like to mess with a winning formula." Then his uncle sobered and draped an arm over Dylan's shoulder, lowering his voice as the two of them walked toward the office. "Thank God you came when I called. I can't manage this place on my own. You know Virginia—she was my right *and* my left hand here. I'm just…lost without her."

Dylan could see that in his uncle's eyes, hear it in his voice. He'd never known anyone who loved another person as much as Virginia and Ty had loved each other. They'd had movie love, the kind you only saw in some Nicholas Sparks flick. And now, Virginia was gone, and Uncle Ty looked like he was marooned on a de-serted island.

"Whatever you need," Dylan said. "I've got a couple weeks where I don't have to be anywhere. I can start on some of the maintenance or—"

Ty drew in a deep breath. "Actually, I want you to

work with the kids. At least for today. I'm just having a…well, a rough afternoon and I can't do it."

The statement hung in the stale air of Ty's office. For a second, Dylan thought he hadn't heard his uncle right. "Work…with the kids? Me?"

Uncle Ty ran a hand through his thinning hair. His face was lined, his eyes tired. His usual smile had disappeared, as if he'd lost it and couldn't remember where it was. "I just can't. It's not that I don't still love all these kids and love my job, but it's too much right now. How am I supposed to tell these kids how to get their lives on track when mine is so far off the rails? I'm doing all I can to manage the books and clean the bathrooms once in a while."

"Uncle Ty, I don't have a degree in child psychology like Aunt Virginia, or a background in social work like you do."

"No, but you have life experience. And sometimes, that's what gets through to the tough cases better than any therapy you throw at them."

Yeah, he had life experience, but it wasn't the kind he figured these kids should have. Like running away from home at seventeen. Hitchhiking from here to California, funding his way with odd jobs. He'd been picked up by the cops a few times—mainly for loitering and underage drinking—and wound his way around the country ever since, never staying in any one place long. He'd worked fishing charters in Florida, potato farms in Idaho, building projects in Minnesota. He'd feel like a hypocrite if he told the kids that settling down and working hard would make them happy in the end. What did he know about settling down—or finding happiness? "I don't think I can do this, Uncle Ty. I'm not cut out for it at all."

"I know you think that," Ty said, "but you're more suited than anyone I know. You grew up here—"

"And didn't exactly turn out to be a Nobel Prize winner."

"No, but you did turn into a hell of a good man."

Dylan shook that off. If there was one adjective he'd use for himself, it sure wasn't *good*. "Can't you hire someone? Someone with a degree or something?"

"You know this place has always operated on a shoe-string budget, Dylan. Anyone I hired would have to be working for almost nothing." Ty put a hand on his nephew's shoulder. "Just give it a try for a little while. For me, please?"

Dylan took another look at his uncle. Ty's shoulders sagged low, and there was a blankness in his features that Dylan had never seen before, as if Uncle Ty was a fading photo. He'd lost the love of his life, and it had drained every bit of the color out of his world.

"All right. You can count on me, but only for a temporary gig, okay?" Dylan said, with a lot more conviction than he felt. Dylan never had been the kind of guy anyone—especially anyone in this town—had counted on for anything more than a ride to the liquor store on Friday night.

Relief flooded Ty's face. "Thank you, Dylan. It's just for a few days. I need to…find myself again, you know? Without Virginia, I'm…half of who I used to be."

Ty and Virginia had loved each other in that way most people aspired to and never found. Dylan had no such aspirations. He didn't want to be tied down, to any one place or any one person. He was here now, but he wasn't planning on staying one second longer than necessary.

Dylan slung his backpack into the corner beside a teetering stack of boxes and the world's largest supply of colored construction paper. He still wasn't sure he was cut out for this, but maybe if he gave Ty a day or two off, things would get back to normal. "Just tell me what to do."

"The little kids are doing okay. Mavis has them making some kind of rainbow thing with beads." Ty gestured toward the round table, headed by the generously sized, warm and affectionate African American woman. The kids gravitated to her like ants to honey, and from the smile on her face, Mavis loved every minute with them.

"She was awesome when I was a kid," Dylan said. "I'm glad she's still volunteering here."

"Me, too. Though she has fewer hours to spare, since she's running the inn with Della Barlow." Ty nodded, then he waved toward the sofas. "Take the teen circle, will you? The rest of them will be here any minute. All you have to do is prompt them to talk, and believe me, they'll talk your ear off. Remind them to keep it positive."

"Uncle Ty—"

Ty put a hand on Dylan's arm, cutting off his protest. "You've walked the walk and talked the talk and broken the same rules these kids have. But then you turned yourself around, got a great job with that company up in Maine… I can't think of a better person than you to connect with them."

His uncle had a point. If there was one thing Dylan had succeeded at in life, it was being a rebellious teenager. He'd broken pretty much every rule his parents had set forth, and quite a few put in place by the state of North Carolina. If there was a way to get away with doing the wrong thing, Dylan knew it. These kids, sprawled across the sofas like human afghans, weren't going to be able to get anything past him. And whether they knew it or not, they shared some common ground with him.

The door to the center opened and a leggy brunette woman carrying a briefcase strode in, followed by a singing four-year-old and a sullen teenage boy who looked like he'd rather disappear inside his gray hoodie than be here. The smaller kid peeled off and beelined for Mavis's table, while the teenager propped himself against the wall closest to the door. But Dylan's gaze remained on the brunette.

Stunning. That was the only word that came to mind.

She had long brown hair that tumbled around her shoulders. Her eyes were masked by sunglasses, but they couldn't hide a face that had that kind of delicate bone structure that made him think of Aunt Virginia's porcelain teacups. The woman was wearing a dark navy skirt, a white button-down blouse with the cuffs turned back and a bright red beaded necklace swinging down to her waist. Then there were the heels—tall, spiky, dark blue shoes that offset incredible legs and made something deep inside Dylan go hot.

"Ty, sorry I'm late." She strode forward, passing

Dylan as if he didn't even exist. "I got out of work late and then had to track down Cody, who, as usual, wasn't where he was supposed to be." She blew a lock of hair off her face. "I swear, that kid is going to be the death of me."

Uncle Ty put a hand on her shoulder. "It's fine, Abby, really. Cody will settle in soon and Jacob is already up to his elbows in glue."

She glanced over at the table, where Jacob—the youngest one, Dylan assumed—had already taken a seat and was sprinkling beads across bright blue construction paper. Mavis sent up a little wave, signaling *I've got this, honey.*

"Okay." Abby let out a long sigh. "If you don't mind, I have a proposal I need to work on. Can I…" She waved toward the office and gave Ty a smile.

For some weird reason, that smile—directed toward his uncle—sent a little flicker of jealousy through Dylan.

"Of course. Use my office. But first, I want you to meet my nephew, Dylan." Ty turned to Dylan and gestured between the two of them. "Dylan Millwright, meet Abigail Cooper, but everyone calls her Abby. Abby, my nephew. He's going to be helping out with the teen program."

For the first time in his life, Dylan wished he was the kind of guy who wore a suit and tie. His battered jeans, faded concert T-shirt and black leather boots didn't exactly match the polished, pressed woman beside him. "Nice to meet you," he said, extending his hand.

She gave him a surprisingly firm handshake, considering how delicate she seemed at first blush. She was all business, not a spark of interest in her eyes. "You, too."

He was about to say something witty back, but before he could come up with a handful of words more charming than *uh, you're beautiful*, she was picking up the briefcase and heading for Ty's office. A second later, the glass door closed and Abby settled herself behind Ty's desk. She pulled a laptop out of her bag, set it up and started typing.

"I can see you watching her," Uncle Ty said, putting a hand on Dylan's shoulder. "And I can read interest in your eyes. I'm tellin' you right now, Abby isn't..."

"Isn't the kind of woman who would date a guy like me?"

Ty turned to his nephew and the lines around his eyes softened. "I wasn't going to say that. You're a good man, Dylan—"

Dylan scoffed.

"*A good man*," Ty repeated with emphasis, "or I wouldn't have you here. As for Abby, she's...complicated. One of those women juggling a whole lot of balls and not interested in having a man help catch a single one of them. Her ex was a real jerk, who let her and her boys down in a big way."

"I'm not here to date anyone," Dylan said and turned away from the office to prove his point. "Don't you worry about that."

But as he walked away and crossed toward the teenagers waiting on the sofas, Dylan wondered if he'd still be singing that tune if Abby Cooper had looked at him with even an ounce of interest. Either way, the last thing he needed was a small-town single mom with worka-holic tendencies. If anything screamed *complete oppo-site from you*, that fit the bill.

He dropped into the lone armchair sitting in front of the sofas and propped his elbows on his knees. "Hey, guys, I'm Dylan. How about we talk about breaking the rules?"

Abby stared at the report in front of her. She'd spent the better part of the day putting it together, but it still didn't feel right. Had she missed some data points? Forgotten to add the case study? She scrolled through the document, checked it against her list, then read the pages over again.

Ever since she'd taken the promotion to director of brand development at Davis Marketing, she'd worried that she'd bitten off more than she could chew. Worried that they were going to see her as a fraud, as a woman who was only pretending to be up to the job.

Because she was.

Hell, her whole life seemed to be about pretending she could handle everything, whether she actually could or not. Get up in the morning, drag Cody out of bed, feed Jake, shoo Cody out the door and pray he made it to high school this time instead of heading for the park or the mall or somewhere with his friends. Then drop Jake off at preschool, making sure he'd taken his snack and a change of clothes for just in case at daycare later and that he didn't have anything after school that she was supposed to go to. After all that, finally head off to work. Eight or more hours later, head home and repeat the process in reverse. Sometime in that window, she was supposed to cook healthy dinners, make the house spotless, draw baths and read bedtime stories. Oh and have "me" time, with rose-petal filled bubble baths and meaty novels.

Because that was what the magazines said "women who had it all" managed to do. She'd yet to find a way to even come close to that, but it didn't stop her from trying.

Tears sprang to her eyes and a burst of panic made her heart race. Abby drew in a deep breath, counted to ten, then whisked the tears away. There was no time to get distracted or lose her focus.

She read the pages once again, hit Send on the report, then closed the laptop. There was more on her To Do list, but it could wait until after Jake went to bed. That would mean another late night again, but her Mommy Guilt was kicking into overdrive, especially after Jake had asked in the car if she was going to work "again," with that pouty sound in his voice and disappointment swimming in his big brown eyes.

She emerged from Ty's office and crossed to the little kids' table. Two more kids had arrived and now seven of them sat in pint-size chairs on either side of Mavis. She loved those kids and welcomed them like they were all her own little ducklings.

"How are you, Mavis?" Abby said. She placed a hand on the older woman's shoulder. Mavis covered it with her own and gave Abby's hand a friendly pat.

"Just fine, just fine." She turned to the kids and grinned at them. "I have the best table of kittens—"

"We're not kittens, Miss Mavis," Jake said with a

laugh in his voice. He was the happy one of her two boys, always ready with a smile or a laugh. Abby loved that about him and reached over to ruffle his hair.

"Well, I don't know about that, Jakester," Abby teased. "You drink milk, right?"

"Uh-huh."

"And you like to sleep a lot."

Jacob laughed and cocked his head to the side, causing one lock of hair to do a little flip-flop. "That's cuz I'm tired."

"And you have a big old mop of fur—" She nuzzled his dark hair.

"Mommy, that's hair! I'm a boy!"

She leaned back and pretended to study him, tapping a finger against her lip. "Well, now, I think you might be right about that. Now that I look a little closer, I see you are indeed a boy. A cute one at that." She gave Mavis a smile, then placed a kiss on her son's forehead. "Keep on working on your picture, Jake. I'll be back in a minute."

She crossed the room, pausing by the watercooler, filling a paper cup and pretending to get a drink, but really trying to see how Cody was doing. Of the two boys, Cody had taken their father's sudden departure the hardest. It had been easier when Keith had left the first time, because Cody was only two, but ten years later, when Keith had returned to try again, Cody had started to put trust in his father. The problem was Keith had never fully committed to his family and had never really intended to stay forever.

The second time, Cody had turned twelve the day

before and gone to sleep believing the world was perfect because he had a new bike and another game for his Xbox. When he got up the next morning, there'd been an empty spot at the kitchen table and a dark oil stain on the driveway where Keith's Malibu used to be.

Keith had walked out the door, leaving her with a newborn baby, forty dollars in the bank, a sheaf of bills as high as her elbow and the Herculean task of explaining why to two boys who didn't understand.

There were days when she wanted to throttle her exhusband for what he had done to their family, for how he had hurt his children. She had known he'd wanted out for a long time, but had never thought he'd up and move, to live with the twenty-year-old college student who was the "love of his life."

Keith Cooper had been irresponsible and selfish, two traits that Abby had been blind to for far too long. She'd kept thinking he would change, that he would settle down, find a career, not just a job, and become the family man she'd foolishly hoped he'd be.

She'd been wrong.

Abby leaned against the wall beside the watercooler, a paper cone of cool water in her hand, and watched Cody. He was hunched into the corner of one of the sofas, looking angry and sullen. Par for the course with a sixteen-year-old who thought his life sucked.

To his left sat Dylan Millwright, Ty's nephew. He was a good-looking guy—tall and lean, with dark hair and green-brown eyes. She hadn't really noticed him before, but she did now.

He had a roguish look to him, with the scuffed black

boots, the battered jeans, the faded T-shirt. Like one of those guys in a modern-day fairy tale who roared up on a motorcycle and whisked the bored debutante away for a life of adventure.

Except Abby knew full well those kinds of guys didn't make good boyfriend or husband material. They were as temporal as spring weather, gone with the next gust of wind.

"Hey, Cody, want to join us?" Dylan asked.

Cody shrugged and hunkered down more, as if his hoodie could hide him from the world.

"We're just talking," Dylan said.

One of the other kids, a fair-haired tattooed kid wearing a T-shirt with Kurt Cobain's picture, leaned forward. "Yeah, like about girls and crap."

Another boy, with long dark hair and a dirty white T-shirt, leaned back against the couch. "My girl's all mad at me today. I spent the day in solitary and she's acting like I did it on purpose."

In solitary was slang for in-school suspension, something Abby knew all too well from Cody's frequent trips down that hall. She leaned back against the wall, waiting to see where the conversation would lead.

"Well, did you?" Dylan said.

Long Dark Hair snorted. "No. Who gets suspended on purpose?"

Dylan chuckled. "Some of us have done that. So I can sympathize."

"What do you know about our lives, man?" Cobain Fan scoffed. "What'd you do, skip a class? Blow off an essay?"

"I was a lot like you guys. One of those angry kids who thought he knew better than any adult. Now I—"

"Let me guess," Cody said. He had pushed the hoodie off his head. He had the same mop of dark brown hair as his little brother and his father, except he wore his long on the top and shaved on the sides. "You grew up, got a good job, bought a sweet house in the suburbs where you mow the lawn on Saturdays and crap like that. Matt's right. You don't know anything about how tough our lives are."

"I'm not claiming to be an expert, even if you all think I'm too old to understand," Dylan said. "Just someone who has made my fair share of mistakes."

"Doesn't mean you know anything about us," Matt—previously known as Cobain Fan—said.

"True. But it doesn't hurt to talk about your lives, does it? Maybe I can learn a thing or two from you guys, too." Dylan shrugged. "So let's talk."

Cody cursed. "Talking doesn't change jack. Waste of time."

"Hey, I get it that you all don't really want to sit here and go on and on about your lives. I'm not exactly Mr. Conversation myself. But I don't think sitting around here—" Dylan waved at the motley set of battered sofas "—pissed at the world is going to change anything. And I'm betting every one of you has something he wants to change about his life. So let's talk."

Abby couldn't have been more surprised if Dylan had stood up and started singing "The Star-Spangled Banner." She never would have imagined—given his appearance—that he would be so smart and intuitive with how he handled these kids. There was color in Cody's cheeks, interest in his eyes—

Two things Abby hadn't seen in a long, long time. Abby clutched the paper cup so hard it crumpled, praying her son would open up, stop shutting himself off from the world.

"Whatever, dude," Cody said finally, then got to his feet, flipping the hoodie back over his head as he rose. "I'm not here to have a Dr. Phil moment with some guy I don't even know. I'm just trying to survive."

Then he headed out the door, snagging a basketball from the bin as he went. The door shut behind him with a solid *thunk*.

Abby looked at Dylan. She could see the same disappointment in his face that she felt herself. For one brief second, Abby had felt like she had an ally.

And that was a dangerous thing to depend on, Abby reminded herself. She knew full well how a man could let her—and more, her sons—down. So she went back into the office and went back to work, doing the only thing she knew how to do, to—

Survive.

Chapter Two

Dylan straightened the sofas, replaced the cushions and pillows and picked up the empty soda cans from the scarred coffee table. The rest of the teenagers had headed outside after Cody, a sort of group mutiny. Dylan could hear the ping-ping of a basketball hitting the pavement.

Well, that hadn't gone too well. He'd hoped maybe he could connect with the teenagers, have an open discussion, maybe warn them off from making the same mistakes as he had. But so far, his batting average at being a teen group leader was pretty close to zero. For the hundredth time, he wondered why Uncle Ty had thought he could be good at this.

The little kids had finished their craft project, and were sitting in a circle on the carpet while Mavis read them a story about a lost kangaroo. Maybe that was the age when Dylan should be telling them to stay in school. When they still thought books and stories held magic, and when they weren't scarred by the world.

Uncle Ty came over and picked up a cushion that had fallen on the floor. "That went pretty well. I liked how you handled them."

Dylan turned to his uncle. "Really? They all walked out on me."

Ty waved that off. "It happens. The last thing teenagers want you to know is that they're listening to you and agreeing with you. The first time I led a teen group, it lasted maybe ten minutes before the whole lot of them walked out the door. I didn't have the basketball court or the game stations then, so they all went home. Your group lasted a lot longer than that."

"Maybe. But they still left." Dylan sighed.

"No, they're still here." Ty pointed to the boys outside the window, shooting layups and teasing each other between shots. "Getting teenagers to listen is like turning a cruise ship. You don't yank the wheel hard to the right. You nudge it, a little at a time, so the passengers don't even feel the turn."

Dylan chuckled. "Covert counseling?"

"Exactly."

"I'll keep that in mind." Talking to the teenagers had been like talking to his former self, if he could have done that fifteen or sixteen years ago and with better results. Of course, Dylan hadn't listened to anyone back then, not even his uncle. Dylan had been so angry at the world, so ready to leave Stone Gap. Maybe if he'd listened years ago, his path wouldn't have been so rocky, and he wouldn't be thirty-two and still trying to figure out what he wanted to be when he grew up.

"Don't worry so much. You're doing great." Ty looked around the room and let out a long breath. "There's so much to do here. I put everything on hold when Virginia got sick because I kept thinking she'd get better and I'd have time, but…" Ty shook his head. "I need to repaint. Replace that carpet. Repair a few of the chairs and sofas, fix the kitchen cabinets, replace a chunk of countertop that rotted when we had a water pipe burst. One of the toilets is leaking and there's a hole in the roof, two broken windows, a big hole in the hallway wall and another over there. That's just the big stuff, not to mention all the little things that need to be done around this place. I don't even know where to start."

He could hear the stress in Ty's voice. The center was, indeed, in need of a major overhaul. Major overhauls—of buildings at least—were something Dylan could do. He draped an arm over his uncle's shoulders. "It's like steering a cruise ship, Uncle Ty. One thing at a time. Show me where the tools are and I'll start on the repairs today."

Gratitude eased the worry in Ty's face. His uncle looked tired, worn down by the last few weeks. "I'll get my toolbox. I have a list as long as my arm of things I need to buy at the hardware store—"

"Give it to me. Go home tonight, let me lock up. The center's only open for another hour, and I'm sure I can handle things for that long. I'll run over to Ernie's hardware store in the morning and start the repair work tomorrow." It was the least he could do for his uncle during his time here. And, it would keep Dylan busy, which would also keep him from running into his brother. Or think about what he was going to do next, after he was done in Stone Gap. He had a job offer from his boss to manage a construction project in Maine. It was a multi-year commitment starting in the spring, for a slew of new housing. His boss had taken Dylan under his wing a couple years ago, even paid for Dylan to take the contractor's exam, to make him official. Jay was a good man, who had a similar history to Dylan's, and they'd hit it off from the start. It was the longest Dylan had ever stayed with one job, and most of that was due to Jay's support.

Dylan had put off the decision, telling Jay he needed to go to Stone Gap first. Be there for Uncle Ty and then…

Dylan would see. Taking the job from Jay would mean staying in one place, something Dylan wasn't so sure he wanted.

"Thank you, Dylan." Ty's eyes watered. "If Virginia and I had ever had a son…"

The emotion chafed at Dylan. He never knew quite what to do with emotions, his own or other people's. "Don't go getting all sentimental on me, Uncle Ty. Or I'll be the one heading out to the basketball court."

"Point taken." Ty chuckled. He dropped his keys into Dylan's palm. "Thank you. I'll see you in the morning."

Dylan squeezed his uncle's shoulder. "Don't worry. I've got it all under control. See you tomorrow."

As his uncle walked out of the building, the brunette—Cody's mother, Abby—emerged from Ty's office for the second time. Dylan had noticed her standing by the watercooler earlier. He didn't know how much, if any, she'd overheard of the conversation between him and the teenagers, or if she'd just been standing there to get a drink of water.

Abby and Mavis talked for a moment. Then Abby gave Mavis a nod and headed over to Dylan, with her little boy in tow. He was a younger version of Cody, but with a bright, inquisitive face and a ready smile.

"Mavis asked me to set up the snack for everyone because she has to leave early today. And she suggested I get some help, because there are a whole lot of hungry kids here."

He grinned. "So you're asking me to be crowd control?"

"Pretty much, yes. But if you're busy…"

"No, not at all." He could have been in the middle of building the Taj Mahal, and he would have told her he had plenty of time. Something about her blue-green eyes drew him in, made him want to know more about her. They were…

Intoxicating.

A tug on the hem of Dylan's T-shirt drew his attention. He glanced down and saw Abby's youngest son peering up at him, with eyes a deeper green than his mother's. He was a cute kid, only three feet tall, wearing a Transformers T-shirt, jeans and sneakers that blinked red lights when he walked. "I wanna snack. Miss Mavis said you're gonna make me one."

Abby put a hand on her son's shoulder. "Jake, that

isn't what Miss Mavis said. Mommy's gonna make the snack."

Jacob gave his mother a doubtful look. "But you don't cook very good, Mommy."

Abby's cheeks flushed. Dylan liked that. The blush made her seem open, vulnerable. "I'm going to head into the kitchen now before my son spills any more family secrets."

Dylan chuckled. "That's okay. I used to do that to my older brother all the time when we were kids. Especially if he had a girlfriend over. I once told Wendy Simmons about the time Sam got a hornet stuck in his shorts. I thought Sam was going to kill me."

That made Abby smile. She had a nice smile. Warm, friendly. "Sam… Sam Millwright? He's your brother? I've met him a couple times. He sold my boss the property that houses our offices."

"Yup. Sam's my brother." Dylan fell into step beside her as they walked toward the small kitchen at the back of the community center. "Almost five years older, but he thinks he's twenty years older. Like he's my father and needs to remind me how to be responsible."

Okay, so maybe a little more resentment leaked into his voice than he would have liked. No need to spill his own family secrets to a person who was, essentially, a stranger.

"I have a younger sister like that. She's the one who did it all right. Married the perfect man, works the perfect job at a magazine, lives in the perfect house in Connecticut." Abby sighed. "According to her, I'm…a mess." Then she blushed again, as if she wanted to suck the words back inside.

It was another moment of vulnerability, a chink in her armor. He suspected she rarely let anyone see her with her guard down.

"For what it's worth, I don't think you are a mess at all. When you walked in, it made me wish I was wearing something a little less…rock-concert-leftover, just so I could impress you. Like a suit or something." Damn, where had that come from? When was the last time he'd confessed anything like that? Maybe it was because she'd given him a peek inside. Or maybe it was the way Abby carried herself, all poised and confident, that had him feeling like she was, well…a little out of his league. Okay, a *lot*.

She arched a brow. "A suit?"

"I do own one, contrary to what my current attire suggests. Last time I wore it was at my grandfather's funeral and I think my mother still has it in a box somewhere. But I was ten, so I'm not so sure it would still fit me."

She laughed, then pushed on the swinging door. As soon as the three of them entered the kitchen, Jacob scrambled onto one of the stainless steel stools and sat at the counter. He set the picture he'd been working on aside, propped his elbows on the counter and sat up tall. "I'm ready to help, Mommy."

"That's great, Jakester. We're making peanut butter and jelly sandwiches." She tossed Dylan a look. The laughter had disappeared from her voice, and she was all business again. "Despite my son's one-star rating, I can handle those. Really. I'm sure you have other things to do and I hate to put you out. I'll be fine on my own. Really."

The teenagers had finished their basketball game and began to file into the building in a hum of conversation and heavy footsteps. As they headed for the couches, they glanced over at the kitchen. "Yo, man, where's the food?" Matt called out.

"Coming soon," Dylan said. He turned back to Abby. He got the distinct feeling she was giving him the brush-off. She had, after all, asked for his help, then promptly changed her mind. "I don't mind helping at all. And, I have the skills. I have, after all, been making my own sandwiches for almost twenty years now. In fact, I even have Expert Sandwich Maker on my résumé."

"And did you actually get hired somewhere because of that?"

"I think it was my Great Ninja Skills section that impressed the bosses." He winked at Jacob. "I bet you're a great ninja, Jake."

"I am. I scare Mommy all the time cuz I go like this." He hopped down off the stool, then tiptoed forward, with his hands bent like T. rex arms. "I'm super quiet."

Abby ruffled his hair. "You're four, Jake. I don't think *quiet* is an adjective for you yet."

Jake squirmed in his seat, as if proving the point that he was neither stealthy nor quiet. "Did you see my picture I made?"

Abby glanced at the paper. "Very good, Jake. I like your doggy."

From where Dylan stood, he wasn't sure how Abby

discerned the brown blob on the paper was a dog, but then again, Dylan wasn't exactly an art critic. Nor could he draw worth a damn. The pot couldn't exactly pass judgment on the kettle here.

"You know why I drew it?" Jake bounced up and down on his knees. "Cuz I love dogs."

Abby smiled. "I know. If there's one thing you talk about more than dinosaurs, my little non-ninja, it's dogs."

Jake studied his drawing, his lips thinned in concentration. "Can we get a puppy, Mommy? Mrs. Reynolds next door said her dog had puppies and I can has one if I want."

"It's *have*, and no, we're not getting a puppy right now. I have my hands full with you guys." She waved toward the sink. "Go wash your hands, buddy, then sit down again and you can lay out the bread. I'll put on the peanut butter and jelly."

"Or, I can do the peanut butter and you can do the jelly," Dylan said. Somehow, they had ended up inches apart. He could catch the floral notes of her perfume, see the lower lashes that dusted under her eyes. "Assembly-line style."

Why was he trying so hard? Even though Mavis had the little ones under control, Dylan did need to check on the older kids in the center and keep working on that list of repairs, and making sandwiches wasn't a job she couldn't handle.

"I've got it." She handed Jake the loaf of bread, then retrieved the peanut butter from the shelf. "Thanks."

The *thanks* was a clear dismissal. She had obviously

changed her mind about his help. She was also intelligent and beautiful and light-years out of his league. He should take the hint and leave her be.

Instead, he reached into the fridge for the jelly before she could grab it. "An extra set of hands makes the job go faster," Dylan said. "I have no doubt you are fully capable of making a couple dozen sandwiches all by yourself. But there are hungry kids out there who don't care who's slapping on the peanut butter, just as long as it's ready yesterday."

She glanced at the teenagers, who were watching the whole conversation from where they sat. At the same time, Mavis finished the book she was reading, and the little kids scrambled to their feet and dashed to sit at the tables. Mavis waved toward the door, a question in her face, and Abby nodded. "Okay. But only because the kids shouldn't have to wait."

It wasn't exactly her saying she'd been so charmed by his smile that she couldn't say no, but he'd take it.

Dylan slipped in beside her. Jake handed his mother a piece of bread, Abby slathered peanut butter on it, then Dylan spread jelly across the surface and topped it with a second slice of bread. "Are you always this difficult to help?" he asked.

"I'm not difficult. It's just…" She handed him the next piece of peanut-buttered bread. "In my experience, it's better to do things on my own than to count on someone else to help."

Someone had let this woman down. More than once. Dylan wouldn't consider himself Mr. Dependable, but he was the kind of guy who kept his word. He made three more sandwiches before he spoke again. "Well, maybe you've been counting on the wrong people."

She sent him a sideways glance. "Or maybe it's just better to count on myself. No surprises that way."

"Maybe. Or maybe not." He slapped the last piece of bread onto the final sandwich, then pulled a knife out of the drawer and cut the stacks in half.

"Diagonal," Abby said softly. "That's how my mom did it."

"Mine, too."

They shared a glance for a heartbeat, heat filling the space between them, then she spun toward the fridge and filled a tote with juice boxes. A second later, they'd put the snacks onto the sill between the kitchen and the main room. The kids descended like locusts, and before Dylan could blink, every last crumb was gone. Jacob wolfed down half a sandwich, then dashed off with the others to play with a bucket of Legos. That left Dylan and Abby alone in the kitchen.

"Well, I'd say you got a five-star rating on your peanut butter and jelly sandwiches." Dylan retrieved the empty tray and put it in the sink.

A grin flickered across her face. "Maybe I should add that to my résumé."

"Seems to me like you're the kind of girl who already has one hell of a résumé."

Interest sparked in her eyes. "And what makes you say that?"

"Because you are smart and talented. Not to mention beautiful, which isn't a résumé thing, I know, but—" He stopped before his mouth ran away from him.

Her gaze narrowed. "Are you making a pass at me?"

"I'm..." Was he? He wasn't sure. He wasn't in town long, and even if he was staying, he wasn't a guy who did long-term. Abby was completely out of his league and definitely had *long-term* written all over her. That reality reined him back in. "Just making an observation."

"Oh. Well, uh, thank you. That's...that's very nice of you to say." She spun away from the sink and started loading the leftover juice boxes back into the refrigerator.

Dylan knew a brush-off when he saw one, and Abby had just flicked him off like a cobweb on her shoulder. Dylan gave Abby one more look, then headed back out to the main room.

Abby washed the platter and knives, then dried them and stored them on the shelves of the kitchen. She glanced around the room and noticed the peeling paint, the nearly bare shelves, the broken cabinets, the missing chunk of countertop. She'd been bringing her kids here for a year and had never seen it this...lonely. When Virginia had been alive, the kitchen had been full and sparklingly clean. Now it just seemed tired.

Dylan stuck his head in the door. "Hey, we're closing soon. Do you need anything?"

"No. But I think this place does." She let out a sigh. "Things started falling apart when Virginia got sick, but since she died...it just hasn't been the same around here."

Dylan came inside and let the door swing shut behind him. "My aunt Virginia was one of a kind."

"I didn't know her long, but I'd agree with you. She was like a second mother to the kids." Abby folded the dish towel in thirds and laid it on the counter. Maybe it was his help with the sandwiches, maybe it was seeing him try so hard to talk to Cody, but Abby found herself opening up ever so slightly. "When I first started coming here with the boys, Virginia was the one who connected with Cody. Jacob, he's the kind of kid who connects with anyone, but Cody…he hasn't been the same since his father left."

Dylan leaned against the counter and crossed his arms over his chest. He looked so solid there, like the kind of guy she could lean against. "My aunt was like that with me, too. I didn't get along with my dad, and Uncle Ty and Aunt Virginia became more like my parents." Dylan shifted his weight. "How long has it been since Cody's dad left? Sorry. Ty told me a little about your situation."

She should have been angry. Abby tended to keep her personal life to herself. But she saw something in Dylan, something that reminded her of her boys. He had, after all, gotten Ty's stamp of approval which wasn't given to just anyone. Maybe this guy knew something about how hard it was for her to be mom, dad and breadwinner all at the same time. Or maybe she'd just liked the way he smiled at her earlier. In a day filled with stress, that had made her feel good for a second.

"You want to hear about the first or the second time?" She shook her head. "I was stupid enough to take him back and try again. He was gone again the day I found out I was pregnant with Jacob. Despite all the promises he made, when it came down to it, my ex wasn't exactly interested in being a father." She shrugged, like it was no big deal. She'd gotten over the hurt long ago, but there were days when she wanted to throttle the boys' father for the looks of disappointment in their eyes. He'd barely done more than send a birthday card while Cody was growing up, but she'd thought Keith had changed during those few months when he came back. Believed him when he said he wanted a second chance. She'd foolishly thought maybe having Jacob would change things. It hadn't.

"Well, at least the boys got a great mother," Dylan said.

She didn't feel that great on the days when she got truancy notices about Cody and difficult questions from a curious Jake who was beginning to notice he didn't have a father. "And how do you know I'm a great mother?"

"I don't. But your kids seem to be good kids, and that doesn't happen by accident." He pushed off from the counter and crossed to her. "I've never had kids, but I know how important it is to have a good influence in your life."

This was not a topic Abby wanted to discuss. All it did was remind her of how she had picked the wrong man—twice. She averted her gaze and concentrated on wiping up some crumbs. "It's great that you're helping Ty."

"Yeah, well, I'm not really doing much."

He seemed embarrassed by the praise. She wanted to know why, if he was just a naturally humble guy or if he didn't think he deserved it. But she didn't ask, because she had enough on her plate and caring about one more person would tip her over the edge.

Cody was a minute away from being kicked out of school. Jake was doing okay, but he was having trouble paying attention in preschool, and she was worried that he was going to end up following his older brother down a difficult path.

At least they have a great mother—she wasn't so sure about that. She glanced through the half window at Jake, sitting in a chair by the window, no longer interacting with the other kids, while Cody was draped across an armchair, lost in his phone, sullen and angry again. Whatever momentary good mood he'd experienced earlier was gone now.

She sighed. This was why she couldn't get involved with anyone. Couldn't even think about a personal life, no matter how nice Dylan's smile was or how kind his eyes seemed. Because she was barely holding her own life together.

Chapter Three

The Stone Gap Inn looked like the kind of home Dylan had seen on the cover of *Southern Living* magazine. A wide, welcoming front porch with twin rockers, a gorgeous oak door with a brass knocker, opening into a picturesque foyer with a curved staircase.

Mavis grabbed Dylan as soon as he walked in the door that night and gathered him into another big hug. "Oh, it was so good to see you this afternoon," she said. "Your uncle was sure glad you came back to town."

"I'm glad to be here." He pressed a kiss to Mavis's cheek, then drew back. "Tell me you're still making your rhubarb pie."

"You know I am." She grinned. "And I have a piece waiting for you."

"I've been looking forward to it all day." He followed

Mavis down the hall into a sunny yellow kitchen. "You guys have done amazing work with this place."

Mavis beamed, clearly proud of the B&B. "That was all the doing of Della's boys and her new daughter-in-law. They put in a whole lot of blood, sweat and tears to take this place from decrepit to delightful."

Dylan had grown up with the Barlow brothers. He wasn't surprised they'd all pitched in together to help Della rebuild this place. He'd always thought he and Sam would be close like that, but...

Ancient history. There was no sense wishing for things that weren't going to change. "How's business been?" Dylan asked.

"Getting better every day, as word spreads and people hear about my rhubarb pie." She winked as she laid a hearty slice before him.

"I take it the pie is in the Yelp reviews?"

"Of course." Mavis settled into the chair opposite him. "So, I bet you being back in town has the ladies down at Sadie's Clip 'n' Curl buzzing."

Dylan shook his head and chuckled. "Stone Gap hasn't changed a bit."

Mavis's hand covered his. "That's what makes it so great."

He scoffed. "For you, maybe. I'm only in town to help Uncle Ty and then—"

"Back to running away."

"I'm not running away, Mavis. I'm too old to do that."

She peered at him over her reading glasses "You most certainly are. So maybe this time you could consider staying. You've got family here, Dylan, and that's not something you can find growing like blueberries in Maine. Your uncle told me you were thinking about taking a permanent job up there. It's no Stone Gap, you know. Now, enjoy your pie. I already made up your room, second one on the left at the top of the stairs. You're staying in the Asheville. Oh, and don't forget, there'll be waffles in the morning."

She left Dylan to finish his pie. He washed his plate and fork, loaded them into the drying rack, then went to bed. Mavis was wrong about him, but he knew her well and knew trying to change her mind was like trying to shift the direction of the Mississippi River.

The next morning, Dylan headed into the community center shortly after eight, his belly full of homemade waffles and rich maple syrup. He'd planned to arrive earlier, but he'd had to wait for Ernie's hardware store to open up so he could buy the list of supplies Uncle Ty had given him. His uncle had kept the list at a bare minimum, so Dylan added a few things—okay, a lot of things—to the cart before he checked out. Dylan had enough savings to cover the costs, because he suspected Uncle Ty didn't have any kind of budget. Some of the bigger items would have to be ordered from a big-box store, but Ernie carried enough to get Dylan started.

Uncle Ty wasn't in, so Dylan used the key from yesterday to let himself into the building. He flicked on the lights, pausing a moment in the doorway to notice the quiet. He'd never been in the community center when it was empty. The place seemed sad, as if all the life left it when the kids went home.

He decided to start with the projects that were safety issues. The list of things to do was long, but if he worked his way backward from the areas where the kids congregated first, he could minimize the risk of anyone getting hurt. First, he tackled a broken electrical outlet, then moved on to repair a wonky light switch. The community center didn't officially open until two, when the older kids got out of school, so that gave Dylan a few hours to work.

Dylan was getting ready to patch a hole in the wall when the front door opened. He pivoted, expecting Uncle Ty. "Cody. What are you doing here?"

The teenager shrugged. He slid his backpack off one shoulder and dropped it in the corner. "Just needed a break."

Dylan glanced at his watch. "It's only ten in the morning. Aren't you supposed to be in school?"

Cody shrugged again. He dropped onto a love seat and propped his boots on the opposite end. He draped an arm over his eyes and leaned his head back.

Dylan watched him for a minute. He recognized that don't-care attitude, the slouched shoulders, the ripped jeans and faded concert T. "Yo, this isn't a motel."

Cody didn't respond.

Undoubtedly, the kid was skipping school. Dylan debated whether he should call Abby and realized he didn't have her number. And Cody probably wouldn't give it up.

"Listen, let me take you back to school. Finish up the day, then come back here."

Cody shook his head. "No. No way."

"You can't skip school, Cody," Dylan said.

"Why not? I'm practically failing anyway. What's the point?"

"Getting a diploma so you won't be stuck serving fries to ten-year-olds when you're fifty?"

"I don't care about that. All I care about is being left alone." Cody jerked up his backpack and turned to go. "I don't need a lecture from you, too."

Dylan sighed. He could see what was going to happen as soon as the boy walked out the door. It was pretty much Dylan's history repeating itself. Dylan knew that look and knew it well—

Cody would leave here and get into trouble faster than the wind could shift on a fall afternoon.

He thought of the stress on Abby's face the day before. How overwhelmed she seemed, being both father and mother. The last thing he wanted to do was add to her troubles. Cody was safe here—albeit skipping school—and if Dylan kept him occupied, at least there'd be something good to come out of the whole thing.

"Before you go, Cody…" Dylan unloaded his supplies and set them beside his toolbox. A square of Sheetrock, a small handsaw, some plaster and a putty knife. He looked at the hole in the wall—a deep circular indent that was probably from some angry teen's fist—and then back at Cody. "I could use a hand, if you have a minute."

Cody didn't move. "Where's Ty?"

"Not here." Dylan wasn't about to explain to a sixteen-year-old how his uncle was mourning the loss of the love of his life, and doing what he had done ever since Virginia died—sitting in his house, trying to get the motivation to go to the center she had loved so much and that echoed without her presence. Dylan had stopped by last night for a little bit, and seen the loss of the love of his life hanging over Ty like a cloud. At Cody's age, relationships started in homeroom and ended by sixth period. "Come on, dude, help me out."

Cody stood there a moment longer, then let out a long sigh, then dropped his backpack into the corner again. He glanced over at the wall. "That wasn't my fault, you know."

"Whose fault was it?"

"Leon. That dude's got an anger management issue. Meaning, he doesn't manage it at all." Cody traced the outline of the hole. "He got pissed because somebody changed the channel without asking him first, like he's the warden around here."

Dylan tried to think back to the names of the kids who'd been in the circle last afternoon. "Was he here yesterday?"

"Nah, Ty kicked him out and told him not to come back. He does that with any of us who break the rules."

Dylan chuckled. "Some things never change." Uncle Ty had been a little more lenient with Dylan, but there'd been times he'd skated on the edge of banishment.

Cody gestured toward the wall. "So, uh, what do you have to do here?"

"The hole is too big for an ordinary patch," Dylan said. "I'm going to trim the Sheetrock to fill in the space, then attach it to the stud behind the hole. We'll put a patch over that, and in a few hours, it'll dry and be good as new."

"Sounds pretty simple."

"It is. Here, hold this." Dylan handed him the Sheet-rock without asking if he wanted to help. Keeping the kid busy was a good policy regardless, Dylan figured.

Cody held the square of Sheetrock, bracing it against the floor, while Dylan sawed off a piece big enough to fill the hole. A couple times, he glanced back over his shoulder to assess the right shape, then perfect the cutout.

"How do you know all this stuff?" Cody asked. "Did your dad teach you?"

His dad. Jonathon Millwright had favored Sam, the eldest. Sam was the one who could do no wrong, who got good grades, who married his high school sweet-heart, had a career and a couple of kids. Dylan spent his entire childhood being compared to his brother—and always came up lacking. No one had been on his side. Their mother had supported her critical, controlling husband, no matter what.

"My dad and I didn't exactly get along. He was never real hands-on, especially with me." Dylan shrugged. Better to keep the story short and simple than to explain decades of troubled history. "Uncle Ty taught me some stuff, and I learned the rest along the way."

Cody slipped the piece into the space in the wall, then held it while Dylan screwed it into place. "What do you mean, along the way?"

Should he tell Cody the truth? Would the kid see it as a journey to be emulated or an example of what not to do? "I dropped out when I was your age. Hitched a ride out of here and took whatever jobs I could so I could afford a place to stay warm and something to eat."

"Sounds awesome."

"It was the exact opposite of awesome." Dylan lowered the screw gun. "Some nights I slept on the ground or in a doorway. Many days I didn't have anything to eat because I couldn't catch a ride or find a job. It sucked, a lot."

"Yeah, but it worked out okay for you. Didn't it?"

"I took the long road to get here. If I had been smart and listened to the advice I was given, I might have taken a few less detours." Dylan peeled the lid off the plaster and held out the putty knife to Cody. "Here, you do this."

"I don't know how." Cody scuffed at the floor. The hood of his sweatshirt obscured his face. "My dad didn't show me anything, either. He's never been anything more than a sperm donor."

Dylan could hear the hurt in the kid's voice. Dylan might have had a strained relationship with his father, but at least he'd had one, and he'd had Uncle Ty to pick up the slack. Cody looked like he could use an Uncle Ty of his own, or at least a reasonable facsimile.

Dylan, however, was the only one here. He didn't even begin to think he was role model material, but maybe he could at least teach Cody a couple things and steer him away from the bad decisions Dylan had made at his age.

That was a lot to ask from a piece of Sheetrock and some plaster, but he was going to try.

"Here," Dylan said, placing the putty knife in Cody's palm. "I'll show you."

Cody brushed the hood back, then glanced over at Dylan. "For real?"

"Yeah." Dylan grinned at Cody. "I might not know everything, but I do know how to fix a hole in a wall."

Not a hole in a kid's life. That was a task way outside of Dylan's skill set.

Abby rushed into the community center, breathless and angry. She'd gotten the call from the high school truant officer a little after eleven and spent the better part of her lunch hour trying to find Cody. He wasn't at home, he wasn't at the park. Finally, she thought of the community center. Ty was known to let the kids hang out during the day if they wanted a place to chill, usually calling their parents so they wouldn't worry. She hadn't gotten a call, so she'd worked on the assumption Cody was spending his hooky time elsewhere. But she'd run out of other places to look.

There was a car in front of the building, not Ty's green pickup but a battered red Jeep. She remembered seeing the same car yesterday and realized it must be Dylan's. She parked and hurried into the building.

Then stuttered to a stop.

Dylan and Cody were working together, repairing a broken window screen. Dylan was holding the frame while Cody rolled some tool along the edge, that reinserted the plastic line that held it in place. Dylan was explaining how the tool worked while Cody listened, his eyes bright, his face attentive. They were so engrossed in the task, they didn't hear her enter.

"So, what did you mean earlier about taking the long road?" Cody asked.

Abby started to open her mouth to yell at Cody for

skipping school when she heard Dylan start to speak. She hung by the door, watching and listening.

"I was young and stupid. I thought it didn't matter if I graduated high school or went to college," Dylan said. "You start ditching class when you're young, and it gets easier to ditch the other important things in life. Like a job. Like an interview. Like a date. I became someone who quit. A lot."

Cody snorted. "Is this going to be one of those *kid, you should stay in school* speeches? Because I get enough of that already."

"Nope. I'm not telling you what to do. You probably wouldn't listen any better than I did." Dylan sighed. "I will tell you, though, that I learned my lesson when I was washing dishes until my hands bled from the hot water—or when they were frozen stiff from hauling hundred-pound bags of potatoes off of trucks for hours in the cold. That's when I wished I had stayed in school."

She wouldn't have thought Dylan had a past like that. He was a little rough around the edges, but he seemed responsible, smart, strong. Or maybe it was just his smile that blinded her to everything else.

"I hate school," Cody said. "I just wanna blow that place so bad."

Dylan turned to Cody. "Stick it out. I know it's hard, dude. At the time, it's going to seem like the hardest thing you've ever done. But if you stay with school and graduate, that's success."

"Success? What, graduating at the bottom of the class?" Cody snorted and shook his head. And this was where Abby usually lost the argument. Because his grades were so bad, Cody saw graduating as a lost cause. Instead of trying hard to change that, he gave up.

"You gotta learn to finish what you start." Dylan shifted the screen and stretched the material over the frame. "Dropping out puts you behind the curve before you even get out of the gate. It's a hell of a lot harder to get where you're going if you start five steps behind than if you start in the middle."

Cody didn't say anything, but Abby could see that he was mulling over Dylan's words. They were the same ones Abby had said, over and over again, but this time, Cody actually seemed to be taking them in. Maybe it was because it was advice from a stranger, given in a rougher language than she would have used. Maybe because Dylan had been down Cody's path already and spoke from experience.

Dylan stepped back and assessed their work on the screen. "Looks good. We'll just trim the extra bit of screen along the edge, and it'll be good as new," Dylan held out the tool to Cody. "Here, you want to try? Be careful. The blade is sharp."

Cody took the retractable knife from Dylan, then slid it along the edge of the new rubber spline, trimming the extra sliver of mesh. "Hey, that was pretty easy." Cody leaned back, and looked the window over. "It looks like it was never torn."

"The magic of a good repair job. Let's hang this—" Dylan cut off the sentence when he turned and noticed Abby standing there. "Oh, hey, Abby."

Cody let out a low curse, then turned toward his mother. "Mom, I can explain—"

"And you'd better. You know what the principal said about you skipping." She crossed to her son, taking a moment to be glad he was okay and not drinking or doing drugs or getting into some other kind of trouble. The last couple years with Cody had been rocky at best, which was why she had started bringing him to the community center. She'd hoped he'd find a good outlet for all the angst and anger that came with being sixteen and essentially abandoned by his father. Up until now, Cody hadn't done much more than make a token effort at being involved here. Seeing him working with Dylan had been a revelation…but it didn't stop her frustration.

"Don't you understand that you are one bad move away from being expelled? You only have one job, Cody. Go to school."

The light in Cody's eyes dimmed. "I know. I just got all stressed because Mrs. Deets was on my back again, so I ditched and came here."

"We talked about how you can't just do this, Cody." She ran a hand through her hair and let out a gust. "I'm worried about your future."

Cody cursed under his breath. "I heard the lecture already, Mom. I don't need another one."

She spun toward Dylan. "And why didn't you bring him back?"

"Because I figured he'd be gone again five minutes later. So I thought I'd give him something constructive to do. I let him stay, but he had to promise me he'd go to school every day next week. He's been helping me with the repairs around here. We fixed the small hole in that wall, tightened a leaky faucet in the kitchen, and now we're working on the window screens. He did a great job."

The praise lifted Cody's head. He shot Dylan a look that was a mixture of surprise and joy. Cody had had very few male role models in his life, and none that he had warmed to as quickly as he had warmed to Dylan.

"I even learned how to patch a hole, Mom," Cody said. He gestured toward the wall. "You wouldn't even know Leon put his fist through there."

She could see pride in her son's face. Interest. It was more than she'd seen in months, and the moment caused a little catch in her throat. Her anger evaporated. "That's great, Code. Really great."

"I know you're probably going to drag me back to school," Cody said, his voice low, his gaze on the floor. "But Dylan really needed some help with the windows today. One of them is broken, and Dylan's worried somebody might try to break in."

She opened her mouth to protest and to tell Cody she had, indeed, been here to bring him back to school. But she took one look at his face, at the enthusiasm written all over him and decided one more missed day wasn't going to hurt anything. Maybe a little bit of success would help Cody find his footing again. It was, after all, only one day. "Sure. That sounds like a good thing to do. Why don't I run out and get you guys some lunch? I bet you're starving."

"You mean I can stay?" Surprise lit Cody's voice. He almost sounded like he was Jake's age again, shocked she had let him stay at the playground for an extra half hour. There was no argument in him, none of the sullenness that was usually part of his daily wardrobe. For a split second, he was Cody again, the son she had been missing for a long, long time.

And that was worth one missed day of school.

"Yeah, you can stay." She glanced at Dylan. "As long as that's okay with you."

Dylan nodded and turned to her son. "Totally cool with me. As long as you go to school next week, like we agreed. No skipping."

"Deal," Cody said.

"Great. I'll be back with some subs." She turned away, before Cody saw the tears that were threatening at the back of her eyes. She pushed on the door and stepped out into the North Carolina sunshine.

"Hey, thanks for letting Cody stay."

She spun at the sound of Dylan's voice behind her. She tried to work a smile onto her face, but it wobbled. Her composure was on the brink of disappearing. She fumbled for her sunglasses in her purse and slipped them on. "Thank you for letting him help. He's never really gotten to do any of that stuff before, and he looks like he's enjoying the work."

"He's a good kid." Dylan eased the door shut and stepped out onto the porch with Abby. "I know you've had some problems with him lately, with cutting class and getting in trouble."

"He told you that?"

"Not in so many words. I..." Dylan looked back over his shoulder at the door. "I see a lot of myself in him. I was like that at his age. Mad at the world, ready to run at the slightest hint of a problem."

In a few words, Dylan had summarized all the fears and worries that Abby had been keeping to herself. She shook her head, and the tears she'd been trying to hold back began to spill onto her lashes.

Abby worked so hard to be strong, to handle everything herself. But right now, the stress, the worry, seemed too heavy, too much. Jake wanting a puppy, something normal kids all over the world asked for, had been something she couldn't even entertain. She was barely holding herself together, never mind her kids and her life. When the school had called, it had crushed the very fragile hold on her stress. And now, the relief that Cody was okay, that he was actually doing something constructive—that had her teetering on the edge of a sob. "It's been hard, you know? Being mom and dad at the same time. My friends don't understand, because they've all got partners or grandparents around to pick up the slack, but it's just me, and Cody is at that age where he needs a man who can be a good influence. Ty was a good role model to him, but then Virginia died—Ty started withdrawing and Cody went off the rails again and..."

Dylan took her hand, and her babbling brook of words ceased. His touch was warm and strong, comforting. He gave her a little squeeze. "Hey, it's going to be okay. He's a good kid."

Abby raised her gaze to Dylan's. For just a moment, she needed that reassurance. In a second, she told herself, she'd go back to being strong and independent. "You really think so? I mean, that he'll be okay?"

What was she doing? Asking a perfect stranger to predict her kid's future? Maybe she was hormonal. Or maybe it was simply that Abby was exhausted, drained by the simple task of raising two boys on her own while trying to build a career at the marketing agency and keep everyone fed and clothed—and feeling like she wasn't doing any of the above well.

"I don't have a crystal ball, but I do think he's ready to find a better way to do things," Dylan said. "Maybe spending some time helping out around here will give him a sense of accomplishment. I know I found my way by going into renovation and new construction work. There's just something about seeing a room or a house or even a table take shape under your own two hands that makes you feel like you have control over your world."

She liked how Dylan described his work. And for Cody, she got a sense that that feeling of control and accomplishment was important. Her oldest had struggled so much with having a father who barely cared. The therapist she'd taken him to a few times had said that Cody really needed to find an outlet for his emotions, a way to express himself. Jake did that through his art, but Cody tended to bottle up his feelings. Both times he had been with Dylan, she had seen Cody come out of his shell and quite literally come out from under the security of his hoodie. A wave of reassurance swept over her, because for a moment, she wasn't alone. "Cody needs that. He needs it a lot."

"Then let him hang here with me. Tomorrow's Saturday, and if he wants to come over here bright and early, he can help me fix the broken cabinet in the kitchen and some busted tiles. Ty's got a long list of needs for this place, and I want to do as much as I can to help him while I'm here."

"I noticed that things had gotten out of hand when I was looking around the kitchen. I was thinking maybe I could go to the store and get some supplies for the center this weekend. It seems like Ty is out of everything."

"Virginia did all the ordering for him. He's kinda lost without her. I think everyone is." Dylan released her hand, as if he'd just realized he'd been holding it.

A little flutter of disappointment went through her, but she was determined not to show it. She knew better than to depend on anyone other than herself. Already she was starting to like this guy, to crave more time with him. She could see why Cody liked him so much. Dylan was confident and quiet, yet patient and warm. Not to mention, he cared—about Cody, about his aunt and uncle. That caring nature was something she could get used to—and even considering getting used to counting on someone meant she was treading on dangerous ground. "Uh…what kind of sub do you want?"

"I'm not picky." He grinned. "Surprise me."

"I'd hate to disappoint you."

"You won't, Abby. Believe me." He started into the building, then turned back and put a hand on her arm.

This time, his touch sent a flutter through her veins. She lifted her gaze, surprised at the electricity, the intensity that a simple touch could bring. She had the strangest urge to press her lips to the slight dusting of stubble on his chin, to inhale his cologne.

"I have an idea," Dylan said.

"Oh, yeah?" Her voice shook a little, damn it.

"Why don't I pick you and both the boys up tomorrow morning? That way, I can help you get the supplies for the kitchen, and you all can go with me to the home improvement store. I need to order some things that Ernie doesn't carry, and I'm sure both boys will love being around power tools and forklifts."

For a second there, she'd thought Dylan was going to ask her out on a date. It took a moment for her brain to process what he was saying. That it wasn't a date at all. Disappointment sank in her gut, which was completely insane. She didn't have time or room in her life for another person with testosterone. "Sure. If you don't mind. The boys would love that."

"Great." He grinned. "Then it's a date?"

No, it's not. She worked a smile onto her face. "Of course."

But as Abby climbed into her car and headed away from the community center, she did her best to ignore her disappointment. She ignored it. The last thing she wanted to do was fall for another man with a charming smile and all the right words. Because in the end, the words were empty and the ones who got hurt were the boys she was trying so hard to protect.

She flicked a gaze at the rearview mirror and saw Dylan, talking to Cody by their newly repaired window. Her heart cracked a little, and she whispered a silent prayer that this time she was wrong about that man and his smile.

Chapter Four

Dylan borrowed Ty's extended cab pickup truck early the next morning. The Ford rattled and shook its way down the road, yet another thing on its last legs. Dylan made a mental note to take a look under the hood later this afternoon. He was no mechanic, but he knew his way around basic engine maintenance.

He pulled into Abby's driveway. She lived in a small bungalow on Peach Street, a cul-de-sac filled with kids' bicycles, swing sets and a basketball hoop at the end of the curve. Her house was older, maybe built in the fifties, but it was neat and tidy, with a row of red geraniums along the front. A wooden swing hung from eyehooks on the porch and swung gently in the breeze.

He half expected a white picket fence and a golden retriever to come running out the door. Abby lived in the kind of house he'd expect to see in some sitcom. The kind of home he'd avoided all his life. It smacked of commitment, domesticity and—

Shackles. Expectations.

Jake poked his head up from the porch. He had a gold-colored dog in his arms, as if providing the final key to Dylan's view of the perfect family life. He waved like crazy at Dylan, keeping the puppy balanced in one hand. Abby came out onto the porch, bent down and scolded her youngest son, who trudged next door, dropped the puppy into an outdoor playpen, then headed back, his eyes downcast and his face full of pout.

The front door opened again, and Cody emerged, looking half asleep and angry to be woken up so early on a weekend. At the door, Abby touched Jake's shoulder, and the little boy turned around. Abby bent down and zipped the front of Jake's spring jacket. She placed a hand on her son's chest and gave him a smile. He smiled back, then leaned forward on his toes and wrapped his arms around his mother.

Something in Dylan's heart squeezed. The whole scene—Abby and her sons in the shade of the front porch, a dark-haired trio framed by the pale yellow house—smacked of domesticity. Dylan should have felt more cynical. Jaded.

Instead he felt…

Envy.

Crazy thoughts. He lived his life like a tumbleweed. He wasn't the kind to get wrapped up in geraniums and porch swings. Dylan jerked his attention back to the present, rolled down the passenger-side window and leaned across the cab. "Good morning, everyone. You all set?"

"Yup." Jake beamed, his frown gone. "Mommy says we're gonna see a fork truck."

Dylan chuckled. "A forklift, and yes, we'll see at least one of those today."

Abby gave Jake a nudge. "Boys, why don't you get in the truck so we don't keep Dylan waiting?"

At his mother's reminder, Cody opened the back door for his little brother, installed a booster seat, and then the boys climbed in back. "Hi, Dylan," Jake said, leaning over the seat and halfway into the front. "I can't wait to build stuff today. Can we build a doghouse someday? In case I get a puppy?"

Abby shot him a glance and shook her head.

"Uh, maybe," he said, then directed his attention to the teenager. "Hey, Cody."

Cody gave Dylan a half nod. "Hey."

Well, at least he hadn't turned into a zombie. For a second there, Dylan wasn't sure. And he might not be peppy, but Cody's usual attitude seemed to be at a minimum. All good signs for the day ahead.

Abby climbed into the passenger's seat. She'd dressed in jeans, a worn gray T-shirt and a blue hooded sweatshirt that was unzipped. Her hair was in a ponytail that swung along her neck and her makeup was light. She looked beautiful. Sweet.

Damn. He was turning into a walking poem. Had to be the early morning and lack of caffeine. He'd been running late and he'd headed out of the B&B without his usual cup of joe. Yeah, that was it.

"Good morning," Abby said.

"Good morning." He shot her a grin. "I see you're ready to work."

"I have almost no handyman skills, but I do have a good attitude."

"That's half the battle. The rest can be taught." He glanced in the rearview mirror at Cody. The teenager was sitting with his arms crossed over his chest, a scowl on his face. Apparently the good attitude hadn't taken root in all members of the Cooper family.

"Hey, Jake, Cody, buckle up. Okay?"

Cody rolled his eyes but did as he was told. Jake sat back in the seat, dragged his seatbelt across his lap, clicked it into place, then crossed his arms in his lap, his face eager.

A big-box grocery store and a home improvement store were located just outside of Stone Gap, about twenty minutes away. Jake started chattering before the truck even left the driveway. "What are we gonna build, Dylan? Do I get to use a hammer?"

He chuckled. "Maybe. First we have to pick up the supplies. Then we'll decide what we want to fix first."

"I don't know how to hammer stuff," Jake said.

"That's okay. I'll teach you." Dylan glanced over at Abby. She had a slight smile on her face, and when she caught him looking, she averted her gaze. "I can teach your mom, too."

She laughed. "I might be a hopeless case. Give me a marketing presentation to write, and I'm in my element. But fixing a leaky toilet or hanging a picture…

Let's just say I've used a lot of superglue and duct tape to repair stuff in my house."

"Hey, those are valid home-repair tools." He shot her a grin. "Seriously, though, if you need help with something at your house, I'd be glad to step in. Fixing houses is pretty much how I make a living."

"I'll keep that in mind."

He wondered if she was being polite or if she really meant that. And why he cared when he wasn't planning on staying in Stone Gap. He reminded himself that Abby was one of those women who settled down, planted geraniums. And he was the kind of guy who moved on before the geraniums bloomed.

Jake kept up his chatter, asking about hammers and nails and doors and pretty much anything he could think to ask about. The conversation went in loopy circles, detouring from hammers to dogs then back again to nails. Dylan glanced at Abby, who clearly was used to Jake's roundabout style.

"Is this pretty much how it always is with a kid?" he asked her, keeping his voice low.

She chuckled. "Yup. Jake's mind moves a million miles a minute, and he's one of the most creative kids I've ever met. You'll get used to it."

Dylan wanted to contradict her, but figured if he announced he wasn't staying long, he'd spoil the light mood in the truck and also indicate that he cared more than he did. Abby was a friend, and her kids were just... help for the day. Albeit, chatty, inexperienced help.

Once they parked at the home improvement store, Jake and Cody got out of the truck and followed along behind Dylan and Abby. Dylan grabbed a bright orange cart, then headed down the aisles. Jake kept on talking as Dylan shopped, picking up Sheetrock, some plywood, a box of replacement tiles for the bathrooms and a stack of other supplies. "Well, I think we've about emptied the store," Dylan said. "Let me just drop off this order for the countertop at the front desk and we can check out."

Cody hadn't said two words the entire time. He'd barely shown any interest in anything Dylan bought, eyes glued to his phone. Abby tried to engage her teenage son several times but didn't receive much more than grunts in return.

"Cody, why don't you help me load the truck while your mom and Jake grab us some hot dogs?" Dylan turned to Abby and handed her some money. "If you don't mind. There's a vendor right outside the store."

"Not at all." She took Jake's hand. "Come on, Jakester, let's get some hot dogs."

"I love hot dogs!" Jake looked up at his older brother. "Do you love them, Cody?"

Cody shrugged. "They're okay."

"I'll get you one. Okay?" Jake gave his brother a wide grin, which Cody half returned, then Jake headed outside with his mother.

Dylan placed his order, paid for his purchase and walked to the truck with Cody. "I know you probably don't want to be here—"

"Are you really going to do it?" Cody spun toward him.

"Do what?"

"Teach Jake how to fix stuff? You're not going to just ditch him at home or something, are you?"

"No, of course not. Why would I…?" Dylan's voice trailed off as he put the pieces together. The absentee father, the boys who had been raised by a single mom. The stoic, seemingly emotionless teenage boy, making sure his little brother wasn't disappointed again. Dylan saw so much of Sam and himself in these two boys—or at least him and his brother when they were younger and got along. He could see the flicker of hope in Cody's face, gone almost as fast as it appeared.

"I meant what I said, Cody." He met the teenager's gaze and held it. "I'm going to teach both of you how to fix things. And your mom, if she wants to learn, too."

Cody considered that, then slid the plywood into the bed of the truck. "Okay. Good."

They put the rest of the supplies in the truck, finishing up just as Jake and Abby returned with the hot dogs. She glanced at her oldest son, then at Dylan. Cody hadn't said much, but his mood had considerably brightened and Dylan could see the relief in Abby's face.

"Hey, thanks for grabbing lunch," Dylan said.

"You're welcome. Though your arteries might argue with the menu choice." She handed him one of the hot dogs. "Isn't stopping me from having one, though. I swear, it's been years since I ate a hot dog. I'm not big on junk food, as my boys will attest."

He shifted closer to her. "Life is short, Abby. You should have some really good junk food once in a while. It makes you appreciate the healthy stuff later."

She laughed. "I don't know if I agree with that logic. But I'll give it a try."

Cody took his lunch and climbed into the truck cab. Jake clambered up beside his big brother and started talking a mile a minute about the hot dog vendor, the bird he saw in the parking lot, the dollop of mustard on his shirt.

Abby watched her sons with a bittersweet look in her eyes. "Those two boys are like night and day. I swear, Jake was born happy and talkative. Cody was always my quiet one. The good kid when he was a baby—a good sleeper, good eater. Jake had enough energy for ten kids—always squirming, never wanted to sleep. Now Cody's become…" She sighed. "Maybe it's just teenage stuff."

Dylan gave the cart a shove and sent it sailing into the corral. It nestled with the others with a soft clank. "They're both good kids, Abby."

"Thanks." A shy smile filled her face, and he could tell, this was the place where she was most easily touched. When it came to her kids, Abby allowed that wall to wobble ever so slightly. He liked that.

He wasn't going to slip into their lives and become Ward Cleaver, but he could enjoy a Saturday morning in her company and make it fun for her kids. Dylan took her trash and tossed it in a nearby can. "Let's get back to the center. I can drop you off at home on the way, if you want, then bring the boys home when we're done working. You don't have to help."

"I want to. The center is important to me, too." Abby climbed into her side of the truck and waited while

Dylan got in the driver's seat. "I've been trying to get Ty a grant so he can do some big improvements, maybe even expand. But grant writing isn't my specialty, so I haven't been successful yet."

He glanced over at her. Abby was the first person outside his aunt and uncle who seemed to care as deeply about the center as he did. It was an encouraging sign. A team effort, after all, worked far better than a solitary one. For the first time since he arrived, Dylan had a flicker of hope that maybe the center could be saved after all. "That's great. I didn't even know there was such a thing."

Abby shrugged. "It's only great if it works out."

Dylan pulled into the parking lot of the grocery store. Abby was an efficient shopper and they were in and out of the first stop in less than thirty minutes. The boys helped load everything, then hopped back in for the short ride to the center. In the back seat, Cody had his head back, asleep, while Jake was working a handheld game. Quiet, for now. "I'm sure you'll get that grant," Dylan said. "Either way, everything you're doing today is going to be appreciated. Ty can use all the help he can get, especially when it comes to getting that place back in shape."

"Even if it's from people who can barely hold a hammer?"

He shot her a grin. "By the end of the day, you'll be an expert and the boys will be ready to open their own renovation business."

"I'm counting on that, Dylan." She turned her attention to the window, her gaze on the passing houses.

She didn't share any of the troubles on her mind, not that he expected her to. Abby was clearly a woman used to shouldering her burdens alone, and given what little he'd heard about the boys' father, Dylan suspected she'd been doing so for a long time.

Abby glanced over at her sons from time to time, as if making sure they were still there. She checked her phone but otherwise kept to herself. A few minutes later, they pulled into the parking lot for the center.

On Saturdays, the center didn't open until three, a big departure from the early morning opening time that Dylan remembered. The hand-lettered sign announcing the new weekend times was undoubtedly put there by Ty, to minimize his hours at the center. In the old days, Ty and Virginia had planned game days and movie nights for Saturdays, but the schedule on the door was blank. Dylan wondered how long it had been since the center had been running at full speed. That river of guilt flowed over him again. If he had been here…

But he hadn't been, and there was nothing he could do to change that fact. Nothing except make the present better.

When Dylan parked, Cody jerked awake. "We're here, guys. Let's get the truck unloaded and get to work. We only have a few hours before the kids arrive."

Cody slipped out of the truck without a word, and stood by the tailgate, perfecting his teenage attitude. Jake bounced up and down beside Dylan. "What are we gonna work on first? Are we gonna build something? Should I wear a tool belt? I don't have one, but I can make one." He tugged on the belt loops of his jeans.

Dylan chuckled. "You're good, Jake. And the first thing we're going to work on is repairing the broken cabinets in the kitchen so that we can load in all the food and stuff we bought this morning."

"Cool!" Jake grabbed a bag of supplies and hurried over to the shelter door. He kept on bouncing, impatient for Dylan to grab a load and unlock the door. As soon as the door was open, Jake beelined for the kitchen.

"I wish everyone who worked with me was that eager," Dylan said to Abby.

"Heck, I wish he was that eager about cleaning his room." She shed her jacket once inside the building, then motioned to Cody. "Come on, Code. Let's get started."

Cody muttered under his breath about it being too early, but came inside and dropped his coat on one of the sofas. He followed Dylan into the kitchen, where Abby was already waiting with Jake.

Dylan laughed. "Okay, it's only one cabinet, so I don't need that much help. So why don't I get you and Cody working on removing the broken tiles in the bathroom? It's pretty easy and foolproof because the tiles are already broken and the grout is old and dried out."

"A job I can't screw up?" Abby grinned. "Put me to work, sir."

The *sir* had his mind derailing down a whole other path. Dylan yanked himself back to the present, and to the toolbox. He found a couple hammers, chisels and a putty knife and handed them to Abby and Cody. "Jake, can you find me four of these screws—" he held up a wood screw, then handed Jake a small plastic tub "—while I show your mom and Cody what to do?"

"Sure!" Jake scrambled onto one of the stools and started sorting through the container.

Dylan, Abby and Cody headed for the single restroom. Down the road, Dylan would love to add another bathroom, just to help handle the amount of traffic. When Ty and Virginia opened this place, they converted an old house, which meant it also had old plumbing, old wiring and an old layout.

Then he remembered that down the road, he'd be moving on. Which meant someone else would worry about the additional bathroom, the major changes the center would still need, even after he repaired and updated what he could in the space of a couple of weeks.

"Okay, how do we do this?"

He glanced at Abby and Cody, the two of them waiting in the small room for him to get his act together. He took a set of tools from her and knelt on the floor. "We only want to remove the broken tiles. First, you have to scrape out the grout." He showed them how to do that with the edge of the chisel. "Be careful not to chip the nearby tiles. Then, use the hammer and chisel to break it up and remove it."

"Looks easy enough." Abby put her hands out for the tools.

"Not yet. You both need these." He reached into his pocket and took out two pairs of safety glasses.

"No way, man," Cody said, warding them off. "I'm not wearing those dork goggles."

"You will if you don't want tile chips in your eyes. Trust me, that's no fun." Dylan handed Abby a pair. She slipped them on, and he thought no one in the world had ever looked as cute with safety glasses on as she did. For a second, he imagined being alone in the close quarters of the bathroom with her. Then he glanced at her and remembered that Abby came with an entire package that he had no business being around.

"Well, uh, you guys let me know if you run into any problems. I'll be in the kitchen."

Then he headed back to the cabinets before he lingered too long with a woman who made him think about everything but the reason he was really here.

Abby knelt beside Cody and started working on the first tile while her son worked on one a few feet away. "I think we can handle this. What do you think, Cody?"

Cody grunted.

Abby sighed and sat back on her heels. "Cody, will you talk to me?"

"I am."

"A grunt and two words is not talking to me. How's school, how are your friends, how's—"

"School sucks. My friends are cool and I don't want to talk about anything else." He bent down and started chiseling away at the grout.

"Be careful, remember what Dylan said—"

"I'm not a baby, Mom. Quit telling me what to do."

Abby sighed again. When had everything shifted between her and Cody? When had the boy who had rushed into her arms at the end of the school day turned into this distant almost-man?

A part of her was envious that Dylan had gotten through to her eldest. What secret was she missing?

They worked together for the next half hour. Abby tried, over and over, to get Cody to talk, but he'd gone back to grunts and single-word answers. The chisels made more noise in the bathroom than her son did.

"I've finished my section." Abby got to her feet and wiped the dust off her jeans. "I'm just going to check on your brother. Or do you want me to help…?"

"I've got it, Mom." Cody kept his back to her and went on working.

Abby headed toward the kitchen, her mind still heavy with worry about her eldest son. Every day, he seemed to grow more and more detached. Did he blame her for his father's absence? For the long hours she worked to make ends meet? Or was it all normal teenage attitude?

As she neared the kitchen, she could hear Jake talking to Dylan. Her youngest was, as always, excited and chipper, going a mile a minute, telling him all about the puppies next door and how he'd named them and thought the littlest one was the cutest and the loneliest. Dylan was indulgent and patient with Jake, which made Abby like him even more. He had a way of relating to her kids that was nice. Reassuring.

Easy to get attached to.

That sent the red warning flag up in her head. Something she had better pay attention to, regardless of how a few conversations went.

"Can we fix more stuff, Dylan?" Jake was saying. "Can we fix my window? Cuz Mommy says it's broken and when it's hot, I wanna open my window. And if I get a puppy, he'll get hot, too."

Dylan chuckled. "I can fix that later. But right now,

let's fix the stuff we have here. Now, do you want to help me replace the wall outside the office?"

"A whole wall? Sure!"

Dylan emerged from the kitchen and drew up short when he saw Abby. "Hey."

"Hey." She stood there like an idiot for a long second, then remembered why she had sought him out. "We finished taking out the broken tiles."

"Great. I'll lay the new ones when the center closes for the night. They need time to set before people start walking on them."

"Did you finish the cabinet repair?"

"Yup. Me and my trusty helper. Then we put the groceries away. They might not be exactly where Ty expects them to be but—"

"I'm sure it's all fine. Thank you, Dylan. It was really sweet." She shifted closer to him, intrigued, attracted, despite her common sense. This man, who connected with her kids, did thoughtful things to help her out... Every time she saw him, all she did was crave more of all that.

He shrugged, but his gaze locked on hers, held. A heartbeat filled the space between them. Another. "No problem."

Jake sauntered out of the kitchen then, a kid-size hammer tucked in his jeans pocket. "I was a big help, Mommy. Dylan said so."

"That's right. And now he's going to help me fix a wall." Dylan looked at Abby. "You want in on that fun, too?"

"Sure." She flexed a biceps. "I'll add it to my list of skills."

"Stick with me and you'll have a killer handywoman résumé in no time." Dylan grinned, then headed out to the truck.

Stick with me. Why did those words impact her? Why did her gaze linger on him, and more, her thoughts? She'd found herself smiling a hundred times more today than she had in weeks. She told herself it was because she was spending time with her boys. Nothing more.

When Dylan returned with two panels of Sheetrock, with a thrilled Jake rushing to hold the door and start up his endless stream of questions again, Abby found that smile returning. Even though she had a stack of work waiting for her at home, she felt light, happy. Unstressed.

Dylan laid the Sheetrock against the wall, then popped his head in the bathroom. "Cody, wanna help do some demo work?"

"Does that mean I get to destroy something?" Cody said.

"Yup. Bring your hammer."

"Cool." Cody ambled into the room, his hammer tucked in his pocket, just like Jake. His little brother ran up beside him, mimicking Cody's stance. Cody leaned over and ruffled Jake's hair.

Well, heck, if that's what it took to get her teenager to come out from under that perpetual dark storm cloud, maybe she should have Dylan come over and figure out something they could demo in her house. Of course, that would probably mean Dylan would get sweaty and have to take off his shirt—

Not productive. Not one bit.

Dylan positioned the three of them along the long wall in the hallway. Water damage from a leak in the roof last spring had crumbled part of the wall, left the rest a rusty tan color. "All right, Cody, you start here. Jake, you start over here, and Abby, you start here."

"Wait, me?" she said when she realized Dylan had moved her to a place at the end.

Dylan shifted closer to her. His smile drew her in, like the proverbial moth to the flame. He had an easy smile that fit him well, like a comfortable pair of jeans. "You have a little stress you want to work off?"

"Uh…yeah." Except it wasn't stress burning in her right now. It was the curiosity about kissing him. Wondering what it would be like to be in his arms.

This man was all wrong for her—a charmer, a wanderer. A man who didn't seem to want or need any ties.

Yet that didn't stop her from wanting more. From fantasizing about him. From wanting him. And from "accidentally" bumping into him a couple times today. All of which left her discombobulated and flustered.

"Yeah, uh, I have some stress," she said. "Where do I hit?"

Dylan pulled a marker out of his back pocket and drew three X's on the wall. "Right there. After you punch a hole in the wall, start tearing out the old Sheetrock. Trust me, this is going to be better than therapy."

"What about the electricity?" She pointed at the wall

socket. "The mom in me doesn't want to make any emergency room trips today."

"I turned off the power already, and I'm handling the section with the wiring, as a double precaution. You guys should be just fine." He waved toward the wall. "So...have at it."

Jake hit the wall first, making a hammer-size dent. Cody followed, sending his hammer through with a crash. A chunk of wall tumbled onto the floor. Dylan and Cody turned to look at her.

"Have at it, Abby," Dylan said. "Let her rip."

Abby gripped her hammer with two hands, took a deep breath, then swung it at the X. She hit a little wide of the target, but hard enough to punch a hole in the wall. Sheetrock cracked, then dropped to her feet. "Wow. I did it."

"You did." Dylan's eyes held a measure of pride and wonder. "Now let's rip the rest of the wall down."

They went at the damaged Sheetrock like a pack of wolves, hitting, tearing and yanking, then tossing the debris on the floor. Most of it yielded easily, softened by the water leak. Abby latched on to an edge, pulled, then leaned back and pulled some more. The wall tore in one giant, satisfying piece.

A few minutes later, the four of them stepped back and assessed their work. All that remained was a few wires from the electrical outlet and the studs.

Abby had had no idea how awesome it would feel to tear something apart. The whole experience was... liberating. Powerful. Unleashed. Wild. All the things she had avoided in her life for so long.

"Well, that was great," Abby said. "More therapeutic than I expected."

"Can I say I told you so?" Dylan said.

She laughed. "I think I deserve that. Okay, what do we get to demo next?"

"Hold on there, Bob Vila. Let's clean this up, hang the new wall, then move on to another project."

"That was so cool, Dylan!" Jake said. "I hit it with my hammer. Lots of times!"

"You did great, Jake," Dylan said, then turned to her oldest. "You, too, Cody. You're a natural at this."

"Thanks." Cody toed at the floor. "Can I, uh, help you hang up the new wall?"

Abby glanced at Dylan. Cody had been an unwilling participant today until just now. She half expected Dylan to do what her ex always did, tell the kids no, and do the job himself. Her ex-husband had been around so little that the boys were perpetually hopeful whenever he was home that he'd let them spend time with him—help out while he did stuff around the house. He'd always said it was easier, faster to do the work himself. And the boys would be left watching from the outside while their dad hung a picture or changed the brake pads in his car.

"Sure, Cody. Let's just get the old stuff cleaned up and then I'll show both you and your brother how to hang the new wall." Dylan swung a trash can into place. "The least fun part of demo—cleaning up."

Cody nodded, then grabbed a big dustpan and scooped up the chunks, dumping them into the trash without complaint. Jake did his best, but his littler hands didn't do the job of his older brother. When they were done, Cody took the initiative to grab the first piece of Sheetrock.

Dylan nodded toward the wall. "Go ahead, put it up. Then the three of us will nail it into place." He dropped some nails into Abby's palm.

They worked together as a team. Cody held the wall while Abby hammered on one end and Dylan and Jake did the other end. Dylan would drive a couple nails, then hold one for Jake and let him take a swing at it. Even when Jake hit Dylan's thumb a few times, Dylan went on letting Jake try. It was sweet, and for a moment, Abby found herself wondering what their childhoods would have been like if Dylan had been around the boys in those days without a father.

Then she drew herself up and faced reality—she already knew what happened with men like him. Men who had no real ties or commitments. They might be good for a while, but eventually, they left. And they let her down. More than that, they let her sons down.

And that was the one price Abby wasn't willing to pay, no matter how much she liked Dylan's smile.

With his motley crew, Dylan managed to make his way through a lot of the repairs before three. For sure, the wall demo had been the most popular activity of the day. The boys had been cooperative—Jake clearly eager to learn; Cody unable to pretend he didn't care. Even Abby had been enthusiastic and, in the process, picked up a few skills.

Abby.

Every time he'd looked at her, he lost his concentration. She had this way of knitting her brows when she was struggling to understand something. He thought it was…

Cute.

Okay, so he really was becoming a softie. It had to be being back in this town. Being around all these kids. Even now, several hours after he'd brought Abby and her boys back home, and he'd returned to run the center for the rest of the day, he found his mind straying to her. Wondering what she was doing.

At six, he said goodbye to the last of the teens as they left, shut the doors and turned off most of the lights. He spent an hour laying the new tile in the bathroom, then picked up his phone. No texts from Abby. No contact at all.

He didn't know why he was disappointed. After all, they weren't dating, weren't even really friends. She was a woman he'd met a couple days ago who'd helped him tear down a wall. Nothing more. And either way, he wasn't the kind of man who settled down with a dog—as soon as Jake wore Abby down—and kids. He wasn't even remotely cut out for that. He needed to remind himself of that.

He locked the building and headed out to the parking lot. And saw his older brother, Sam, waiting for him.

Sam hadn't aged much in the years they'd been apart. His hair was a little shorter, his frame a little heavier, and the scowl Dylan had come to know well still sat on Sam's face.

"When were you going to tell me you were in town?" Sam asked.

Dylan rolled his eyes. Why was he surprised Sam had started with criticism? "Hello to you, too."

"I would have said hello if I didn't have to find out from Sadie at the grocery store, who found out from Mavis Beacham, that my long-lost brother has returned to Stone Gap. And is staying at the Stone Gap Inn, but apparently forgot to call and let his older brother know."

As usual, Sam had attacked first, assuming the worst. When had their relationship turned into this adversarial clash of swords? It seemed like one day they'd been normal brothers, the next, antagonists from different planets.

"I didn't call you because I'm pretty sure the last words you said to me were *don't bother calling me, I won't pick up.* Forgive me if I didn't want to rush into a confrontation with you." Dylan shook his head. Every time he and Sam got together, it was an argument.

Sam let out a gust. "It's the same old thing with you, isn't it? Blame everyone but yourself."

Dylan threw up his hands. "I don't have time for this conversation."

Sam looked away. He stood there for a long moment, as if mulling his next words. His gaze swung back to Dylan. "What are you doing here anyway?"

Dylan debated not answering. He thought about just getting in his Jeep and leaving. His relationship with Sam had been rocky for years, and that wasn't going to change anytime soon. Sam still saw him as the family screwup, while Sam was the one who did it all right. Settled down, got married, had kids. Even after his wife died, Sam had stayed here, juggling kids and work and now, a new fiancée. The storybook life—the same one Dylan had stayed away from. Because he'd learned years ago that family could let you down. Family could hurt you. And family could turn away when you needed them most.

His older brother was the one who was supposed to support and protect him. Be there, no matter what. But Sam's love had limits, it turned out. The last time Dylan had gotten in trouble and Sam had gone to the Stone Gap Police Department to pick him up, Sam had been by his brother's side. But when it was all over, Sam stood in the driveway and shook his head in disgust. "I give up. Nothing gets through to you," Sam had said. The words had hurt then, and still did.

Yet, there was a part of Dylan that remembered the older brother who had given his little brother a hoisting hand up into their tree house. The older brother who had skipped math to sneak out to the playground and confront a bully preying on Dylan at recess. The same older brother shielded him from their father's anger, who had tucked Dylan in on the nights when the house reverberated with shouting and anger. Was any of that still there, in Sam? Or was it a lost cause? Was Dylan an idiot for hoping again?

"I'm working at the center," Dylan said. Maybe if he told Sam about that, his brother would offer to pitch in. The two of them, working together, like when they were young. "Helping Uncle Ty out. He's not up to running it since he lost Aunt Virginia."

Sam arched a brow. "Ty put *you* in charge?"

"Yeah." Dylan bristled. "Why wouldn't he?"

"Because you're not going to be here in five minutes, Dylan. I know you, and I know you have all the sticking power of wet tape."

Dylan let out a gust. Why had he let himself get sentimental? "Same old Sam. Telling me all the ways I screw up my life. Thanks for the reminder, big brother, that I'm not as perfect as you."

"I'm not saying that." Sam took a step closer. "I just don't want to see Uncle Ty left in a bind when you leave."

The implication was clear—that Dylan would let the family down again. He'd had a long day and didn't need to deal with this. Not now, not ever. Sam had been here to deliver a lecture, not a reunion.

Dylan thumbed the remote for his Jeep and unlocked the doors. "Thanks for the vote of confidence. See you around, Sam."

Then he climbed in the truck and left, before he said something he'd regret. In the rearview mirror, he saw Sam, still standing in the parking lot and watching him leave. For a second, Dylan debated turning around. Then he caught a green light and the urge disappeared.

Chapter Five

Dusk had fallen over Stone Gap, broken by porch lights flicking on and streetlights that dropped yellow pools on the road. Dylan stopped at the intersection in the center of downtown. Left took him back to the Stone Gap Inn. Right took him to Abby's house. After the conversation with Sam, a part of Dylan just wanted to go to a bar and forget it all with a few beers. But all that would give him was a headache and a few more regrets. He hesitated and then turned right.

He made one stop before he got there and pulled into Abby's driveway a little before eight. The lights were still on, and he could hear the sound of a radio. He climbed the porch steps and through the large front windows, he saw Abby.

Dancing. With Jake.

She swung back and forth, laughing, while Jake kept time with his mother, the two of them holding hands and stepping together. The radio was playing an old seventies song, one of those catchy one-hit wonders that struck a familiar chord.

What hit him hardest, though, was how…homey the whole scene was. How warm. Just a mom and her son, dancing in the living room on a Saturday night. It was a world so foreign to him, something he didn't think really existed. If he'd been a different man, maybe he would have dreamed of such a scene. But he wasn't, and he shouldn't.

He almost hated to ring the doorbell. Came close to turning around and leaving, because he didn't want to intrude on Abby and her sons. Then he remembered the stop he'd made and figured he had a good enough reason for being here.

Dylan pressed the doorbell. Abby flicked off the music and peeked through the window, her face narrow with suspicion. By the time she opened the door to him, the suspicion had been replaced by a smile. "Dylan. What are you doing here?"

It was the second time he'd been asked that question in the space of twenty minutes. But coming from Abby, the words sounded sweet, genuine. "I, uh, wanted to thank you guys for your hard work today. So I brought ice cream." He held up the bag in his hand.

"Ice cream!" Jake raced to the door and poked his head outside. "What kind? I love ice cream! I love chocolate the best. Or maybe cookie dough. I love that one, too."

Abby blushed and put a calming hand on Jake's shoulder. "Sorry. You just happen to have brought over Jake's favorite dessert."

Was it also her favorite dessert? He wanted to ask but figured that would show interest, and Dylan wasn't interested in Abby.

Uh-huh. That's why he was on her doorstep with three melting quarts of ice cream instead of back at the bed-and-breakfast, getting a good night's sleep after a very long day.

"I did get cookie dough, Jake," Dylan said. "And chocolate. And vanilla. Just in case."

Abby smiled. "Something to make everyone happy."

"As long as I grabbed your favorite, that is." Then he caught himself and added, "and, uh, Cody's."

"Cody is out with his friends. And I'm a chocolate kind of girl." She hesitated a second, then opened the door wider. "Come on in, Dylan."

Abby's house was just as welcoming as he'd expected it to be. Wide wood floors, pale cream walls, and a dark brown leather couch that looked as soft as a marshmallow. Framed photos of her boys filled the walls of the hallway, and dominated the fireplace mantel. A pile of clean, folded shirts sat on the second step, with a basket of toys on the first. The house was organized but comfortable.

He felt both at home and out of place, following her down the hall to the sunny yellow kitchen with a bright spray of flowers in the center of the round maple table. Before they reached the kitchen, Abby's doorbell rang again. Jake spun on his heel and barreled for the door.

"I get the door, Jake, not you." Abby put a hand on his shoulder, then opened the door. "Besides, buddy, it's past your bedtime."

An elderly woman stood on the other side, holding the same puppy Dylan had seen before. "I thought I'd bring this little guy by for Jake to play with."

"Mrs. Reynolds, it's late and Jake has to get to bed. Besides, we can't get a dog. I work so many hours—"

"I know, dear." The older woman had a kind face behind cat's-eye glasses. She put a hand on Abby's and gave her a soft smile. "But Jake loves these dogs so much, and if he can play with them a little, it wears the little guys out and gives Jake his puppy fix."

"Can I, Mommy? Can I? Please?" Jake bounced up and down, all but lunging for the dog.

"Okay, but only for a few minutes. Bedtime, re-member?" Jake leaned forward, took the dog from Mrs. Reynolds, then spun around. "And keep him in the kitchen. I don't want any accidents on the carpet."

"I'll be back in a little bit," Mrs. Reynolds said.

"Thanks." Abby shut the door, then let out a long sigh. "How can I keep telling him no? He's going to get attached."

"That might not be such a bad thing," Dylan said. "Dogs teach kids responsibility."

"He's four years old, so let's not pretend most of the responsibility would fall on him. I have my hands full, Mr. Single and Unattached to So Much as a Pot-ted Plant. The last thing I need is another mouth to feed and clean up after." Abby shook her head. "You wouldn't understand."

She was right about him. He had no attachments. But as he watched Jake love on that puppy with tight hugs and hundreds of kisses, he wondered if that was such a good thing. Jake talked to the dog nonstop for a solid five minutes, clearly attached despite Abby's wishes, before Abby said it was time to bring Dudley—the dog's name, according to Jake—home. "He needs to go to bed early," Abby said. "And then you can come back and have ice cream."

"Okay." Jake frowned. He plodded behind his mother, and the two of them returned the dog while Dylan waited in the kitchen. By the time they returned, Abby must have said something because Jake was back to his usual bouncy self. He spied the tubs of ice cream melting on the counter and reached for one of the containers. "I want a lot of ice cream," Jake said. "Please, Mommy?"

She grabbed three bowls out of the cabinet and set them on the counter. "First, wash your hands."

Jake rose on his tiptoes and rubbed his hands under the water from the kitchen faucet. Abby dished up the ice cream, chocolate in one bowl, cookie dough in another. She hesitated over the third bowl. "Which is your favorite, Dylan?"

"Oh, I…" He looked at the sunflower-printed dish towel hanging off the stove. The refrigerator peppered with Jake's drawings and candid photos of the boys. The carved wooden sign above the window that read simply Family. "I wasn't planning on staying. I just wanted to drop that off as a thank-you."

"You're not staying?" Jake pouted. "But I wanted to show you my dinosaurs."

Dylan arched a brow. "Dinosaurs?"

"Jake's favorite thing in the whole world, besides a P-U-P-P-Y, is dinosaurs." Abby ignored his answer about not staying and put a bowl of half chocolate and half vanilla in front of him. "I'll warn you, though, once you get him started talking about them, it's hard to get him to stop."

Dinosaurs.

Dylan saw another kitchen in his mind, heard another boy's voice. The memory slid through him, crystal clear and just as biting all these years later. His father, coming home after a long day at the office. He could still see Dad setting his briefcase in its customary place by the front door with one hand while he loosened his tie with the other. Dylan had been four or five, still caught in that world where he believed his father would one day just come home and be a dad like the ones on TV. With piggyback rides and baseball lessons and campfire stories. *Dad, look at my dinosaur! Mom bought it for me today. Because I was good in the store. It's a T. rex and he's mean! Rrrr!*

His dad had given the toy a half a glance, then told Dylan to go outside to play. *I need a moment to breathe when I get home, not a kid and a bunch of toys all over me. Where's Sam? I want to see his book report.*

Maybe that was when Dylan had started to pull away. When he'd stopped believing in happy homes and loving parents. When he'd realized that, beside his brother, there wasn't going to be a male role model there to make a big deal about his new dinosaur or teach him how to pop a fly ball or tell him a ghost story on a camping trip.

As Dylan ate his ice cream, he looked over at Jake, who was sitting at the bar, a ring of ice cream around his mouth, his eyes wide and waiting. And hopeful.

How could Dylan let him down? The kid had just had to give back a puppy, for Pete's sake. Dylan couldn't say no to this request. Even if Dylan was far from father material, he could at least do this.

"Sure, I'd love to see your dinosaurs. They're my favorite, too," Dylan said. "I used to have some when I was your age."

Jake's eyes widened. "You did? Did you have a bron-o-saurus?"

"I did. My favorite was Tyrannosaurus rex. Do you have one of those?"

"I do! Lemme go get him!" Jake scrambled off the chair, the last of his ice cream forgotten. He barreled out of the room, then ran back in five seconds later, his arms stuffed with plastic dinosaurs of all shapes, sizes and colors. He stopped in the center of the kitchen and let the pile tumble to the floor. "Look at all my dinosaurs, Dylan."

Dylan gave Abby a grin. "You weren't kidding about the collection."

"Makes birthday gifts pretty easy." She nodded toward her son. "Jake, why don't you show Dylan your triceratops?"

Jake dug through the pile of plastic toys until he found the three-horned dinosaur. "I named him Joe."

Dylan chuckled. "Joe's a great name."

"And this one is Mack and this one is…" Jake went through every single dinosaur—maybe three dozen in all—and told Dylan their names and explained what he knew about what they ate. Kid clearly knew his dinosaurs. Maybe better than Dylan had at that age. Jake then started going on about movies with dinosaurs— apparently there was one with many sequels—and scientists who studied dinosaurs, and books that had dinosaurs in them, until his mother put a hand on his shoulder.

"Jakester, why don't you take the dinosaurs back up to your room and get ready for bed? I'm going to talk to Dylan for a minute, then I'll come tuck you in."

Jake pouted, but did as he was told and gathered up his toys. "Do I have to brush my teeth?"

Abby smiled. "Always."

Jake trudged out of the room and up the stairs. A second later, they heard the clatter of the dinosaurs hitting the floor, followed by the sound of running water.

"Thank you for indulging him." Abby said. "I'm sorry he ran on so much."

Dylan waved that off. "I was just like him when I was young. My dad didn't really care all that much, and I always wanted him to. Uncle Ty was the one who would listen to my stories about dinosaurs or ask me to draw a picture and hang it in his office."

"Your uncle is such a great guy. Everyone needs an Uncle Ty."

He nodded. "They do indeed." As far as he could tell, Abby's boys didn't have a close male relative. And given how depressed Ty had been lately, he probably wasn't being much of a surrogate relative to Abby's kids, either. If listening to Jake talk about dinosaurs for a little while could help with that, Dylan would do it.

"Also, thank you for the ice cream," Abby said. She was leaning against the counter, her empty bowl beside her hand. "It was a nice thing to do."

He shrugged. "It was no big deal. I wanted to thank you all for helping me so much." And have a chance to see her again, though he didn't say that out loud. Because that would mean admitting he was interested in her, that he was thinking about her—and wishing he wasn't leaving at the end of his two weeks.

Abby had changed into a fresh pair of jeans and a soft coral sweater with an enticing V-neck. Her feet were bare, bright red toenails a contrast to the light tile.

There was something both innocent and sexy about her standing there barefooted. That drew him to her, like a chain coiling into a winch. He got to his feet, grabbed his empty bowl, then closed the distance between them. Abby raised her gaze to Dylan's, her eyes wide. Her lips parted and her cheeks flushed, but she didn't move.

The heat from her body merged with his. Her perfume floated in the space between them, something darkly floral. It enticed him, drew him even closer. He leaned over her shoulder and reached behind her to ostensibly put down the bowl. "I should put this in the sink."

She stayed where she was, her chest rising and falling with each breath. "Thanks." The word escaped in a whisper.

As he drew back, Dylan paused and pressed a kiss to the valley of her neck. Damn, she tasted good. Better than the ice cream. Better, in fact, than anything he could remember tasting in a long, long time. He kissed farther up her neck, her skin soft and sweet and warm. Another kiss, a fourth, inching his way along that delicate curve, then the underside of her jaw.

Abby let out a little mew, then drew in a sharp breath and leaned toward him. Dylan planted his hands on either side of her, then kissed her jaw, the soft fullness of her cheek, then drifted closer to her mouth. Her breathing hastened but she stood stock-still, waiting, anticipating.

When his lips finally met hers, Abby opened to him. Her arms slid around and up his back. Dylan planted his legs on either side of her, and she shifted into that space. Desire surged inside him, overriding common sense, the dozens of reasons he had for not getting involved. All he knew right now was Abby. All he wanted was Abby. Their kiss deepened, becoming hotter, faster, hands sliding along backs and waists and—

"Mommy? You coming to tuck me in?" Jake's voice, echoing in the staircase.

Abby jerked back and put her hands on Dylan's chest. "Uh, yeah, Jake." She turned back to Dylan. Even though her cheeks were flushed and she was still breathing hard, cool distance had replaced the warmth in her. "You should go. I have... I have..."

"People to tuck in," he finished for her.

"Yes." She stepped to the side and smoothed her

hair. She cleared her throat. "Uh, thank you for the ice cream. It was a nice thing to do."

"You said that already." Dylan grinned. Was it possible that the strong and confident Abby was just as flustered as he was by that kiss? A little part of him hoped so.

"Oh, well, yes, uh, I forgot." She started walking out of the kitchen, with Dylan following behind. She opened the front door, the message clear—*leave now, we're not returning to that kiss.* "Thank you again."

"Anytime." The word was one of those throwaway ones, the kind people said without really thinking about it. But when Dylan thought of stopping by Abby's *anytime*, a little rush ran through him.

Insane. She represented home and hearth and kids— and he was unattached, unburdened, unhomey. Just because he enjoyed a dish of ice cream in her kitchen or got a little sentimental when he watched her dance with her son didn't mean he walked in the same world she did. Or even should.

"See you at the center." Dylan reached for the door handle.

"Mommy, can Dylan read me my story tonight? Please?"

Dylan turned and saw Jake, wearing dinosaur pajamas, the buttons a little askew, and holding a hardcover book. Dylan could see himself in those pajamas, with that book, waiting for a dad who was never going to get involved, never going to take the time to read a story. His mom had done the work of two parents, always excusing her husband from his parental duties with excuses about stress or exhaustion. *Dad's tired tonight.* Or *Dad had a hard day at work.* Or *Dad's grumpy because he's stressed about work.*

Sam had read Dylan stories at night—the two of them propped up against Dylan's headboard in the room that they shared. Sam had read about pirates and lost treasures, adventurous dogs and amateur detective twins. Then Sam had gotten older, found girls and basketball and moved into his own room that had been cobbled together from an unused corner of the basement. By then Dylan could read on his own, of course, but he remembered being hurt and wondering why his brother no longer hung out with him in the evenings.

Can Dylan read me my story tonight? Please? He could see the hope in Jake's face, the need in his voice.

"Jake, Dylan's going home," Abby said. "He—"

"Would love to read a story," Dylan said.

She turned toward him. "Really, you don't have to. I mean, it's a lot for Jake to ask."

"I don't mind, Abby. I remember being that age and wanting the same thing." Besides, how hard could it be? Dylan could read—way better than when he was a kid, after all—and Jake was just a little boy. It would take five, ten minutes, tops.

Besides, Jake was kind of growing on Dylan. He was a cute kid, who was curious and bright and funny. And reading to Jake might make Dylan a little more comfortable relating to the kids at the community center.

Yeah, that's why he was doing it. To relate better. Not because he could hear the echoes of his own childhood in Jake's voice.

"Okay," Abby said to Jake. "But just one story."

"Aw, Mom…"

"One." She and Dylan made their way up the stairs to the first room on the right. It was a small bedroom, with a twin bed in the shape of a red race car, a set of bookshelves filled with toys and books, and two toy chests overrun with stuffed animals and cars and robots. Jake's dinosaurs were in a pile at the foot of his bed, with Joe the triceratops on Jake's nightstand, basking under the light of a dinosaur-themed lamp.

Jake scooted over on his bed. "Dylan, you can sit here. I mades room."

"Uh, okay." Dylan lowered himself onto Jake's bed and sat back against the headboard. He settled in, while Abby went back downstairs to load the dishwasher.

"Here. I wanna read this book." Jake gave him a hardcover copy of a book about a lonely dinosaur who goes on a cross-country adventure.

Dylan opened the book and started to read. At first, the words were as stiff as Dylan's posture, but as he read, he settled into both. Jake shifted, then snuggled up against Dylan, his little head resting on Dylan's left arm. Dylan hesitated for a moment, caught in the middle of a sentence.

"Uh, and then the dinosaur said…" Dylan looked at the page, then over at Jake's head, nestled into the soft cotton of Dylan's T-shirt. It could have been him and Sam, years ago. And something in Dylan's heart melted.

"He said he wanted a friend," Jake said. "And then he meets a friend. And then he's happy. And then they go on adventures. I love this story. Mommy reads it a lot."

Which made Dylan wonder anew why Jake wanted him to read the book. Had Jake tired of his mother's reading? Or was there something more here, something that Dylan didn't want to see?

That maybe Jake had already latched on to Dylan and begun to see him as a pseudo-father figure? If so, that was far from the role Dylan, of all people, should be playing. Sam was the one with kids, the one who had settled down, made a life in this town. Dylan was only here for a short time, and then he'd be gone. And with his past, he wasn't cut out to be anyone's father, substitute or otherwise.

But was it worse to let Jake down tonight or to give him this time to be happy and then let him down weeks from now? Either choice would leave this little boy with heartbreak. The last thing Dylan wanted to see on any child's face.

Or on the face of that child's mother.

Abby paused outside Jake's bedroom door. Her breath caught in her throat, lodging with a thick lump. Jake sitting there, curled up against Dylan, a smile on his face, while Dylan read about the lonely dinosaur traveling the world to find a friend. The book was a favorite of Jake's, one she herself had read to him, oh, two hundred times.

The scene before her was one she had prayed for a thousand times when she'd been married to Keith. She'd always thought, given the chance, that he would step up and be a good dad. Take Jake on piggyback rides and shoot hoops with Cody. But in the end, Keith had checked out, spending more of his time away from home than with his family.

But this was just a scene, a blip in time, and she knew better than to put her stock in a man who was only going to let her down. And worse, let her sons down. They had had enough of that for one lifetime. Even today, seeing Jake's face when they brought back the dog, she'd wanted to cry. She felt like a terrible mother, saying no when she really wanted to say yes. Her baby had had to give up so much already—she hated the thought of him losing even more.

Her tender feelings were about more than that, she knew. She was starting to care about Dylan. Enjoying spending time with him, seeing the way he smiled at her, the way he patiently taught her how to work on the floors and the walls, and the way being around him made her heart race like it hadn't in a long, long time.

Dylan finished the book and closed the cover. Jake had nodded off, so Dylan slid out from under him and pulled the covers up to Jake's shoulders. He turned, then noticed Abby. "Oh, hey. Didn't see you there."

"I was only here for a second." Long enough to see the look of adoration and hope on Jake's face, the little smile that lingered after he fell asleep. Long enough to know that men like Dylan didn't hang around and that she was going to be the one left to pick up the pieces in his wake, for her kids and herself. Better to remember that than to let a smile and a racing pulse affect her decisions.

Dylan stepped into the hall, leaving Jake's door ajar. "He's a busy kid, but fun and smart."

"He is." Abby smiled. "I got lucky. A lot of women say their second child is more difficult but Jake has been sweet from the day he was born."

"I think a lot of that is due to you. You're so great with him, with both boys."

Here, in the dim hall, Abby was a hundred times more aware of Dylan. Their kiss still simmered on her lips, and the desire still rumbled in her veins. A part of her wanted to take his hand and bring him down the hall to her bedroom and finish what they had started.

The insane part, clearly. Her son was starting to lean on and believe in a man who wasn't going to stay—but he still believed in Santa Claus and the tooth fairy, too. It was crazy of her to do the same thing.

"Well, thanks again," she said. "I'll show you out."

"No problem." He followed her down the stairs and back to the front door. At the last second, he pivoted back to face her. "Tomorrow, the center is closed, so I have a rare day off. I was going to do some reno work in the morning, but what do you think about going fishing later in the morning? Uncle Ty has a pontoon boat he keeps down at Stone Gap Lake, and he said I'm welcome to use it. I'm hoping I can get him out, too, to get some sun and maybe catch a few bass."

"Fishing?"

"It'll be fun. I'll even bait your hook for you."

She put a fist on her hip. "Do you think I look so girly I can't do that?"

"Well, no, but you know, most women I've known don't like to handle worms and stuff like that."

She gave him a sassy look. "I'll have you know I've

been fishing since I was five years old. In fact, I bet I'll be the first one to catch a fish."

He grinned. "Are you challenging me? Because I've been fishing all my life, too. And Uncle Ty has won a few titles, in the years he isn't beaten by Ernie Morris."

This was where she was comfortable, with teasing and jokes and activities. Not with those quiet moments in her kitchen when she imagined things that were never going to come true. When she started to fall for a man who wasn't going to be here down the road. So she'd fish with him and leave it at that.

She put out her hand. "Want to put a wager on it?"

"Okay." He thought a second. "Ten bucks says I catch a fish faster than you do."

"Make it twenty and I'm in." They shook and she laughed. As she watched him leave, she realized she was feeling light, happy and, most of all, anticipating spending another day with Dylan.

Damn it. Just when she had convinced herself to let him leave and not see him again, Dylan had come up with an idea she couldn't resist. She didn't want to like this guy—

But she did.

And the worst part? Her sons liked him, too.

thing. "Your superior fishing ability
my inability to hook anything."

Ty sat back in his recliner
mote. He'd muted the TV wh
ages of Bruce Willis and
screen in one of thos
and not a lot of plo
Uncle Ty said fi
"And sittin
"Aunt Vir
that. Sh
ing
vo

Uncle Ty put his feet up and shook his head. "You kids go without me. I've got a football game to watch later."

Dylan looked around at Ty's ranch-style house. He and Aunt Virginia had lived here for their entire marriage. When Aunt Virginia had been alive, the house had been bright, merry. But now, it seemed as if the light had gone out of the space. The curtains hung despondent and limp and the air held a musty, sad scent. "I need you on my team, Uncle Ty. I made a bet with Abby that I could catch the first fish."

Uncle Ty scoffed. "Dylan, you know I love you like a son, but your fishing skills suck."

"Exactly why I need you along." And one of the things Dylan didn't want to admit to Abby. Call it manly pride, but he didn't want her to think he was bad at any-

should balance out

and fiddled with the re-
when Dylan came in. The im-
a Sylvester Stallone filled the
e guy movies with a lot of guns
t. "I wouldn't be good company,"
nally.
g here all day is better?" Dylan sighed.
ginia would be mad as hell at you for doing
e'd want you to get out of the house and go fish-
with Abby and her boys. Not to mention your fa-
rite nephew."

Ty let out a short laugh and shook his head. "You're a pain in the butt, you know that?"

"Yup. I do indeed." Dylan held out the canvas hat he had grabbed from the hook by the door earlier. His uncle didn't take it. "Here's your lucky fishing cap. All it needs is you to be wearing it."

Ty didn't say anything for so long, Dylan was sure he wasn't going to go. Then Ty flicked off the TV, popped the footrest back into his recliner and got to his feet. He reached for the cap and plopped it on his head. "How much money do we have riding on this bet?"

Dylan chuckled. "With you on my side, not nearly enough."

There was a small shift in Uncle Ty's mood as he headed out of the house. His steps hesitated when he approached the truck, but he got in and made small talk while Dylan drove.

On the way over to the lake, Dylan stopped at the

community center to show Uncle Ty the renovations he'd done so far, hoping maybe that would bring his uncle out of his funk. Ty made all the appropriate sounds and words, but his enthusiasm for the center was still low. *Give it time*, Dylan told himself. Soon enough, Ty would be back at work, and that meant Dylan could get back up to Maine and to the job waiting for him there.

All of this—the ice cream, the fishing, the work at the center—was temporary. His real life was far from Stone Gap, far from women like Abby Cooper. Yet he forgot all of that the second he saw her and started thinking about the kind of life he was far from equipped to have.

They pulled up to the dock and got out of the Jeep. Abby and her sons were already waiting there, Cody leaning against Abby's car and texting on his phone, Jake holding his mother's hand and dancing from foot to foot. "Dylan! We're goin' fishin'!"

Dylan chuckled. "Yup, we are. But first, you're gonna need this." He reached over and into the pontoon and pulled out a life jacket.

Jake pouted and argued, but in the end, Abby told him he had to wear the life jacket or forget fishing. Abby bent down and fitted the life jacket around a wriggling, impatient Jake. When she was done, Jake looked down at the thick orange vest with a pout. "But Cody isn't wearing one."

"Cody, you know how to swim?" Dylan said.

Cody shrugged. "Sorta."

Dylan grabbed a second life jacket and tossed it at Cody. The teenager caught it with one hand. "Then you get to wear one, too."

"Yay! Me and Cody are the same now!" Jake ran over to his brother. "Mine has a whistle on it. Does yours have a whistle? Can we blow the whistle?"

"That's just for emergencies, Jake," Dylan said. "Like if you fall in and you need us to come get you."

Jake's eyes widened. His gaze darted from Dylan to Abby, to the water and back again. "Am I gonna fall in?"

"No, sweetie, you won't fall in." Abby put a hand on her son's shoulder and knelt down to his level. She checked the belt on the life jacket and tightened it a bit. "Just be sure to listen to Dylan and Ty, okay? They're the bosses today."

Dylan had to laugh at the idea of being the boss of anyone. Sure, he'd run construction crews before, but that was different than commanding a family of three on a fishing trip. Uncle Ty was the one used to being in charge, but as he glanced at his uncle, he saw that Ty still wore a look of disengagement. Somehow, Dylan had to get his uncle to plug in today. Maybe then the cloud over Ty would begin to lighten.

Dylan glanced at the group, all of them waiting on him to do or say something. "Well, it looks like everyone's all set. How about we get on that boat and catch us some dinner?"

"Wait. I brought a cooler," Abby said. She reached into her back seat and pulled out a small dark blue container. "Snacks and some water bottles, in case we're out here a long time."

A smile flickered on Ty's face. "And that, nephew, is why you always invite a woman on a fishing trip. They think of the important things like food and drinks.

Your Aunt Virginia always made me two ham-and-cheese sandwiches and tucked my favorite soda into the cooler." His eyes misted and he shook his head. When he spoke again, his voice was thick, and his hands trembled. "I sure miss those sandwiches."

Abby put a hand on Ty's shoulder, kindness and understanding filling her features. "I thought you might be feeling that way, Ty, so I made you two ham-and-cheese sandwiches and packed a Dr. Pepper."

Ty's eyes widened. "How did you know?"

Dylan wondered the same thing. It was such a sweet gesture from Abby, and one that left Dylan feeling a weird bit of envy. He'd never dated a woman who paid attention like that, who did thoughtful things for him, with no expectations in return.

"You're not the only one who talked about your spouse with a whole lot of love." Abby's smile was tender, soft. "Virginia used to tell me how much she loved taking care of you."

"And she did a wonderful job of it." Ty cleared his throat, then resettled his fishing cap on his head. "The fish are biting, so we better get a move on while they're still hungry."

The shift in his uncle was nearly imperceptible, but it was there, and it gave Dylan hope that maybe things were starting to turn around. And maybe this outing was going to go better than he expected.

Uncle Ty boarded first, then put out a hand to help Jake and Cody up the gangplank and onto the pontoon boat. Dylan reached for Abby's hand as she stepped onto the wobbly crossing. She glanced at him but didn't take his hand. "Thanks. I've got it."

Of course, she was a grown woman, not a kid like Jake. And from what she'd said the previous night, he knew she had been on a boat before and knew how to steady herself. Even knowing all that, a little shiver of disappointment went through Dylan. He shook it off and climbed onto the boat, unlatched the gangplank and released the ropes holding the boat to the dock.

Uncle Ty hadn't stepped up to start the engine or steer the pontoon out into the water. He dropped the keys into Dylan's palm, then took a seat on one of the cushioned benches at the front of the boat. Jake clambered up beside him, kneeling on the seat to look over the bow. Abby sat down beside her son and put a cautionary hand on his back. Cody joined them, still immersed in his phone.

Dylan started the boat and began to back away from the dock, then pivoted the pontoon toward the open water of the lake. It was a sunny day, and the deep blue lake sparkled with gold. A few boats dotted the expanse of Stone Gap Lake, most of them fishermen out for an afternoon of fun and maybe a good catch.

"Uncle Ty, where's that great fishing place you always go to?" Dylan knew the answer but figured asking might engage Ty a little more. The melancholy mood was washing over Ty in waves. For a second, the waters would be calm, then his grief and depression would roll in again and the light in his eyes would dim.

His uncle sat there, staring out at the lake, sadness heavy on his shoulders. "Wherever you think, Dylan."

"I remember this spot over by a little grove of trees

that we used to go to a lot. Sort of tucked away? Which direction is that?"

Ty waved vaguely toward the east side of the lake, and Dylan turned. The old pontoon boat—not made for speed—putt-putted across the lake, its cranky engine clearly in need of a tune-up. Item number 753 on the things Dylan needed to do for his uncle before going back to Maine.

Abby came up beside him. The breeze made her hair dance around her shoulders, and the slight chill in the air added a little color to her cheeks. She was wearing jeans and a thick sweatshirt. The outfit made her look casual, comfortable, like the kind of woman a man could come home to at the end of the day and share a pizza with.

Where the hell had that thought come from? It was the ham sandwiches, Dylan told himself. One touching moment, and he got all hearth-and-home.

"In case I forget to say it, thank you for today," she said.

He shot her a grin. "We haven't even started fishing yet."

"I know. But Jake is already having the time of his life. Even Cody is starting to loosen up a little."

At the front of the boat, Cody had moved next to his little brother. The two of them were talking, with Ty throwing in a word or two, about the water, what kind of fish they would catch, how fast the boat was moving. Jake did most of the talking, of course. Still, Dylan could see the engagement in Cody's face, the relaxed posture. And the phone that was now tucked in his back pocket.

Abby sighed and leaned against the railing beside Dylan. "It's been hard, being both mom and dad. And working full-time." Then she shook her head. "Sorry. I don't usually complain about my life."

"Or rely on anyone else?"

She let out a short laugh. "You noticed that?"

"I do believe you gave me a good lecture about that when we were making PB&Js." He didn't add that it had intrigued him, the way she had been both stubborn and confident. He'd met very few women who challenged him like Abby did. He liked that. A lot. Maybe too much.

"I'm sorry. I've just been let down so many times..." She shrugged. "It's just easier to have no expectations. I grew up relying on myself and I guess it was easier just to keep on doing that."

Dylan wanted to shake some sense into the man who had left Abby to raise her sons alone. Even though he wasn't a father, if he'd had children of his own, he never would have done that. Kids required parents who were there, parents who supported instead of criticized. Abby was like that, and Dylan had no doubt her sons were lucky to have a mother like her.

He thought about what she'd said, growing up and relying on herself, and realized he had more in common with her than he'd thought. "Where were your parents when you were a kid?"

"In a bar or on the road." Abby shrugged, like it was no big deal, but he could see the lingering pain in her eyes. "My mom was busy with her things and my dad traveled for work. Most of the time, it was just me and my sister, home alone. I learned how to make my own breakfast at five, and by the time I was ten, I was getting myself ready and out the door for school every day."

"That had to be tough." It was a life he understood, a childhood that seemed deflated, empty of the essentials other kids had. "You turned out pretty well, though, considering."

She shrugged again. "I grew up, I became a different mom. It all worked out."

"My parents weren't too plugged in, either. I had an older brother, as you know, but once he got to high school... I was kind of left behind, being a not-so-cool middle schooler still. When I was seventeen, I went out on my own and pretty much never looked back." His gaze scanned the water's edge. Stone Gap lay just beyond the trees, a small town so many people loved—so many people other than him. "I've lived everywhere but here."

"Why not here?"

"I'm not much for small-town life." The expectations that came with that. The disappointments. Far better to keep his roots loose and movable.

"So neither one of us relies on other people." She gave him a half smile, her eyes unreadable behind dark sunglasses. "I wouldn't have thought we had that in common."

He wouldn't have, either. From the minute he met Abby, he saw her as the two-point-five kids, white-picket fence, house and husband type, the kind who built connections and relationships with everyone around her. But she was far more complex than that, and ten times more independent. Every layer of her that he uncovered made him like and admire her more. She'd done things he couldn't imagine doing—like raising two kids alone.

"For the most part, I'm the kind who doesn't rely on others, but I have found that sometimes people surprise you." Dylan turned a little more north, aiming for the outcropping of trees that marked the edge of Uncle Ty's fishing spot. "First time I ever ran a construction crew, I had a hard time letting go, letting the guys do their thing. I only trusted myself, you know? I had this one kid who worked for me. He was maybe nineteen or twenty and a real go-getter. Always trying to go above and beyond, prove himself to the guys who had a few years on him. He'd ask me, over and over, for more responsibility."

"Did you give it to him?"

He chuckled. "Eventually, he wore me down. So I put him in charge of a tile job that had to be done over the weekend. Figured he could handle it—he'd laid tile with me dozens of times and this job was fairly small. I took the day off, thinking I'd come back and check on his progress that afternoon." Dylan slowed the boat as they neared the trees. A few more minutes, and they'd drop anchor.

"What happened?"

"When I got there in the afternoon, the kid was gone. The guys said he was there for an hour that morning, then said he was going to grab coffee and never came back. I was really ticked off. I finished up the job with the other guys, then went to his house. He wasn't there. His mom said he hadn't come home." Dylan turned a little left, to avoid the stump he knew lurked underneath the lake's tranquil waters. Uncle Ty had hit it more than once. Dinged up the boat one time badly enough that they'd had to do an emergency repair before heading for home. "I decided I wasn't going to trust anyone again. Do it all myself, you know, and not let anyone let me down again. A month later, who comes back to work, but the kid."

"Really?"

"Yup. A part of me was mad as hell at him, but another part was glad to see him. Because you know what?" Dylan stopped the boat and shut off the motor. At the bow, Uncle Ty was showing Jake the best place to cast his line. Dylan paused a moment, watching a stick float by them. "I saw myself in that kid. I used to be the person no one could depend on. The one who would take off at the slightest issue. He got scared that day, he said, worried that he would screw up and ruin the job, so he left. I did that once, too, when I was around his age. Responsibility mixed with someone whose age still ends in *teen* doesn't always work. Eventually, I grew up. Realized that wasn't the way to live my life. Though some would say I'm still as undependable as I was when I was a teenager."

Some people like Sam. His parents. Dylan's family had never seen him as anything other than an irresponsible, fickle kid. Yeah, maybe he'd switched from job to job more than the average person, and maybe he did move often, but once he'd grown up and got a clue, he'd never walked out on a job, never let a boss down. Never walked away from someone who needed him.

"Did you hire the kid back?"

"Yup." Dylan tossed the anchor over, then leaned

back against the console. "Turned out to be one of the smartest things I ever did. I gave him a second chance and a big lecture, and he turned out to be one of the best workers I've ever had."

"That gives me hope," Abby said quietly. Her gaze was on the water, far from him.

"Hope for what?" Dylan asked.

But she didn't answer. Instead Abby pushed off from the railing and crossed to her boys. "Who's ready for Mom to teach them some killer fishing skills?"

Abby concentrated on fishing and not on Dylan. Or at least, she tried to. The five of them were at the bow of the boat, a wide and generous space because the steering wheel was close to the rear. Ty, Dylan and Cody were fishing on one side of the boat while Abby and Jake fished from the other side.

Jake was eager to learn but impatient with the fish. Every ten seconds he thought he had a nibble and yanked his pole up. "Mommy, when am I going to catch a fish?"

"When you sit down and wait a bit," Abby said. "You have to be patient."

Jake sighed and plopped onto the seat. "Okay."

Abby glanced over at Dylan. He'd surprised her, with the story about the kid who worked for him. Based on how he was with the teens at the center and with Cody, she could see him doing exactly that with one of his workers—but she understood how he had seen himself in that kid, too. He seemed to be a good guy, but there was a lot of wanderlust in him. Ty had mentioned once that his nephew Dylan had worked all over the country, the kind of guy who got tired of the day-to-day grind and would constantly set off on another adventure.

Exactly the kind of man she didn't need in her life. Nor did she need her boys relying on someone like that. At the same time, she couldn't deny the connection the boys had with Dylan. The way they talked to him, asked him for advice, and interacted with him. Cody was engaging with them, and Jake was slowing down, paying attention, learning whatever Dylan had to share. For the first time in a long time, she was seeing a change in her sons, and she wasn't ready to walk away from that yet.

Not to mention the attraction she felt for him. He was sweet and tender, and a hundred times she caught him watching her. She found herself glancing at him just as often, wondering if he was thinking of her as much as she was thinking of him.

Across from them, Cody let out a whoop. "Hey! I got one."

"Great job, Code," Dylan said, clapping him on the back. "You beat your mom, too."

"Let me see!" Jake ran across the bow just as Abby grabbed his pole and saved it from landing in the water. "Wow! It's a big fishy!"

"Awesome, Cody," Abby said. "You might beat us all."

"There's a competition?" Cody asked.

Dylan grinned at Abby, and she smiled back. "Well, it was a bet between Abby and me, but I think we should include everyone. Whoever catches the most fish..." His voice trailed off, leaving her to fill in the blanks.

"Gets to decide where we go for dinner," Abby said.

Cody perked up at that. "Even if it's fast food?"

The forbidden food that Abby only allowed her boys to eat once in a while. Most nights, she had something healthy that she made in the slow cooker, which constantly earned complaints from Cody, who would live on a diet of cheeseburgers and pizza if she let him.

Fast food or not, this was one of the few times she'd seen her son interested and she wasn't about to let that go over some fries.

"Even if it's fast food," Abby said. She cast her line into the water. "But if I win, we're going to that vegetarian place on Fourth Street."

Cody groaned. "God, Mom, I hate that place."

"Then you better get fishing." She grinned at her son, and for just a second, he smiled back. It was a start. A really nice start.

Dylan's gaze connected with hers. For a second, she thought how nice this was, a family moment, with her boys laughing and having fun. But it was, she reminded herself, just a moment. Dylan wasn't her husband or even her boyfriend. He was just a guy, a guy who would one day be far away and not here to depend upon.

When they pulled back up to the dock, Dylan would leave and she would go back to being a single mom. Far better to focus on that than imagine a future that was never going to happen.

Chapter Seven

Dylan stowed the fishing poles in the storage bins on the pontoon boat, then grabbed Abby's cooler and joined everyone on the dock. Uncle Ty looked tired, which surprised Dylan, who remembered a constantly moving, optimistic uncle with more energy than a roomful of preschoolers. Ty said a quick goodbye to Abby and her boys, then headed off to Dylan's truck, climbed inside and laid his head against the headrest.

Dylan sighed. The day had been a moderate success. Uncle Ty hadn't been his usual jovial self, but he had helped Jake fish and taught Cody a few things about giving the line well-timed tugs to entice the fish closer. After Cody noticed the lures attached to Ty's lucky cap, they had a long talk about the benefits of spinnerbaits over crankbaits.

But it was Abby whom Dylan noticed the most. She hadn't been kidding—she was a great fisherman. For the first time since he'd met her, he saw her truly relax, her mood light, her smile wide, as she hooked one fish after another. Cody had the lead until the very end, when his mother nabbed two fish back-to-back. They threw all their catches back into the lake, mostly because Jake worried that the fish were going to miss their families. It was kinda cute and something Dylan remembered saying when he was Jake's age.

He was stacking the life jackets in the bin at the front of the boat when Cody came up beside him. "Hey, Cody."

"Thanks for the fishing," Cody said. "I had a good time. I've never gone, and it just seemed so...peaceful." The teenager shook his head. "That sounds all weird and nerdy."

"Nah, it doesn't," Dylan said. "When the water is as smooth as glass and the sun is warm on your back, it feels like the world has stopped for a second. Now *I* sound weird and nerdy and like some Walt Whitman poem."

Cody laughed. "Yeah, I get that. Makes me forget about homework and grades and stuff like that."

Dylan arched a brow. "Are you saying homework is usually the first thing on your mind?"

Cody scoffed. "Yeah, I guess not. But I was thinking about it a lot and I kinda want to change that. I guess I need school to have a job doing stuff like building houses or something."

The thought that Cody might follow in Dylan's career footsteps warmed him. He wondered if that was what it was like to be a parent, to see your child admire and emulate you. Then a part of him remembered he was no role model for a troubled kid. Dylan may have gotten his life back on track but not without a lot of effort and missteps.

"Building houses is all about figuring out angles and reading blueprints and negotiating contracts. If you want to get a contractor's license, you have to take a test. So yeah, you kinda need to pay attention in school."

Cody toed at the deck, his face shadowed by the hood of his sweatshirt. "Can I ask you something?"

"Sure." Dylan straightened and leaned against the railing.

"You said you and your dad didn't get along and, like, he wasn't there much."

"Yeah. I mean, he lived with us, but he worked a lot. And when he was home, he was closer to my older brother and I was the one who always seemed to be in trouble. But I had my Uncle Ty to take me fishing and teach me how to fix stuff."

"So, like, did you ever—" Cody let out a breath "—did you ever tell your dad that bothered you?"

"Yeah." It had been more than a decade, but Dylan could still hear the words ringing in his head, words he had flung at his father before Dylan packed his bags and hit the road. *I was never anything but a disappointment to you.*

His father had stood there, silent. Even after the door shut and Dylan climbed in his car, Jonathon had stayed inside, stubborn to the very end. In the years since, there'd only been a handful of stilted phone calls on holidays and birthdays. In every one of them, his father had talked about how good Sam had turned out, with the implication that Dylan was still nothing but a disappointment.

"I was hoping he'd change," Dylan said, "but some people never do. The only way you find out if they're gonna change, though, is to give them the opportunity." He thought of the kid he had hired, the kid who had screwed up but come back twice as good after Dylan gave him a second chance.

"I don't think my dad's gonna change," Cody said. He shrugged, as if it didn't matter, but clearly it did. "Thanks for the fishing."

"Anytime, Cody." The teenager ambled off. Dylan waited a few minutes, busying himself with tidying up the pontoon boat, before following.

Dylan stowed the coolers in the back of Abby's car, then turned and noticed her holding a sleeping Jake in her arms and struggling under the weight of the four-year-old. Cody was already sitting in his mother's car, ready to leave. The hoodie was over his face, and he was glued to his phone.

"Here, let me take Jake," Dylan said to Abby, reaching for her son.

"You don't have to—"

"I know I don't." He put his arms out. Abby relented and transferred her son, who barely stirred.

Jake's weight settled over Dylan like a thick, heavy blanket. Dylan had never held a kid like this before. He'd had friends who had babies and kids, of course, but he'd never held any of them. There was something warm and nice about the way Jake nestled into Dylan's shoulder, his arms going tight around Dylan's back. He smelled of Johnson's Baby Shampoo, which rocketed Dylan back to after-dinner baths and water fights with his brother.

He followed Abby to her car and waited while she unlocked the doors. As he moved to lower Jake into his booster seat, the boy stirred. "T'ank you for fishing," he said. "I had fun, Uncle Dylan."

Uncle Dylan?

"Glad you had fun, Jake," Dylan said, because he didn't know what to say to the uncle thing, so instead he latched Jake's seat belt.

"Can we go again? Soon?" Jake asked. Beside his brother, Cody watched for Dylan's answer, feigning teenage indifference.

"Uh, sure." But as Dylan made the promise, he realized he couldn't necessarily keep it. Another week, and he was due to be in Maine. The projects at the center would be done by then, and hopefully Ty would be back at work, which would let Dylan hit the road. Leave Stone Gap.

Leave Jake and Cody. And Abby.

It would be best for all of them, he told himself. Before they all got too attached. Like Jake with the puppy. Except...the little boy had become attached to that dog within seconds.

Abby stowed her purse in the car, then slipped into the driver's seat. "Thank you, Dylan. I agree with Jake. It was a great day."

"You're welcome. Glad you all had fun. And congrats on winning the fishing contest." He gave her a grin. "I might have exaggerated my fishing skills."

She laughed. "You caught one. That's better than none. And you still get to partake in the winner's prize, if you want to come to dinner with us."

"Do we really have to go to that vegetarian place?" Cody leaned over the seat. "I hate that food, Mom. It makes me want to barf."

Abby chuckled, her mood still light and fun. Dylan liked her like this, unfettered, unstressed. "How about a compromise," she said to her eldest son, "since you were one heck of a fisherman yourself today. Burgers on the grill?"

Cody brightened, then he dimmed the emotion as if he was afraid to be caught looking happy. "Sure, that would be okay, I guess."

"Dylan, are you comin' to our bar-b-cue?" Jake asked.

Dylan hesitated. Abby had invited him to the restaurant a second ago, but he wasn't sure if it was a real invitation or one of those people threw out to be polite. He should probably get some more work done anyway. The clock to his departure was ticktocking away. And the more he tied himself up with this family—this woman—the harder it would be to leave.

"Jake, I'm sure Dylan has other things to do tonight," Abby said. "We've already taken so much of his time."

"But I want him to come, Mom. He's my friend."

The word hit Dylan smack in the chest. *Friend. Uncle Dylan.* In just a few short days, Jake had bonded with Dylan.

The little boy didn't see Dylan's past or Dylan's shortcomings. He took him at face value and saw him as a buddy. Someone with a shared affinity for dinosaurs and burgers.

Which Dylan realized wasn't such a bad feeling. He glanced over at Cody and saw the older boy was also waiting for Dylan's answer. The two of them, depending on him. He wasn't the kind of guy they could depend on, but he didn't say that. There was something… magical in the air right now, that floated in the happy mood between the Cooper family and himself. Dylan didn't want to be the one who brought that back to earth.

Besides, it was just a barbecue, he told himself. Not a lifetime commitment.

"How about I bring some potato salad?" he said.

A smile curved across Abby's face. "Sure. That would be nice. Come by after five."

"Great. See you then." He waved to the boys, then shut Abby's car door and headed back to his truck, his steps lighter. A barbecue. It didn't get more American, apple-pie than that. Dylan climbed inside his Jeep and started the engine.

"She's a keeper," Uncle Ty said.

"Who?"

His uncle gave him an unamused look. "Just because I'm old and a little slow doesn't mean I'm dim-witted, too. Abby is who. She's the kind of woman a smart man keeps for a lifetime."

Dylan put up his hands. "Whoa, whoa. I'm just going to a barbecue, Uncle Ty. Not a wedding."

"Then be careful. I saw how those boys look at you. They already see you as part of the family. And Abby…"

"Abby what?" Dylan prompted. He was curious and also didn't want to know at the same time. Because he already knew how Jake felt—*Uncle Dylan*—and if Abby was starting to depend on him, think about a future…

Ty didn't say anything for a moment. Dylan turned out of the parking lot, heading in the opposite direction of Abby. A moment later, her car disappeared from his rearview.

"Just don't break her heart," his uncle said finally. "She's a good woman, and like I told you, she's been through a lot."

Dylan let out a gust. "Why does everyone expect the worst of me?"

Ty shifted in his seat and gave his nephew a hard look. "I never said you were no good for her. I just said be careful and don't hurt her. I know you're not planning on staying around, and Abby is the staying-around kind."

"I know that already." It was the exact war he'd been having in his own head.

"I see how you look at her. It's the same way I looked at Virginia when I first met her."

Dylan took a right, then a left, winding his way through Stone Gap and back to Uncle Ty's house, a few blocks away from the center. When the weather was good, Ty and Virginia would walk to and from the center, hand in hand, talking the whole way, their laughter so frequent, it seemed to bubble between them with each step. Dylan had always thought his aunt and uncle had it right and perfect, one of those rare relationships where the two made for perfect complements.

"Well, what you and Aunt Virginia had is about as common as a two-headed penny."

"That doesn't mean it can't happen to you, if you ever decide to stay in one place longer than five minutes and hitch your star to one woman."

Dylan scowled. "How did a simple fishing trip turn into a lecture about me settling down and getting married?"

Ty grinned, the first smile Dylan had seen in hours on his uncle's face. "Don't you know, Dylan? Sometimes when you go fishing, you catch something completely unexpected. A real prize."

Abby took a long hot shower after she got home from fishing. She shaved her legs, curled her hair, spritzed on a little perfume and redid her makeup.

For a barbecue.

She changed her outfit twice, finally settling on a pair of skinny jeans and a navy blue loose flowy blouse. She straightened a house that didn't need straightening, rummaged through her pantry for a boxed dessert that she could whip up, then made the hamburger patties.

When her phone rang at four thirty, Abby steeled herself, sure it was Dylan calling to cancel. Telling herself that would be best, because she was already starting to fall for him.

Instead of Dylan, her sister Melanie's name lit up

the phone. "Hey, Mel," Abby said when she answered. "How are you?"

"Driving home from work in rush-hour traffic from hell. I thought leaving a little early would help me miss it, but no." Melanie sighed. "I've got to go to a big meeting with an advertiser tonight. You know, fancy restaurant, the whole schmoozing thing."

"I can't remember the last time I was in a fancy restaurant," Abby said. "So how's Adam?"

A hesitation on Melanie's end. "Everyone's great. Just great. You know, the usual, working a lot, spending a lot, sleeping too little. I think we might take our winter vacation in Europe this year."

"Europe, huh?" Abby had to admit she felt a pang of envy. That was the kind of vacation she'd never be able to afford for her kids. Melanie was free and loose, without kids to tie her down. "Glad everything is going well. You sound great."

"Yeah, yeah. I am."

There was something off in Melanie's voice, though, something that nagged at Abby. Maybe her sister wasn't as happy as she made herself out to be. Or maybe the traffic just had her off center. "You doing okay?" Abby asked. "I mean, you don't call me that often and—"

"I'm just catching up, Abs." Melanie let out an irritated sigh. "Why are you giving me the third degree?"

"Sorry." Abby switched topics, and forced a brightness into her tone. "Your birthday is coming up. Why don't I buy you a plane ticket, and you can come down here and visit me? I know the kids would love to see you. Oh, and do you remember Harris McCarthy from high school? He's been back in town recently. He's a builder or something and was working on a project nearby for some retired baseball player. I saw it in the paper the other day. Small world, isn't it?"

Her sister seemed to hesitate. "Harris McCarthy? From high school? I… I hardly remember him."

Abby laughed. "Right. You were head over heels for him in high school. I always thought you two would end up together. Guess you hit the jackpot elsewhere, though."

"Yeah, well, happy endings don't always come true." Melanie let out a breath, then her voice brightened. "Anyway, I should go. I've got…traffic. Meeting. All that stuff. Bye, Ab!"

Her sister was gone. Abby worried about Melanie's out-of-the-blue call for a second, then brushed it off. Melanie had that jet-set life, was editor of a major magazine, married to a man who used to be a model. So what if she rarely called? Maybe reaching out signaled a change in their relationship. Besides, if there was one thing Melanie didn't need, it was someone worrying.

A little before five, her doorbell rang. Abby checked her hair and makeup in the hall mirror, then cursed herself for worrying what she looked like. This wasn't a date, it was a cookout—a cookout her son had invited Dylan to attend. But when she pulled her door open and saw Dylan, it was a little hard to remember that.

Dylan had showered and changed, too, and she could smell the soapy freshness of his skin. His hair was still damp, the longish dark brown locks curling at his neck and by his ears. He had on jeans and a dark green T-shirt that hugged his chest, rolling and dipping over muscles that seemed to beg her to touch. Abby had to remind herself to breathe.

"Potato salad," Dylan said, handing her a ceramic bowl topped with plastic wrap.

She arched a brow. "Did you make this yourself?"

"Nope." He chuckled. "I have no cooking ability, remember? I asked Della where to find the best potato salad in Stone Gap, and she said, 'right here in my own kitchen.' Then she made up a batch and told me to make sure Jake and Cody got these for later, and for just them, not us grownups." Dylan handed her a plastic sandwich bag stuffed with chocolate chip cookies.

"Good thing I made brownies too, so I get my chocolate fix. Della is awesome. She spoils my boys rotten. I swear, she's like everyone's grandma." Abby opened the door wider and waved Dylan in and then started talking a mile a minute to cover for her nerves. "For a while, she was babysitting your brother's two kids. Jake and Henry got along really well. In fact, Henry and Libby are at the center at least once a week. You'll probably see them soon. You should see how big Henry's gotten. He talks as much as Jake, and when they're together at preschool, they go on and on more than a Congressional debate. It's nice to see how Sam's kids have blossomed since Katie came into their lives."

"I've, ah, never met Libby or Henry." Dylan grabbed the tray of hamburger patties and followed Abby into the backyard. "And who's Katie?"

He didn't know about his brother's fiancée? That seemed strange. Then she remembered he had said he didn't get along that well with his brother anymore. She wondered what had driven them apart. She'd met Sam briefly—she knew his kids and fiancée much better—and found him to be a nice guy, sort of an older version of Dylan.

"Katie is a sister to one of the Barlows and moved here a little while ago." Abby pressed the button to light the grill. Flames whooshed under the steel grate. "Sam hired her to be his nanny, and five minutes later, he fell in love. You should see him. Sam goes around town, grinning like a total fool. They're getting married at the end of the month."

"Guess I have been gone a long time." A mix of emotions ran across Dylan's features. She could see he was hurt that his brother had left him out of the loop about his life. Maybe, given enough time in Stone Gap, Dylan and Sam could mend their broken fences.

Jake came barreling across the yard and plowed straight into Dylan's legs. "You came to our party!"

Abby laughed. "Jake, one guest doesn't make a party."

Dylan bent down to her son's level. "Thank you for inviting me, Jake," he said. "And I think it's a party if you have balloons."

Jake pouted. "I don't have any balloons. Cuz it's not my birthday."

Dylan fished in his pocket and pulled out a handful of brightly colored uninflated balloons. "If you help me blow these up, then we'll have balloons. Even if it's not anybody's birthday."

Abby tended the burgers while Dylan and Jake competed to blow up balloons the fastest. In minutes, they had a dozen filled, and Jake took off, playing kickball with one of them and laughing when it floated away from his foot. Cody helped, too, tying the balloons for Jake and inflating a few of his own. Mrs. Reynolds came over and brought the puppies, who tumbled over their big feet, running after Jake and the balloons. Jake's smile was as wide and bright as the North Carolina sky. Dylan dropped to the ground, while the puppies and Jake climbed all over him.

She watched them and had the same feeling she'd had out on the lake. That this was what a family with two parents—two involved, caring parents—could look like. It was a dangerous thought, a very dangerous thought. She knew better than to dream of an impossible future.

She'd always thought of herself as pragmatic, sensible. But when it came to her boys and the family she dreamed of having, the hopeless romantic kept trying to make her believe in some white picket fantasy. This was just a barbecue, just a handful of balloons. Not a life.

And this man, no matter how much she was attracted to him or how much she craved his touch, wasn't interested in anything permanent.

"That was thoughtful of you to bring those. The kids are really having fun," Abby said to Dylan. Such a simple thing, a handful of balloons, but the joy on Jake's face caused a lump in Abby's throat.

How she didn't want to like this guy, or rely on him, or bring him any further into their lives. Every time she thought she had resolve, he did something sweet, and all her resistance melted.

Dylan shrugged. "I used to be a kid once. I saw these at the center when I stopped by there this morning with my uncle and thought Jake might like them. They're not puppies, but they're still fun."

Damn him for being so considerate. She turned away and concentrated on the burgers. Because that was easier than dealing with the conflicting emotions running through her.

Dylan moved into the space beside her. The heat from his body mingled with the heat from the grill. She wanted to reach out and touch him, feel the muscles underneath his shirt. Lean into him for another of those amazing kisses.

"Hey, you had a hard day," Dylan said. "Hell, a hard week, between working, helping at the center, and taking care of the boys. Why don't you let me grill?"

"I thought you couldn't cook."

"I can't. But when it comes to tending something on a fire, I'm your man." He flexed a biceps and gave her a grin.

I'm your man.

The words hit her hard and carved a chink in that wall Abby had kept around her heart for years. How she wanted to believe those words, even if he was saying them as a joke. How she wanted to trust that he was the kind of man who would stay around, who would be a role model for her boys, who would share the workload that weighed heavy on her shoulders, who would treat her with kindness and love.

But she knew better. Dylan himself had told her he

wasn't hanging around. That he wasn't the kind of guy to put down roots.

"Thanks for the offer, but I'm okay on my own," Abby said and pivoted away before Dylan could see the truth in her eyes.

Something had shifted in Abby after Dylan had given Jake the balloons. For a second, he'd seen her open up, warming to him, then that wall went up again and she was cool and distant.

Maybe she'd read the change in Dylan after hearing about Sam's fiancée. It had taken him a moment to absorb the news about the upcoming wedding—to which he hadn't been invited—and to push his disappointment to the side. A part of Dylan was hurt that this information hadn't come from Sam, but he knew that was par for the course. They rarely talked, and their last few exchanges had been terse.

He was happy Sam had found love again. He and his older brother might not get along, but Dylan still wanted to see Sam and his kids happy and content. If Dylan hung around town long enough, maybe he could at least meet this fiancée, even if he wasn't invited to the wedding.

Wait. Hung around town long enough? He only had a week left before he had to drive to Maine. After these next few days, Dylan would be hundreds of miles away from Sam. From Jake and Cody. From Uncle Ty.

From Abby.

And that fact, Dylan was pretty damned sure, was the reason why Abby kept putting distance between them. He had made her no promises, nothing beyond his short stay here. But as he watched her, helping Jake dish some potato salad onto his plate, he caught her glancing at him, and something in his chest leaped.

Cody left a minute later, as soon as his plate was clean, saying he was going to hang out with a friend. With dinner over, the still tired Jake went inside, sat down to watch TV and promptly fell asleep on the sofa, a plastic dinosaur clutched in his hand. Dylan helped Abby carry the dishes into the house, then started the water to wash them before she could.

"You don't have to do that," she said.

"I know." He nodded toward the dish towel. "You want to dry?"

He half expected her to make up another excuse to be away from him like she had earlier. When they'd all sat down to eat, Cody and Jake had sat together on one side of the picnic table, leaving Abby and Dylan on the other. But instead of sitting beside him, Abby had gotten up to shut off the grill, then bring everyone refills of their drinks, then extra napkins they didn't need.

He wondered if she'd done that because she wasn't interested in him or because she *was* interested and was afraid to take it any further. He knew he hadn't imagined the undercurrent between them, her responses to his kisses, his touch. He didn't want the day to end, and if doing the dishes, heck, cleaning her whole house, kept him here a little longer, he was game. Even if he knew he was only prolonging a connection he couldn't keep.

Abby hesitated a second, then grabbed the towel and slipped into place beside him. He caught the dark floral notes of her perfume, a compliment to the sweet scent of the dish soap. Earlier, when the evening had been hotter, Abby had put her hair up into a clip, and he'd had the strongest urge to kiss the valley of her neck, then peel back the edge of her shirt and kiss the divot beside her shoulder—

He turned, halfway through washing a plate. "Go out with me."

"Outside? We brought everything in already."

"I meant on a date." The words had been spontaneous, but the sentiment had been there since the day he'd met her. Abby intrigued him, with the way she was both strong and fragile at the same time. The side of her that danced with her four-year-old son to oldies was such a beautiful contrast to the resilient, confident woman who baited her own hooks.

He knew he was asking a lot. Knew he was leaving town soon, and there was no way this relationship could progress, and that a man like him shouldn't be in a relationship, especially not one that was a package deal. But he also didn't want to head to Maine without spending at least one night alone with Abby. Hearing her laugh. Seeing her smile. Holding her in his arms.

Abby took the plate he'd washed and dried it. "I don't know, Dylan. I mean, I suppose Cody could watch Jake, but he's not always the most reliable teenager..."

"Della could watch Jake. She told me herself she loves that kid. Or my uncle Ty. He's great with kids, and having Jake around might bring him out of his grief for a little while." He rinsed another plate and handed it to her. "When was the last time you went on a date?"

She scoffed. "I can't remember. How sad is that?"

Pretty damned sad if you asked him. Abby was a smart, beautiful woman. Any man with half a brain cell in his head would ask her out. For the hundredth time, Dylan wondered what had made her ex-husband so blind to how amazing she was.

"That's all the more reason why we should go out." He handed her another plate. She dried it in slow, concentric circles, turned to put it away and paused.

"Why?" she asked. "Why go out on a date when you told me yourself you're not staying in town? That this is a temporary stop for you?"

She'd nailed the truth about him in a few words. The thought of leaving caused an ache in his chest, but Dylan told himself that feeling would ease. For right here, right now, he wanted to get to know Abby more. Find out what made her laugh. What she felt like beneath him. He wanted more—even though he knew she was right and he had no business asking her for anything.

"Does everything in your life have to be permanent, Abby? We can go out, have fun and leave it at that." One night. That would be enough. Wouldn't it? He turned off the water, let it drain and put his back to the sink. "Loosen the reins a bit, Abby."

She shook her head. "I don't do that, Dylan. I don't change my schedule, I don't take impromptu trips. This whole thing here—" she waved to indicate the house, her kids "—is like a well-oiled machine. Take one cog out and it falls apart."

"You spent a Saturday tearing down a wall, took

an impromptu fishing trip, had a last-minute barbecue. Nothing fell apart." He leaned closer to her, caught those blue-green eyes with his own. "I think you're just scared."

She raised her chin. "I'm not scared to go out on a date."

"Then prove it. The center closes at six, so I'll pick you up at six thirty tomorrow night. Wear something comfortable."

"I have a presentation to work on—"

He leaned toward her, kissed that valley of her neck, then her lips. The protest died in her throat.

She let out a soft sound as his lips continued their path along her neckline. That simple sound almost undid him. Her hands went to his waist, and her body swayed into his. Everything in him wanted to sweep her into his arms and carry her into her bedroom and take his sweet time exploring the lines of her curves. Instead, he pulled back, aware that a sleeping Jake was only a room away. Later, he told himself, later they could see where this led. "I'll see you tomorrow night, Abby."

A smile curved across her face. "You're stubborn, you know that?"

"That's what my mother tells me." He almost hated to go but knew there was work to be done at the center yet tonight, so it could be ready for the kids tomorrow. And maybe getting out of this house, with all the toys and bedroom stories and warmth, would keep him from dreaming of things he couldn't have. "Thanks for dinner."

"You did the cooking. And brought the side dish. All I did was provide a picnic table."

"And brownies. Don't forget the brownies. It's always nice to end with something sweet." He grinned, then took Della's clean dish and headed toward the door with Abby walking beside him. Jake was still sleeping on the couch as they walked by, so Dylan leaned over and gave Abby a quick kiss goodbye. "See you tomorrow."

"See you tomorrow, Dylan." She said his name with a soft lilt in the middle. A lilt that almost had him staying.

He left Abby's house, his chest filled with anticipation. She lingered in his mind as he went to work at the center, repairing loose floorboards, grouting the new tiles and painting the wall the four of them had put up two days ago.

He headed back to the inn a few hours later, his muscles tired, but his brain still running a mile a minute. That alone was a sign he was in too deep with Abby. He couldn't remember the last time a woman had occupied his every waking thought. Hell, she'd been in his dreams, too. If he was honest with himself, he thought about her pretty much all the time.

When he walked into the bed-and-breakfast, he saw the kitchen light burning. He headed down the hall and found Della Barlow sitting at the table, a pile of recipe books and a notepad beside her.

"Oh, hi, Dylan. I'm just working on the menu for next week. We've got a few more visitors coming in on Friday."

Dylan put the clean dish away, then sank into the opposite chair. "That's great. Business is doing well?"

"Better than expected." She pushed a covered plate toward him. "More of those chocolate chip cookies I made for the boys."

"Thank God." He grabbed two and took a bite out of one. "I have to admit, I was a little jealous watching Jake eat them. Your cooking is the best, Della. The potato salad was a huge hit, too." He was sure he'd gained at least five pounds in the time he'd been here, eating Della's cooking. Not to mention the little treats Mavis often brought into the center.

"You're welcome." She set her pen down and crossed her hands over the notepad. Her reading glasses slipped down on her nose, and she took them off. "How was the barbecue? How's Abby?"

"It was great. And Abby is…" He shrugged, as if he was blasé about the whole subject, but then a smile winged its way across his face. Hell, he could feel that smile all the way to his toes.

"Something special, isn't she?" Della gave him a knowing glance. "She's only lived in Stone Gap for a few years, but she's really been a great addition to town. She worked with Mavis and me on some marketing materials for the inn when we first opened. Wouldn't take a dime for her time, either."

That sounded like the woman he knew. Stubborn yet generous with her time and talents. Like the way she helped at the center, kept applying for those grants, despite a demanding job and life as a single mom. "Well, whatever she did, it seems to be working if you're booking up that fast."

"So," Della said, fiddling with the pen. "Are you

thinking about extending your stay here? There's always plenty of renovation work in this area, especially being so close to the city. I know you're only booked through the end of next week, but it seems you've fit back into Stone Gap like a missing puzzle piece."

"I never fit this puzzle, Della," Dylan said. "I'm not a small town kind of guy."

"And what's so bad about small towns?"

"They close in on you. I like space, room to move and breathe." He thought of all the judgment and expectations that came with this place.

"And you can't find that here?"

"There's not much for me here, Della. That's why I left a long time ago." There was his uncle, of course, and now Abby, but all of that came with the one thing he didn't do—settling down. Staying put.

Della covered Dylan's hand with her own. He often wondered what it would have been like to grow up as a Barlow instead of a Millwright. "There's a lot more than you think. Your uncle, the community center, your brother—"

Dylan scoffed. "We don't exactly get along. Uncle Ty will eventually get back to running the center alone and I'll…"

"Move on, leave." Her kind eyes met his. As long as he'd known Della, she'd been a surrogate mom to everyone she met. Wise, kind and giving. "Or is it more running away again?"

And right on the money. He kept telling himself this wasn't running away…

Except wasn't that exactly what he was doing? Running before he got too close? Running before he found himself stuck here? Running…because it was easier than facing all the things he'd left in the first place? All those fears meeting Abby had awakened in him?

"I'm too old to run away," he said, though he wasn't sure if he was telling Della or himself.

Della nodded and got to her feet. "Good. I'm glad we agree on that. So, put you down for another week? Until you find a place of your own?"

Dylan put up his hands. "Whoa, whoa. I'm not moving back to Stone Gap. I have a job waiting for me in Maine—"

"And a family needing you here." Della stacked up her recipe books and stowed them on a shelf. "If there's one thing I've learned in my life after raising three boys and welcoming a stepson and a whole bunch of daughters-in-law into the family, it's that family is the most important thing in your life. You can find a new job. You can find a new house. But finding a new family… That's not something you can just pluck out of the classified ads."

"I have commitments in Maine, Della. I can't just break them."

"Okay. Can't blame me for trying to keep you around, and don't think this means I won't mention it again sometime. You've always been like an extra son to me." Della put a hand on his shoulder. "Good night, Dylan. Mavis is making waffles for tomorrow morning's breakfast. She knows you like them." Della went home to her husband Bobby every night while single Mavis lived at the inn. They took turns doing the cooking and cleaning, with Mavis mainly handling the morning routines and Della taking over at night.

"Thanks, Della." He waited until he heard her leave. Then he snagged another cookie and headed up to his room. But the last chocolate chip cookie didn't taste as sweet. And sleep took a long time to come.

Chapter Eight

Abby spent her workday distracted. Twice, she'd been caught daydreaming in a client meeting. Her mind kept drifting to the date she had tonight. With Dylan. A man who was all wrong for her, but she couldn't seem to remember that whenever he was nearby.

She left work a few minutes early, then headed to the community center to pick up the boys. When she walked in, Jake scrambled to his feet, leaving his craft project on the table. He plowed into her legs and gave her a tight hug. She hoisted Jake onto her hip—he was almost too heavy for her to keep doing this—then asked him about his day.

Cody was sitting on the sofas with the other boys, in a repeat of the other day. Dylan sat in the armchair at the center of the group, talking with the teenagers about the latest *Star Wars* movie. He looked up, saw her and gave her a quick, private smile. A little thrill ran through Abby and she felt her face heat.

Dylan excused himself from the teen circle and crossed to her. "Hey. You're here early."

"I wanted to get the boys over to Ty's house so I'd have time to change out of my work clothes." Just the thought of changing clothes had her mind derailing to thoughts of being in a bedroom with Dylan, taking off her shirt—

She cleared her throat. "Are you sure Ty is okay with watching them?"

Dylan nodded. "I talked to him earlier today. I think the fishing trip really helped bring him out of his dark mood. The boys are good for him."

"Good." She shifted Jake's weight, aware her youngest son was paying attention to every word of the adult conversation. "Well… I…uh, should get going. See you at six thirty?"

"You can count on it." He smiled at her, and heat rushed through every inch of Abby.

Oh, this was bad. Very bad.

But that didn't stop her from humming under her breath as she gathered her sons and headed out of the community center. She drove over to Ty's house with the boys, her mind on Dylan instead of on the continual stream of chatter from Jake, who interjected *can we get a puppy* in between every sentence.

Ty came out onto the porch when she pulled in. He still looked too thin and too pale, but there was a little more spring in his step. "How you doing, Abby?"

"Great. Brought you a couple of troublemakers to keep you company."

Jake looked up at his mother. "I'm not a trouble-maker."

Abby laughed. "I know, Jakester. I was just joking."

Ty chuckled. "Well, they're my favorite troublemak-ers in this whole town. Boys, I rented a movie and or-dered a pizza. Sound good to you?"

Cody nodded. "Yeah, sure."

She'd expected Cody to complain and ask to go to a friend's house. But he seemed okay staying here with his brother, so she didn't question it. "You guys all set? I have to run home and change before I go out tonight."

Jake nodded, then bounced up and down when he noticed the video in Ty's hands. "I'm gonna help Ty put the movie on! It's about dinosaurs!"

"Somebody told me they're your favorite thing," Ty said. He glanced at Abby. "My nephew apparently was very impressed with Jake's knowledge of T. rexes."

Dylan had remembered and thought to tell Ty, so Jake would have a good time. Every time she thought she had this guy figured out, he did something that sur-prised her, like kissing her in her kitchen and leaving her breathless and thinking of him long into the night.

Abby gave Jake a kiss and a hug, then Ty and Jake headed down the hall. Abby turned to go.

"Wait, Mom." Cody reached in his backpack. "Can you, uh, sign my progress report?"

By the end of the last school year, Cody had been on the edge of failing. After multiple meetings with his teachers, they'd finally settled on a weekly progress report that Abby had to sign, so everyone could keep an eye on his grades. She'd asked the teachers for his junior year to keep the practice in place, so she wouldn't be caught off guard and end up having to send Cody to summer school again.

She took the paper from him, expecting the same report as always. Lots of Ds and Fs, and a whole lot of *needs to participate more, missing assignments, negative attitude* in the comments column. She hadn't seen a grade with any of the first three letters of the alphabet in at least a year.

She scanned the pink sheet, then read it again. Four Ds, no Fs, and one C in math. *Attitude improved. Did all homework this week.* Abby raised her gaze to her son. "You brought up your math grade?"

Cody shrugged. "Dylan helped me with my homework. I finally get the Pythagorean theorem. It's not really that hard. He just told me to think about it like building a house."

Abby stared at Cody. Was this the same son she'd been nagging a week ago to bring a book home once in a while? The same son who had told her he wanted to drop out? The same son who said math was pointless? "That's...that's great, Cody. Way to go. I'm really proud of you."

Cody toed at the floor. "Yeah, like I said, it was no big deal."

Before her son could escape, she drew him into a tight hug. Cody stood there, stiff, for a moment, then eased into his mother's embrace. "Well, it's a big deal to me, Cody. And I'm really, really proud."

Cody untangled himself and stepped back. "Yeah, well, I'm gonna go see what Ty has to eat." Cody ambled off, and Abby had to choke back some tears when she got back in her car.

Dylan was changing her son's life. Redirecting her lost teenager. Bringing light into her world.

And making it extremely hard for Abby to remember why she shouldn't get involved with him.

Dylan had never been a man who was known for romantic gestures. That kind of thing had always befuddled him, and he'd usually opted for the easy way out, with a fast casual dinner in some chain restaurant. But tonight, with Abby, he wanted to make it special. To make *her* feel special.

He'd debated all afternoon between some big grand gesture, a few smaller ones, or just eschewing the romantic part all together. But then he'd think of Abby and how hard she worked to raise her sons, to do her job and to help other people, and decided she deserved far more than a half-hearted effort on his part. Not to mention a part of him wanted to impress her, to see her smile light her eyes.

At 6:29, he was standing on her doorstep, a thin bead of sweat on his forehead and a too-tight collar on his neck. He'd run around like a crazy man after he left the center and barely made it to her house in time. There was no music coming from inside, no dancing this afternoon. The boys, Dylan knew, were already at his uncle's house. He'd stopped by there first, to make sure Ty had it under control, and was surprised to see his uncle sitting at the coffee table, playing Monopoly with Cody while Jake watched a cartoon movie about dinosaurs.

Abby opened the door, and Dylan had to remind himself to breathe. She looked stunning, in hip-hugging dark jeans, a blue patterned V-neck shirt and a soft cream cardigan. Her hair was down, curling loosely around her shoulders, and she was wearing a soft red lipstick that begged him to kiss her.

"Hi," she said, her voice quiet and shy.

"Hi." It was like they hardly knew each other. He blamed it on the collared shirt, so foreign to Dylan that it might as well have been a straitjacket.

"Nice shirt." Abby smirked.

"Figured I'd try to impress you." He held out his hands. "Did it work?"

"Well, to be honest, even though you look handsome—"

He heard the *handsome* and figured that was worth this strangulation collar.

"—what someone wears doesn't impress me." Abby grabbed her purse and pulled the door shut behind her. "Actions do."

It was a good policy. Dylan had always hired workers based on the way they handled the job, not on what color their hair was, how many piercings they had, or whether they had a sleeve of tattoos. But her words had him wondering if his actions had been the impressive type, because he was really starting to fall for this woman. "So how am I doing in the actions department?"

The shy smile filled her face again. "Not bad, Dylan. Not bad at all."

Damn. When she looked at him like that, it took all he had not to run up the stairs with her and make love to her. He cleared his throat. "Are you ready to go?"

She locked the door and pivoted toward him, nearly colliding. She caught her breath, her eyes wide and luminous in the dim light from the porch. "Am I, uh, dressed okay? You said to wear something comfortable."

"You're perfect, Abby. Absolutely perfect." The words hung in the tense, heavy air between them. He wanted to say more but was afraid the words would trip in his throat, make promises he couldn't keep.

A blush filled her cheeks. She held his gaze for a moment, then looked away. "We should probably get going. I don't want to leave the boys at Ty's too late."

He led her down to his Jeep, opening the door for her before coming around to the driver's side. He'd taken it to the car wash early this morning, scrubbing down almost every surface inside and out until the leather and glass resembled its much-former new self. As he drove, they exchanged small talk about the center, the nice weather Stone Gap had been enjoying all week, Jake's newest toy dinosaur.

"So, you grew up here?" Abby asked.

"Yup. Born and raised."

"Did you like Stone Gap when you were a kid?"

Dylan thought about that for a moment. "I guess I did when I was little. The town, anyway. My school. My friends. My brother. It wasn't until I got older, high school age, that my mind changed."

She shifted in the seat to face him. "So what happened? I'm not trying to pry, I'm just...trying to understand my own son."

"Because you see a lot of Cody in me?"

"In who you used to be," she said.

Who he used to be. Had he really changed all that much? He thought of what Della had said, about how he was only running away again. Was he really? Or was he just moving on to the next opportunity?

He liked to think he had grown up, changed, evolved. But he was in his thirties and had yet to put down roots or even have a relationship that lasted longer than a few months. He'd never really fallen in love, never really connected with anyone too much. His entire life, it seemed, was transitory. For years, he'd liked that, but now, admitting it out loud made it all sound...sad.

"It was gradual," Dylan said. "I was always close to Sam, and he made life here good. We'd go fishing, build forts in the woods, stay up too late watching movies and eating junk food. Then my brother grew up, got a car and his own life. My dad was never much of a father, especially to me. I think he resented having a second child because it meant he had to work more, you know? Sam was always the one who could do no wrong, and when Sam was gone, my father laid into me twice as hard. So instead of trying harder, I rebelled. Flunking out of school, committed a string of petty crimes, that kind of thing."

"A rebel without a cause?"

He chuckled. "Yeah, I guess that's how you could describe it. But really, I spent more time with the truant officer and talking to the Stone Gap cops than anyone should. I guess I just felt like Stone Gap had all these rules and restrictions, and I just wanted to escape them."

"Like you wanted to with your father," Abby said softly.

He'd never thought of it that way. When he'd run away, he'd told everyone it was because he was sick of being held down, of being told what to do, of being in trouble. He'd thought he was escaping the town that seemed to judge his every move, the neighbors who shied away because they thought he was trouble. The brother who had rejected him.

He'd never seen it as an escape from his father.

"I understand that," Abby said. "I was so anxious to get out on my own and get away from my parents that I married the first guy who asked. I'd say it was the biggest mistake of my life, but I was blessed with two sons from that relationship so... I guess it had its pluses."

"Everything in life has an up and a down side." Dylan shook his head. "Now I sound like some fortune cookie philosopher."

It was being around Abby and her boys that had him thinking like that. Had him questioning his choices, decisions. Made him wonder how his life would have been different if he had followed the same route as Sam. Would he be married to a woman like Abby? Raising a couple of boys? Maybe a little girl?

Speculation, that's all that was. His life was what it was, and he liked it. He wasn't lacking for anything. And he certainly wasn't cut from the same cloth as Sam, who seemed made for the role of family man.

But as he glanced at the beautiful woman beside him, he had to wonder if he was fooling himself.

They wound their way through the town and at last Dylan turned onto a dirt road that led to the edge of Stone Gap Lake, away from the few private homes on the lake and the dock where Ty's pontoon was parked, and down to the western side of the lake. The Jeep bounced a little on the rough surface, sending Abby's arm crashing into his. He didn't complain.

A quartet of small cabins sat on either side of the road's end. To the right, stacked logs formed a circle around a stone firepit. The rest of the buildings had fallen into disrepair, but these four still stood strong. Maybe they'd been built later or with better materials. Whatever the reason, he was glad they were still here. There were some things in Stone Gap that he liked to be able to count on. This place was one of them.

"Where are we?" Abby asked.

"It used to be a campground. I went here in the summers with my uncle, my brother and some of my friends. It was a group outing that Ty organized every year. The campground shut down about ten years ago when the owner died."

He had hundreds of happy memories from those years. When he and Sam had first started going to the Little Otter Summer Camp, Dylan had been only five, his brother almost ten. He and Sam had roomed together, staying up late long into the night talking or playing card games. Those were the years filled with swimming and boating and fishing and bonds Dylan was sure would never break.

But just like the campground had fallen apart, so, too, had his relationship with Sam. *I give up on you*, Sam had said as the police left after Sam had gotten Dylan out of yet another scrape. *You're just going to let everyone down again.*

Dylan wasn't that kid anymore. He'd cleaned up his act, stopped doing stupid things like knocking over mailboxes or spray-painting the sides of buildings. That night in the police station had been the wake-up call he'd needed. The problem? Sam didn't see any of those changes in Dylan and probably never would. And until Sam stopped seeing him as the family screwup, their relationship was destined to be a failure.

"This must have been a great place to camp," Abby said. "What a view."

"It was. It's one of my favorite places in Stone Gap." He parked, shut off the car.

The lake spread before them, blue and deep. The sun was setting, and the lake began to tint with purples and pinks. They got out of the car and Dylan came around to the passenger's side. He took Abby's hand and led her down the trail to the water's edge and to the little tableau he'd set up earlier.

He'd borrowed a thick blanket from Della and spread it on the grass. He'd set a cooler on one corner, then laid two wineglasses and a chilling bottle of white wine in the center, flanked by a spray of wildflowers. It was simple and rustic and he prayed she liked it.

"Wow. This is really nice, Dylan." Abby gave him a smile. "I love it."

The praise warmed him. He hadn't realized until then

that he'd been holding his breath, waiting for her reaction. All that told him that he was in too deep, but right now, in this place, with this woman, the first woman he'd ever taken here, Dylan didn't care.

"Thanks. I... I didn't know what you liked so I got a few different things to eat." He knelt on the blanket, pulled a book of matches out of his pocket and lit two candles sitting in mason jars. The gold light flickered over the blue patterned quilt. "There. Ambiance."

"Perfect." Abby lowered herself into a sitting position on the blanket, then leaned back on her hands. "The lake is so quiet and still."

Dylan sat beside her. "This used to be my favorite time of day when I camped here in the summers. I'd sneak out after dinner started and sit here to eat. Most of the fishermen were gone, and the swimmers were out of the water, so it was just me, a few loons and the occasional fish jumping. I liked the quiet. I still do."

"Do you find a lot of that where you live?"

"Yeah. When I'm not working, I'm doing the same thing. Either camping in the woods or fishing in a lake. I've always loved being outdoors."

"Me, too. Though I spend far too much time indoors. When I was a little girl, my grandpa would take me fishing. My dad was never much for that kind of thing, nor was my sister, so it was just me and my grandpa." Abby smiled. "Whenever I visited him in Connecticut, I made sure to get at least one afternoon out on the water with him. He died five years ago, and I haven't been fishing since you took us out on the water. I was so glad to share that with my boys, especially Jake, who has never got-ten to do those things."

"Is that where you grew up? Connecticut?" He couldn't imagine her in a place like Connecticut, which had always seemed so upper crust to him. Abby was more like...

Well, more like Stone Gap. At least the good parts of it. The parts he used to love.

He'd never met a woman like her. He'd dated all kinds of women, but none had that calm centeredness mixed with sweet temptation that Abby had. It was a contradiction that intrigued him and attracted him in ways he'd never felt before.

"I grew up in a little town much like this one," Abby said. "I moved down here after I got divorced. I really wanted a small town for my kids to grow up in, and when I got the job offer at the marketing agency a cou-ple towns over, I looked at a house here in Stone Gap and fell in love with the area. I've been here ever since."

He scoffed. He didn't get people who said they fell in love with this sleepy North Carolina town. "All I wanted to do when I got older was leave this place. I can't understand anyone who wants to stay."

"But why? Stone Gap is a great place. You have a job that can go anywhere. And you have family here—"

"I'm only close to my uncle. My parents moved to Arizona a few years back and I rarely see them. That leaves just my brother, Sam, and my niece and nephew."

"Why not try to make amends with Sam?" Abby said. "I've met him, and he seems like a really nice guy."

You're just going to let everyone down again.

"My brother still sees me as the same headstrong foolish seventeen-year-old who dropped out of school and took off on his own." The teenager who hit the road and never looked back. The adult who hadn't been there when Sam's wife died, or when Aunt Virginia died. The man who had let his family down too many times to count. If he could go back and make amends for all that, Dylan would. But life just didn't work that way.

"That's…sad," Abby said. "I don't get along really well with my sister, but I am glad she's part of my life. We talk a couple times a month. We can trade stories about my mom's apple pie or what our uncle Sal is up to now. There's no one else you can do that with but family."

Dylan turned and reached in the cooler. The topic of his family was a sore one for him, the kind that made him question all his life choices. Maybe if things had been different… But they hadn't been, so dwelling on that didn't do anyone any good.

"So, I brought some roast chicken, a salad and this pasta thing that looked good at the market."

Abby laughed. "Change of subject?"

"Yup." He held up the container of chicken. "Do you want some?"

"Let's start with the wine and watch the sun set."

"Sounds like a plan." Dylan pushed Play on his phone, sending a soft undertone of Sinatra into the air while he poured two glasses of wine. The music calmed the tension in his chest, recentered him to the quiet of the setting, the beauty of the woman beside him. "To unforgettable evenings," he said and clinked his glass against hers.

"Sinatra? Wine? A sweet toast? You surprise me, Dylan Millwright."

"Good. That was my plan." He was sure there were other men who could do something far more romantic and memorable, but when Abby settled against his shoulder, he figured he'd added just the right amount of romance. They sipped their wine and watched the world ease into dark while Frank Sinatra crooned in the background.

Being with Abby was so enjoyable, unpressured, unhurried. He liked being around her, having her close. She was the kind of woman he didn't feel he had to force conversation with. The silence between them felt…relaxed. A first for him on a date. At the same time, every inch of him was acutely aware of her, of the scent of her perfume, of how close she sat, close enough to be warmed by the heat from her body.

"This is nice," Abby said with a long, happy sigh. "Really nice. I can't remember the last time I just…sat and enjoyed an evening."

"Me, either. Most days I'm too exhausted to do much more than eat and go to bed. The projects I get hired to work on are usually so time-consuming, I haven't had too many weekends off." He also hadn't had the desire to have time off. Work kept him from thinking, kept him from dwelling on his choices, his life. Nor had he had a woman he wanted to spend time with as much as he wanted to be with Abby. He'd seen her every day since he arrived in Stone Gap, and still it didn't feel like enough.

She turned to him, her eyes bright in the moonlight. "You're a good man, you know that?"

The words took him by surprise, especially since Uncle Ty had said them just a few days ago. The praise didn't feel as if it fit him, like an oversize suit. "What makes you say that?"

"The way you pitched in with your uncle, how you led the teen group. And how you're changing my boys' lives."

He shook his head. She had him all wrong. "I'm not doing anything really."

"You're doing more than you know. Cody's math grade went up." Abby clasped Dylan's hand and met his gaze. "I haven't seen that boy get anything higher than a D in a *year*. This week, he has a C in math. He did all his homework for the week and he said he finally understands the Pythagorean theorem, and all because of you."

Dylan hadn't been sure that Cody was listening when they'd talked. The conversation about solving triangle problems came up when they'd been working together on the repairs for the center. "I didn't do much. Just put it into terms he understood. He really likes working with his hands and doing construction work, so when I rephrased the word problems into that kind of thing, he understood it."

"It's more than that, though, Dylan. My boys have been...lost for a while. I really do the best I can, but I'm a mom, not a dad. And I think it's important for them to

have a strong male role model. It's why I started bringing them to the community center. By then Ty pretty
much checked out, and it wasn't until they met you
that I saw real changes, especially in Cody." Her eyes
welled. "I thought I'd lost him. And now... I think he's
coming around."

Dylan wanted to tell her she was putting her faith in
the wrong man, that he wasn't this picture-perfect man
she painted him out to be. And strong male role model?
He was the last man on earth anyone should hold up like
that. "I told you, you're a great mom. That's important,
more important than a fishing trip or a few minutes repairing a wall and talking about math problems."

She shifted to sit up and lean over him. "You made
a difference, and I can't begin to tell you how much I
appreciate that."

"You're...welcome." The words didn't feel right, because he didn't feel like he'd earned them. And yet,
he wasn't going to argue any further with her because
he had to admit he really liked seeing the gratitude
in Abby's face, seeing her so happy. And all because
he'd helped Cody solve for C in a triangle. "I just... I
really like you, Abby, and hanging out with your kids
seemed natural."

"You really like me?"

He grinned. That was a lot easier to say than *you're
on my mind all the time and I'm not sure what to do
about that.* "You think I break out the Sinatra for every
girl I meet?"

"Well, I don't know. Do you? For all I know, the
Little Otter Summer Camp could be your secret love

nest." Her smile was edged with something devilish. Something he liked very much.

He cupped her jaw and ran his thumb along the edge of her lips. "It's most definitely not. It is my favorite place in this town, but I've never taken anyone I dated here before."

"Why me?"

"Because I wanted to give you something…special. Because… I'm falling for you, Abby Cooper."

Damn. He'd said that out loud. The words hung in the air. He shouldn't have said them, shouldn't have taken this any further, knowing he was leaving in a week. But every time he looked in her eyes or felt her touch, all rational thought fled.

"I'm falling for you, too, Dylan," she whispered.

His heart soared and he didn't give a damn about timelines or expectations or anything other than being with Abby. He'd worry about tomorrow in the morning.

He pulled her down to him, until she was on his chest, and her mouth was inches from his. "This could get dangerous."

"I'm kinda hoping it does." Then she smiled again, and that was all the answer Dylan needed.

He kissed Abby, not a soft, easy kiss like before, but hard, hot, fast. The desire he'd tamped down from the minute he met her surged to the surface. She met his fire with equal passion, running her hands down his shirt, over the buttons, then as his kiss deepened and the desire became a full-on inferno, she fumbled with the buttons, undoing them one at a time.

Dylan was tempted to rip the shirt off, but there was

something sexy and sweet about her unbuttoning his shirt. He vowed to wear this kind of shirt around her often. A lot more often.

She parted the panels of his shirt, then slid a hand along his chest. "God, your chest is…amazing," she said. "So sexy."

"Hang enough Sheetrock and you can have these muscles, too."

"No thank you, sir. I'll stick to my computer and my weak biceps." She straddled him. "And running my fingers over your chest instead." She did just that and he groaned. Her hands were smooth and soft, her touch igniting every nerve she brushed against.

"I think we should be equal in that regard." He slipped off her sweater, then slid his palms under her shirt and lifted it over her head. She wore a lacy pink bra underneath, and he wondered if she had done that on purpose, for him. He sure hoped so.

His fingers danced above the lacy edge, and her nipples hardened against his palms. Damn. "You are beautiful."

She blushed, and for some reason, that made him fall for her even more. Abby had no idea how mesmerizing she was, how amazing, and he liked that little bit of vulnerability. It was damned sexy.

Dylan rose into a sitting position, with Abby settling in his lap. He kissed her again, his hands tangling in her long, dark hair, then slid his palms down her back, to the tiny clasp at the back of the bra. Abby gasped when the lace cups fell forward, exposing her skin to the cool night air.

He was hard beneath her, his body urging him to hurry up, to quench the need burning inside him, but he didn't want to rush this. He wanted to savor her, to savor this moment, the beauty of her in the moonlight. He bent his head, kissing a trail from her shoulders to the top of her breasts. When he brushed against her nipple, Abby arched against him.

He took her nipple in his mouth, tasting it delicately at first, then harder, teasing the bud until she was gasping and writhing against him. "Good Lord, Dylan," she said. "Just that...and oh...oh my. Yes, that."

She ran her fingers through his hair, urging his mouth closer. He switched to the other side, and in an instant, she was moaning again. He lifted his head, cupping her jaw with his hands, and kissed her, deep, slow, easy. Then he pulled back and shifted to the side, laying her down on the blanket.

The moonlight danced on her bare skin, and he took a moment just to drink in that image. Then she smiled that sexy, devilish smile again, and he forgot all about moonlight and savoring. He undid the clasp on her jeans, slid them over her hips and tossed them to the side, then did the same with his own jeans.

"Are we really doing this?" Abby asked.

"Do you want to?"

She nodded. "But...it's been a long time for me, and... I may be out of practice."

"Then I say we practice." He ran a finger under the edge of her pink lace panties. "A lot."

"That sounds like an incredibly good idea, Mr. Mill-wright." Her laughter was throaty, sexy, and when she surged into his arms, he lost all rational thought. A second later, they were both naked under the moonlight, the food and wine forgotten, and he was fumbling for the condom in his wallet.

When he entered her, she arched and gasped, digging her fingers into his back. Being inside Abby felt like coming home, warm, sweet, delicious and perfect. She matched him, stroke for stroke, their lovemaking hard and furious and hungry. She cried out, her voice lost among the trees and the night birds.

He increased his pace and she gasped his name in his ear, over and over again, until her orgasm crested and she let out a long, happy sigh. He came a minute later, holding tight to her long after they were finished. For those endless sweet minutes, the world was perfect, and there was nothing in his mind, in his heart, except for Abby Cooper.

He rolled to the side, curling her against his chest, and realized one thing. Dylan had fallen hard for Abby Cooper—

And leaving Stone Gap was not going to be as easy as he'd thought.

Chapter Nine

Abby woke up the next morning, long before the alarm rang. Her day stretched before her, filled with To Do lists and lunches to make and kids to worry about, but her mind lingered on the night before. On the picnic with Dylan. The lovemaking that had left her more satisfied than she could ever remember—twice.

He had been a considerate and tender lover, especially the second time. In those moments under the moon, she had felt special and treasured and—

Hooked.

As much as she hadn't wanted to, Abby had fallen in love with sweet and considerate Dylan Millwright. The man who was all wrong for her, and was undoubtedly going to leave her brokenhearted. Except there was the tiny part of her that saw the way he connected with this town, with his uncle, with the center and with her and her boys, and began to hope that maybe he was going to stay.

She got up, pulled on a robe and went out to the kitchen. The coffeepot, set on a timer the night before, already had fresh hot brew waiting for her. She poured a cup, powered up her laptop and got to work, first checking on the status of a grant she'd applied for a month ago for the center, then on a client presentation she needed to make on Friday. She had about an hour before the boys had to get up for school, and instead of trying to chase elusive sleep, she'd be smart to work.

Because when it came down to it, focusing on a man wasn't going to pay her bills or feed her children. The only one she could rely on to do that was herself.

Uh-huh. Then why did her thoughts keep roaming to last night? To being touched by him, kissed by him, and wanting so much more in that private little grove by the campground. Abby shook her head and refocused on work. On being practical.

She answered what felt like a thousand emails in between typing up presentation notes and creating a few more PowerPoint slides. Three cups of coffee later, Jake came bounding into the kitchen. "Morning, Mommy!"

"Morning, Jakester." Abby refilled her coffee again, then set a cereal bowl on the kitchen table. "You're up bright and early and all by yourself. Good job, buddy."

He'd even dressed himself, in a striped T-shirt and a worn pair of jeans. His socks didn't match, but she let that go. Just the fact that Jake had taken the initiative to get ready on his own told her that her littlest son was growing up. As proud as she was, a tiny part of her was sad.

Jake climbed into the chair and waited for his mother to pour him some cereal. "I wanna go help Dylan build more things today!"

"You can't sweetie. It's a school day. You and Cody have to get ready." She grabbed the milk and added some to Jake's bowl, then got him a spoon. "After school, you can go to the center. Mavis will be there, so you can make a new craft."

"I wanna build things. Like a house. For my dinosaurs!" Jake dug into his cereal, hurrying through his breakfast. "Can I do that? I don't wanna do a craft."

Abby chuckled. "Well, let me talk to Dylan later and see if he needs your help. Right now, I need you and your brother to get ready for school." She dropped her attention back to the presentation. Just one more slide—

"Cody's not goin'," Jake said between spoonfuls. "He came in my room and told me. He said he had to go somewhere else."

The hairs on the back of Abby's neck rose. She froze. "Somewhere else?"

Jake nodded. "Can I watch SpongeBob?"

Abby flicked on the TV, breaking her no-television-during-meals rule, just to keep Jake distracted for a minute. There was no way Cody was going to skip school again. He'd promised her, promised Dylan. His grades were improving; he'd be crazy to start skipping again. Maybe Jake had misunderstood.

She headed down the hall toward Cody's room. The door was closed, as usual, with its bright red Keep Out sign tacked outside. Abby knocked twice. "Cody? Time to get up for school."

No reply.

She knocked again, harder. "Cody? Come on, wake up. I'll make you some eggs if you want. Or one of those burritos you can eat in the car. Let's go, I don't want to be late for work."

No response. Par for the course with a teenager who slept like the dead and hated waking up before seven. Abby turned the handle, opened the door and poked her head inside. Cody's room was dark, save for the soft blue glow coming from his computer's power supply. She took a few steps into the room. "Cody? Hey, sleeping in is—"

The bed was empty. The covers shoved aside, the pillow on the floor.

And the bedroom window open. A chilly breeze floated the dark blue curtains in, out, in, out. She crossed to the window and saw nothing outside except for the deep impression of two footprints in the dewy grass, then a trail leading around to the side of the house.

That couldn't be from Cody. He had to be here somewhere. He'd never run away before. And things were going so well—why would he do that now?

Abby spun on her heel and darted into the bathroom the boys shared. Empty. She checked Jake's room, her bathroom and bedroom, the living room. No Cody. She paused on the stairs, looked out into the yard and noticed Cody's bike wasn't in its customary spot propped against the side of the shed.

Abby ran into the kitchen, her heart in her throat, panic rising in her chest. Jake was still at the table, eating while SpongeBob prattled on about Krabby Patties. "Jake? What did Cody say to you this morning? *Exactly.*"

Jake shrugged, his gaze on SpongeBob's debate with Mr. Krabs. "I dunno. He said goodbye."

Goodbye didn't mean anything. Cody could have gone to school early or to a friend's house—

But there was no text on her phone, no note on the table. Not that Cody told her when he was going to skip school. Something about this departure, though, felt different, wrong, and Abby's Mom SpideySense was tingling.

"Did he say where he was going?" Every word got shriller, worry hitting her in a wave. Cody skipped school, broke curfew and snuck out at night when he was grounded, but never had he left early in the morning, without a word.

Jake turned and looked at his mother. "Mommy, what's wrong?"

"Cody's not in his room," Abby said, and saying it made it real, and the feeling of wrongness multiplied. *Calm down*, she told herself, *don't get Jake all worked up. It's probably nothing.* "He's not in trouble, but I do need to know where he told you he was going, because moms should always know where their kids are, right? So, Jake, can you think really hard and tell me everything he said to you?"

Jake thought a minute. "He said, 'Bye-bye, Jakester.

I gotta go. I'm gonna go see Dad.' He said Dylan said he should."

Keith lived two states away, in Georgia. She wasn't even sure Cody had his father's address, since it had been at least a year since the boys had received so much as a Christmas card. Cody had no money, no means of transportation beside his bike. How on earth was he going to get there?

"Come on, Jake, we have to go now." She picked up the half-empty bowl and put it in the sink. "Go get your shoes on as fast as you can. We're not going to school today."

"Yay! Are we gonna go see Dylan?"

"Yes," Abby said, the word ground out between her teeth. "We are definitely starting with Dylan."

Dylan had arrived at the community center shortly after six in the morning, his To Do list long and full, the pressure to finish doubled after a late-night phone call from his boss in Maine. The job's timeline had been moved up, and Jay wanted him back as soon as possible—and if Dylan wasn't able to return to take on the role, he'd need to immediately hire someone else. Which meant instead of a week before he had to hit the road, Dylan had two days.

Today was Tuesday. He needed to drive back to Maine on Thursday, meet with his boss as soon as he got back and be ready to break ground on the first house in the development on Monday.

But after last night with Abby, Dylan's desire to leave quickly had been cut in half. He wanted the full week, wanted every minute he could have with her. He knew it was impossible to make this new relationship last once he returned to Maine, but—

He still wanted to see if there was a way. Abby was strong and confident and beautiful and unlike any woman he had ever met. She lingered in his mind, hung on the fringes of every thought, every breath.

So he got to work, because that was the only thing that kept him from running back over to Abby's house, just to see her smile, or even better, kiss her, touch her again. Given how often that urge hit him, he was going to end up renovating the entire building in a single day.

The door to the center opened, and even though Dylan knew it was too early and that she was undoubtedly either dropping kids at school or heading to work, his heart hoped to see Abby walking in. Instead, Uncle Ty headed inside and Dylan had to pretend he wasn't disappointed.

"Hey, Uncle Ty." He put down his paintbrush, crossed the room and gave his uncle a quick hug. "What are you doing here so early?"

Ty rocked back on his heels, paused a minute before he spoke. "Here to help, if you want a hand."

Dylan swallowed his surprise. "That would be great."

"Sorry it took me so long to get back on track." His uncle drew in a deep breath. "I always believed life was a journey on a winding road, you know? You hit a bump, you get up and keep going. Until I hit a detour and lost my Virginia and I came to a dead stop." His eyes watered. "But I gotta keep moving, even if it's harder than hell. Like you said, Virginia wouldn't want me sitting around, living in shadows the rest of my life. She'd want me to…"

"Move forward." Instead of staying in one place. That had always been Dylan's reasoning for moving from place to place, job to job. He'd told himself he was moving forward. But for some reason lately, it felt an awful lot like staying in the same place.

His uncle glanced around the center, at the newly repaired walls, the fixed window, the broken door that had been rehung. "You've done a great job here, Dylan, in a really short amount of time."

Uncle Ty had always been more of a father to Dylan than his own father, and his uncle's praise warmed him. "Thanks."

Ty brushed his hands together. "All right. Enough of that emotional crap. Where do we start?"

"Actually, I have to run over to the home improvement store and pick up the replacement piece of countertop I ordered." Dylan thumbed toward the paint and brush he had left in the corner. "If you want to finish painting that game cabinet while I'm gone, that would be great."

"Sure. Sounds good."

"When I get back, I have a few things to finish up here, then I thought I'd check out your truck this afternoon. Sounds like you need a tune-up. And then…" Dylan took in a deep breath. Better to say it sooner than later, even if the anticipation he'd felt earlier when he'd talked to Jay had begun to wither. "I've got to go back to Maine a little sooner than I expected. The timeline for the new build got moved up. My boss wants to put me in charge of the entire project, but only if I can get there in the next few days."

"That's great," Ty said, beaming at his nephew. "I always knew you'd be a success."

Dylan scoffed. Success? He wasn't sure he even thought of himself that way. Sure, he'd gotten his GED, advanced in the construction world until he became a general contractor, but it wasn't like he'd cured cancer or anything. "*Nobody* thought I'd be a success."

Ty put a hand on his nephew's heart. "Doesn't matter what anyone else thinks. If you're a success in here, then you are. As long as you're proud of yourself, that's all that matters."

Dylan had never thought about that before. Was he proud of who he was? What he had become in those years since he'd left this town? The man he'd been for the last couple weeks?

The same man who was leaving all this in his rear-view mirror soon?

Instead of answering those questions, he nodded toward the door. "I should get the countertop."

Uncle Ty reached in his back pocket and tugged out his wallet. "Let me pay you for—"

"You don't owe me anything, Uncle Ty. Not a single dime." Dylan pushed the wallet away. "You changed my life when I was younger, and that's payment enough."

"Success, right there." Ty gave his nephew a wide smile. "That's what makes me proud of myself, Dylan. It's not the money I've made or the house I've bought. It's opening this place and changing a life, one person at a time. It's why Virginia and I put so many years into this place and why I'm back again. You change one kid's life, and I'll tell you, it's the best feeling in the world. It's the kind of feeling that makes you want to stay around and keep on doing that."

Dylan grinned. "Is that a hint?"

"Well, I'm not getting any younger, and this center's going to need someone to keep it going. Someone young and enthusiastic." Ty arched a brow. "Hint, hint."

Him? Run the center? Dylan had enjoyed his time here, no doubt about that, but he didn't see himself as the kind of person who should be influencing kids. He didn't have the steady way that Ty had or Aunt Virginia's experience. "Nobody could replace you, Uncle Ty."

"No, there's one somebody who could." Ty gave him another smile, then gestured toward the door. "Go ahead, go get the countertop. I'll hold down the fort here. But think about what I said, okay?"

"Yeah." Dylan walked out of the center and climbed in his Jeep. Uncle Ty was crazy if he thought Dylan should be the one to take over the center. Dylan certainly hadn't done much to change anyone's life here in the past week or so—one changed grade for Cody didn't equal a life-changing moment—and he doubted he'd ever be the kind of role model Ty had been to him.

No, it was best if he got on the road and got back to Maine. Before he got any more wrapped up in a fantasy life he wasn't made for having.

Abby tried Dylan's phone but there was no answer. She tried calling Cody, leaving several messages, but he didn't answer, either. She drove through town toward the community center, frantic, looking for her son and his bike.

Nothing. She told herself Cody couldn't have gone that far. It had only been, what, at most an hour since he left? She didn't know for sure, and that was what scared her most. Cody could be anywhere by now.

Maybe he was just blowing off some steam. But no matter how many times she checked her phone, she didn't see a message from Dylan or Cody.

"Mommy, where are we going?"

Jake had sat in the back seat, playing with one of his dinosaurs, unaware of the rising worry in Abby's mind. "I was thinking we'd stop by and see Dylan, then maybe you can play at Ty's house today." She tried to keep her voice light, happy, in the this-is-an-adventure tone. She glanced at Jake in the rearview mirror. "Does that sound good?"

"Yup. I like Ty. He's really nice and he made me popcorn. And he likes dinosaurs, too."

"That's great," Abby said, barely hearing as Jake went on about Ty's favorite prehistoric creatures. Her mind raced while her gaze darted from one side to the other, peering down every street she passed. No sign of her son, of his bike.

A little after seven, Abby pulled up to the community center. Dylan's car wasn't in the lot, but Ty's was. She parked, not bothering to stay within the lines, then unbuckled Jake and dashed inside. She slowed her steps when she got inside, said a quick hello to Dylan's uncle, then plopped Jake in front of the TV. "Why don't you watch a cartoon while I talk to Ty?"

"SpongeBob?"

"Sure, sure." She handed Jake the remote, then crossed the room to Ty. "Has Cody been here?"

Ty paused in touching up the paint job on a cabinet that usually held games and books. "No, I haven't. Isn't he supposed to be in school?"

Abby lowered her voice and tried to curb her growing worry and impatience. "He told Jake he was leaving to go see his father. He said that Dylan told him to do it."

"Dylan?" Ty's brows creased. "He wouldn't tell Cody to run away."

But hadn't Dylan been a runaway himself? Had he told Cody about his life and Cody had taken that as a sign he should do the same? Didn't it stand to reason that if Dylan could persuade Cody to do his math homework, he could also influence him in running away? Or was she just being overly suspicious because she was worried and scared?

"Maybe he didn't. But maybe he just made his choices sound glamorous to a teenager who didn't need a negative influence." She let out a gusty sigh. She should have known better than to trust a man who had wanderlust in his blood. "I never should have fallen for him."

"Whoa, whoa. Don't blame this all on Dylan. Let's talk to Cody first—"

Abby threw up her hands. "I don't know where he is. He's on his bike and he doesn't have any money, and I don't know what to do." Tears burned the backs of her eyes, but she willed them away. She had to hold it together, had to think. "I tried calling Dylan, but he didn't answer."

Ty nodded toward the table. "Left his cell here when he ran over to the home improvement store. He should be back in about a half hour."

"I don't have that kind of time, Ty. I need to find Cody before he does something stupid." She glanced around the center again, as if she could find her eldest son asleep on a sofa, unnoticed by everyone. All she saw was Jake, thankfully engrossed in the cartoon and unaware of her worry. "Can you stay here, watch Jake and call me if Cody shows up?"

"Of course. And when Dylan gets back—"

Dylan. The mistake she'd made. He had gotten close to her and her boys and just when she'd let down her defenses, he'd gone and told Cody something stupid. Or if he hadn't said the words, he'd at the very least set the example.

"He's made things bad enough. I don't need his help." Then she turned and headed out of the building.

Doing exactly what she should have done all along—relying on herself and no one else.

Chapter Ten

They were a family.

Dylan sat at the stop sign in downtown Stone Gap and watched his brother with his fiancée and his kids in the park. Laughing, smiling. Having fun.

The kids, both brown-haired like Dylan and Sam had been as kids, were dressed in jackets, with book bags and lunchboxes set on the bench. Probably making a quick stop at the park before school. It seemed like something Sam would do. Sam always had been the nurturing kind. Dylan had no doubt he was an excellent dad.

Dylan sat at the stop sign, his Jeep idling, for a long time, debating. Then someone pulled up behind him and beeped, forcing him into a decision. Dylan went through the intersection, pulled into a space on the right, then jogged across the street.

He didn't know what made him enter the park. Something deep inside him urged him closer to his brother, to that picture-perfect family on the swing set. Maybe it was the sense of things unfinished or the urge to set things right before he left again. Or maybe it was seeing Sam's kids, laughing and playing together, that reminded him of days like that decades ago.

When Dylan neared, Sam stopped pushing the swing his daughter was on and raised a brow in surprise. "Dylan. What are you doing here?"

The distrust in Sam's voice almost made Dylan turn around. But then he looked at the two kids, a girl about eight and a little boy the same age as Jake, and he saw himself and Sam in their curious faces. Dylan thought of Jake and Cody and how awful it would be if the two of them grew up and stopped talking to each other. Jake clearly idolized Cody, and Cody had a way of being protective and tender with his little brother, much like Sam had always been with Dylan. Before Dylan took several wrong turns and their relationship went south.

Why had he gone so many years without talking to Sam? Did it really matter what they had said to each other when they were both still young and hot-headed? Dylan's heart ached for the connection he'd once had with Sam. The memories he'd missed out on, the conversations they hadn't had.

More than a decade had passed. Wasn't it time to let go and move on?

Dylan took two steps forward. "Meeting my brother's family, if that's okay. Sorry it took me so long to get here."

Sam glanced at the brunette woman beside him—Katie was her name, Dylan remembered. She gave Sam a slight nod and a tender smile. Sam stepped away from the swing, and Katie slipped into his place and started pushing Libby first, then Henry, alternating between the kids.

Dylan held his breath. Sam stood there another minute, assessing Dylan. Finally, the steel in Sam's face eased. The two of them, so alike, so close. Dylan could almost feel the years of animosity rolling back.

"Better late than never," Sam said. He reached forward, and drew Dylan into a hug. Dylan held stone still for a second, surprised, then as Sam kept on hugging him, he was five again, scared of the sounds of yet another argument floating up the staircase. Sam telling him it was all going to be all right. Making up a story about a pirate and a hidden treasure, until Sam's voice drowned out the anger on the floor below them.

His older brother. Not just a sibling but a friend. A friend he had missed more than he realized.

"Damn, I'm sorry, Sam, for everything," Dylan said, drawing back. All the words that Dylan hadn't spoken, words that had lain in wait for the moment when he was ready to face his past, repair his mistakes. "I didn't mean to drag you into my trouble all those years ago. I should have called Dad the night I was arrested instead of you but you were...you were my best friend."

Sam had been the only one Dylan trusted. The only one he'd ever felt was on his side.

"Don't apologize. I'm glad you called me," Sam said. "Dad would have just yelled at you and probably left you in that police station overnight. I never understood why he had such a beef with you."

Dylan had done a lot of thinking about that very fact ever since he'd left home. It had taken years for him to see his father clearly, to understand the anger and criticism. Now he was older, presumably wiser, he could see his father's viewpoint. Didn't mean he agreed with it, but it brought some peace to Dylan to know it wasn't really personal. "I heard him and Mom arguing one time and he said he would have left her a long time ago, except she got pregnant again. I think he just always saw me as the reason he had to work so many hours and not get whatever life he wanted."

Sam shook his head in disgust. "That's just wrong. I'd never think that about one of my kids."

"That's why you're the kind of dad everyone wishes they had." Dylan glanced at Henry and Libby, who were clearly happy and content. How would Dylan's life had been different—or for that matter, Jake and Cody's lives—with two loving, supportive parents? "That's why I called you that night. I knew you'd take care of me."

And Sam had. After he'd bailed Dylan out, he'd talked to the police and the shop owner, getting them to drop all charges so that Dylan could go free. Then Sam had come home and started lecturing Dylan, not out of some need to emulate their father, Dylan realized now, but out of fear that his little brother was going to end up in jail or worse. Dylan had been too angry in those years to see what his brother had done for him. Too immature to realize that leaving town wasn't the answer to his problems. Facing them and tackling them was.

Sam smiled. "You think I'm a good dad?"

"You know I do. But if you ask me in public, I'll deny everything."

The brothers laughed, then Dylan sighed and faced all the things that he had avoided for so long, all the mistakes he had made. Sam hadn't let Dylan down— he'd been trying to protect him. Whereas Dylan, caught in misguided resentment, had left Sam alone when he needed support the most. "I'm sorry I missed out on getting to know Libby and Henry earlier. Or not being here after your wife died. I was too caught up in my own crap to be good brother. I'm so, so sorry."

"I don't blame you. Hell, I wouldn't have talked to me, either." Sam shook his head. "I said a lot of things to you that night that I never should have. I was young and I was just…"

"Just what?" Dylan prompted when Sam stopped talking.

His brother watched his kids swinging for a while. "I was mad. You were leaving, Dylan. Leaving me, leaving me with them. And I was mad that you were getting out of here and I was…staying behind."

Dylan had never looked at it that way. For so many years, his own hurt feelings had gotten in the way of him seeing things from Sam's point of view. When Dylan was away, Sam had handled their parents, dealt with them almost daily. Helped them move to their retirement home in Arizona. "I had no idea. I didn't leave town because I was mad at you. I left because I didn't see another way out."

Sam considered those words, then waved a hand in dismissal. There was the Sam that Dylan had known as a kid, quick to forgive and forget. "It's been more than ten years. I think that's long enough, don't you?"

"Yeah," Dylan said. "More than long enough."

Sam's face broke into a wide grin. He clapped Dylan on the shoulder, then drew him into another hug. And just like that, the brothers erased years of distance. The renewed connection to Sam settled over Dylan like a warm summer day. It was nice. Really nice.

"Come on, Dylan." Sam thumbed toward the swing set. "I'd like to introduce you to my family."

As they crossed to the playground, Dylan saw Katie's face light up. She smiled at Sam first, one of those private smiles of someone in love. His brother had the same goofy grin on his face. A little surge of envy ran through Dylan. What would it be like to come home to a woman who smiled at him like that every day? Who made his world light up?

Like Abby had, in the few days they'd been together. He pushed that thought away, to deal with when he wasn't feeling all dorky and sentimental.

"Dylan, this is my fiancée, Katie," Sam said. "She's related to the Barlows, but it's a long story. I'll tell you sometime over a beer." Sam said that as if Dylan was putting down roots. Planning on being here for the next family barbecue or birthday party. The Barlows had—well, every one of them had settled into town. They'd been here for generations, the kind of people who put down roots. Like Sam had.

Dylan had no doubt that he could return to Stone Gap in ten years and still find the Barlows here, and see Sam and Katie, happier than ever. And where would Dylan be?

He had no idea. He could be in Maine, he could be in Florida, he could be in Timbuktu. For the first time that he could remember, that thought didn't fill him with anticipation.

"Nice to meet you, Katie," Dylan said. "You must be a patient woman to put up with my brother."

Katie smiled up at Sam. "Oh, he's not so bad."

"Yeah, he's not," Dylan said. "I'm happy for you both."

Sam called over his kids and introduced them. Libby and Henry were both cute, amiable kids. "You guys must know Jake Cooper," Dylan said. "His mom said you two come to the community center sometimes."

Libby nodded. "We go on Tuesdays, when Mom Katie works late. She helps my daddy with his company."

Sam chuckled. "I don't think being a corporate Realtor means I have a company of my own, but yeah, Katie helps me with the accounting." He wrapped an arm around his soon-to-be-wife. She beamed up at him and put a hand on his chest. "She's brilliant with numbers."

For a second, Dylan wanted to tell Sam about Abby, to add that his girlfriend was brilliant at marketing, that she had helped put the Stone Gap Inn on the map. But calling her his girlfriend implied something more permanent. Something that meant staying in town.

As he said goodbye to his brother's family, promising to stop by for dinner the next night, he had to wonder if maybe taking the road out of town had taken him in the wrong direction. Away from the very thing that Sam had and Dylan hadn't thought he wanted until he saw how precious it was.

Abby spent another hour scouring Stone Gap and calling Cody's cell phone. No response and no sign of her son. She called his school, texted his friends, but no one had seen or heard from him. She swung back by the community center, relieved to see Dylan's car back in the parking lot. Finally.

He was just getting out of his truck as she pulled in. He gave her a wave, then opened the back of his Jeep to pull out the section of countertop he'd ordered a few days ago. "Hey, Abby."

"Don't you 'hey' me," she said. Her temper was full-on now, powered by an almost frantic worry about where Cody could be. "What did you say to my son?"

Dylan gave her a confused look. "Say to your son? Which one? Jake? Cody?"

"Cody. He ran away and told Jake it was because of what *you* said." She came closer, pointing at his chest. "What did you say to him? Did you tell him how great it was to run away? How it would be some kind of cool adventure or something?"

Dylan shook his head. "I never told him to run away, Abby. That's the last thing I'd say to any kid."

She let out a gust. "Did you tell him to go look for his father?"

"No. We never really talked about his father." Dylan thought a minute. "Wait, yeah, we did one time, but only briefly."

"And what *exactly* did you say to him?"

"He asked me if I'd ever confronted my dad about how he treated me when I was a kid. I told him that I had and that it hadn't gone well. Cody asked if there was hope for his dad, and I said he wouldn't know until he asked him. I'm sorry, Abby. I never thought he'd take off and go do that."

Cody, still aching for the father he'd never really had. The man who had provided him with DNA and not much else. Her heart broke for her son, who was looking for answers he might never get. "So you told him to go see his father and confront him?"

"No. I didn't. And Cody didn't mention that he wanted to." Dylan put the countertop down, then took Abby's hands in his. "You have to believe me, Abby. I would never tell him to leave."

She wanted to lean into his touch, into the comfort of someone who knew Cody, someone who wanted to support her, but Dylan was the whole reason she was here. Maybe his intentions had been good, but the results were disastrous. She pulled her hands out of his. "Whatever you said, it made my son sneak out of the house before I woke up and get on his bike. His father lives in *Georgia*, Dylan. Is he planning on riding all the way there? Or God forbid, hitchhike? He has maybe ten bucks to his name. What do you think is going to happen to him out there?" Her voice had risen into that shrill panic again. Her heart thudded in her chest, the worry quadrupling as she realized how much she'd counted on Dylan having the answers she needed.

Another dead end. Her son was out there, somewhere, and she couldn't find him. Oh, God.

She had already called the police, but they were nonchalant about a sixteen-year-old who had a history of not showing up at school. She was going to call again, and maybe they'd take her seriously this time.

"Calm down, Abby. I'm sure if we think about it together, we can figure out where he is or what route he might have taken."

Calm down? Didn't he realize what she was going through? The catastrophe his "words of advice" had created in her life? If something happened to Cody while he was out on the road...

"I'm not doing anything together with you, Dylan. All you did is show up in this town, screw up my life and now you're going to leave again, like a storm that blew through. Do me a favor and stay away from me and my boys." She got back in her car and left the parking lot, then headed for the streets again.

Alone. Because that was the best choice for her, all around.

Dylan watched Abby go, and for the second time in his life, felt like he had failed at everything. Had an innocuous conversation really driven Cody to try to make his way to Georgia? On a ten-speed and with ten bucks?

He replayed the words he'd exchanged with Cody in

his head again and again. There'd been nothing in their few words at the end of the fishing trip that said, *run away and settle this*, Dylan was sure of it.

Cody was a smart kid. He would know he couldn't travel through two states on a bike. And even if he was trying, chances were good he was still close by. But where?

And if Abby hadn't been able to find him, what made Dylan think he'd have better luck?

He grabbed the countertop and headed into the center. Jake was sitting at a table, working on some kind of craft with glue and construction paper while Uncle Ty was fixing a loose door handle. When he saw Dylan, Ty stopped what he was doing and gestured toward the kitchen.

Dylan laid the replacement countertop into the open slot, then turned to face his uncle. He kept his voice low, aware Jake was just a room away. "What happened? I just saw Abby in the parking lot and she said Cody ran away?"

"I don't know much more than you." Worry etched the lines in Ty's face. The kids at the center were Ty's family, and whenever one of them got in trouble, got sick or hurt, it hit his uncle as hard as it did the parents. "She came here about an hour ago, looking for you. You'd forgotten your cell—"

Dylan patted his pocket and cursed. Of all times to not have his phone on him.

"So she left Jake here and went out searching." Ty shook his head. "I told her you'd never say anything like that to Cody."

"And I didn't. Not exactly." Dylan recounted what he had told Abby in the parking lot. "I didn't mean anything other than calling his dad up and having a conversation, if he thought it would help. Not take off and go there on his own. Even if he tried that, I don't think Cody could have gotten very far."

"Unless he ditched the bike and started hitchhiking. Like you did."

The thought made Dylan shiver. Would Cody do that? Would he, like Dylan once had, think that thumbing his way from here to Georgia was a cool idea?

Two years before Dylan left Stone Gap for good, he'd had a blowout fight with his father over his grades and lack of ambition and whatever else his father was mad at him for that day. Dylan had taken off on his bike, riding hard until the sun went down and the road ahead seemed endless. He'd hit a rock, blown a tire and been forced to leave the bike on the side of the road, then stick out a thumb.

In the movies, hitchhiking always looked so cool. Some guy with an interesting story to tell picked up the lonely wanderer and they embarked on an adventure, building a lifelong friendship as the miles passed. But the first car that stopped was driven by a man who gave Dylan a long look that made his hair stand on end. He'd refused the ride and walked away, feeling the dark crowding in on him.

A second set of headlights came up behind him a few seconds later and Dylan had started to break into a run, sure the creepy guy was coming to get him. Grab him and drag him away, in one of those hitchhiker scenarios that didn't end with a fun adventure.

But when he'd turned, he'd seen the headlights of a pickup truck, not a sedan. And behind the wheel, a much welcome and familiar face.

"You brought me home that night," Dylan said to his uncle. The gratitude he'd felt on that stretch of road still rung in his heart. "Somehow you found me, and you picked me up."

Before anything bad happened. The words were unspoken but had always hovered in the air. It was one of hundreds of tiny moments that had tied Dylan's loyalty to his uncle. Ty was a good man, a good role model and one of the best things in Stone Gap. When Dylan had left town, he'd missed his uncle every single day.

"It was easy to find you, Dylan. I knew you and figured you'd head for that campground on Stone Gap Lake. We did that group camping trip there every summer. You always loved that campground and said it was your favorite place in the world." Ty shrugged, like it was no big deal, but for Dylan, who had grown up with a father who'd never understood him, Ty's perceptiveness mattered. A lot.

"I'm glad you remembered that, Uncle Ty. I don't know what I would have done if you hadn't come along."

"Well, I'm glad I did. Though I'm not so sure you liked the lecture I gave you on the way home about making smart choices. About staying around instead of running from your problems."

"I guess I didn't really listen, since I was on the road again two years later." He had hurt his uncle, hurt his brother, and now, he realized also hurt himself by severing these relationships that meant so much to him.

Ty smiled. "You always were a stubborn learner, Dylan, but you came around. And hopefully you've stopped running."

Dylan didn't know how to answer that. Was going back to his job in Maine running away? Or was it just doing the sensible thing? "I honestly don't know, Uncle Ty."

"Did I ever tell you how I ran away from home when I was about that age?" When Dylan shook his head, Ty continued, "Probably because I didn't want you to think it was a cool idea. But I'd had a fight with my parents, probably over the same things kids fight with their parents about now, and I decided I was better off on my own. I made it two miles out of town and spent the night camping in the woods. By the time I got back home, my mother was a mess and my father was talking to the police in the driveway. I've always regretted hurting them like that. When I saw the worry on their faces, I knew running away was the wrong choice. So when you did the same thing, I found you by thinking like I had when I ran away. That's how you can help Abby find Cody. Which direction do you think he would go? And where do you think he would stop when it got scary and lonely?"

Dylan didn't know Cody that well. He'd only met the kid a little over a week ago. But from the start, he'd felt like they were kindred spirits. Loners with troubled relationships with their fathers.

It wasn't much to go on. But it was a start.

Chapter Eleven

Abby sat in her house and cried. She'd been all over Stone Gap, up and down every single street, then driving the outskirts, even hitting the highway for several miles in each direction, trying to find any sign of her son. She'd called all his friends, then the friends' mothers, searched the penny candy store and the arcade and the bowling alley—

No Cody.

She picked up her phone and made the last call she wanted to make. When her ex-husband picked up, Abby braced herself. "Keith, I just wanted to let you know Cody might be on his way up to see you."

He sighed. "Did you kick him out or something?"

The implication that it was her fault. "No. He's just upset with you and I think he wants to talk to you in person. He didn't think it through and just took off on his bike."

He cursed. "Can't you keep an eye on those kids? I don't have time to deal with this."

"Those kids are your *sons*, Keith." How many times had she said those words and it hadn't changed anything?

When they first met, she'd been fresh out of high school and seen city-born and much older Keith as charming, exciting. A man who traveled the world, lived for experiences and spontaneity. It wasn't until she was married and pregnant that she'd realized all of those things rotated around the very small axis of Keith. When he'd come back into her life, begging for a second chance, she'd convinced herself that he had changed, that the fairy tale she had dreamed of was finally coming to life. In the end, Keith had gone right back to focusing on the only thing that mattered—himself.

"I'm the one who is here with them full-time, feeding them, raising them, so yes, I do keep an eye on them."

"Here we go again." He sighed. "The bad-dad lecture."

"I don't have to give you a lecture. You *know* you're a terrible father. You haven't been there for either one of them for longer than five minutes." Keith had had brief moments of clarity when he'd come back into her life, vowing to be different, to try again to create a family with her. To stop wasting money on gambling and alcohol and idiocy. She'd thought the change was real, something to depend upon. But in the end, he'd gone right back to his old behavior, leaving her with two kids and a nearly empty bank account.

"I have to work, Abby. It's not like I just sit around all day. I'm busy."

"Too busy for your children?" She drew in a breath and bit her tongue before she said anything more and re-tread an argument she'd had five thousand times. None of that brought her son home. "Will you please just let me know if you hear from or see Cody?"

"I don't think I'll see him. I've got meetings and sales calls and—"

"Just text me or call me. Please." She hung up, even more frustrated than she'd been before she had dialed. Keith was never going to step into fatherhood and be a good role model. The kind who read bedtime stories and took his sons fishing and showed them how to fix whatever was broken.

Only one man had done that. Dylan.

But he'd also given her son advice that had put her sixteen-year-old out on the road alone. Cody had been gone for five hours now, and she was no closer to finding him than she had been this morning.

Abby sank into a chair and started to sob again. She'd failed as a parent. Failed to keep her child safe. Failed to be there when he needed her. And now, she may have lost Cody altogether.

When Dylan left Uncle Ty at the shelter with Jake, the two of them were working together to install the new countertop. The activity kept Jake distracted, kept him from asking every few minutes where his mother was and when his brother was coming back. On the other hand, the little boy peppered Uncle Ty with so many questions about the installation process—and everything else under the sun, including Ty's favorite kind of dinosaur and whether he thought Jake should have a puppy—that the older man had no time to dwell on his grief. Dylan could see Ty's enthusiasm for working with kids returning the more he interacted with Jake.

Which meant Ty no longer really needed Dylan. He'd finished all the repairs on the center except for the roof and an engine tune-up for Ty's aged pickup. If he had enough time before he left, he wanted to give the pontoon boat a spruce-up. And there was also the broken window at Abby's—

If he wanted to, Dylan could easily find enough things to keep him busy in Stone Gap for a month. The problem—he didn't have a month. He had two days. And right now, the entire To Do list was on hold until he found Cody.

He thought of what Uncle Ty had said, about trying to see Cody's perspective and using that to figure out where he might have gone. For a while, Dylan drove aimlessly, while his mind turned over every conversation he'd had with the boy.

Then, as he made his second loop of Stone Gap, his mind latched on to an idea. It was a long shot, but maybe...

Dylan turned right, and as the Jeep left the main areas of Stone Gap, he began to accelerate. The long shot became more of a possibility the farther he drove. He turned off the main road, down a path he had taken just a couple days ago. His battered Jeep bumped and lurched over the dirt road, squeaky axles protesting the rough treatment.

There was a flash of silver ahead of him. The frame of a bike, left in the grass of a ditch. Dylan's chest squeezed. For a second, that was his bike and he was back on the road and trying to get away from the scary man in the sedan.

What if the same thing had happened to Cody? What if Dylan was too late?

The pocked road forced him to slow the Jeep. It had rained the night before, and the path that had been smooth just twenty-four hours earlier was now filled with muddy divots that were hardening in the North Carolina sun. He braced himself on the roof while he urged the Jeep farther down the path.

Finally, Dylan rounded a corner and stopped. Stone Gap Lake lay before him, blue and sparkling and inviting. On any other day, the sight would have made Dylan feel peaceful.

But when he noticed the empty dock, the space where Uncle Ty's pontoon boat usually sat, any sense of peace evaporated. Undoubtedly the key tucked in the box under the steering wheel was used to start it, by a kid who had paid attention on a fishing trip.

Dylan debated calling Abby. But he wasn't sure that was Cody's bike, and the pontoon could have been borrowed by one of Ty's friends. Still, Dylan's instincts told him otherwise. He'd check it out, then call her if he found something.

Better to be sure than disappoint her again. He'd seen

the look in her eyes, the hurt, the betrayal. Why did it seem that no matter how hard he tried, he still ended up hurting the people he cared about?

Dylan jogged down the shore, until he reached the spit of land that held Ray Prescott's cabin. At the top of the hill, he saw Jack Barlow, installing a new back deck on Ray's house. His old friend from high school still had the haircut and lean body of his military days. "Hey, Jack!"

The youngest Barlow son turned and gave Dylan a wave. Jack put down his hammer and the board in his hands, then ambled down the embankment. "Dylan! Nice to see you. My mom told me you were back in town."

He wasn't surprised Della had mentioned his return to her sons, probably thinking they would all get together. Now was not the time to catch up, though. "Yeah, I've been here for almost two weeks. Listen, can I borrow Ray's boat?"

Jack shrugged. "Sure. I don't think he'd mind. Is Ty's broken down?"

"No." Dylan sighed. "I think Abby Cooper's son Cody is out on the water in it. Abby's been looking all over for him, and she's frantic."

"Come to think of it, I did hear a boat go by maybe a couple hours ago. I was busy and didn't look to see whose boat it was. But it went to the eastern side of the lake."

"Thanks, Jack." Dylan turned to go back down the hill. Eastern side? Maybe Cody had taken the boat out fishing. Or maybe it wasn't Cody at all and Dylan was chasing his own tail.

"Hey, Dylan?"

He turned back. "Yeah?"

"It's good to have you back in town. Maybe after you get this Cody thing straightened out, you could come to dinner at my house. Meri would love to see you, too."

Meri, clearly now Jack's wife, given the gold ring on Jack's left hand. "Sure. That'd be great." He didn't want to tell Jack that his time in Stone Gap was limited and the chances of dinner with them were slim. He thanked him again, then jogged down to the pier and untied Ray's flat-bottom fishing boat from the cleats.

There was water in the boat, from the rainstorm. Dylan scooped it out with furious moves, then turned to start the motor. The engine took a couple good pulls before it finally roared to life.

Dylan steered the boat through the lake, scanning the wide expanse of water. He headed east, passing Uncle Ty's favorite fishing spot on the way. No pontoon. No Cody.

Dylan pushed the little outboard to go faster. He skirted the outside of the lake, then slowed to skim past the thick pocket of lilies that carpeted the water between the tiny island in the center of Stone Gap Lake and the water's edge. Just as he rounded the island, he saw the pontoon.

And Cody, sitting on the seats at the bow, his head on his knees. Relief flooded Dylan. He took out his cell phone to call Abby, but out here on the lake, he didn't have a signal.

Dylan pulled up alongside the pontoon, tied the fishing boat to the railing, then climbed aboard. "Cody! Hey, dude, we've been looking all over for you."

The teenager scowled. "I didn't want to be found. I wanted to get out of here for a while."

He could have been parroting back Dylan's exact words when he was that age. He could see the anger and distance in the set of Cody's jaw, the hardness of his shoulders.

Was anything Dylan could say going to make it better? Or would he only send Cody in the wrong direction again?

He thought of that long drive home with Uncle Ty all those years ago, the words his uncle had said. Words Dylan hadn't been ready to hear then, but maybe Cody would respond differently.

Dylan lowered himself to the bench seat beside Cody. "Your mom said you were thinking of going to your dad's house in Georgia."

"Yeah, well, he doesn't want to see me. I called him and he said he was busy and maybe he could get me a plane ticket sometime instead." Cody cursed. "I should have known he wasn't going to change."

Dylan's heart broke for Cody. He knew that disappointment. He wished he could wave a magic wand and make everything better, but life wasn't a movie that ended with happy tears and rolling credits.

"Some people never change," Dylan said. "But if you ask me, your dad is the one losing out, not you. You're a great kid, Cody. You're smart and strong and so good to Jake." Much like Sam had been with Dylan.

Cody lifted his head. "You think I'm a great kid?"

"Yeah, I do. I've really enjoyed getting to know you and spending time with you while I've been here."

Cody picked at the railing, his gaze averted. "My mom says you're leaving."

"I have a job in Maine. So yes, I am leaving." But the thought made Dylan's chest ache. He looked out over the glass-smooth water, sparkling in the bright sun. It was a perfect day to be out here, absorbing some peace and quiet. He was going to miss this lake. Miss—

This kid. His brother. And most of all, their mom.

"So you're gonna be just like my dad and bail." Cody cursed and got to his feet. "Why don't you just leave already? We don't need you."

The sharp words slivered through Dylan. He could see the wall going up in Cody again, the boy adding the bricks as fast as he could, to head off another hurt. "I'm not bailing, Cody. I have a job and—"

"There are jobs here, fixing up houses and running the center and things like that. You told me so yourself. That if I graduated and learned more of this stuff, I could work with a construction crew like you do."

"Yes, I could work here. But..." Dylan searched for an explanation, one that Cody would understand. And came up empty. "Maine is where my job is. I'm sorry."

"Just go, Dylan." Cody's face darkened and he waved Dylan off. "You don't have to stay here and babysit me. I'm fine."

"Then why were you sitting on the bow? Not fishing or moving?"

"Engine died." He shrugged. "But I'll just wait a

bit and start it again. I mean, I don't know much about engines, but I figured maybe it was just overheated or something."

There was no way Dylan was going to leave this kid on the water in a boat that wasn't working. Though honestly, he wasn't about to leave him until he was safe and back home with his mother.

"Let me look at the motor." Dylan waved to Cody. "Come on, you can help me."

They went to the back of the boat. Dylan tried starting the outboard himself, but it wouldn't catch, so he tipped it forward and removed the cover. "We can check the spark plug and the fuel lines. See if the plug is bad or if one of the fuel lines is leaking." He pointed out the parts to Cody as he went through the engine. "All of this seems to be okay."

"Then are we stuck out here?"

"Nope. Couple more things we can check." Dylan lowered the engine back into place, then pointed at a hatch. "Open that up and we'll check the fuel vent."

Cody lifted the hatch, looked at the tank below him, then up at Dylan with confusion. "Uh, where's the fuel vent?"

"See that circular thing right there, attached to the fuel line? When that gets blocked, the engine can't draw any fuel and it won't start."

Cody looked inside, peered at the vent. "It looks like there's some mud in there."

"Mud daubers—they're **kind** of like wasps—like to build nests in there." **Dylan** took out his penknife and handed it to Cody. "Be careful, but go ahead and clean that out."

"Me?"

"You can do it, Code." Dylan sat back and watched while the teenager cleaned the vent, then closed the hatch. "Okay, try to start it."

Cody turned the key. The outboard sputtered for a minute, then roared to life. Pride lit Cody's face. "I did it."

"Yup." Another victory in the life of a kid who'd had way too much disappointment, especially today. Dylan couldn't repair all that, but he could fix this moment. "Now, let's head for home."

Cody shook his head. "I can't do that. My mom's gonna kill me."

"She'll be mad, yes. But she'll also be so glad to see you that she's probably going to hug you for a year." Now whether Abby would forgive Dylan that quickly was a whole other story. He wasn't going to put a wager on that, not after their argument this morning.

Cody fiddled with the steering wheel. "She's not such a bad mom, is she?"

"She's one of the best." The kind of mom every kid deserved to have. A woman unlike any other that Dylan had ever met.

Cody let out a long breath. "Is my dad ever going to change?"

The question hung in the warm October air, heavy and thick. Dylan heard his own voice in Cody's and would have done anything in that moment to fix everything for the boy. "I don't know the answer to that,

Cody. My dad is still the same as he was when I was a kid. I don't know if people really change all that much."

"But you did, didn't you? My friend Matt said his mom used to know you. She said you, like, dropped out and stuff, and people thought you were going to end up in jail, cuz you got arrested a lot when you were a kid."

Yeah, that was his reputation. People didn't forget in this town, and he might as well have tattooed the information on his forehead.

Except there were some people—Sam, Abby, her sons, Uncle Ty—who didn't see Dylan's past when they looked at him. They just saw him, as he was. *You're a good man*, Abby had said.

Words that Dylan still wasn't sure he believed. He wondered if Abby still believed them, or if he'd let her down too much, too.

"Once. I got arrested once," Dylan said to Cody. "I was young and stupid and didn't listen to anyone. My brother bailed me out and the charges were dropped, but it could have ended much, much worse, Cody. And yes, I did drop out, and floated around for years before I finally figured out what I wanted. If I could go back and do it all over again, I'd do a lot of things differently."

Cody waved that off. "All adults say that."

"Because it's true." Dylan glanced out over the water. "You know, you've got a great mom, a great life here. And a great future, if you just accept it instead of running from it. I ran from my life for too long, and I don't want to do that anymore. There's something nice about knowing where you're going to be tomorrow and the day after that."

Cody thought about that for a second. "And where are you going to be, Dylan?"

Dylan didn't answer. He just took the wheel and steered the pontoon boat back to the dock.

Abby grabbed her car keys and headed out the door. She needed to make another sweep of Stone Gap, and if she still didn't find Cody, she was going to call the police. Keith had texted to say he heard from Cody and told him not to come to Georgia. That they'd see each other another time.

At least that took a two-state hitchhiking journey off the table. But it didn't tell her where her son was.

She pulled out her phone to call Ty and ask him to keep Jake a little longer when a Jeep pulled in her driveway. Dylan's car. With Cody in the passenger seat. Thank God.

Abby barreled down the stairs and flung open the car door. All the worry and anger disappeared the second she saw her son's face.

"Mom, I'm sorry—"

"Thank God you're okay." She grabbed Cody in a bear hug, the tightest hug she'd given him since the day he was six and fell off the monkey bars and banged his head on the ground. She'd picked her son up that day and held him tight and long, thinking she would have died if she'd lost him. And now, ten years later, she felt exactly the same way. "I love you, Cody. I'm so glad you're home."

Cody hugged his mother, just as he had when he was six. For the first time in a long time, Abby felt like she had her son truly and totally back. Gratitude overflowed in her heart and spilled out in her tears.

"Don't you ever do that again, Cody. You worried me so much." Her words were muffled by his shoulder.

"I won't, Mom. I'm sorry. I wasn't thinking."

"You're home now. That's all that matters." She hugged him tighter still. Over Cody's head, she saw Dylan. She mouthed *thank you*. Dylan nodded in return, his face unreadable.

After a while, Cody drew back. "Hey, where's Jake?"

"Over at the community center with Ty." Abby brushed Cody's hair off his forehead. He looked embarrassed but didn't stop her. "We can go over there. I know he'll be glad to see you."

"Why don't we all go over there?" Dylan said. "Hop in, Abby. I'll give you a ride."

She climbed in the back of the Jeep and the three of them made the short drive to the community center.

Abby could hardly take her eyes off her son. He'd only been gone a few hours, but it had felt like a lifetime. Later, they would talk, maybe one of those late-night conversations she used to have with Cody before Keith left and Jake came along. She'd make him some hot cocoa and they'd sit at the kitchen table and get back to where they used to be before the schedules and the organization and the turmoil over grades and curfews.

If there was one thing she'd learned in the last couple of weeks, it was that ditching the schedule sometimes didn't necessarily result in catastrophe. It was in those moments when she'd had unscripted fun with her boys—fishing, barbecuing, tearing down a wall—when she had seen the connection knit more tightly between the three of them. In the future, she vowed, there'd be far more of that and far less of the rigid lines that had filled her life before.

As soon as Dylan parked, Cody hopped out and headed inside. Abby lingered by the car. She'd loosened up with her kids in the last few weeks, and it had changed things in good ways, overall. Maybe it was time she loosened the cage she kept around her heart, too, and let someone in again. "Dylan, wait. I wanted to talk to you."

He turned back. "Sure."

"Thank you so much for finding Cody." Abby could tell Dylan thank-you a thousand times and it still wouldn't be enough to express the depths of her gratitude. He didn't have to help her, didn't have to come back here, knowing how she blamed him. But he had, and that meant a lot. "How did you do it? I looked everywhere, called all his friends."

"I was like him one time, and my uncle found me by thinking about where I would go. So I did the same with him. He said something to me on the fishing boat about how when he was out on the water, nothing bugged him. I thought he might have borrowed Ty's boat."

The fishing trip. Of course. Cody had been open and relaxed that day, back to the son she remembered before his father had left for the second time. "Thank God you did. I was about to call the police and demand they put out a missing person report." She shook her head, and now that the elation had passed, regret filled all the spaces inside her. "I feel like such a bad mom. How could I not see that he was hurting so badly?"

Dylan put a hand on her shoulder and met her gaze. "At that age, they're pretty good at keeping their feelings to themselves. Don't beat yourself up."

She leaned into his touch, into the confidence he had in her. For so long, Abby had felt alone, struggling to balance a thousand things at once. But this man understood her, understood what she was going through. "It's hard not to. When you're the mom, you feel responsible for everything."

"Cody thinks you're a great mom, Abby. Actually, he said, 'she's not a bad mom.'"

She laughed. "Well, there's a rousing endorsement, but I'll take it." Coming from a sixteen-year-old, that was the equivalent of a gold medal, Abby figured.

Dylan stepped forward and tucked an errant lock of her hair behind her ear. She wanted to hold on to that moment, but his hand was already gone. "I think you're not a bad woman myself."

"You're a good man, Dylan. You really are." She held his gaze and felt her body warm, responding to him as easily as a flower opening to the midday sun. She liked this man, liked him a lot.

No, not just liked. *Loved.*

She had fallen in love with Dylan Millwright somewhere between tearing down the wall and casting the first fishing line. He was considerate and tender and, most of all, welcomed the package deal that was Abby and her boys. She loved his smile, loved the way he touched her and the way he looked at her. Like maybe…

he loved her, too. But instead of asking about that, she slipped into the easier space of a joke. "Not a bad woman, huh? I'll take that as a compliment, too."

"Actually, you're pretty incredible, Abby." He cupped her jaw, and his thumb traced over her lips. She wanted him to kiss her. Wanted him to hold her. Wanted him to hold on and never let go. "I'm gonna miss you when I leave."

It took a moment. Then the reality of those words hit her, hard and cold. He was leaving. It wasn't like she hadn't known this all along, but some silly part of her had hoped he would fall in love with Stone Gap—fall in love with her—and stay. "So you really are going to Maine?"

He gave her a sad nod. "The job's starting earlier than I expected so I'm leaving Thursday afternoon."

Less than forty-eight hours. She'd thought he would be here at least until the end of the weekend. But he hadn't made her any promises, hadn't made any plans for the future. She should have known better than to fall in love with a man who had no intentions of staying put.

"That's what you do, isn't it? You leave?" She shook her head and willed the tears threatening her eyes to stay back. "Why did I think there was a chance you'd change your mind?"

"I never promised you anything, Abby. You knew all along that I had to go back to my job."

"No, you didn't promise me. But I thought—" She shook her head, cursed, then drew in a breath. "I thought you had found something here that you couldn't find in Maine or Virginia or Iowa."

Something like me. And my boys.

Dylan started to protest, but she cut him off. "I've got to get inside. My boys and I need to go home. We'll get a ride from Ty. We've had a long day, and I think we just need to order some Chinese food and chill tonight and go back to being a family of three."

She didn't invite him over. Didn't ask him to join them. They were back to being just three, and Abby told herself that was fine. She was fine. Or...

She *would* be fine. Once she forgot about Dylan.

Just when she'd started to fall for him. To see him as the kind of man she'd always wanted. Before Dylan could stop her, or twist her heart into another knot, Abby turned on her heel and went inside the center. It wasn't until the door shut behind her that she allowed her tears to fall.

Chapter Twelve

Dylan sat in his Jeep on the hill overlooking Stone Gap on Thursday afternoon. The town lay before him, sleepy and still in the warm sunshine. It was the third time he'd sat here and looked at this town. Once to say goodbye, once to say hello. And now—

The Jeep idled while Dylan debated. If he said goodbye, it would probably be for a long time. The project in Maine was two years' worth of work, and the scale of the project meant it was something that would undoubtedly eat up all his free time.

That's what you do, isn't it? You leave?

Abby's words had haunted his thoughts ever since Tuesday night. When she'd confronted him, a part of Dylan had wanted to leave right then and there, get back on the road, where no one expected anything of him—

And where he wouldn't let anybody down.

That was the crux of it, wasn't it? That he didn't want to disappoint anyone again. But who had he really disappointed?

Not Uncle Ty, who had said to him this morning that Dylan had brought him back from the edge of his despair. Ty had given him a long hug and thanked his nephew over and over again for all he had done. There'd been tears in Ty's eyes and genuine love in his voice.

Not Cody, who had come up to Dylan at the center today to show him his math test, with a very proud B in red at the top. Cody thanked Dylan for making the equations understandable. *And for turning me around when I got lost*, the teenager had added.

Then there had been Jake, who had run into the center this afternoon, calling out *Uncle Dylan* with such joy in his voice that it nearly made Dylan choke up.

And Abby—

Dylan couldn't even think about her without his chest tightening. She was the one person he had let down, and hurt. He could still see the tears in her eyes, hear the catch in her words. Damn. He sat in the Jeep for a long, long time, watching Stone Gap wind down for the day, families going home to each other, sitting down at the dinner table, passing rolls and jokes.

Then he put the Jeep in gear and started to drive.

As soon as Abby pulled into the driveway on Thursday night, the boys were out of the car, dashing inside with the pizza she had picked up on the way home and the latest superhero movie she had rented. For all her talk about wanting to enjoy more spontaneity with her boys, though, all Abby wanted to do right now was crawl into bed and cry.

Dylan had stopped in at the center this afternoon, said goodbye to both her sons and Ty, then stopped to say goodbye to her. His words were short, to the point. Nothing flowery, nothing romantic. He could have been saying goodbye to his dentist for all the emotion in his sentences.

Her heart ached, her eyes burned, but she kept putting one foot in front of the other. Kept being the responsible one, the one who stayed and built roots.

After she set the boys up with the movie, she poured a rare midweek glass of wine and went out to sit in the rocker on her front porch. How long had it been since she'd sat here and enjoyed watching Stone Gap ease into night? She used to love seeing the streetlights wink on, the parents coming home at the end of the day, the families getting in one last game of catch before bedtime.

But tonight, all that made her incredibly sad. She sipped her wine and wondered if it was worse to try to go back inside and pretend she actually cared if a group of superheroes saved the world.

Her phone rang, and her sister's name lit up the screen. Two calls in the space of a week? Melanie must be either bored or homesick. "Hey, Mel."

"What's up? You don't sound like yourself."

"Just…" What was she supposed to say? *I was let down by another charmer? I fell for Mr. Wrong again?* "Drinking some wine and trying to forget a guy."

"It's always about a guy, isn't it?" Melanie sighed. "Was he nice?"

"Yeah. And smart and good with the boys and... gone."

"Gone for good or just for now?"

"I don't know." She didn't quite want to accept yet that Dylan might never return to Stone Gap. A stubborn part of her clung to hope. Stubborn and stupid. She'd learned this lesson once before. She needed to let go of the fantasy of Dylan and accept the reality.

"If you find a guy who's smart and good with the boys and treats you well, hold on tight," Melanie said. "Trust me, those men don't come along every day."

"Good advice," Abby said. But the words stung her throat. The man had come along and left again. There was no way to hold on to him—because he didn't want to stay.

"Listen, I think I will come down and visit you. Let me take a look at my schedule and see when I can fit in a visit, okay? I really need..." Melanie paused "...some sister time."

Abby thought of yesterday, of how overjoyed Jake had been to see his brother home again. She prayed her sons never lost that connection and stayed close long after they were adults. "I do, too, Mel. I really do."

They chatted a little while longer, while Abby went down to the box, retrieved the mail, then returned to her seat. After she hung up with her sister, Abby went through the envelopes—a thick stack because she'd forgotten all about getting the mail in yesterday's madness.

Bills, flyers, catalogs, an ad for a spa opening in a

nearby town, then a letter. She opened the envelope and scanned the contents. She had to read it twice before she believed the words before her.

She got up, opened the front door to go inside and make a call when a pair of headlights swung into her driveway. She blocked her eyes from the sudden glare, then blinked. She knew those headlights. Knew that vehicle.

Knew that man.

The engine cut off, the headlights blinked into darkness. The Jeep's door opened and Dylan stepped out. He hesitated a second, reaching into the truck for something. Abby's heart leaped, but she cautioned herself not to get too excited. He could be here because he forgot something or wanted to say goodbye to the boys again. She put down her wineglass and got to her feet.

"So," Dylan said as he approached, his voice still making her heart flip, "turns out I had a little trouble leaving town."

"Car trouble?"

"Nope." Then he came into the light and she saw what he had in his hands. One of the puppies from next door. Not just any puppy, but the puppy that Jake had named Dudley. The dog had fallen asleep but stirred when Abby approached. "I sat on the hill outside of town for a good hour, trying to find the motivation to get on the road and head to Maine. But as I looked down into Stone Gap, I realized everything I ever wanted was at the bottom of that hill, not a thousand miles away from here."

"Everything you ever wanted? As in a dog?" She

didn't dare let the hope come to life again. Almost didn't dare to meet his gaze. She wanted to tell him about the letter she had received—the grant that had come through for the community center—but if he wasn't staying, it wouldn't matter to him.

"I've been an idiot, Abby," Dylan said. He put the dog on the chair on the porch, then took her hands in his and held tight. "I've spent my whole life running from this town because I thought I hated it. What I really hated was the person I used to be when I lived here. I was running away from him. From the mistakes I made, the reputation I had. But I couldn't put enough miles in between all that. Not until I came back here and faced my past. And met you and your boys."

She held her breath, not sure where the conversation was going to go next. Only knowing she wanted him to keep talking. Even the yellow Lab was watching, tail beating a soft tune against the cushions. The hope in her chest began to bloom again.

"You changed my life, Abby. From the minute we met, you looked at me and you saw just me. And you made me crave the very things I never thought I wanted. A family. A dog. And most of all, a woman who looks at me the way you look at me."

Her breath caught in her throat. "And how do I look at you?"

"Like you love me."

She dipped her gaze. What if he didn't love her in return? What if she was still being the foolish one? Because she did love him and couldn't bear it if he didn't feel the same.

The puppy scrambled down from the chair and pawed at Dylan's leg. He picked the dog up with one arm, then turned back to Abby. Dylan tipped her chin until she was looking at him. "And I look back at you like I love you, too."

"You do?"

He smiled. "I do. I love the way you laugh and the way you smile. I love how you love your sons. I love how good you are at fishing and how easy you are to please, and most of all, I love how I feel when I'm with you."

"And how is that?"

"Like I've come home, Abby. For the first time in my life." He brushed away a tendril of her hair, and had such tenderness in his eyes, she nearly cried. "So I decided it's about time I put down some roots and stayed here in Stone Gap. With you. And Dudley, if you'll have us."

She wrapped her arms around him and the puppy, and laid her head on his shoulder. Everything she had dreamed of was all coming together in this one instant. She thought of her sister's words, about finding a good man and holding on tight. She intended to do that, starting right now.

"A PUPPY!!" Jake came barreling down the hallway, slamming into Abby's legs. "I knew it!"

Or maybe she'd do that in a minute, when they were alone again.

Dylan bent down and handed the little dog over to Jake, making sure he had a solid grip on the squirming bundle of fur. "Dudley needs a home," he said. "Think you can give him a good one?"

Jake nodded. And nodded again. And nodded until Abby thought her son's head might bounce off. "I can. I promise."

"You know, Jake… I think you're going to need some help with this puppy," Dylan added. "Walking him, training him. I should tell you, I am a pretty good puppy trainer."

"You are?" Jake's eyes widened. "Can you help me?"

"I'm planning on it, kid." Dylan ruffled Jake's hair.

Cody stood in the hallway, watching it all, his face hopeful and scared and vulnerable. His chin jutted up and he eyed Dylan with a flicker of mistrust. "You mean it?"

Dylan rose. He took Abby's hand and drew her to his side. "I do."

Cody studied him for a long time, then gave Dylan a nod and a flash of a smile. An understanding passed between them, and the guardedness that Cody wore like an extra shirt began to melt. Cody put a hand on Jake's shoulder. "Hey, squirt, what's this mutt's name again?"

"Dudley. And he's not a mutt."

Cody laughed. "I know. Come on. Let's take him outside and let Mom talk to Dylan."

The boys headed outside, a burst of conversation flowing between them about the dog and a dog house and who was going to walk him first. When the back door opened, a breeze whispered through the house. Abby could swear it carried the scent of happiness.

"Now where were we?" Abby asked.

"I was right..." He pulled her against his chest. "Here. Exactly where I should be." He kissed her then, long and slow and sweet, while the night birds began their evening calls and the families around them wound down for the day. Her grandfather used to call it the magic hour, and as Abby curved against Dylan, she thought that was a perfect description. An absolutely perfect description.

Epilogue

The grant for the community center had given them enough money to expand, adding a game room, a second bathroom and a bank of computers for the kids to use for homework. The center buzzed with life every day, just as it should. Ty was a new man, dividing his time between working there and working on his fishing skills.

Dylan stood in the middle of the center and saw happy, busy kids. He'd started his construction business last month and already had contracts to build two new houses in nearby towns. He worked part-time at the center with his uncle, keeping his hours on the construction sites flexible enough to be here most afternoons.

"Hey, Dylan, I had an idea."

Dylan turned to Cody. The kid had filled out in the last couple months. His grades were up, his eyes brighter, his face happier. He worked with Dylan on the weekends and really seemed to have a knack for building. "Sure. What is it?"

"How about I lead the teen group today? I was thinking, you know, the whole peer-to-peer thing might work well."

Dylan nodded. "I think that's a great idea. Go right ahead."

Cody grinned, then headed over to the center of the sofas. He got the attention of the other teenagers and exchanged a little small talk before turning the conversation to school and grades. "You know, I hate to say it, and probably wouldn't in front of my mom, but doing homework actually does make the rest of it easier. I'm even thinking about going to college."

The other kids scoffed. "Why go to more school?" Matt asked.

"Because it opens up doors," Cody said. "Opportunities. Choices. And I like the idea of more choices. I like having more options?"

The others nodded agreement, and the conversation shifted to jobs, then colleges. There were still several naysayers in the group, but Dylan heard many of the boys chiming in, supporting Cody.

"He's becoming quite the leader," Uncle Ty said.

"Yep. I'm proud of him." And he was. It was weird, because Dylan wasn't really Cody's dad, but every day he spent with the two boys, he fell into that role more and more. There'd been more fishing trips, a couple overnight trips to the old campground, and a trip to a dinosaur museum with Jake. Every time he saw them, the bond between them grew until it felt like Cody and Jake had always been part of his life.

"He reminds me of someone else I knew at that age." Ty clapped Dylan on the back. "Good job, Dylan. You've really turned this place around."

"I'd say that was a team effort."

Ty smiled. "We do have one heck of a great team here, don't we?"

Dylan grinned. "We do indeed." Between the boys, himself, Ty and Abby, the center had become a new place, even better than before. Aunt Virginia's picture hung on the wall, her smile seeming to say she was well pleased with how her legacy was continuing.

The door to the center opened, and Abby hurried in, with Jake by her side. Dudley brought up the rear, still all gangly puppy legs and too-big paws, but perfectly content to trot along beside Jake, who spoiled the dog rotten. Truth be told, Abby and Dylan did, too, and Cody had sneaked him bites at dinner more than once. The Lab had made a perfect addition to their family, and although Dylan came by every day to let the dog out and walk him, it wasn't the same as actually going to sleep in the same house with Abby, Jake, Cody and Dudley.

Abby stopped when she saw Dylan and smiled that smile he loved. Dylan patted his pocket and worked a smile to his own face, then strode forward to greet her. "Glad you're here."

"Sorry I'm late. That presentation ran over, but it worked out well anyway. The agency landed the contract and put me in charge of the new account." Abby beamed.

"That's great, Abby. I'm thrilled for you." He ruffled Jake's hair. "And how was school today?"

"We talked about dinosaurs! Did you know a person who studies dinosaurs is called a pale-o-tologist?" Jake said. "That's what I want to be when I grow up. Or maybe a vet...vetra-narian. Cuz I love dogs."

"Or maybe both, Jake." Dylan pointed to the craft table. "Hey, I think Mavis is waiting for you."

"Great! Thanks!" Jake bounded off. His dog bounded after him, then settled at his feet under the table.

Dylan grabbed Abby's hand before she could head into the office to do any last-minute work. "Hold on a second. I want to show you something."

She gave him a curious glance. "Okay."

He led her through the center and into the hall where the four of them had installed a new wall just a few short months ago. His heart pounded in his throat, but the rest of him felt sure and confident. In fact, he'd never been surer about anything in his life.

"There's a problem with the wall we put in," he said. "I don't know if it's going to last. It might need a stronger foundation. Why don't you take a look at it and tell me what you think?"

Abby stood back and assessed the wall. "I don't see anything wrong, Dylan." She paused, looked closer. The confusion on her face yielded to something tentative, cautious. "Wait. Did you write something on here?"

By the time Abby read the words he'd scrawled on the unpainted wall earlier today, Dylan was already on one knee, the velvet ring box propped open. She turned to him and stared, mouth agape. "Dylan...what...what are you doing?"

"The second smart thing I've done in a long time. The first was not going to Maine." He leaned toward her. "Will you marry me, Abby?"

Her smile bloomed into the biggest one he'd ever seen. She barely hesitated before the joy lit her eyes. "Yes, Dylan, yes! Of course I'll marry you."

He let out a whoop, then rose and slid the ring onto her finger. He leaned around the corner and called out to his sons. He'd sat both of them down yesterday and asked them for permission to marry their mom. If the boys hadn't been on board, Dylan would have waited. But both kids had been as overjoyed as Abby. And when Jake asked if he could call Dylan Dad, he almost broke down and cried. They were his sons, now and forever, and this was his family. Dylan was a bit overjoyed himself. "Cody, Jake, she said yes!"

The boys rushed in and gathered Abby and Dylan in a celebratory hug. The four of them stood in the hall where they'd once rebuilt something that had been torn down, and now began to build a new family together. The family Dylan had always wanted, and the home he'd searched the world for and only found when he came back to the very place he left.

* * * * *

COMING SOON!

MILLS & BOON

Coming next month

FALLING FOR THE PREGNANT HEIRESS
Susan Meier

"It kills me how you cannot understand that if I left you, your brother would be furious."

"He will be on his honeymoon."

Trent groaned. Always practical Sabrina would be the death of him. "He'll hear about this sometime and when he does all he'll see is that you were in a life crisis and I abandoned you."

"This isn't a crisis. It's a situation."

He gaped at her. "Does everything have to be so logical for you? Can you just once get mad? That man, Pierre—" he said the name with a disdain that rolled off his tongue like fiery darts "—didn't deserve the time he got with you."

No man really deserved her. She was soft and sweet. But hardened by a childhood with a father who expected her to be a perfect little doll. The man she finally let loose with, was honest with, had to be someone special. Someone who would see she deserved to be treated with kindness and love.

Not merely passion.

And right now the feelings he had for her were nothing but passion. He was angry, but she was gorgeous, sexy. He could picture every move of making love to her. He could almost see her reactions. Hear her coos and sighs of delight.

He scrubbed his hand across his mouth. It sounded as if he wanted to be that man. And he had to admit he liked the heat that raced through his veins when he thought about keeping her in his life, but that was wrong. He was a man made to be single, to enjoy life, to forge his own path. She was pregnant with another man's child, a woman who would need stability to bring order to her world right now.

And if both of those weren't enough, she was the sister of his best friend, which made her strictly hands-off.

Continue reading
FALLING FOR THE PREGNANT HEIRESS
Susan Meier

Available next month
www.millsandboon.co.uk

LET'S TALK
Romance

For exclusive extracts, competitions
and special offers, find us online:

f facebook.com/millsandboon

🐦 @MillsandBoon

📷 @MillsandBoonUK

Get in touch on 01413 063232

For all the latest titles coming soon, visit
millsandboon.co.uk/nextmonth